民國文化與文學研究文叢

十 編

李 怡 主編

第 13 冊

從危機詩學到地域小說：
中國現代文學中英論文集

鄭 怡 著

國家圖書館出版品預行編目資料

從危機詩學到地域小說：中國現代文學中英論文集／鄭怡 著—
初版—新北市：花木蘭文化事業有限公司，2018〔民 107〕
序 2+ 目 2+202 面；19×26 公分
（民國文化與文學研究文叢 十編：第 13 冊）
ISBN 978-986-485-530-8（精裝）
1. 中國當代文學 2. 文學評論
820.9   107011810

ISBN-978-986-485-530-8

9 789864 855308

民國文化與文學研究文叢
十　編　第十三冊　　　　　　ISBN：978-986-485-530-8

從危機詩學到地域小說：中國現代文學中英論文集

作　　者　鄭　怡
主　　編　李　怡
企　　劃　四川大學中國詩歌研究院
總 編 輯　杜潔祥
副總編輯　楊嘉樂
編　　輯　許郁翎、王　筑　美術編輯　陳逸婷
出　　版　花木蘭文化事業有限公司
發 行 人　高小娟
聯絡地址　235 新北市中和區中安街七二號十三樓
　　　　　電話：02-2923-1455／傳真：02-2923-1452
網　　址　http://www.huamulan.tw 信箱 hml 810518@gmail.com
印　　刷　普羅文化出版廣告事業
初　　版　2018 年 9 月
全書字數　334288 字
定　　價　十編 14 冊（精裝）新台幣 26,000 元

從危機詩學到地域小說：
中國現代文學中英論文集

鄭怡　著

作者簡介

鄭怡，美國匹茲堡大學比較文學和文化學博士，澳大利亞新南威爾士大學人文語言學院中國文學，比較文學副教授，中國四川大學文學新聞學院講座教授。曾為柏林高級研究院，特拉維夫大學波特爾比較詩學研究所博士後研究員，新加坡國立大學亞洲研究所高級（客座）研究員，悉尼大學語言文化學院高級研究員。主要學術研究方向為：現當代中國文學，文化學；比較文學；比較美學史。著有 *From Burke and Wordsworth to the Modern Sublime in Chinese Literature*（Purdue University Press 2011）, *Contemporary Chinese Print Media: Cultivating Middleclass Taste*（Routledge 2013）等，與人合編 *Orbits, Routes and Vessels: Motion and Knowledge in the Changing Early Modern World*（Springer 2014）, *Post-Mao, Post-Bourdieu: Class and Taste in Contemporary China,*（Portal Journal of Multidisciplinary International Studies Special Issue, Vol. 6 No. 22 July 2009）, *Travelling Facts: the Construction, Distribution, and Accumulation of Knowledge*（Campus Verlag 2004）。

提　要

　　文集第一部分為「地方──歷史空間和現代中國小說」，集中分析李劼人的長篇歷史小說，師陀的系列地域短篇，張恨水的都市言情和金庸的武俠小說。從三十年代長篇和系列短篇小說敘事中歷史與地域關係的重置、時空的互緣共構、其對鄉土變遷的世界背景視景式的呈現，到二十世紀上半葉至中葉的通俗小說中對「江湖」作為文化概念以及敘述結構的重新想像，來探討現代小說對歷史──無論是大事件還是日常生活變遷──的把握與企求，以及這種企求對其敘述形式，尤其是對探索空間性敘事方式的影響。

　　第二部分為「危機的詩意──現代中國文學的歷史審美建構」，以郭沫若的早期詩作，張愛玲的邊緣人短篇，和現代主義作為一種歷史審美寫作形式在二十世紀中國的興衰為契，主要討論新詩詩學和五四新文化對歷史「危機」作為審美情感、「詩意」以及新文化之基石的可能性的建構；三四十年代小說中生存美學作為歷史視野的存在；現代主義的宿命；語言詞匯的更新與思想、文化、文學變化的關係等。

在民國史料中重新發現現代文學
——《民國文化與文學研究文叢》第十輯引言

李 怡

　　研究中國現代文學需要有更大的文學的視野，也就是說，能夠成為「文學研究」關注的對象應該更為充分和廣泛，甚至是更多的「文學之外」的色彩斑斕的各種文字現象「大文學」現象需要的是更廣闊的史料，是為「大史料」。如何才能發現「文學」之「大」，進而擴充我們的「史料」範圍呢？這就需要還原現代文學的歷史現場，在客觀的「民國」空間中容納各種現代、非現代的文學現象，這就叫做「在民國史料中重新發現攜帶文學」。

　　但是這樣一個結論卻可能讓人疑竇重重：文獻史料是一切學術工作的基礎，無論什麼時代、無論什麼國度，都理當如此。如果這是一個簡單的常識，那麼，我們這個判斷可能就有點奇怪了：為什麼要如此強調「在民國史料中發現」呢？其實，在這裡我們想強調的是：文獻史料的發掘、整理並不像表面上看去那麼簡單，並不是只需要冷靜、耐性和客觀就能夠獲得，它依然承受了意識形態的種種印記，文獻史料的發掘、運用同時也是一件具有特殊思想意味的工作。

　　對於現代文學學科而言，系統的文獻史料工作開始於 1980 年代以後，即所謂的「新時期」。沒有當時思想領域的撥亂反正，就不會有對大量現代文學現象的重新評價，就不會有對胡適等自由主義作家的「平反」，甚至也不會有對 1930 年代左翼文學的重新認識，中國社科院主持的「文學史史料彙編」工程更不復存在。而且，這樣的文獻史料的發掘整理也依然存在一個逐步展開的過程，其展開的速度、程度都取決於思想開放的速度和程度。例如在一開始，我們對文學史的思想認識和歷史描述中出現了「主流」說——當然是將左翼文學的發生發展視作不容置疑的「主流」，這樣一來至少比認定文學史只存在一種聲音要好：有「主流」就有「支流」，甚至還可以有「逆流」。這些「主」「次」之分無論多麼簡陋和經不起推敲，也都在事實上為多種文學現象的出場（即便是羞羞答答的出場）打開了通道。

即便如此，在二三十年前，要更充分地、更自由地呈現現代文學的史料也還是阻力重重。因為，更大的歷史認知框架首先規定了那個時代的社會性質：民國不是歷史進程的客觀時段，而是包含著鮮明的意識形態判斷的對象，更常見的稱謂是「舊中國」「舊社會」。在這樣一種認知框架下，百年來的中國文學發展史常常被描繪為一部你死我活的「階級鬥爭史」，是「新中國」戰勝「民國」的歷史，也是「黨的」「人民的」「正義」的力量不斷戰勝「封建的」「反動的」「腐朽的」力量的歷史。

這樣的歷史認知框架產生了 1980 年代的「三流」文學——「主流」「支流」和「逆流」。當然，我們能夠讀到的主要是「主流」的史料，能夠理所當然進入討論話題的也屬於「主流文學現象」——就是在今天，也依然通過對「歷史進步方向」「新文學主潮」的種種認定不斷圈定了文獻史料的發現領域，影響著我們文獻整理的態度和視野。例如因為確立了「五四」新文學的「方向」，一切偏離這一方向的文學走向和文化傾向都飽受質疑，在很長一段時期中難以獲得足夠充分的重視：接近國民黨官方的文學潮流如此，保守主義的文學如此，市民通俗文學如此，舊體詩詞更是如此。甚至對一些文體發展史的描述也遵循這一模式。例如我們的認知框架一旦認定從《嘗試集》到《女神》再到「新月派」「現代派」以及「中國新詩派」就是現代新詩的發展軌跡，那麼，游離於這一線索之外的可能數量更多的新詩文本包括詩人本身就可能遭遇被忽視、被淹沒的命運，無法進入文獻研究的視野，例如稍稍晚於《嘗試集》的葉伯和的《詩歌集》，以及創作數量眾多卻被小說家身份所遮蔽的詩人徐舒。再比如小說史領域，因為我們將魯迅的《狂人日記》判定為「現代第一篇白話小說」，就根本不再顧及四川作家李劼人早在 1918 年之前就發表過白話小說的事實。

同樣的情況也出現在文學思潮的認定框架中。過去的文學史研究是將抗戰文學的中心與主流定位於抗日救亡，這樣，出現在當時的許多豐富而複雜的文學現象就只有備受冷落了。長期以來，我們重視的就僅僅是抗戰歌謠、「歷史劇」等等，描述的中心也是重慶的「進步作家」。西南聯大位居抗戰「邊緣」的昆明，自然就不受重視。即便是抗戰陪都的重慶，也僅僅以「文協」或接近中國共產黨的作家爲中心。近年來，隨著這些抗戰文學認知的逐步更新，西南聯大的文學活動才引起了相當的關注，而重慶文壇在抗戰歷史劇之外的、處於「邊緣」的如北碚復旦大學等的文學活動也開始成爲碩士甚至博士論文的選題。這無疑得益於學術界在觀念上的重大變化：從「一切爲了抗戰」到「抗戰爲了人」的重大變化。文學作爲關注人類精神生活的重要方式，最有價值的恰恰是它能夠記錄和展示人在不同生存境遇中的心靈變化。

在我看來，能夠引起文學史認知框架重要突破的原因就在於我們的現代文學史觀正越來越回到對國家歷史情態的尊重，同時解構過去那種以政黨爲中心的歷史評價體系。而推動這種觀念革新的，就是現代文學研究的「民國視野」的出現。中國現代文學發生於民國，與民國的體制有關，與民國的社會環境有關，與民國的精神氛圍有關，也與民國本身的歷史命運有關。這本來是個簡單的事實，但是對於習慣於二元對立鬥爭邏輯的我們來說，卻意味著一種歷史框架的大解構和大重建——只有當作爲歷史概念的「民國」能夠「祛除」意識形態色彩、成爲歷史描述的時間定位與背景呈現之時，現代歷史（包括文學史）最豐富多彩的景象才眞正凸顯了出來。

最近10來年，現代文學研究出現了對「民國」的重視，「民國文學史」「民國史視角」「民國機制」「民國性」等研究方法漸次提出，有力地推動了學術的發展。正是在這樣的新的思想方法的啓迪下，我們才眞正突破了新中國／舊中國的對立認知，發現了現代文學的廣闊天地：中國文學的歷史性巨變出現在清末民初，此時的中國開始步入了「現代」，一個全新的歷史空間得以打開。在這個新的歷史空間中，伴隨著文化交融、體制變革以及近代知識分子的艱苦求索，中國文學的樣式、構成和格局都發生了巨大的變化。具體而言，就是在「民國」之中發生著前所未有的嬗變——雖然錢基博說當時的某些前朝遺民不認「民國」，自己在無奈中啓用了文學的「現代」之名，但事實上，視「民國乃敵國」的文化人畢竟稀少——中國的「現代」之路就是因爲有了「民國」的旗幟才光明正大地開闢出來。大多數的「現代」作家還是願意將自己的夢想寄託在這樣一個「人民之國」——民國，並且在如此的「新中國」中積累自己的「現代」經驗。中國的「現代經驗」孕育於「民國」，或者說「民國」開啓了中國人眞正的「現代」經驗「新中國」與「民國」原本不是對立的意義，自清末以降，如何建構起一個「人民之國」的「新中國」就是幾代民族先賢與新知識階層的強烈願望。可惜的是，在現實的「新中國」建立之後，爲了清算歷史的舊賬，在批判民國腐朽政權的同時，我們來不及爲曾經光榮的「民國理想」留下一席之地。久而久之「民國」就等同於「民國政府」，「民國」的記憶幾乎完全被北洋軍閥、國民黨反動派所淤塞，恰恰其中最值得珍惜的部分——民國文化被一再排除。殊不知，後者也包含了中國共產黨及許多進步文化力量的努力和奮鬥。當「民國文化」不能獲得必要的尊重，現代中國文學（文化）的遺產實際上也就被大大簡化了。

民國時期的中國文學也是民國文化當然的組成部分，當文化的記憶被簡化甚至刪除，那麼其中的文學的史料與文獻也就屈指可數了。在今天，在今後，現代文學文獻史料的進一步發掘整理，就有必要正視民國歷史的豐富與複雜，在袪除意識形態干擾的前提下將歷史交還給歷史自己。

嚴格說來，我們也是這些民國文獻搜集整理的見證人。民國文獻，是中華民族自古代轉向現代的精神歷程的最重要的記錄。但是，歲月流逝，政治變動，都一再使這些珍貴的文獻面臨散失、淹沒的命運，如何更及時地搜集、整理、出版這些珍貴的財富，越來越顯得刻不容緩！十五年前，我在重慶張天授老先生家讀到大量的民國珍品，張先生是重慶復旦大學的畢業生，收藏多種抗戰時期文學期刊和文學出版物。十五年之後，張老先生已經不在人世，大量珍品不知所終。三年前，我和張堂錡教授一起拜訪了臺灣政治大學的名譽教授尉天聰先生，在他家翻閱整套的《赤光》雜誌。《赤光》是中國共產黨旅法支部的機關刊物，由周恩來與當時的領導人任卓宣負責，鄧小平親自刻印鋼板，這幾位參與者的大名已經足以說明《赤光》的歷史價值了。三年後的今天，激情四溢的尉先生已經因爲車禍失去行動能力，再也不能親臨研討現場爲大家展示他的珍藏了。作爲歷史文物的見證人，更悲哀的可能還在於，我們或許同時也會成爲這些歷史即將消失的見證人！如果我們這一代人還不能爲這些文獻的保存、出版做出切實的努力，那麼，這段文化歷史的文獻就可能最後消失。爲了搜求、保存現代文學文獻，還有許許多多的學人節衣縮食，竭盡所能，將自己原本狹小的蝸居改造成了歷史的檔案館，文獻史料在客廳、臥室甚至過道堆積如山。中國社科院文學所的劉福春教授可謂中國新詩收藏第一人，這「第一人」的位置卻凝聚了他無數的付出，其中充滿了一位歷史保存人的種種辛酸：他每天都不得不在文獻的過道中側身穿行，他的家人從大人到小孩每一位都被書砸傷劃傷過！民國歷史文獻不僅銘記在我們的思想中，也直接在我們的身體上留下了斑斑印痕！

由此一來，好像更是證明了這些民國文獻的珍貴性，證明了這些文獻收藏的特殊意義。在我們看來，其中所包含的還是一代代文學的創造者、一代代文獻的收藏人的誠摯和理想。在一個理想不斷喪失的時代，我們如果能夠小心地呵護這些歷史記憶，並將這樣的記憶轉化成我們自己的記憶，那就是文學之福音，也是歷史之福音。

民國時期的中國文學是色彩、品種、形態都無比豐富的「大文學」。「大文學」就理所當然地需要「大史料」——無限廣闊的史料範圍，沒有禁區的文獻收藏，堅持不懈的研究整理。這既需要觀念的更新，也需要來自社會多個階層——學術界、出版界、讀書界、收藏界——的共同的理想和情懷。

2018 年 6 月 28 日於成都

從危機詩學到地域小說——短序

　　什麼是現代中國文學的核心問題？它對自身何爲的焦慮？與政治文化過於緊密的聯繫？我們又該怎樣看待它對「現代」作爲新內容新概念的嚮往，新形式的實驗？對傳統的摒棄和依戀及其試圖建立新文化審美傳統的野心？文集涵括了作者多年來對現代中國文學形式和意義的思考，通過對個體作家文本的研討，側重探索現代中國詩歌和小說與現代中國史及其世界背景自覺的衍生關係，提出其發展過程中的歷史審美主義傾向，強調新詩和現代小說，尤其是二十世紀三十年代重興的長篇和系列小說對於審美和文類形式的建構與其參與歷史進程的企圖息息相關。以不同的詩學情感形態和虛構敘事想像來追溯過去，感懷評說甚還重塑影響現世變遷，是這些不同文類，作家，作品的共同追求。

　　文集分爲兩部分。第一部分爲「地方—歷史空間和現代中國小說」，從三十年代長篇和系列短篇小說敘事中歷史與地域關係的重置、時空的互緣共構、其對鄉土變遷的世界背景視景式的呈現，到二十世紀上半葉至中葉的通俗小說中對「江湖」作爲文化概念以及敘述結構的重新想像，來探討現代小說對歷史——無論是大事件還是日常生活變遷——的把握與企求，以及這種企求對其敘述形式，尤其是對探索空間性敘事方式的影響。

　　第二部分爲「危機的詩意——現代中國文學的歷史審美建構」，主要討論新詩詩學和五四新文化對歷史「危機」作爲審美情感、「詩意」以及新文化之基石的可能性的建構；三四十年代小說中生存美學作爲歷史視野的存在；「現代主義」作爲二十世紀的文學概念、思潮和創作形式在中國的興衰；語言詞匯的更新與思想、文化、文學變化的關係等。

　　雖然篇幅不多，且以對作家個體文本的研究爲主，文集還是體現了作者對中國現代文學從史到作品的思慮。是爲短序。

目

次

一、地方──歷史空間和現代中國小說

A La Mode: The Cosmopolitan and the Provincial

Yi Zheng

This chapter addresses the constitutive relationship between the cosmopolitan (*yang*) and the provincial (*tu*) in the fashioning of a modern Chinese urbanity. It understands fashion change as "communicative" and "institutional" (Barthes 2006), thus intimately at the same time broadly social: located in sartorial and other cultural material details as well as changing ideas and practices of urbanity. It examines these changes as they are figured in modern and contemporary Chinese city narratives in terms of the multidirectional dynamics of the cosmopolitan and the provincial, demonstrating that a place-specific narrative is needed to account for the making of a grounded modern Chinese urbanity. Conventional time-centered stories tend to obliterate the spatial specificity and thus the very make-up of such urbanity because of their emphases on the coming-into-being of a modern urbanity in a temporal progression. This study proposes a place-centered framework to examine the process. It also aims to provide a revisionist aesthetic and historical parameter within which to understand anew the cultural history of a fashionable Chinese modernity as well as modern Chinese narrative practices.

Time, Place, and Fashinable Modernity

Fashion, the domain of change, seems the prerogative of the modern in its twentieth century Chinese connotation. 〔註 1〕 Indeed, for all its cultural and historical ambiguities, fashion has "acquired positive meaning as the spectacle of the Modern" (Ko 1999: 144). In "Jazzing into Modernity," Dorothy Ko notes that the concept of fashion in its short Republican history was reconfigured from *shimao* (current mode) to *modeng* (modern). 〔註 2〕 However, the substitution from the French *a la mode* to the English "modern" does not indicate changing perceptions of the world map of fashion and fashionable places. As numerous accounts of Republican or Shanghai fashion make clear, Paris was the modern fashion source for the Chinese metropolis (Shi 2005). But the changing terminology does confirm the hegemony of the modern not only in sartorial trends, but also in narratives of cultural and social fashion in twentieth-century Chinese life. It accentuates the predominance of time in the story of the fashioning of a Chinese modernity.

Stories of trends and fashionable tastes in twentieth-century China often treat fashion as the marker of time. This tendency is reinforced in the late-twentieth century adaptation of fashion into *shishang* (trends and longings of the times). In the picture-memoir *minguo wanxiang: shishang* (The Republic Panorama: Fashion), a wistful re-invocation of real and imagined Republican bourgeois life, fashion in vogue (*liuxing shishang*) is equated with metropolitan progress in a tradition of constant change:

> Only in the metropolis can trends and fashion move as fast as the stars, and adhere to constant change. Only there can customs and new needs fuse into one and metamorphose into endless novel incarnations and in turn manifest themselves in the details of everyday life, and, then, spread far and wide into other places. (Shi 2005:6) 〔註 3〕

〔註 1〕 On dress and Republican modernity, see Finnane (1999: 119-23); Huang (1999: 133-40); Ko (1999: 141-53); and, on dressing the modern Socialist body, V. Wilson (1999: 167-86); Chen (2003: 361-93).

〔註 2〕 Peter Carroll, however, tells us that *shimao* emerged from the late nineteenth-century Shanghai brothel demi-monde as a new coinage for "fashion/popular'" to describe the burgeoning, often hybrid Chinese-foreign consumer culture of the treaty port. It is therefore a case of true cosmopolitan hybridization rather than direct linguistic cultural translation (Carroll 2003: 443-74).

〔註 3〕 This and all other translations from the Chinese are my own.

The metropolis in this case is figured as the hotbed of modern process, predicated on its aura of fluidity, its happy insouciance to old customs and tireless fascination with novelty. If the modern metropolis has a tradition, it is one of constant change, signposted by the whirlwinds of shifting fashion. It is a tradition that manifests a foreign-sourced cosmopolitanism where all that is left for the locals to do is to catch up in time. The fashionable then is to be progressive.

In this retroactive tale, what defines fashion and fashionable modernity is urbanity, constant change, and timely progress. The other image that dominates the lovingly remembered Shanghai fashion scene is the proximity of the megametropolises of the epicentres of world civilization (*wenming*) where fashion is marked not by space, but time:

> It only takes three to four months for what is most fashionable in
> Paris to be in vogue in Shanghai […]. So are other things, like the
> timely new outfits from Japan, and the 'puffed quilt' style for women
> worn by the Hollywood stars […]. (Shi 2005: 84)

What is fashionable is necessarily cosmopolitan, though the map of the world is presented only to be compressed to represent the movement of time. This compression of specific spatial location along one progressive timeline, what I call "the verticalization of space and change," is characteristic of the changing fashion stories leading up to modernity. In the contemporary postreform reminiscences about the older modern urbanity it is exemplified by the glittering and fashionable possibilities of the treat port megametropolis of the presocialist era. These possibilities are often figured as a lost dreamland ready to be picked up again in China's postsocialist bid to be rejoined with the globalizing world. One might call this a peculiar postsocialist Chinese retro-fashion, redolent with brash contemporary politics. But this retroaction is nonetheless a logical continuation of the once fashionable story of modern progress·

Against the grain of stories that chart Chinese urbanity as temporal progress, there are other city narratives that highlight place not only as scene of action, but also as constitutive of modern cultural and social fashion. In these processes of modernity are often complicated and spatialized as concurrent vignettes rather than sequential scenes. And the materiality of cosmopolitanism is perceived as more than fancy goods, even in accounts where fashion still dominates. Finnane (2003) certainly centralizes the significance of place in framing the "fashionable impulses" of a particular city in its- not-so-easily-delineable process of becoming modern. Here a history of fashion that is understood by reference to "place" can still be used to support a temporal schema, that is, as history. Finnane's placing of this periodization in the sartorial practices of Yangzhou problematizes modernity's lineal progression. For example, if indeed fashion in China is by and large the domain of the modern period, its conceptual beginning is much earlier, and has multiple sources. Finnane (2003) explains,

> By the late seventeenth century, if not earlier […] "Suzhou style" and "Yangzhou style" (*Su sh*i and *Yang shi*) emerged as parallel, notionally contrasts, but probably mutually influential modes of dress. Educated men in China began to bemoan the instability manifest in the rise of "contemporary styles" (*shiyang*) of clothing and its unhappy consequences for social order. (Finnane: 401)

And from around 1795, "there was an observable decline in the urban economy as the salt trade entered an era of crisis" (404) but according to chronicles of the time, this was not accompanied by any diminishing interest in fashion or other forms of novelty and pleasure seeking in the city (Finnane 2003: 394-96). In this chapter, fashion changes occur in particular locales for multiple reasons, among which contingency is as significant as social and economic trends. However, what is more interesting in Finnane's emplaced account of fashionable modernity is her characterization of the presence of the cosmopolitan in shaping the local sartorial trends. This is presented not so much as modern progress, but as the presence of a "world context" (Finnane 2003: 392). The object, then, in following place-specific changes in modern Chinese urban fashion, including sartorial details, would be to seek the meanings of this presence of the world context in local places.

A La Mode: the Cosmopolitan and the Provincial

The cosmopolitan and its other, the provincial—understood as the bounded local place—are usually thought of as a contrasting couplet. Like Raymond Williams' country and city, they are structuring understandings of central organizing principles in "fundamental ways of life," and they often stand for a much wider structure of sensibility than what is entailed in our physical environs (Williams 1973: 1). In Keith's understanding, Williams' insinuation of the country and city into a way of thinking about everyday life is always about something more than just a descriptive vocabulary. Keith (2005) writes that "this opposition invoked sets of social relations and power relations that were crystallized in specific buildings, aesthetics, characters and moralities" (26). Williams's characterization of these structures of sensibility with their attendant urban and rural values is deeply culturally and historically rooted. It can nonetheless be borrowed to understand the stock imageries of the contrasting modern/ cosmopolitan/ urban and the outmoded/backwaters/rural in the usual stories of the Chinese modern, which are just as deeply rooted. The smaller cities, including the not-so-small provincial centres, are often vaguely delegated back in time into the rural as cultural location in these depictions. The cosmopolitan and the provincial thus delineated are emphatically associated with modern values. In the sense of fashion as stylistic configuration, while the metropolis is seen insouciantly seeking the endless progress of cosmopolitan novelty, the provinces and the country are forever stuck in nonchange, or worse, slow and bad imitation. The fashionable impulses of the provincial in this context seem an oxymoron; those who dare to wear them on their sleeves are cast as impostors aping foreign manners (*jiayangguizi*). The cosmopolitan and the provincial in these associations are temporal rather than spatial constructions.

Cosmopolitanism has always been figured as an ideal against fear and distrust of the other. This is certainly the case in Anthony Appiah's (2006) celebration of a metric of human scale, in which love of and comfort with the other is simply necessary and good ethics in a world of strangers. By this logic the colonial adventures of Richard Burton are as admirable as the ex-colonized African's migration to the metropolis. 〔註4〕Appiah's cosmopolitan citizen is of one world and many, a portrait in line with, but extending beyond, both its classic Greek and modern Kantian origin. It has moved from the man who traverses the Greek cosmos, and then the "universal" and "eternal peace"—if one can interpret eternal peace as a general well-being—to the pluralist "one world and many." "One world and many" is therefore more heterogeneous than the Greek islands, and worldlier and more humanly possible than eternal peace. In this way it is a more historically grounded and realistic, moral-ethical calculus. The other recent model is Homi Bhabha's reframing of the problem of the cosmopolitan through a language of geographical scale. And according to Keith it is based on a notion of "affiliative hybridization," which appeals to a very different politics of location, such as "the unknowable nature of the city habitus [and] the ecological certainties of a finite globe" (Keith 128). Here what is to Keith a frame of multiple perspectives within an uncertain register is, to me, Bhabha's most significant cosmopolitan formulation. His language of geography is built on, rather than dismissive or transcendent of, places. His cosmopolitan vision is grounded in a spatial consciousness.

> [For] a radical cosmopolitan concern can only articulate itself by conceiving the rapidly accelerating and expanding world as somehow "incomplete," narrower than the horizon of human totality, in contention with the modernist myth of linear progress elsewhere (Bhabha 2003: 1) .

In current discussions of cosmopolitanism, however, the metropolitan centres are its central if not exclusive referent. They either speak of the "diversity of routes of arrival and roots of origin of the populations of today's cities" or point "towards a different way of seeing the city, an acknowledgement of the heterogeneity of contemporary social reality." Cosmopolitanism is often envisioned as an ethical project that aims to resolve the moral questions that arise from the attempt to reconcile various differences in the context of contemporary global cities (Keith 2005: 39).

〔註 4〕In Appiah's (auto) biography, Burton not only travelled, but was adept at understanding other people's cultures. He was such a wonderful reader and translator of the civilization of others that the fact that he had begun from the colonizing end seems irrelevant. One might take this with some irony, though Appiah does not seem to intend it. This is one point of discomfort for the author in accessing Appiah's otherwise fine thesis.

However, heterogeneity of origins, routes of arrival, modes of life, and cultural preferences can be understood as characteristic of many kinds of urban formations and are therefore not attributes peculiar to the contemporary megametropolis. Furthermore, cosmopolitanism as we inherit it today is an historical category. The process of Appiah's one world and many extends hack more than two centuries, as do the modern Chinese stories of fashion and urbanity. And as a historical possibility, one that can serve as the foundation for any contemporary ethical choice, its location has to be extended. The presence of the world has been felt in many places other than the rnegametropolis of the former world empires, as is attested to by both historical and fictional accounts. In fact, the traversing of different worlds, whether by guile, force, or happy volition, is the very stuff that makes up the genealogy of the modern world. In the process of modernization, cosmopolitanism became no longer simply an ethical but a future ideal; it became an adventure and a romance (like the story of Richard Burton). As an historical possibility and practice, it is grounded in its particular routes and locations. In some parts of the world, notably the home places of the "others" of the colonial or imperial European powers, cosmopolitanism is experienced as the "world" coming to the local places, converging with the extant "heterogeneity of origins, routes of arrival, modes of life and cultural preferences" of the local inhabitants. And in this sense it is bound with its other—the local-bounded place and locale-based perceptions. In other words, to understand cosmopolitanism historically and in place, one has to juxtapose it with categories that emplace—define it in terms of place and scale—such as the provincial.

In the context of the development of a modern Chinese urbanity, cosmopolitanism is best understood as the presence of one world and many. In terms of cultural and social fashion in these urban formations, its process is indicated by the historical linguistic popularity of the word *yang* (the oceanic, that which comes from overseas) since the mid-nineteenth century (Feng 2001). In fact, the gradual popularity of the associations and connotations of *yang* became the best approximation of the grounded cosmopolitanism that developed in China's protracted, often traumatic modernization process. Although as a historically denoted term and concept *yang* keeps oscillating in its emotive connotation and value judgment—from cosmopolitan longing to morally derisive exclusion—it is still the one term that is most popularly used in what might be called an everyday modern Chinese urbanity and its imaginative representation. The provincial, on the other hand, is usually defined not only as that which belongs to or comes from the provinces, but as that which is unsophisticated and unwilling to accept new ideas or ways of life. The equivalents in Chinese language are *waishengde, difangde, xiangjiande* as well as *xiangqide, cuyiede, pianxiade*. In terms of style, the provincial is at best associated with a certain plain primitive charm, at worst the plain bad taste of country bumpkins. It is therefore the opposite of *yang* in fashion—*tu* (of and belonging to earth, countryside, unsophisticated, parochial). As contrasting stylistic and cultural conceptual configurations, *yang* gradually went beyond its connotation of mere foreign exotica to stand for the trendy, timely, and modern progressive, whereas *tu* became something not only too local in place, but also backwards in time.

However, these associations seem to have little to do with the actual historical and contemporary importance of Chinese provinces and the province-based political economy. Franz Michael, for example, has established that regionalism has been one of the most important phenomena in Chinese imperial history (Michael 1971). 〔註 5〕Goodman's studies of political and social changes in provincial China, on the other hand, are significant for understanding twentieth-century and contemporary China (Goodman 1997). 〔註 6〕In his reflection on "The Province, the Nation, and the World," Levenson (1967) delineated the intricate relationships between these three concepts as mutually

---

〔註 5〕For Michael, this is largely due to the dynamic role played by the gentry between the state and the autonomy of the sphere of the Confucian social order. The dynamics between the gentry, the imperial state, and the relative autonomy of the sphere of the Confucian social order can be seen played out as the complications that underwrite part of the social, cultural and sartorial fashion changes in Li Jieren's (1997b) historical city novel *Great Waves* (da bo) on which my discussion will focus in the third part of this essay.

〔註 6〕I would also like to thank Professor Goodman for providing me the essential sources for the study of provincialism.

constitutive rather than diagonally opposing. For him, rather than a transcendental moral program, they are historically changing categories, which have specific temporal and spatial connotations. The cosmopolitan strain in twentieth- century China, sometimes appearing as nationalism itself and sometimes against it in Levenson's delineation, is bound with its other, the provincial, both literally—as the inevitable locus of the local part to the national or cosmopolitan whole—and figuratively as the imagined whole's stagnant past. The provincial, both as political economic locus and its cultural sentimental imaginary, is therefore essential in recounting the modern Chinese story, including narratives of its fashionable urbanity.

City Novels and Local Cosmopolitanism

It is useful to think of modern Chinese urbanity as characterized by the presence of the cosmopolitan—the world as context. That is, ideas, things, and people from the world beyond China (*yang*) having a significant presence in local places. The world I am referring to here is Appiah's one world and many, sometimes vaguely denoted in the transitional Chinese language as the West Ocean (*xiyang*), the East Ocean (*dongyang*) and the South Ocean (*nanyang*). As numerous stories of city life and fashion demonstrate, what is present in any particular place at the various modernizing junctures are intersections of different and coexisting worlds. The provincial is thus a constitutive part of the world as context in the story of a fashionable Chinese modernity, rather than its antithesis. Following this lead, Finnane's (2003) tale of Yangzhou cosmopolitan/local fashion and Zamperini's (2003) account of fashion and identity in late Qing Shanghai use city memoirs and city novels as revealing particulars of local, but at the same time temporal, sartorial practices. Zamperini argues that most premodern Chinese fiction writers took pains to provide their readers with detailed descriptions of their characters' clothes because they believed in the power of clothes to reveal moral orientation and cultivation, in addition to social status, gender, and class. And, what is most interesting in the early modern city novels that came out of the late Qing period is the tension between these microcosmic and the macrocosmic ways of identifying. As Zamperini notes, "Clothes start marking the time of the body and of the society in which it operates. For the first time in Chinese fiction, dresses reveal the time and the space in which the characters live" (Zamperini 303).

Zamperini's argument for the importance of sartorial description in Chinese fiction both insightfully delineates a tradition and notes the incipient moment of Change. But city novels as loci for social and cultural fashion, including the fictional and sartorial change, can be understood even more fundamentally in their generic construction. The descriptive details in the urban setting not only reveal character development in historical context, but also firmly locate changes in place. Detailed descriptions of scene and the vignette dramatizations of characters' relationships are most often the key components of these novels. The stories present change in location, rather than focusing on the allegorical *Bildungsroman* of a burgeoning nation, which emphasizes change in time. A focus on description, from the sartorial to other material or sentimental signs of a fashionable urbanity, can thus lead to a rethinking of the modern novel as genre as well as location for a multilayered Chinese cultural and affective modernity.

"Light, Heat and Power!" is the famous opening gambit for showcasing the startling urbanity of Shanghai in Mao Dun's *ziye* (Midnight), first published in 1931. Old Mr. Wu, a *bona fide* member of the provincial gentry running away from peasant riots to his capitalist son's mansion in the French Concession, is confronted on his first entry into Shanghai with the sound and fury of the nightless metropolis:

> What is most startling, however, are the extraordinary large-sized
> neon-light advertisements high on all foreign looking buildings? They
> blare out scarlet beams and green beams, fiery and phosphorescent:
> Light, Heat and Power! (Mao 1986, 1)〔註7〕

But what really scares Old Mr. Wu to death (literally, even the recitation of the Confucian classic *taishang ganyingpian* (Treatise on Response and Retribution), a timeless practice for moral guidance, did net revive him) is a sartorial detail. To his detriment, Old Wu sees the naked-looking thighs (actually clad in transparent silk

---

〔註 7〕 The last three words are in English in the original.

stockings) of a woman sitting on a rickshaw, sticking out of the high-cut slits of her satiny *cheosagsam*. The perilous urbanity/modernity here embodied in the metropolis is not narrated in the development of Old Wu's character. In fact, the narrative of Old Wu ends when he dies before the dawn of next day. What remain in the reader's mind and stand for the lethal modernity/urbanity of a "morbidly prosperous" 〔註 8〕 metropolis are the spatialized descriptive details of the startlingly clad resident female bodies, and their deadly effect on the old and provincial. This generic specificity, that is, the importance of the spatial descriptive, is also borne out by Mu Shiying's "New Sensationalism" in its capturing of his most beloved and most loathed night scene in Shanghai:

> "The Great Evening Post!" The paper boy opened his blue mouth, with its blue teeth and blue-tipped tongue. Opposite, tilted towards it is the blue neon-lit high-heeled pump. "The Great Evening Post!" Suddenly he acquired a red-mouth, from which a tongue stuck out, and from the wine bottle opposite wine is pouring out. Red street, green street, blue street, purple street. […] Oh, the metropolis decked out with such contrasting-hued cosmetics! (Mu 1933: 71)

A bit awkwardly, Mu seeks to record his urban sensations with what he conceives as fresh visual images. He is keen to show off what he has learnt from the cinematic art itself—part of the fashionable cultural urbanity—the juxtaposition of nonsequential，parallel scenes in montage. One can argue that this is simply a classic example of the New Sensationalist School, in which the eschewing of sequential narrative is expected. However, Mao Dun is a textbook social-realist. *Ziye*, like most of his other novels, aims to represent the most typical, therefore the truest, aspects of his society and times. But, as demonstrated in the example of the opening scene, Mao Dun's representative realism is to be found as much, if not more, in his description as in the structure of his narrative. The truest and most typical are represented here in the demonstration of the visual sensual details of an urbanity/modernity that is as much the web-like setting as part of the unfolding of the story. In other words, the different kinds of modernity/urbanity of the characters

---

〔註 8〕 A catchphrase used in Socialist China to describe Shanghai modernity before 1949.

and events are dramatized and made real in descriptions of clothes, architecture and streetscapes, and in scenes of multilayered human interaction. This means one can extend the usual definition of novelistic realism from representing progression in time, to demonstrating the typical, detailed and locale-based presence of one world and many. Modern novels, then, especially those that proclaim a self-conscious realism, not only lend themselves to the most proper form of the "national allegorical" (Jameson 1986), but, more important, are the most vivid and emplaced demonstrations of the coming-into-being of one world and many. 〔註9〕 The latter is the process and consequence of what can be called our shared modernity. If in Mao Dun's metropolitan perception, the cosmopolitan and the provincial are diagonally opposed—they kill each other—in Mu Shiying's visual capturing of Shanghai as his home city, the cosmopolitan is localized: his neonlights of wine and high heels are the local scene par excellence.

Li Jieren's multivolume historical city trilogy *da bo* (Li 1997a, 1997b, first pub. 1937)—or *Great Waves*—might serve as a better example of the modern Chinese novel as the spatial-descriptive; that is, as vignettes that produce emplaced modern urbanity and offer an understanding of the interplay between the cosmopolitan and the provincial in local places. For, although Li tried in later years to join the "nation and narration" and reshape his ambitious and sprawling *oeuvre* into the progressive and historical mode, the volumes remain hopelessly "naturalistic" and locale bound (S. Li 1986: 207-49). The minutiae of the provincial city life refuse to settle themselves into the local colours of a national temporal whole. They take over as the main players in the unfolding of a non-progressive, often disjointed and emplaced process of change—the binding of one world and many. *Great Waves* is also a case in point because it professes, like Flaubert's *Madame Bovary* (1857/2005), to be a study of provincial manners at particular historical junctures. To look at the minutiae of the waves of change in social and cultural fashion in Li's provincial "city novel" (Hanan 1998) is to embark on a number of things. First, it joins a complex set of narratives that reach far beyond

---

〔註 9〕 The term emplaced is used here to mean located in the most specific setting and embodied in nameable details of people and things.

the tension between tradition and modernity in narrating modern China and Chinese fashion (Edwards 2007). Li's scenes of the great foreboding waves in the gentry and plebeian lives of the provincial city showcase an impressive cultural complexity in sartorial details as well as other material and sentimental signs of urbanity. And they undo the conventional account that posits fashion trends in China variously as the desire for modernity or the echo of tradition. Li's *naturalism*—a critical term often applied negatively to his compulsion to describe lives and times in great detail—is vindicated in vignettes of the *fin de siècle* whirlwinds of gentry activism—and plebeian movements in the provincial city of Chengdu. It is highlighted in the minutiae of unpredictable sea-change in local lives and perceptions. Fashion shifts in clothes, cityscape, and social (in particular, gender) relations become central as signs of a provincial modernity that is not necessarily progressive, but is nonetheless cosmopolitan. These shifts dramatize the material and sentimental presence of different worlds as the context for the emergence of such modern urbanity. The constitutive presence of the cosmopolitan (*yang*) and the provincial (*tu*) can thus serve as "structures of attention" (S. H. Donald 2006) in examining Li's provincial historical vision enacted and demonstrated in multiple spatial-descriptive "eat drink man woman" (*yinsi nannu*) plus clothing scenarios of local urban life.

S. H. Donald (2006) defines "structures of attention," through Williams, as ways to understand city dwellers' and sojourners' affective as well as structural relations to their environs in the production and consumption of the idea of the city; as organizations of perception and feeling (65-67). She provides useful analytical focal points for a reading Li's city novel. One should not only look at how Li structures our attention—what he wants us to see—but also what we notice, that is, the scenes and things in the "city life" carefully choreographed to catch our attention. In this sense, it is significant that Li begins his *Great Waves* with the ripples in the dead pond of a small town. The first volume of the sprawling novel, called *Sishui weilan* (Ripples in a Dead Pond, 1997c), was first published in 1935. It is set in Tianhui, a small country town outside Chengdu in the last decades of the nineteenth century. The reader's first encounter with the presence of what might be called cosmopolitan fashion is in the ingenious sartorial activities of an unusual and unusually charming woman. She is a woman who, with her extraordinary feminine capability and peculiar location, straddles town and country, and moves with the same ease and cheeky audacity amongst the peasants, the gentry, the city plebeians, and the foreign mission, and is thus often the harbinger of tidings between the different worlds.

Deng Yaogu has small bond feet, and embroiders her own lotus shoes. But this seems not to have hindered her from going places with, as well as without, her husbands. One consequence of her frequent traversing is unequivocally demonstrated in her clothes. When asked how she manages to pin her headscarf so prettily, she shakes her head and laughs out loud:

> Miss, if I tell you, you will laugh at me. […] This is what I saw during the Winter Month two years ago, when I went with Boy Jin's current Father Gu to do the Foreign Winter festival. There was a foreign woman who wore it like this. […] Do you think it looks good? (Li 1997b: 12)

This ability to take advantage of different worlds makes Deng exceedingly stylish in the eyes of the city-gentry-boy narrator:

> [T]he cuffs of her lotus-pink purple wide-legged trousers are bound with one wide strip of black foreign satin, and then trimmed again with light greenish-blue braided lace. I could not tell what is the colour and material of her padded jacket, as it is covered by a layer of clean scallion white unlined outer jacket made of foreign cotton cloth, trimmed at both shoulder and cuff with wide black bands. On it she also wears a royal blue cloth apron. On the necklines of both her inner and outer garments fashionable low collars are sewn, revealing a long section of her neck, though not very white, but looks extremely soft, textured and satiny. (Li 19976: 13)

With the episode of Deng, whose country-town, *tu-yang* exploits make her a modern adventuress, Li demonstrates the presence of the world in a local place's modern awakening. The change is first illustrated as ripples in a dead pond, dramatized *avant la letter* as material and sentimental signs of a provincial traversal of different worlds as in Deng's imaginative "aping" of foreign fashion. The significance of her sartorial ingenuity lies not so much in her boldness to adopt foreign fashion—the result is a locally recognizable attractive fusion into her late Qing outfit—as in her practice of fashion, something that is recognizable by both country-born adventuress and urban-gentry youth because of her spatial mobility. It is an act that makes the cosmopolitan local. In Li's depiction, Deng becomes a proto-modern type: a semiconscious participant in the trends of the times. This is not because of her progressive consciousness, for she is not shown to have any, but because of her spatial mobility and transgression. This sometimes incongruous but always significant mixing of worlds is demonstrated more emphatically in the cityscape and urban-gentry life, as the novel moves from small town to the provincial capital of Chengdu.

In the provincial capital, the Master of the Hao Mansion, Hao Dasan, like many of his local official-gentry brethren, is only third-generation Sichuanese. This is typical of the *fin de siècle* half-official, half-gentry class in Chengdu. Like some of them, he owns acres of fertile land in the surrounding counties, and numerous shops as well as real estate in the city. Though he is reputed to be well-read (his official title was bought after he passed the county examination), it is also known that he does not understand the New Learning (*xinxue*), which is beginning to be in vogue in the provinces. Nevertheless,

> not understanding New Learning does not interfere with Hao Dasan's dressing and eating routine, especially since he already has the prospects of being a waiting-list prefecture magistrate. There is really no need for him to follow the trend of New Learning and be taken as a Rebel. Thus he can still calmly and leisurely follow the old rules and habits left over by his grandfather, and methodically, comfortably live his own life. (Li 1997b, 178-79)

But then again, in the methodically and leisurely comfortable Hao Mansion, "[t]hough their life style follows the old and the customary, it is nonetheless fused with many a novelty, indeed in the material sense.

"They have purchased, for example, a bronze-shelved and coloured-glass topped lamp that burns foreign kerosene, and learnt from the professional foreign lamp salesmen how to light it properly. In fact, they have replaced, at a great cost, the lighting in the whole estate with foreign kerosene lamps of various shapes and colours. They have also taken great pleasure in having their photographs taken, also at great cost, and it is to their delight that Chengdu finally has its own resident photographers. All in all, …[i]n the Hao Mansion these cosmo-foreign (*yang*) things are really not few. As to the multi-coloured glazed glass windowpanes, the full-length looking-glass with the red sandalwood pearl-inlaid stand, they are obtained long ago through Grandpa's hands. The most recent and useful, in fact the whole household has grown dependent on them, are the very rare toothbrushes, toothpaste, foreign cloth towels, foreign soap, perfumes and so on, small things. How come that foreigners who look so thick and stupid can make these homely things so very well, that once you touch them, you can never live without them? (Li 197b: 179—80)

Love of otherworldly things is not necessarily accompanied by love of other worlds, but it does force certain admiration from the provincial hearts and minds. At least it shows these worlds are very much present in the everyday provincial life, at a great cost, both economically and affectively. This duplicity in reaction is further set up in Hao and his friend's discussion of the Boxers, foreigners, and the imperial affairs at the capital and in the provinces at the end of the volume. In general, Hao and his local gentry-official chums prefer the Boxers to the foreigners because of their pragmatic imperial allegiance (on hearing the Dowager Regent's declared support for them) and dissatisfaction with the rising competing power for land and wealth from local converts (to Christianity). They did not however show any innate parochial distaste for things and people alien. On the whole their attitudes are those of a distant audience to a spectacular show. Both the foreigners and the boxers seem to belong to worlds, which though impinging, are nevertheless still distant, geographically as well as affectively. Interestingly though, they seem as fascinated by the foreign worlds as they are by

the magic of the Boxers. For instance, at the height of the Boxer Rebellion，
Dasan and his friend He Huanzhong have a chat:

> Hao Dasan does not know how many countries the foreigners have,
> nor how many of them are there, so he asks He Huanzhong, who was
> once in Magistrate Yu's retinue and had been to Shanghai. And thus has
> some knowledge of the New Learning. (Li 1997a: 186)

Mr. He recounted the number of foreign countries he knew, mostly those that the
Magistrate had business dealings with or were visible in Shanghai. Hao suddenly
remembered the United States of America, where his foreign kerosene came from.
The conversation then turns from gleeful applauding of the Boxers' heroic deeds to
anxieties about the sources of their everyday delights. Hao worries out loud:

> If they do break into the Beijing embassies, I wonder if the
> foreigners will ever come again. It'd be a real worry if they won't. All
> our nice *yang* goods, where would they come from then? (Li 1997b:
> 186)

The dubious love for foreign goods, which shows the ambiguity of the provincial
gentry's reaction to the presence of other worlds in the midst of their familiar
environs, is part of Li's careful structuring of attention. It reminds us that the
cosmopolitan has come to the heart of the local provincial at a time when the
age-old Confucian ideal of its imperial cosmos—all under heaven—is dramatically
and traumatically coming apart. The unraveling and reforming of this
end-of-the-world world are demonstrated by the material and affective comfort and
duplicity with the provincial city's cosmopolitan elements on the part of the gentry.
In Li's description it is not so much the fledgling nation-state, but the wide world,
that is its context. The citified gentry, whose presence, together with that of the
urban merchants, craftsmen, and plebeians (Li's city story covers them all), already
signalling the heterogeneity of origins, different routes of travel and modes of
arrival of this *fin de siècle* world, are neither conservatives nor progressives of this
history. As Li goes on to narrate it over several decades, these city dwellers, from
gentry men to plebeian women, continue to be the heroes and heroines, villains and
losers, of this gradual becoming of a modern Chinese urbanity. They are

jugglers—opportunists—in a process of slowly fusing other worlds with their own, punctured alternately with enthusiastic embraces, revolutions, and rebellions, in their daily juggling of a simultaneously cosmopolitan and provincial existence. For Li the modern Chinese story is indeed the story of changing places. It is the coming-into-being of one world and many at the very heart of the provinces.

Understood in this way, the nonlinearl locale-based city narratives are the most representative modern Chinese stories of urbanity. While they do not hurry along to propel history to its "end," which is a historical perception and narrative practice that sweeps away the multiple players and especially the textures and structures of life and feelings of history, they demonstrate the complicated constituents of change and process. In this context, the cosmopolitan and the provincial always implicate and condition each other. The cosmopolitan, therefore, should indeed he understood as the world context of local urban transformations in fashion, cultural perception, and practice. And the coming-to-be of the modern provincial is the process of becoming one world and many in the bounded local place.

The World of Twentieth-Century Chinese Popular Fiction: *From Shanghai Express* to *Rivers and Lakes of Knights-Errant*

Yi Zheng

The origins of modern Chinese popular fiction can be traced to vernacular narrative traditions that flourished in "transformation" (*bianzuen*) narratives and chantefables of Tang (618-907), "records (*zhi*) of Song (960-1279), "drama" (*zaju*) of Yuan (1271-1368), "popular tale" (*pinghua*) of Yuan and Ming (1368-1644), and "novels" (*xiaoshuo*) of Ming and Qing (1644-1911) periods. These narratives retained a close relationship with the oral and folkloric as well as the classical and literary *(wenyan)* traditions (Hanan 1981:1-11). The development of popular fiction in modern China is also credited to the copious translations of Western novels at the turn of the twentieth century, which spurred stylistic innovations and incipient mordernitien that had been in full swing (Hanan 2004; D. Wang 1997; Chen Pingyuan 2010). Moreover, translation also contributed to the formation of the vernacular as a formal narrative medium (Hanan 1981:6).

Recent attention to the unprecedented experimentation in fiction writing from the mid-nineteenth to the early twentieth century established the late Qing (1849-1911) era as a pivotal moment in modern Chinese fiction in its transformation from the traditional to the modern. This heightened interest in late Qing fiction demonstrates a revisionist effort to recover repressed modernities from the monolithic, linear history that champions the May Fourth culture, calling attention instead to the historical *longue durée* and complexity of formal as well as affective changes in modern Chinese culture. This shift also highlights the importance of genre novels, in which the popular and the political interchange. The new account now challenges the history of modern Chinese fiction that progressively links such monuments as Liang Qichao's call for "revolution in fiction" as part of a political reform to the May Fourth radical disassociation with tradition, allowing the inclusion of social transformation with its cultural and effective consequences at different levels of Chinese society during a particularly turbulent time. Besides the political and intellectual reformers (often doubled as the New Novelists), and the cultural avant-gardes who aimed at total revolution in aesthetic end social realms, the heroes of the historical transformation of modern Chinese fiction now include the self-transforming literati (*wenren*) who competed to shape the cultural makeup of the populace through vernacular narratives. In this respect, the significance of the modern experimentation of genre fiction becomes obvious.

Genre novels are the mainstay of modern Chinese popular fiction. They are usually categorized into prototypes such as romances (*yanqing*), social scandals (*shehui heimu*), court cases (*gong,an*), and knights-errant or martial arts (*haoxia*). Their development is divided into different stages in correspondence to modern Chinese history: before 1949, the most popular and developed genres were romances, social scandals, detective stories, knights-errant, and martial arts, some publicized at the time as the butterfly or 'Saturday" school of fiction. In mainland China from 1949 to 1966, these forms metamorphosed into inadvertent elements of thrilling, comic, romantic, or tragically cathartic relief for socialist realist fiction, making the didactic and ideological familiar and palatable to a public hankering for diversion. Meanwhile, in other Sinophone regions, especially Hong Kong and Taiwan, these genre forms continued to evolve, with the knights-errant and martial arts becoming one of the most popular leisure readings. By the end of the twentieth-century, genre novels have revived in mainland Chinese and remain prosperous elsewhere.

Since late Qing novels have been the subject of significant recent scholarship, either as vanguard of the new novelistic experimentation or precursor to modern Chinese popular fiction, this chapter devotes attention to the early Republican (pre-World War II) butterfly genres and the mid-century émigré knights-errant and martial arts fiction. 〔註１〕 Continuing late Qing experiments in modern vernacular literature, these genre forms embodied thematic, formal, and affective transformations that correlate to dramatic changes in modern China. This embodiment and recreation of a sociocultural world as the carnivalesque (Bakhtin 1984) mirror image of modern China is one of the most significant points of interest in these popular genres, as it allows insights into the affective transformation and cultural aspiration of a *minjian* (folk) society that is the field of production, consumption, and vision of these narrative forms.

Of *Jianghu* and *Minjian* in Popular Fiction

The spatial is essential in the embodiment and transformation of social visions. While butterfly fiction is known for its urbanity (Link 1981), knights-errant and martial arts novels are celebrated for their inimitable spatial imagination, fantastic journey motifs and configurations of a modern world of *jianghu* (literary "river and lake"). As there are also genre mixtures in both narratives, the urban and *jianghu* worlds they delineate supplement each other in projecting the phantasmagoria of a fast-changing China.

This chapter examines the configuration of a modern *jianghu* as affective supplement to new urban spaces and argues that the spatial imagination and structural underpinning—from the social to the topographical—of modern Chinese popular fiction is closely related to the dislocation of culture and home as an overriding modern Chinese experience. The traumatic transformation of sociocultural spaces in twentieth-century China as a consequence of ongoing revolutions, reforms, and wars grounds the affective orientation of writers and readers. The changed role of the Chinese literati and urbanization are two most immediate transformations in modern Chinese socioeconomic life and spatial arrangements that directly impacted

---

〔註 １〕 The metamorphosis of popular genre fiction in mainland China since 1949 is a subject that merits separate attention. Its entanglement with the mandate of socialist and revolutionary literature is particularly interesting.

the flourishing of popular fiction in the first half of the twentieth century. While the former accounts for the dramatic increase in the number of fiction writers, the latter predicates the formation of these genres' vast readership and the structure of their sentiments, which in turn cultivates their reading habits. These are augmented by the massive dislocation of populations. In these contexts, to account for the exotic and outlawed world of knights-errant amongst the untamed *jianghu*, or the folkloric in the metropolis, is to understand the modern configuration of Chinese city space and the affective structure of urban readers.

Jianghu and *minjian* are explored here as crucial concepts and spaces that make up the affective and cultural map of modern Chinese genre fiction. They are figured as rivers and lakes, faraway mountains and untamed waters, as well as train carriages, courtyards, city parks and streets. Admittedly, the history of *jianhu* is not confined to modern Chinese fiction. Though its origin has been the subject of much debate, its continuous employment has made it clear that it is a social-spatial concept despite the varied and shifting references. Many accept that "river" and "lake" originally refer to the three rivers and five lakes of the mid-to-lower Yangze region, and the reference became generalized in the transitional period between Qin and Han (207-200 BC). *The Book of Han* (Hanshu, 111 AD) specifies it as unorthodox societies outside the capital. After Song and Yuan (960-1368), with the increase of migrant populations, the nature of *jianghu* societies began to change, and in Ming and Qing (1368-1911) they often metamorphosed into highly organized underground societies in opposition to the imperial court (Han Yunbo 2003). In its long transmutation, *jianghu* acquires a specific reference and connotes not only a world in nature for heroes to roam and conquer, but also a space at the margins of society in uneasy if not always oppositional relations with state institutions and elite traditions. What modern genre fiction carne to inherit and renew is this historically particularized cultural space. In the early 1920s, when knights-errant fiction became martial arts novels, writers often evoked *jianghu* directly in their titles. 〔註2〕Through *jianghu*, popular fiction writers projected their

---

〔註 2〕Pingjiang Buxiao Sheng, the first notable modern Chinese martial arts novelist, used the word "jianghu" in the titles of quite a few of his novels, including *The Knight Extraordinaire of the River and Lake* (Jianghu qixia zhuan, 1923).

fascination with a cultural tradition as latecomers attempting to capture rampant activities of a volatile modern society, as Zheng Zhengyin did in his "paper *jianghu"* (Han Yunbo 2003:88).

This sense of the pan-jianghuization of a *fin-de-siècle* world is also what grounds David Wang's reinterpretation (1997) of the late Qing as conjoining conventions of the court case and the knight-errant (*youxia*) into one mixed genre. In Wang's understanding, the necessity to combine magisterial authority, traditionally seen resting in the able hands of upright court officials, which is the implicit affective resolution of the court case genre, with the lawless and wilful abandon of knights-errant in carrying out justice for heaven, which is the spiritual underpinning of martial arts fiction, reflects a sense of deepening social crisis. This unlikely marriage of two distinct realms of popular imagination—one for the triumph of orthodoxies and institutional justice, the other for extreme individual moral and physical excess—is for Wang a contemporary compromise of aesthetic tastes that reveals the irredeemable political turmoil and official corruption in late Qing society (D.Wang 2003:2). Letting *jianghu* serve the court is thus a reflection of a desperate turn in public imagination. In late Qing popular novels such as Shi Yukun's *Three Heroes and Five Gallants (Sanxia wuyi,* 1879) and Liu E's *The Travels of Lao Can* (*Laocan youji,* 1907), beliefs in both the sanctity of reliable state power and in the tradition of the uncompromised knight--errant spirit are abandoned (D. Wang 2003:4). The unbridled expansion of *jianghu* in public imagination is thus linked to affective disillusionment during troubled times.

The expanded *jianghu* in modern Chinese fiction can be understood in terms of Chen Sihe's conceptualization of *minjian* (2003:257) as an unorthodox, marginal society. Chen bases his formulation on an extended notion of the folkloric, carrying with it the sense of sociocultural forms traditionally practiced by rural societies and handed down through oral traditions, and connoting perseverance of old ways over change. Chen, however, stresses its oppositional status as a cultural space vis-a-vis the political. He differentiates this space from Jürgen Habermas's civil society and public sphere; whereas civil societies and public spheres are political-spatial understandings grounded in an emerging European bourgeois urban society, *minjian* is mainly a cultural configuration of folk traditions of an agrarian China. In fact, Chen's *minjian* is restricted to the cultural forms of Chinese peasantry, periodically appropriated by the intelligentsia for reformist or oppositional agendas. In this sense, *minjian* is analogous to civil society in one respect but differs in others. The similarity that Chen perceives is the self-organization of a society outside the realm of state power. The Habermasian public sphere presupposes rational democratic participation, whereas *minjian* resonates with the carnivalesque polyphony of the marginal (Bakhtin 1984).

While the self-regulating *minjian* at the margins of the state can be borrowed as a descriptor of modern *jianghu*, Chen's *minjian* overemphasizes the boundary between political and cultural worlds, and the opposition between them. The idea that *minjian* is the conceptual opposite of the state, and that its cultural forms operate outside the state's control, overlooks the historical and structural supplementarity of these social- spatial constructions. Understanding *jianghu* in modern Chinese fiction through *minjian* highlights the latter's phantasmagoric nature vis-a-vis the elite centre of power: rather than a natural place of opposition (such as the unchanging countryside forever preserving an external agrarian past), *jianghu* is a mirror image of the perilous modern China where changes are unpredictable and uninterrupted.

However, to predicate the idea of *minjian* and its assertion on the Yan'an debate on "national form" (*minzu xingshi*) in the 1930s-1940s (Chen Sihe 2003:257) limits the concept's historical valence. The Yan'an debate was initiated by Mao Zedong to signal the emergence of a Marxist political discourse with Chinese ambition. The "national form" is hence a cultural parameter instituted from one of the competing political centers in modern China and has served as a hegemonic framework since then. It is difficult to equate such political employment of the popular with the reassertion of marginal, unsettling cultural forms that *minjian* seeks to elucidate. Moreover, as Chen himself demonstrates, this kind of rediscovery of elements of folk culture at moments of historical crisis by the modernizing Chinese intelligentsia, who otherwise consider such cultures anathema to modern progress in literature and culture since the May Fourth, bespeaks the ambiguity of their choices of modern paths (Chen Sihe 2003:258).

Robert Redfield's anthropological division of the culture of a given society into "great" and "little" traditions (Calhoun 2002:72) is appropriate for a structural understanding of *minjian* as a spatial concept. The distinction here is between the elite cultural institutions and orthodoxies of the ruling intelligentsia, orchestrated by the state and its mechanisms of control, and those informal, popular cultural practices whose realms of activity are at the margins of the direct authority of the state and its intuitions of power. The latter, as divergent cultural practices, often transcend the political ideological status quo and represent life at the lower end of society, expressing and championing the psycho-ethical and aesthetic cultures of the under-represented. Through Yu Yingshi's reformulation of Redfield's cultural division for the Chinese case, Chen Sihe (2003:258-259) sees the "great" tradition historically in court-authorized classics, the civil service examination, and Confucian ethics buttressed by its institutions of education, while locating the "little" tradition almost exclusively in oral traditions of the peasantry. *Minjian* is then what coheres around the agrarian: it is authentic but residual, primitive but unrestricted.

Though insisting on the residual nature of *minjian*，Chen Sihe (2003:258-259) attends to its modern history. For him, it is part of a tripartite structure that underpins the intellectual formation in modern China: it is separate from, but at the same time cuts through, the other two spaces, which he calls the "temple" (*miaotang*) and the "square" (*guanchang*). Unlike *minjian*, the other two represent the places where modern Chinese intelligentsia strive for power, status, and prestige either directly as establishment intellectuals serving the state or as harbingers of new (often transgressive) ideas in the public space. Over the course of the twentieth century, the tripartite spaces are mutually delimiting and penetrating, but for modern Chinese intellectuals, *minjian* is always at best a hidden source for the primitive and raw. The vernacular revolution in Chinese literature is an example.

Hence, an important feature of *minjian* is that it is a place of non-discrimination, tolerance, and conservation, *cangwu nagou*--collecting grime and containing wreckage (Chen Sihe 2003:269). Historically, *minjian* has indeed always offered a place for cultural elites who were banished or retreated from political life. Thus, one can take Chen's charting of its early-twentieth-century formation at three levels but alter the point and level of emphasis. While Chen (2003:259) sees it primarily as persevering the traditions of an agrarian China, an argument can be made for *minjian*'s twentieth-century transformation, in structure and function, into the main container of residual traditional cultural institutions and forms banished from the modernizing centre, and its articulation in an emerging urban popular culture created by the new commercial market and city space.

Indeed, *minjian* became the retreat of literati who chose to uphold traditional cultural forms in opposition to new cultures of the times. But *minjian* also offered chances for those who embraced modernity differently. Thus, it is treated in this chapter not merely as a depository of the residual and agrarian, but as a *seminal* concept with which to approach the *jianghu* world represented in modern Chinese popular fiction. This includes Zhang Henshui's butterfly romances that delineate an urban topography in the turbulent first half of the twentieth century, as well as the mid-century émigré martial arts novels by Jin Yong, whose spatial imagination articulates the longings of millions displaced by a peculiar Chinese geopolitical formation of *liang an san di* (the triangulation of mainland China, Taiwan, and Hong Kong into three separated territories across the Taiwan Strait). While Zhang's realist romances depict the human vicissitudes of a world of sweeping changes, which is the modern equivalent of the unruly *jianghu* for his plebeian, middleclass urban readers, as much as for fictional characters inhabiting his works, Jin Yong's *jianghu* presents forbidden palaces and exotic wilderness of the long ago and far away, and conjures up a different *minjian* vision of a displaced modern China.

From Old Beijing to Shanghai Express: Modern Love in Zhang Henshui's Butterfly Romances

Zhang Henshui is regarded as a major butterfly writer because his vernacular episodic novels are almost exclusively love stories, and they remind readers of traditional scholar-meets-beauty romance (Liu Yangti 1997:4). However, Zhang's love stories seldom end happily in the turbulent world of modern China, and true love is not always rewarded. In fact, modern-day romances in Zhang's voluminous corpus often become nightmarish adventures for his heroes and heroines, in which the traditional and the modern conspire against them. That is why some scholars (Zhang Zhongliang 2011) classify his romances (often published in newspaper instalments) as realist portraits of social customs, conventions, and mentalities of an unruly and often war-torn society. Commenting on his motivation in writing *Flower of Peace* (Taiping hua, 1931), Zhang Henshui (1993: 62; 55) asserts that what he set out to capture is the pain of homelessness and displacement that haunt millions of his fellow citizens, including himself (for he had travelled the length and width of China because of war and for career opportunities). His long career as a newspaper journalist allowed him access to all levels of society and provided him the chance to practice and master the wherewithal of capturing and shaping them through writing.

The stress on Zhang as a socially aware realist novelist, however, concentrates mostly on his painstaking exposure of the society both high and low. The social is understood, in this case, as a critical consciousness akin to social realism, although Zhang is often blamed for hijacking his own realist cause due to his undue sentimentalism or mercenary concerns (Liu Yangti 1997:200-234). Perry Link, on the other hand, understands the social in this case as representations of modern social and spatial formations. The emergence of the class and class culture of "petty city dwellers" (or petite urbanites) is a process that is significantly spatial, for it depends on and generates concurrent urban cultural institutions and practices (Link 1981:4-6). The city as a spatial organization is essential for the development of popular fiction.

Zhang Henshui's romances take place more often in the older-style Beijing than in modern Shanghai, but his Beijing-based *Fate in Tears and Laughter* (*Tixiao yinyan*, 1930; hereafter *Fate*) "establishes the `modern popular' character" of urban fiction in modern China (Link 1981:13). This novel became part of the modern urban entertainment institutions soon after its publication: it was serialized in a popular newspaper; "two movies, several stage plays and many comic book versions were all in circulation at once; a serialization in popular storytelling form was done for radio; the author was suing for his copyright" (Link 1981:13). The social as spatial in Zhang's popular fiction is dependent on his status as a popular writer and the popularity of his writing as genre fiction.

Zhang's novels reveal a worldview that is unmistakably *minjian* in its value. His fictional world is delineated as the space in which protagonists experience the joys and treacheries of love; as the frame of their physical, mental, and affective existence; and as the grid of their movements and actions. His depiction of urban spaces also highlights a field of vision, a repertoire of knowledge, a complex of desires and aspirations, all of which constantly changing and therefore full of surprises. All this is illustrated in Zhang's description of urban topographies of the ancient capital Beijing, the modern metropolis Shanghai, and the wartime capital Chongqing—as the physical stage upon which his characters act, as the demarcation of social formations and life-worlds, as well as the location of these cities' historical memories. Categories such as the "ancient capital" and "modern metropolis" are cultural tropes in modern Chinese literature, which structure cultural imagination, giving a spatial register to changes that are usually perceived as a temporal progression (Y. Zhang 1996:28-29).

Zhang Henshui's Beijing is often taken to be ethnographic as his interest in recounting the layout and minutiae of life therewith far exceeds what is necessary for the background of the story. Places, architecture, and sights such as the *Bridge of Heaven* (Tianqiao)and different kinds of square courtyards (*siheyuan*) are given such appreciative detailing (seen through the admiring eyes of the protagonists) that one can almost read them as items from a city guidebook. Zhang's description of urban life in both high and low societies is so systematically miniscule and elegiac that one suspects that even then he was documenting a disappearing folkloric Beijing culture.

However, Zhang's Beijing is more than a folkloric entity that offers the reader and the protagonist affective reassurance in age-old comfort. His protagonists sojourn in and out of the city, occasionally triumph over but are more often swallowed up by the twists and turns of this exhilarating and at times perilous urban world. In Zhang's depiction, early-twentieth-century Beijing is a *bona fide* modern *jianghu,* where life is rough and. ready, exciting yet menacing, lived with its conflicting lore and logic. This fictional *jianghu* might have offset the tedium of daily modern urban existence, bringing a legendary and distant life close at hand. But more significantly, it represents the *minjian* view on modernity as it is played out in the changing cityscape. The close relationship between journalism and early-twentieth-century Chinese fiction is crucial here, as journalist-writers tended to assume the role of an experienced guide taking readers through cities of their real as well as fictional world (Y. Zhang 1996:302). Besides a journalist, Zhang Henshui (2009:3-54) was also a noted contributor to the literati genre of familiar place essays, especially those on Beijing and Nanjing, two ancient capitals, all written during the war (1944-1945) as nostalgia pieces for himself and his readers in Chongqing. Sure, Zhang's taste in these essays, as well as in scenes and places in his novels, is a continuation of typical literati jottings of landscapes and places. Similar to most of his predecessors, he eulogized winds, flowers, snows, and the moon. However, he was keener on the life of the plebeian—on markets, teahouses, alleyways, and city parks. With palpable pleasures in enumerating the sights, sounds，smells，and tastes of street lives，he came across to his readers as a cityscape portrait artist and a poetic ethnographer. However, Zhang's ancient capitals are not spatial congealment of passing old times. They comprise also of things new and modern: city parks, train carriages, and car rides are commonplace urban scenes and activities as much as traditional teahouses and drum singings. Moreover, Zhang's world is always contemporaneous with the present, and he is a self-conscious *minjian* writer who notes the social and historical of his times from the margins (Zhang Henshui 2009:196)

Zhang's *Fate* lays out the urban topography of old Beijing for its protagonist Fan Jiashu, a novice modern student enjoying his first taste of free city life. Fan comes from an official-gentry family from Hangzhou, a garden-like city near modern Shanghai. The first time he looks around upon his arrival, Fan finds the courtyard belonging to his diplomat uncle charming in a way different from his two-storied new-style house back home. The old-style Beijing architecture conjures up a world he used to read about in classical poetry (Zhang Henshui 1997b: 1-2). Here, Beijing fascinates Fan as the material and emotional embodiment of a split life-world, and he becomes absorbed heart and soul in the city.

The social as spatial thus structures the novel, and *Fate* unfolds as an adventure story in which Fan traverses social and affective spaces as he goes around the city, encountering distinct prototypes and forms of urban China. Critics have argued for the modernity of Zhang's episodic novels: unlike traditional episodic narratives, they are moved not by plot but by characterization (Wen Fengqiao 2005). This means that Fan is the main observer through whom other characters' lives and feelings are filtered through to the reader. His venture into different worlds of Beijing and his responses to people and events he encounters unite and move the narrative along.

Fan's romances with three young women are therefore as much a conventional love triangle as his encounters with three different types of modern Chinese women who represent the sociocultural worlds of Beijing. Shen Fengxi is Fan's primary love object, and their relationship resembles the traditional scholar-meet-beauty type.

However, Shen is not the beautiful, cultivated woman that scholars dream of meeting in spring gardens; rather, she is a pretty drum-singer whom Fan runs into on one of his sojourns into the underbelly of the old capital. Fan's encounter with her thus resembles the act of "slumming" in modern cities by upper-class urban dwellers (Koven 2004). Fengxi's pitiful demeanour and status, plus her comely appearance, unleashes the Eros and altruism in Fan and sets the tone for their relationship. Though Fan tries to save Fengxi from her demi-monde fate by making her a modern girl student, the way it is arranged—clandestinely paying for her fees and her family's upkeep—is too similar to the age-old institution of concubinage to accord Fan the complete satisfaction that theirs is genuine new-style love. Moreover, he cannot fathom the depth of her world and helplessly watches as she becomes prey to the arch-villain warlord General Liu. This is in part her own doing, as she and her family cannot resist the allure of material wealth. She is thus neither loyal nor chaste according to the accepted *jianghu* rules of the game. The perils of the world of the urban poor and the unmediated brutality of warlords and rogue generals are simply beyond the scope of Fan the modern student.

If Fan fails in new-style romance, he is compensated for by a friendship based on *jianghu* principles, which lends the novel its awaited poetic justice. Fan's induction into the modern *jianghu* of Beijing is immediately rewarded by his camaraderie with martial arts master Guan Shoufeng and his daughter Xiugu. While Fan also helps them financially, it is founded on the principle of mutual admiration and genuine altruism. To Fan's delight, Shoufeng and Xiugu are real knights-errant in hiding. Memories of heroic *jianghu* deeds on horsebacks are still vivid on the Guans' mind, and they await their chance to carry out justice: Xiugu avenges Fengxi by killing General Liu. In its old town, Beijing looks like a modern version of *jianghu* where the only heroes are the old-style knights-errant, and justice is kept by their lawlessness.

Just as Late Qing fiction fuses court case and knight-errant novels, Zhang Henshui mixes genre elements and let the Guans embody the just and good in modern *jianhu* and bring plot resolution in *Fate*. Being Fan's second love interest, Xiugu plays a more active part, although the genre convention prevents her from uniting with Fan—a *jianghu* heroine would be of no use once she married a scholar. According to this logic, *Fate* ends with Fan's possible union with He Lina, Fan's third love interest, a new-style socialite from one of Beijing's richest and most powerful families, who brings Fan back to his own social environment. Interestingly, both Fan and He keep close ties with the Guans and appreciate their *jianghu* exploits. *Fate* is thus both a triangular romance and a knight-errant story. Its development is cantered on Fan's emotional and physical adventure into the plebeian bastion of aesthetic and social codes, although his quest ends with both disillusionments and triumphs. Modern scholars with traditional ties like Fan are protected by *minjian* society and share its sentiments, and Zhang Henshui offers a case in which "great traditions" of the literati in exile are preserved in the "little traditions" of urban plebeians in modern China.

In *Shanghai Express* (Shanghai kuaiche,1935), Zhang's vision of modern urban space and traditional *jianghu* is conjoined cogently, if cynically. In this story of lust and deceit, Zhang develops his narrative in the limited space of one train ride from Beijing to Shanghai. The drama is staged mostly in one first-class carriage and the deluxe dining car, while characters traverse to the second and third classes and station platforms occasionally. It becomes clear that, for both Zhang and his readers, the moving train is more than a mode of transportation: it is a symbol of modern life in 1930s China. The train represents a delimited space for urban dwellers who can afford it, separating their life from the vast surrounding country (Zhang Henshui 1997a: 5).

As it turns out, the spatial sense of protection is deceptive, as dangers also lurk within. Train carriages are conveniently used to represent microcosms of different social worlds—segregated but open to movement and transgression. As a spatial structure, the moving train becomes the best vehicle for Zhang's narration that allows him to concentrate on the social as spatial. The social formation and distinction in 1930s China is unmistakably reflected in the separately priced carriages and kinds of passengers traveling in them. While passengers do venture into other carriages, these occasions for mixing prove perilous. As it happens, it is through her alleged high-school classmates who had socially declined and thus had to ride in the third-class carriage that enchantress Liu Xichu conspires to seduce and rob wealthy banker Hu Ziyun. In fact, her scheme begins with a transgression, through deceit and seduction, into Hu's first-class carriage. So Hu's forays into lower-class carriages actually lead to his downfall. Sure, Hu does not go slumming on the Shanghai Express, but he desires a femme fatale who claims to belong to his world. Although they find each ether modern, there is no romance this time. In the enclosed space of the Shanghai Express, the new-style high society mixes with the underworld in a rough *jianghu* fashion—urban lust meets organized crime. The train in this sense is modern *jianghu* at its lowest—traditional *jianghu* survives here as underground crime organizations, and the modern liberated woman is actually in an age-old profession, a demi-monde swindler. There is no knight-errant to save the hero: in its delimited space, without old-fashioned knight-errant as the only modern redeemers of universal justice, all is rough and ruined. This un-principled modern *jianghu* is not only deprived of romance, but it precipitates the latter's perils.

Zhang Henshui (1993:62:103) repeatedly asserts that he writes for "ordinary men and women", which means his genre fiction works on the emotions of urban dwellers, providing them relief and amusement. This is why his butterfly romances, conjoining genres and conventions such as knights-errant, are predicated on a *minjian* vision of modern Chinese life. It concentrates on the phantasmagoria of the urban everyday, an equivalent of modern *jianghu* where new perils and old lore compete and conflict, where traditions persist in plebeian forms and heroic adventures are undertaken by the marginal who redress modern wrongs by ancient deeds. But this is also a world that metamorphosizes in its conventionality, in which ordinary men and women learn to accept urban modernity in and through distrust and suspicion. This fictional *jianghu* with its perils and lore is not only Zhang's consolation to his readers who are weary of the urban mundane, and who are avid for the extraordinary as well as comfortingly familiar, but it also preserves for modern vernacular Chinese fiction a *minjian* place. It keeps vernacular fiction writing in *minjian,* where it originates and continues to flourish.

Across Beautiful, Yet Perilous Mountains and Waters

Jin Yong has been credited for constructing an original, massive *jianghu* in his corpus of martial arts fiction. The world of his knights-errant consists of countless characters from diverse social and cultural backgrounds, different historical periods, and vast landscapes beyond mainland China. Inhabiting snowy mountains or far-off islands and crossing immense lakes and plains, his protagonists fight in palace grounds, invade the walled compounds, wander along streets and grasslands, and fly over rooftops and mountain cliffs. They belong to various schools of martial arts and secret societies, and pledge loyalty to all manners of hermit masters, clandestine Christian groups, and rebel armies.

With his modern recreation of traditional lore and expansive spatial imagination, Jin's novels contribute to the construction of a "cultural China" appealing to complex and conflicting sentiments in the Chinese-speaking world across national and geopolitical divisions. His debut in the mid-twentieth century signals a new development of the vernacular and *minjian* as a counter-tradition: when the course for literature and culture in mainland China was expressly anti-traditionalist, his novels propagated the polyphony of traditional cultural forms and feelings. Written in the British Colony of Hong Kong from the 1950s to the 1970s, these novels attracted myriad readers around the world and became a de facto symbol of a Chinese culture cantered at the margins.

However, rather than a popular pan-Chinese continuation of nation building as some mainland critics would have it (Kong Qingdong 2004: 1), Jin's cultural China is figured exclusively from the *minjian* imagination. Both in its scope and conception, it is a non-national space, a palimpsest of bygone but expansive empires sheltering all grime and wreckage, in which political and elite cultural centers are known to be hostile and utopias always displaced to far-off islands or deserts. And in terms of form, Jin's new-style martial arts fiction is indebted to a modern vernacular genre—knights-errant stories since the late Qing—that continues to capture the popular imagination but nonetheless remains outside the canon of modern Chinese culture. Similar to Zhang Henshui's romances for urban dwellers, Jin's novels are a carnivalesque transformation of both "great" and "little" cultural traditions in compensatory imagination. This supplementary urban imagination is similarly catered to ordinary readers who inhabit wider yet more confined geographical spaces either by volition or force, and who demand consolation or forms of transgression, or simply the pleasure of trespassing. It is by no means surprising that the narrative structure   and imaginative trajectory of Jin's novels are spatial—flights of fancy were one of the few ways to traverse the insurmountable physical as well as geopolitical borders between mainland China, Hong Kong, Taiwan, and other parts of the world during the Cold War (1950s-1980s).

Jin's cultural China is notable for its panoramic grandeur as well as its geographically specific topography. His characters traverse realms of both the fantastic and the mundane. As popular leisure reading, his novels are unusually ambitious: they attempt to capture all aspects of recognizable Chinese traditions— from Confucianism to Taoism and Buddhism, encompassing the everyday, the folkloric, and the foreign—to varying degrees of success. Unlike Zhang Henshui's ancient capitals and modern metropolis, Jin's cultural geographies are less a showcase for exhaustive ethnographic knowledge than a phantasmagoria of a mosaic map of China. This geographically differentiated cultural China underwrites an imaginative topography that serves as the grid for his readers' affective identification, evoking their memories of a historical and physical home, or embodying their longings for cross-generational ancestral spiritual origins. Regardless of how these novels work on their readers' structure of feelings, it is obvious that they offer a counter-realm of cultural historical experience. Through flights of fancy in time and space, his readers are enticed to forget the political and geographical confines of the warring nation-states.

The expansive spatial terrain and diverse geocultural topography of Jin's *jianghu* reminds his diaspora readers—and subsequently postsocialist mainland readers—of the territorial and spiritual splendour of China's imperial past, which stands in stark contrast to the historical trauma of the modern nation-state with all that it forbids and dislocates. Jin's map in this sense not only embodies nostalgia. It can be understood as the playful third space of imaginative freedom produced by popular Chinese fiction, especially martial arts novels and films, in which fantasy conjoins the real and history is transcended by individual choice (Y. Zhang 2011). Jin's imaginative cultural mapping of an alternative historical China is nonetheless a transformative continuation of the twentieth-century vernacular and *minjian* tradition generically. It relocates *minjian* as the site of cultural production to the diaspora.

Spatial movement is the key structure of Jin's new-style martial arts fiction. In this, they are true to type, though they also contain other genre elements such as the picaresque and romance. In the traditional knight-errant genre, traversal of space and distance (*you*) is as important as seeking justice with martial prowess (*xia*). Jin's contribution to modern Chinese vernacular fiction can be said to reside mainly in his extension of the spatial imagination of the knights-errant genre, especially *you*—the journey as motif and structure. Reliance on the spatial is also a recognized feature of traditional Chinese vernacular historical novels and heroic romance. The Fourteenth and Sixteenth-century novels *Romance of Three Kingdoms (Sanguo yanyi)* and *Water Margin (Shui huzhuan)* are famous for their expansive battle scenes. While the former depicts sweeping panoramas of warfare where mountains, plains, and rivers are at the foreground, the latter does not limit its actions to the water margins of Mount Liang, spanning instead its terrain across Shandong to Bianliang in picaresque episodes of its multiple individual heroes. The spatial register in the narrative structure of these novels is meant for presenting vistas, which are featured mainly in scenes rather than movements, even though their characters traverse considerably. A closer prototype for Jin's knight-errant adventures is the mid-sixteenth-century *Journey to the West (Xi youji)*, where the rogue heroic adventures of the Monkey King and his fellow travellers string along fantastic geocultural locations and exotic peoples and customs.

Spatial movement has always been a notable feature that distinguishes modern martial arts novels from the May Fourth fiction, as the latter prefers layered description of single scenes or frequent alteration between scenes. Lu Xun, for example, is most adept at emphatic single scene description, whereas Mao Dun is celebrated for his panoramic portrayal of background events and urban settings. But swift spatial movement is regarded as a significant element of modern martial arts fiction that came to the fore in the 1920s, an element predicated on the concept of *you* as journeying. In knight-errant novels of the 1920s-1930s from writers such as Pingjiang Buxiao Sheng, Zhao Huanting, and Gu Mingdao, *jianghu* is the depth, length, and width of space in which the hero roams. This signifies an important moment in the development of modern-genre fiction, when the martial arts genre separates itself from the court case fiction, and knights-errant become free and mobile again. In modern knights-errant stories, characterization and plot develop along with the spatial movement, through which readers not only appreciate the valence and emotions of the heroes but also marvel at local scenes and customs along the way. This kind of spatial inflection is largely absent from new literature of the day, which is preoccupied instead with the vagaries of time in formal and thematic terms.

When Jin Yong and his colleague Liang Yusheng began serializing their émigré martial arts stories in influential Hong Kong newspapers, the journey home (for some) or simple scenic tours (for others) became a yearning for what was beyond the horizon in the Chinese-speaking world, and all this took on a dream quality when faced with insurmountable borders. It is not surprising that journeying became a requisite element of martial arts fiction in the second half of the twentieth century. Significantly in this context, the realm of Jin's novels is not confined to the landmass of China. The protagonist of *The Heaven Sword and the Dragon Sabre (Yitian tulong ji, 1961)* is born on the Ice and Fire Island near the North Pole, fights his enemies from Wudang Mountain to the Shaolin Temple, leads anti-Yuan rebels across the central north regions, and defeats the alien missionaries from Persia on the ocean. This kind of sweeping moves across vast territories is even more frequent in Jin's later works. His last martial novel, *The Deer and the Cauldron (Luding ji, 1969; Deer* hereafter), pushes the journey motif to the extreme, sending its hero Wei Xiaobao to travel all over China and even to visit Yaksa and Moocow, before he disappears in the vast *jianghu.*

In *The Legend of the Condor Heroes (Shediao yingxiong zhuan*, 1957; English 1994a, *Legend* hereafter), the *jianghu* world is as much an unorthodox battleground beyond the political regimes as a fantastic realm of scenic grandeur and cultural phantasm. Its protagonists Guo Jing and Huang Rong, in a sense, serve as tour guides for Jin's readers of the Cold War era and bring them along a journey of historical recollection and cultural homage amidst contemporary traumas inflicted by contending nations, territories, and ideologies. Unlike Zhang Henshui's modern *jianghu*, which fuses the increasingly new with the reassuringly familiar, the topography of *Legend* covers areas outside the familiar centers of political and cultural authority. Jin, as well as his heroes, appreciates neither the emperors and their capitals nor the cities of the central plain. For the traveling knights, these urban centers are perilous grounds of evil intrigue. Guo Jing and Huang Rong, for instance, are often trapped in towns on their way, even though Huang is well versed in the elite culture. In contrast, the untamed rivers and lakes are places for *jianghu* heroes to rest and rejuvenate. Guo Jing is sheltered in the Mongolian pastures when he runs into dangers (he was raised by the Mongolians), and Huang practices her "Chinese" arts freely only on her father's distant island.

Jin's cultural China is envisioned as a *minjian* world，albeit extended, exoticized, and enlarged. It is for modern urban readers of the Chinese vernacular who can no longer rely on established cities of political or cultural authority as sites for their fantasy or consolation. His *jianghu*, as the mid-century *minjian* for the Chinese-speaking world, must be spatially expansive and psychologically fantastic to alternate as a different realm beyond the margins of the Cold War political regimes. Similar to his outlawed heroes, the reader must be bewildered enough to suspend disbelief and take on a constant journey across sweeping and exotic wilderness.

In Jin's *jianghu*, the world gets better as the radius of power pans out. The places beyond the elite and orthodox political and cultural horizons may not be ideal, for oftentimes they are also beyond the demands of civilization, but they are a less menacing habitat for ordinary local residents as well as for those accustomed to exile. John Hamm (2005:80) points out that，throughout Jin Yong's martial arts novels，there is a dialectic transformation in his depiction of the movement from the centre to the margins: from the scene of exile in his early novels to the consciousness of diaspora in his later ones, which Yingjin Zhang (2011:9) further elaborates as a movement from loss of home and nation to individual reflections on and alternative practices of home and nation.

This sense of the diaspora as new *minjian*，however, is also present in Jin's earlier martial arts fiction. It is already predicated in the historical development of modern Chinese genre fiction in its carnivalesque relation to Chinese cultural tradition. Jin's new diaspora *minjian* is a spatial expansion as well as logical continuation of the previous tradition. The new *minjian* of *liang a san di* can only be cantered in the diaspora as the latter is one of the few remaining margins of cultural possibility vis-a-vis the increasing encroachment of totalitarian and authoritarian regimes. It became the mid-century container of grime and wreckage: a haven for the exiled residuals and a new incubating space for the relocated and expanded vernacular Chinese *minjian* culture. Jin's debut in this sense is more telling than his later novels.

Similar to Jin himself, the hero of the *Romance of the Book and the Sword (Shujian enchou lu*, 1955; English 1994b, hereafter *Romance*) is a fallen literatus stranded in *minjian*, a remainder of the older elite culture and an observer of new cultures in the wildness. But, unlike Fan Jiashu in Zhang Henshui's old Beijing, Jin's residual literati are also martial heroes—they sometimes become leaders in the *minjian* world. Chen Jialuo is a talented scholar from Jiangnan, the traditional centre of late imperial culture. However, even though he was born into the most illustrious local gentry family, he becomes the head of the largest secret society in Qing China and lives in exile. He studies martial arts in Tianshan Mountain at the empire's far western regions and works with the underground Red Flower Society whose members hail from all walks of life from Central, Northeast, and South China.

As a knight-errant hero, Chen Jialuo is a mixture of prototypes, since the novel also has elements of the butterfly romance. He is the fallen scholar but also a martial art master. Torn between his commitments to love and the cause of justice, Chen is burdened with all that is undesirable in a scholar hero—he sticks to residual literati values and acts like a stereotype: he is alternately too impulsive or too hesitant, and as a result loses all he loves and harms his chosen cause. But he remains loyal to his underground society, whose cause of justice is appreciated by the marginal. Even though Jin still differentiates the Han Chinese from its others, such differentiation is not always in favour of the Han Chinese (Wang Yichuan 2007:277). Chen's habitat is, from the outset, the perilous *jianghu* made up of a multiethnic cast of heroes and villains. Though the novel begins with the Red Flower brothers' expedition to the political and cultural centers, and their ill-fated cause of changing history at the centre, it ends with their tragic failure and retreat back to China's Turkic west. The westward journey is an exile for the ex-literati, ex-central plain martial masters, but it is also a homeward passage for them as they become marginal *minjian* heroes.

In Jin's spatial-martial adventure narratives, the protagonists' displacement from the political and cultural centre is an absolute necessity, and theirs are typically journeys of no return. In the course of his long writing career, Jin has become less interested in fallen scholars than in knights-errant of mixed and marginal origins. The heroes of his later fiction, such as Guo Jing of *Legend* and Wei Xiaobao of *Deer, come* directly from the geographical backwater or social underground of the imperial centers and are notably unlearned in elite orthodoxies and cultural arts. The places they inhabit—rivers and lakes, mountain tops and grasslands, far off villages and plebeian urban establishments—look less like places of exile but more like their natural habitat or adopted homes. One may conclude that there are significant changes in Jin's depiction of the movement from the centre to the periphery and, with it, the emergence of a diaspora consciousness.

Indeed, Jin's mid-to-late-century martial *jianghu* is underwritten and complicated by such defining modern experiences as mass migration, displacement, and fragmentation in as much as spaces of the nation-state is concerned. But one should also note that the transformative figuration of such *jianghu* in martial arts fiction as a *minjian* genre is predicated on the transformation and relocation of *minjian* as concept and space in twentieth-century China. Jin re-centers his *jianghu* and his vision of *minjian* as the truly marginal cultural space at the diaspora, just as Zhang Henshui relocated his to the modern Chinese city in the early twentieth century. These relocations sustain *minjian*'s capacity as a cultural space of preservation and recreation, interlocking with but always receding from the contending centers of political and cultural authority. They also re-invigorate modern Chinese popular genre fiction and enable its miraculous flourish in a century of frequent social disruption and austere political and cultural regimes.

References

1. Bakhtin, Mikihail M. 1984. *Rabelais and His world.* Bloomington: Indiana University Press.

2. Calhoun, Craig. 2002. *Dictionary of the Social Sciences*, Oxford, UK: Oxford University Press. Chen, Pingyuan 陳平原.2010. *Zhongguo xiaoshuo xushi moshi de zhuanbian* 中國小銳敘事模式的轉變 (The evolution of the narrative mode in Chinese fiction). Beijing: Beijing daxue chubanshe.

3. Chen, Sihe 陳思和.2003. "*Minjian de fuchen: dui kangzhan dao avenge wenxueshi de yige chang shixing jieshi*', 民間的浮沉:對抗戰到文革文學史的一個嘗試性解釋 (The surfacing and submersion of minjian: A tentative explanation of modern Chinese literary history from the war of resistance to the Cultural Revolution). In *Ershi shiji Zhongguo wenxue shilun*, 二十世紀中國文學史論 (On twentieth-century Chinese literary history). Edited by Wang Xiaoming 王曉明.

4. Shanghai: Dongfang chuban zhongxin, 257-264.

5. Hamm, John Christopher. 2005. Paper Swordsmen: Jin Yong and the Modern Chinese Martial Arts Novel. Honolulu: University of Hawaii Press.

6. Han, Yunbo 韓雲波. 2003. "*Minsu fanshi yu ershi shiji Zhongguo wuxia xiaoshuo*" 民俗範式與 20 世紀中國武俠小說 (The folklore paradigm in twentieth-century Chinese martial arts fiction). *Wuhan ddxue xuebao* 武漢大學學報 (Journal of Wuhan University), 1:86-91.

7. Hunan, Patrick. 1981. *The Chinese Vernacular Story*. Cambridge, MA: Harvard University Press. Hunan. Patrick. 2004. *Chinese Fiction of the Nineteenth and Early Twentieth Centuries: Essays by Patrick Hanan*. New York: Columbia University Press.

8. Jinn Yong 金庸.1994a. *Shediao yingxiong zhuan* 射雕英雄傳 (The legend of condor heroes). Beijing: Sanlian shudian.

9. Jin Yun 金庸.1994b. *Shujian enchou lu* 書劍恩仇錄 (Romance of the book and the sword). Beijing: Sanlian shudian.

10. Kong Qingdong, 孔慶東. 2004. "*Jin Yong yu guomin wenxue* " 金庸與國民文學 (Jin Yong and national literature). Accessed 23 Feb. 2014. http://www. aisixiang.com/data/23633.html.

11. Koven, Seth. 2004. *Slumming: Sexual and Social Politics in Victorian London*. Princeton, NJ: Princeton University Press.

12. Link, E. Perry. 1981. Mandarin Ducks and Butterflies: Popular Fiction in Early Twentieth-century Chinese Cities. Berkeley: University of California Press.

13. Liu, Yangti 劉揚體. 1997. *Liubian zhongde liupai: yuanyang hudie pai xinlun*，流變中的流派：鴛鴦蝴蝶派新論 (The changing trends: a new understanding of the mandarin ducks and butterflies school). Beijing: Zhongguo wenlian chubanshe.

14. Wang, David Der-wei. 1997. Fin-de-siecle Splendor: Repressed Modernities of Late Qing Fiction, 1849- 1911. Stanford, CA: Stanford University Press.

15. Wang, Dewei 王德威. 2003. *Xiandai Zhongguo xiaoshuo shijiang* 現代中國小說十講 (Ten lectures on modern Chinese fiction). Shanghai: Fudan daxue chubanshe.

16. Wang, Yichuan 王一川. 2007. "*Wenhua xugenxing shiqi de xiangxiangxing renting* 文化虛根性時期的想像性認同—金庸的現代性意義 (Imaginative Identification in an Age of Cultural Nihilism—the Modernity of Jin Yong's Novels". In *Jin Yong Pinglun Wushinian*, 金庸評論五十年 (Fifty Years of Jin Yong). Edited by Ge Tao 葛濤. Beijing: Wenhuayishu chubanshe.

17. Wen, Fengqiao 溫奉橋. 2005. *Xiandaixing shiye zhongde Zhang Henshui xiaoshuo* 現代性視野中的張恨水小說 (Zhang Henshui's novels in the perspective of modernity). Qingdao: Zhongguo haiyang daxue chubanshe.

18. Zhang, Henshui 張恨水. 1993. *Zhang Henshui quanji* 張恨水全集 (Complete works of Zhang Henshui). Edited by Xie Zhongyi 謝中一. Taiyuan: Beiyue wenyi chubanshe.

19. Zhang, Henshui. 1997a. *Shanghai Express*. Trans. William A. Lyell. Honolulu: University of Hawaii Press.

20. Zhang, Henshui 張恨水. 1997 b. *T'ixiao yinyua*, 啼笑因緣 (Fate in tears and laughter). In Zhongguo xiandai wenxue baijia 中國現代文學百家：張恨水 (A hundred masterpieces in modern Chinese literature: Zhang Henhsui). Edited by Yu Runqi 于潤奇. Beijing: Huaxia chubanshe.

21. Zhang, Henshui 張恨水. 2009. *Duhe yu fei* 獨鶴與飛 (Flight of a lonely crane). Xi'an: Shaanxi renmin chubanshe.

22. Zhang, Yingjin. 1996. *The City in Modern Chinese Literature and Film: Configuration of Space, Time, and Gender.* Stanford, CA: Stanford University Press.

23. Zhang, Yingjin. 2011. "*Youxi yu lishi zhiwai: disankongjian de lilun yu Jin Yong xiaoshuo de yiyi* 遊戲於歷史之外：第三空間理論與金庸武俠小說的意義 (Play beyond History: Theory of the Third Space and Jin Yong's Martial Arts Novels." In *Jin Yong yu Hanyu Xinwenxue* 金庸與漢語新文學 (Jin Yong and New Chinese Literature). Edited by Zhu Shoutong 朱壽桐. Macau: University of Macau Publication Center. 73-87.

24. Zhang, Zhongliang 張中良. 2011. Zhang Zhongliang jiang xiandaixiaoshuo 張中良講現代小說(Zhang zhongliang on modern Chinese fiction). Changsha: Hunan jiaoyu chubanshe.

1911 in Chengdu: A Novel History

Yi Zheng

I. Scaling the modern historical novel

Georg Lukács' 1937 reflection on the development of the European historical novel is notable in its establishment of a direct link between world-historical events and the evolution of the genre. In his definition this historical novel is "an artistically faithful image of a concrete historical epoch," which could not come about without "the French Revolution, the revolutionary wars and the rise and fall of Napoleon" (19). It is the case not because there exists a causal correlation between the two, but because these momentous events "for the first time made history a mass experience, and moreover on a European scale" (23). For Lukács it is the mass experience of the unprecedented quick succession of upheavals on a grand scale between 1789 and 1814 that gave rise to a different sense of history, when "the masses no longer have the impression of history as a "natural occurrence". And it is the modern sense of history as "an uninterrupted process of changes" which "has a direct effect upon the life of every individual" that necessitated the narrative form for a faithful image of a concrete historical epoch. What is concrete, or specifically historical in this novel image, is not external choices of theme or costume, but "derivation of the individuality of characters from the historical peculiarity of their age" (23). Beyond an oft-noted historical determinism, Lukács emphasizes the spatio-temporal character of people and circumstances with a dual focal point. History becomes a worthy subject of novelistic representation when its effect upon life is felt by every individual as a mass experience with scale. Individuals as historical beings are essential in his plot for the modern historical novel: his analysis of Walter Scott and Leo Tolstoy are famously predicated on their distinctive treatment of "world historical individuals" (47) and the average "mediocre hero" (35). However, like many of his fellow Interwar European writers who lived and wrote in the midst of the "era of crowds", 〔註1〕 the mass and mass experience is also central to his conception of modern history and historical fiction. The historical role of the individual is a manifestation of the historical spirit in the mass experience, and modern history the experience of quick successions of change on a massive scale.

Two years earlier, Lu Xun (1881-1936), a pivotal figure in twentieth century Chinese cultural history, also expounded on the necessity of capacious literary accounts for significant historical events. Lu's interest in the capacity and length of narrative form, against the backdrop of a post-May Fourth (1919) turn to "self", "lyrical" expression and "epistolary" and "diary" form in Chinese fiction in the 1920s (Jaroslav Prusek 1980), like Lukács' emphasis on the scale of history hence historical fiction, betrays an urgent sense of their present. For Lu and his fellow writers, not only is the history of modern China similarly defined by quick succession of unprecedented upheavals, and the mid-1930s in the looming shadow of an impending war, 〔註2〕 it is also a time of reckoning with China's recent past. A suitable form that can account for such tumultuous and wide-ranging world change is thus not only necessary but also timely. For Lu it seems a matter of

---

〔註1〕 For an extensive and insightful account of Interwar European thought and cultural representation of the "the masses", see Stefan Jonsson, *Crowds and Democracy: the idea and Image of the Masses from Revolution to Fascism*, 2013. Jonsson connects the "era of crowds" with the history of Weimar Germany and Austria of the first Republic, covering key thinkers such as Elias Canetti, Hannah Arendt, Georg Simmel, Max Webber, Sigmund Freud, Theodor Adorno, Siegfried Kracauer, Walter Benjamin, and configurations of the crowd and masses in novels, films and plastic art of the period.

〔註2〕 China was on the brink of war with Japan, who had annexed its North-eastern provinces. This war, which lasted eight years, became an important part of World War II, and at its conclusion in 1945 was followed immediately by a four-year civil war that resulted in the post-war geopolitical division of the so-called two-coasts and three-landmasses (*liangan sandi*)—mainland China, Hong Kong and Taiwan.

scaling: "since the last years of the Qing Empire, there is no lack of great historical events: the Opium War, the Sino- French War, Sino-Japanese War, Wuxu Reform, the Boxer Rebellion and Allied Invasion, leading all the way to the Republican Revolution. However as yet there is no historical representation of these that are up to standard, not to mention literary works" (Lu Xun 1991: 287). What is crucial in the call for a modern historical narrative in literary representation is the structure and capacity of a narrative form for recent "great historical events". This is made in his preface to Xiao Jun's (1907-1988) *Village in August* (*bayue de xiangcun*, 1935), one of the earliest full length treatment of the mounting Second Sino-Japanese War. Lu's only reservation about the novel is its lack of real full length—that it reads more like a series of short stories. In this way its structure and characterization do not compare well with Aleksandr A. Fadeyev's *Destruction* (1927). However, for Lu, the novel's promising qualities more than compensated for its structural weakness. "In a taut and tense narrative, the author's heart and blood fuse with the lost sky, the lost earth, the suffering multitude, the tall grasses, the fiery sorghum, the grasshoppers and mosquitoes on the vast prairie; all infused, unfolding and displaying scarlet in front of the readers..." (Lu Xun, 288). As an established master of the prose essay and short story, Lu calls rather urgently for the length and width of the novel. Events such as wars and revolutions that have become regular occurrences since the last days of the Qing Empire (1644-1911) and throughout the short history of the newly-established Republic (1912-1949) merit expansive depictions of a longue durée, as they are experiences of a shifting life world that demand a whole-hearted and full bloodied representation.

Unbeknownst to Lu Xun, in July 1935 Li Jieren (1891-1962) finished *Ripples in a Dead Pond* (*Sishui weilan*), 〔註3〕 the first of his trilogy on the 1911 (*Xin Hai*) Revolution. It was published in early 1936, and was soon followed by *Before the*

〔註 3〕 Of Li's trilogy only the first is translated into English, see *Ripple on Stagnant Water: A Novel of Sichuan in the Age of Treaty Ports,* Trans. Sparling, Bret and Yin Chi, Honolulu: University of Hawai'i Press, 2013; the author suggests however that a better capture of the novel and its title *Sishui weilan* is *Ripples in a Dead Pond*. For this reason and the fact that the other two novels are not translated, the author's own translations will be used throughout the essay for the sake of consistency.

Tempest (*Baofengyu qian*, 1936), and *Great Waves* (*Da bo*, 1937). Immediately upon its publication, fellow writer and historian Guo Moruo (1892-1978) hailed the trilogy as the "modern Chinese history in novel form," a "modern day *Chronicles of Hua Yang* (*huayang guozi*)" (1980: 5). Guo saw in the series' duo ambition regarding modern Chinese history and the novel form the long waited- for new direction for modern Chinese fiction. His categorization places the trilogy in the tradition of a literary form that challenges orthodox history and historiography from the outset, reminding readers of modern Chinese fiction Chinese novel's origin as repositories for alternative versions of the past. 〔註4〕By liking it to *Chronicles of Hua Yang* (Chang Qu 317- 420), the oldest extant gazetteer of Li's region, in which history, geography and individual stories play equal part, Guo also calls attention to Li's ethnohistorical aspiration.

Li's novel history of the monumental revolution is delineated through changing "life modes" (Guo, 1980: 5) and feelings of a geographically rooted provincial community, where the social influences the political, and events that become recorded history are part of or proceeded by cumulative transformations of everyday life. Li defines his novel project as the pursuit of the "historical real (*lishi zhenshi*)": "When you write about political transformations, can you not write about changes in people's lives and thoughts? When you want to capture the stirrings in people's lives, feelings and ideas, can you not describe the political and economic upheavals of the time? Only when you try to delineate the panorama of life and changes of the times can others learn from your writing the historical real there and then" (Li Jieren, "Postscript Vol. 2": 768-69). Li's historical real is time and place bound.

It can be captured and delineated in the panorama of change of that time and place. But for Li, this panorama of historical real is not simply the sum total of social structural and affective transformation, or something revealed in the passions and eruptions of earth- shattering events. It is seen in the interpenetration of political and economic upheavals and the stirrings in people's lives and feelings.

〔註 4〕Owen, Stephen. *Remembrances: The Experience of the Past in Classical Chinese Literature*, 1986: 141-43.

For Li, this interpenetration is what makes modern history a communal (mass) experience with a scale in the Lukácsian sense, and therefore fitting subject for modern historical fiction. Though unlike Lukács' vision of an expanding Europe, Li's scale is defined by the length and width of his native province at a critical moment of its collective experience. His historical fiction of a momentous revolution is also a gazetteer and novel history of a local place. Despite the pioneering status of Li's modern historical novel, however, for most of the twentieth century Li and his work was excluded from official Chinese literary history. Though the publication of the trilogy is acknowledged some sixty years later to have marked a turning point in the development of the modern Chinese novel (Yang Lianfen, 279). In 2015, Kwok-kwan Ng's *The Lost Geopoetic Horizon of Li Jieren: The Crisis of Writing Chengdu in Revolutionary China* for the first time introduced Li's serial novels to an English academic audience. Ng's well-researched study pits Li's geo-poetics against what he perceives as the teleological revolutionary narratives of modern Chinese history and Li's local historical novel against the May Fourth fictional discourse (Ng 48), highlighting Li's unique contribution to modern Chinese fiction. 〔註 5〕

〔註 5〕 Kenny Kwok-kwan Ng, *The Lost Geopoetic Horizon of Li Jieren: The Crisis of Writing Chengdu in Revolutionary China*, 2015. The author agrees with Ng that Li's locale-based historical fiction of the 1911 revolution differs markedly from the Nationalist and PRC versions, and that Li's ambition is vis-a-vis both modern Chinese history and the novel form. The author's main contention is conceptual, that is, on how one conceives Li's historical vision and narrative experimentation. This essay argues that Li's ambition is to write a different version of the revolution, where long term local social and cultural transformations precede and dictate the development of political events. Whereas even though Ng sets Li's fiction against the teleological historical narrative, he at the same time concludes that the revolution as nation-wide historical forces brought about the local social and cultural evolution (42). The author also disagrees with Ng, amongst other things, that Li's local poetics is negative vis-a-vis modern Chinese history, that is, Li recounts historical progress as negative change, and the local place, which is otherwise unchanging, "stagnant" and "decadent", is simply caught up in (then resists against) raging historical progress (46). This essay suggests that Li's local place, which is emphatically not comparable to the countryside or small town in the city-country opposition, but the provincial community of Sichuan best understood in late imperial China's macro-region nexus, is the only site of history, and as such, it is the present, rather than the past (therefore an outside)

II. The novel as gazetteer history of life and feelings of a province in revolution

Li observes in his "Preface" to *Ripples in a Dead Pond* that "since 1925, …I have been considering the possibility of writing a series of linked full-length novels to represent sequentially, in episodes, the changing social phenomena of the last few decades, meaning those events and fragments of life which I have lived through, felt and thought about, and experienced in full, which seem to me significant and are the real turning points of history" (Li Jieren, "Preface", 241). For Li, the subject for historical fiction not only encompasses both notable events and "fragments of life". It is also defined by what the author "experienced in full", thus necessarily encapsulating their processes in time as well as in place. A narrative construction that is "linked full length" and "in episodes" is thus ideal for sequential representations of the "significant and real turning points of history" that this fiction seeks to illuminate. The trilogy, which Li went on to define as an account of the 1911 Revolution that builds up to the events "by tracing their sources and following their currents" (Li, 241), recounts the last days of the Qing Empire (1644-1911) in Chengdu, the capital of the frontier Sichuan province, in three linked episodes: 1) *Ripples in a Dead Pond* begins the epic account in the small market town of Tianhui on the outskirts of Chengdu from 1899 to 1901. Its story dramatizes the grand passions and life and death contests for prowess of a few emerging players at the town's social and economic scene during the turbulent

---

of the history recounted. It provides a perimeter for the narrative that is communal. Individuals whose acts become meaningful in the communal story are historical actors rather than its primitive others, like the local colours of the May Fourth native-soil writers, who are influenced by and can only react to a history that comes from elsewhere. The essay also argues that formally, Li's reinvention of the modern Chinese historical novel draws on Chinese novel's original proximity to history writing, and the gazetteer as a spatial historical form, besides a multitude of European and Chinese social and historical novels. Understanding Li's narrative choice as a French influenced-turn from May Fourth romanticism to realism and naturalism (Ng 42-48) cannot account for the historical-aesthetic ambition of his life-long experimentation with a spatial novel form that can delineate the processes and momentum of a revolution: the interplay of people's life and feelings and the development of events that became recorded history.

years of the Boxer Rebellion. 〔註6〕 *Before the Tempest* follows with the affective and social transformations of the provincial capital from 1902 to 1909, through the family fortune of the Hao household tailing the "New Policies" 〔註7〕 of a dying empire; and *Great Waves* recounts the great agitations leading to the riots of the Sichuan Railway Protection Movement (1911) 〔註8〕 in Chengdu and its escalation throughout the province, which launched the Revolution that formally ended China's imperial history.

Geographic locations, scenes of daily life as well as dramatic events, "fragments" of customs and habitual practice are thus an essential part of the panorama of Li's history as communal world change. Place and place-based narratives are not new to modern Chinese fiction. "Local Colour Stories (*xiangtu xiaoshuo*)" that focus on life and feelings of the authors' native soils and hometowns embody the longing for as well as the anxiety of modernity of the May Fourth and other modern Chinese writers. 〔註9〕 Here the native place with local colours is an epitome of antiquated agrarian civilization, a hotbed for clashes of conflicting values and sentiments. A telling example is Shen Congwen's (1902-1988) *Border Town* (bian cheng, 1934). In the novella the elegiac passing of the idyllic life of a small border town and its surrounding countryside prophesizes

〔註6〕 Officially supported peasant uprising of 1900 that attempted to drive all foreigners from China. "Boxers" was a name that foreigners gave to a Chinese secret society known as the Yihequan ("Righteous and Harmonious Fists"). The group practiced certain boxing and callisthenic rituals in the belief that this made them invulnerable. It was thought to be an offshoot of the Eight Trigrams Society (Baguajiao), which had fomented rebellions against the Qing dynasty in the late 18th and early 19th centuries. Their original aim was the destruction of the dynasty and also of the Westerners who had a privileged position in China, https://www.britannica.com/event/Boxer-Rebellion, accessed 10/8/2016.

〔註7〕 The New Policies (xinzheng) of the late Qing dynasty (1644-1911), also known as the Late Qing Reform, were a series of political, economic, military, cultural and educational reforms that were implemented in the last decade of the Qing dynasty to keep the dynasty in power after the humiliating defeat in the Boxer Rebellion; see William T. Rowe, *China's Last Empire: The Great Qing*, 2009: 255-262.

〔註8〕 Sichuan Railway Protection Movement—a local elites-led popular movement in 1911 to resist railway nationalization which is generally considered the trigger for the Chinese Republican Revolution that ended millennia of imperial rule. See Michael Dillon. *China: A Cultural and Historical Dictionary*, 259.

〔註9〕 See Ding Fan, *A History of Chinese Local-Colour Fiction (zhongguo xiangtu xiaoshuoshi)*, 2007.

the loss of essential humanity in the modern world. Its locale-based poetics showcases Shen's recreation of a Peach Blossom Spring (*tao hua yuan*), the quintessential Chinese otherworldliness in a modern local place. 〔註 10〕 Whereas although Mao Dun's (1896-1981) *Midnight* (zi ye, 1933) is celebrated for its sweeping treatment of Shanghai, modern China's biggest metropolis, its dissection of modern Chinese society is carried out in the opposition between the city and the countryside. In the novel the country towns and villages that stand for an agrarian civilization in its swan song are often the absent foil to the industrial, modernizing and energetic Shanghai, they nonetheless ground its narrative and thematic departure. Mao Dun also wrote novellas and short stories about the changing life and times in small towns and villages. In *The Silk Worm* (chun chan, 1932) and *Lin Family Shop* (linjia puzi, 1932), country places are locations of historical change, but only as static sites of an agrarian life-world menaced by dynamic and foreign forces and on the brink of destruction. Here as in most "Local Colour" literature, changes in place are understood as differences in time. In particular, the distance between city and country is figured as a contrast between the new and the old. It is marked as two different transitional points on the way to a new (modern) civilization. These place centred narratives are thus rather a metaphor for a collective modern Chinese cultural anxiety. Different from these figurations of local worlds, which, in Duara's view stand for the past either to be missed or reformed and transformed, 〔註 11〕 Li's local place is the present of the history recounted.

In Li's trilogy, scenic descriptions underpin events and underline their causes, processes and transformations. They denote a historically formed and transformed geographical, anthropological and political-economic life world. The geographic peculiarity of the region, its endless and steep surrounding mountains and turbulent rivers, which since time immemorial has made human and material traffic a challenge, foreshadows the local passion for ownership and construction of

---

〔註 10〕 Wang Dewei, "The Fall and Temptation of the South: On Su Tong's Fiction", *Food for Angels*, 2002: 18.

〔註 11〕 Prasenjit Duara, "Local Worlds: The Poetics and Politics of the Native Place in Modern China," *South Atlantic Quarterly* 99:1 2000:13-48.

railroads and its intensification into mass agitation. In all three novels, the scenes of life and narratives of events are often delineated with an ethnographic historical orientation. Li seems particularly interested in recounting transformations of local institutions—they mark the changing times as well as reinscribe the setting, influencing further personal and communal actions. The development of opera theatre in Chengdu as a modern urban institution, for instance, runs through both *Before the Tempest* and *Great Waves*. Whilst in the former the reader learns that operas were still only sung for occasions in local place associations or private homes, in the latter registered and named Peking and Sichuan Opera groups were already performing in established theatres newly built or separated from traditional tea houses. Woven intimately into the daily activities of the lead characters, the reader sees from this consequences of the New Policies, as well as the changing location and practice of affective life of the urban dwellers. The theatres have become the new place for hatching plots of love and desire off stage. They harbor courtships as well as encourage harassment of women, whose presence is a constant annoyance for the new municipal police. Whether women should be allowed such public presence also prompts heated debates among the city's cultural worthies—gentry-men who set up and teach in new style schools or write for the newly established local newspapers as an alternative career when the Imperial Civil Service Examination〔註 12〕was abolished in 1902. Wedding ceremonies and marriage customs are also exhibits of Li's ethnohistorical ambition. Each of the novel in the sequence has at least one wedding scene. They record fin-de-siècle displays of local tradition as well as dramatically changing material and cultural fashion, signalling a shifting local world. In *Before the Tempest*, Hao Yousan's wedding to his cousin Ye Wenwan from betrothal to formal ceremony is planned

---

〔註 12〕 The Imperial examinations or *Keju*, were an essential part of the Chinese government administration from their introduction in the Han Dynasty (206 B.C.E. to 220 C.E.) until they were abolished during Qing attempts at modernization in 1905. The examination system was systematized in the Sui Dynasty (581–618) as an official method for recruiting bureaucrats. It was intended to ensure that appointment as a government official was based on merit and not on favoritism or heredity. http://www.newworldencyclopedia.org/entry/Imperial_Examinations_(Keju),accesses 10/8/2016.

and enacted according to age-old rules of ritual perfection for the Sichuan gentry. Even though the Hao household leads the trend in the provincial capital's material and lifestyle change, and Hao and his father are both avid reformers. By the time of *Xin Hai* (1911) however, when Mrs Huang's younger sister is marrying Zhou Hongdao the returnee student from Japan in *Great Waves*, the bride is carried in the traditional bridal sedan chair only to pacify her old mother. It is a compromise in an otherwise completely new style wedding ritual: guests are invited to a party, where the go-betweens, the most distinguished guests, the groom, and even the female guests are called upon to make congratulatory speeches that include references to current affairs and women's education.

Li's ethnohistorical aspiration is not limited to a penchant for elaborating local traditions. Guo is particularly perceptive when he compares the trilogy to a modern day *Chronicles of Hua Yang*, where changes in place and people's life stories are crucial components of the narrative. Li indeed often assumes the role of the gazetteer in his historical fiction. The local place in his historical vision is a life world in crisis. His gazetteer style narrative not only emplaces history, displaying the processes of events in the panorama of everyday world change, it also figures the local place as its only site. This is probably why Li also wrote and rewrote the gazetteer of the Greater Chengdu region at moments of historical crisis. Besides enumerating and recounting at length the geographic register, histories, customs, landscapes, ways of life and feelings of Chengdu city and Sichuan province in the trilogy, he also recorded *The Evolution of the Greater City of Chengdu* in 1949, *The Historical Evolution* of Chengdu in 1953, and *A Street of Chengdu* in 1958, tracing epic historical changes in the minute alterations and ruins of a long-standing place when yet another new world dawned on him and his fellow local inhabitants.

The evocation of a celebrated location-based form that venerates local traditions and locality emplaces events and passions of the times in their deeply set roots, and locates them within changing communal histories. The geographical, anthropological, social and material details of the provincial city and its surrounding towns and countryside in Li's gazetteer-like narrative, make up the ethnohistorical world in which Li situates the pre-histories, processes and feelings of the Revolution.

> It seems to me too abrupt to begin directly from the *Xin Hai* Revolution. As it is by no means a sudden revolution. It has its historical origins and built-ups, like a big melon coming to fruition after a long time accumulation. One can only account for it by tracing its sources and following its currents… I heard about the Allied Invasion, and saw its impact in Chengdu. In the following year the Red Lantern Boxers made a big stir in the city, churches were attacked, then they executed Liao Guanyin these boxers' female leader. These things I remember most vividly. So I decided to begin here, from Geng Zi to Xin Hai, writing about what I heard, what I saw and what I personally experienced…

(Li Jieren, 'My Writing Experience,' 246-47)

Li's place is historical, the location of world change as witnessed and experienced by the author, who, like the traditional gazetteer, is part of the locale and recorded experience. The temporality of this history is embodied and displayed in spatially delimited and demonstrated changing vicissitudes of life and feelings. This spatially defined aesthetic-historical aspiration is best understood in Greg Dening's redefinition of ethnohistory, which goes beyond the inclusion of culture of a particular place in historical accounts. Dening sees its significance in "the ways in which historical consciousness is culturally distinct and socially specific and how, in whatever culture or social circumstances, the past constitutes the present in being known" (Dening, 44-45). The preoccupation with the ethnohistorical in Li, as it is for Dening, is not only to emplace history but also to capture and delineate the "teasing moments", which are the "ethnographic moments" (Dening 43) in history that highlight the "compounded nature of histories" and demonstrate that "the processes of culture and expressed structures are simply writ large in circumstance of extravagant ambiguity" (45). These moments are to be found both in notable historical events and cumulative "everyday social reality" (43).

Like a true gazetteer, Li builds his ethnohistorical world of the *Ripples*, *Tempest* and *Great Waves* with scale and exact measurement:

> From the provincial capital Chengdu heading north to its subsidiary Xindu county people say it is forty li. In fact it is only thirty. The road zigzags amongst endless expanses of flat fields. … But it is still the thoroughfare of northern Sichuan, extending all the way north until the border town Guangyuan, then beyond to Ningqiang county and Hanzhong prefecture of Shaanxi province. This was also the old courier route to Beijing the imperial capital… Goods from all North-western provinces of the empire have to pass through this route.

> At exactly twenty li between Chengdu and Xindu, amongst the vast expanses of fields like embroidered brocades, nestles a town that is neither too big nor too small… This town is the famed Tianhui outside Chengdu's North Gate…

(Li Jieren, *Ripples in a Dead Pond* 2011: 13-15)

Tianhui town, the scene of *Ripples*, and an important reference point for both the *Tempest* and *Great Waves*, is introduced with geographical scale and historical grid as a way station in the human and material flow between the provincial capital and the rest of the empire. As a medium-sized market town at the midway point between Chengdu and one of its county seat, Tianhui's geographical register signals its importance in the grid of what G.W. Skinner defines as the hierarchy of urban systems in late imperial China, in which different levels of cities, market towns, and villages are orderly and hierarchically organized, with the provincial city as the centre of an economic and political macro-region (Skinner, 253-89). In this system cities, towns and villages function differently but maintain a dynamic albeit hierarchical relation around the regional centre both administrative- bureaucratically and economic-commercially. Tianhui is thus part of the vast Qing Empire in turmoil, where the ripples are felt and as the story develops, with irreversible consequences. Spatially Tianhui is and has always been a key pin in the thoroughfare of alternating Chinese empires, at the moment linking a strategically important Qing provincial capital at the margins to its imperial centre. When the story begins it is already a town in the midst of the drastically changing times:

> …the road is so important that from morning till night, no matter rain or shine, you can see hordes of camels carrying all manners of goods jostling between four-carrier official sedans… coming and going in succession. Among the throne of people and traffic you will occasionally glimpse a thin horse…with a military-attired youth on its back, carrying a parcel and umbrella, hurrying away. You will know this is a courier for official documents or imperial edicts. However in recent years because of telegraphs official messengers and their horses became gradually a rare sight…

> (Li Jieren, Ripples in a Dead Pond 2011: 14)

Installing telegraph throughout the empire-wide postal system is the Late Qing court's and elites' attempt to lead and re-direct overwhelming currents of history. Indeed telegraph is not only changing Tianhui town's status on the provincial and imperial map, it is also one of the new technologies that played a critical part in the political upheavals in the last days of the empire (Shi, 129-43). In *Great Waves*, Sichuan Governor Zhao Erfen's order prohibiting the use of telegraph by all parties in communicating the events of the Railway Protection Movement actually abetted the anxiety and passion of the city residents, leading directly to rumours and mass riots (Li Jieren, 387-456).

The incident with which Li begins the *Tempest*, the second of his novel sequence, is the 1903 public execution of the Red Lantern Boxer 〔註 13〕 Liao Guanyin, which, as he explains in the preface to *Ripples*, is one of the seedlings in the fruition of the 1911 Revolution.

> For the ever serene and unperturbed Chengdu city, indeed, no incident is as great as this one. Even if we count the revolt of Short-jacket Li and Lan Dashun, as well as that dramatic time when Shi

---

〔註 13〕 The Red Lanterns were the women's fighting groups organized by village women during the Boxer Rebellion, a violent anti-foreign and anti-Christian uprising between 1899 and 1901; see Joseph W. Esherick, *The Origins of the Boxer Uprising*, 1988.

Dakai was betrayed by that chieftain, captured and tied in a green-felt four-carrier sedan chair, carried to the square in front of the prison gates at the mouth of Ke Jia Alley and executed; or when the Eight Allied Army marched into Beijing in *Geng Zi* year, and the next year Yu the Savage rebelled in North Sichuan. The exhilaration, it is really not the same.

For the four hundred thousand and some residents within the city limits, who does not know that the Red Lanterns are making havoc outside the North Gate?

(Li Jieren, *Before the Tempest* 2011: 1)

For the city residents, the Red Lantern Boxers' crazed foray into the city, and their momentary hold over the heart and mind of the multitude, foretold things to come in their place and lifetime. The impact of the event on the "social mentality" of the residents seems far beyond its immediate outcome, and not comparable to those of a comparable nature. The spectacle of the execution left Hao Yousan, one of the novel's protagonists, and his group of young friends lasting impressions. Whilst it took Hao three days to recover the shock, the exhilaration carried some of his friends onto the path of radical agitation, making Hao an unremarkable but steadfast local reformer. Li sets the event amongst a series of events to highlight its momentum in the succession of the Revolution's sources and currents, and tells its story from the point of view of the city and city residents.

Likewise, Li's gazetteer-style narration of the first public park in Chengdu makes it clear that it is a telling part of local as well as imperial history. Transformations of the cityscape and ways of life are the prehistories of the revolution.

The fact that Chengdu has two cities can be traced to its earliest history…One can see from these records that the Greater City and the Lesser City were indeed two cities. And it was still so in the Song times. They were only merged in the reconstruction of Ming…Then the Banner soldiers of the Manchus came, and a big piece of land towards the western end of the Greater City was partitioned and walled as their residence. People began to call it the Manchu City…

Until after the *Geng Zi* year, the Manchus were going from bad to worse. The poor became poorer, the fallen fell further... Then in the year of *Xuan Tong* there came a general... He knew by then that the Manchus stationed there have come close to their end...So he tried to get the Hans to move in and establish businesses in the Manchu City... and soon after opened up the huge piece of unattended land just inside the Lower East Gate and next to the Guan Di Temple, full of trees and flowers that have grown wild, including a lotus pond, as a park...

This is the first big public park in the history of Chengdu...

(Li Jieren, *Great Waves* 2011: 45-47)

These stories of the city and cityscape spatialize changes in time, tracing the roots and sources of developments vertically, or lay out synchronically the processes of events and human actions in spatially-structured scenes. In this way the momentous history of consequential events is registered in the panorama of everyday space, and earth-shattering change appears both epic and prosaic. Li's gazetteer style presentation accentuates scenes and locations and the scale of monumental events, highlighting their cumulative at the same time contingent processes. This way of accounting for historical change demonstrates that the local is where history takes place and the communal the nodal point of its orchestration. But most importantly, the incorporation of the gazetteer form, where changes in time, landscape and human life seamlessly mesh into each other, allows for a spatially-structured scenic historical novel that accounts for a momentous Chinese revolution as a communal experience with scale,

III. Multifarious actions of a provincial community at the Empire's end

At the occasion of its centennial, Rana Mitter argues that the 1911 Revolution is the most unanchored revolution in modern Chinese history and historiography. Its "highly contested" nature separated it "from any one path of historical interpretation" and "kept its meaning simultaneously uncertain and potent". 〔註14〕 Li Jieren's novel history of the Revolution's undercurrents and defining incidents in the province is an important early twentieth century attempt to anchor it in a form that echoes the Balzacien "historie contemporaine," besides the great historical and social novels of both classical Chinese and European origins that he cites as the sources of his inspiration. Events and experiences of two decades ago are recounted, like in the "historie contemporaine," so that "the resistances of the past are highlighted." However, unlike in the Balzacien novel, they are not to "be overcome by the present narrative". 〔註15〕 Li's multi-volume project to anchor the historical multifariousness of a recent past does not offer "an end to the threat of any hiddenness" by the "explicitness of its narrative promise". He does not "attempt to reconcile the irreconcilable" (Heathcote, 151). Li's historical and historiographical ambition is rather more emphatically manifested in his recreation of the modern historical novel as a form that re-evokes Chinese novel's original ambition as "repositories for alternative versions of the past" (Owen, 141-43). This novelistic ambition to compete in history writing from the margins, as insignificant or unauthorized chronicles (*piguan yeshi, yanyi*) was given full vent in the experimentations of the Late Qing New Fiction writers. 〔註16〕 But it was disfavoured, together with the full-length historical novel, in the New Culture Movement of the May Fourth (1919) and ensuing literary revolution of the 1920s, as a remainder of debilitating tradition. Li's modern historical fiction gives narrative structure to a revolution that launched twentieth century China into a succession of revolutions only to further its multifariousness. It unsettles its seminal status as the founding event of China's first modern nation-state—in Li's capacious story the disintegration of the last empire did not herald in the Republic. Moreover, his gazetteer narrative scales the revolution and its processes as the ethnohistory of a provincial life world, in which

---

〔註14〕 Rana Mitter, "1911: The Unanchored Chinese Revolution," *The China Quarterly*, Vol. 208, December 2011:1009-1020.

〔註15〕 Owen Heathcote, *Balzac and Violence: Representing History, Space, Sexuality and Death in La Comédie humaine*, 2009:151.

〔註16〕 See Chen, Pingyuan, *Transformations of the Narrative Mode of the Chinese Novel (zhongguo xiaoshuo xushi moshi de zhuanbian)*, 2010: 195-221.

political developments that are subsequently considered of national consequence are part and parcel. In this narrative the communal world of the provincial society is both the subject of historical change and the determining parameter through which the changes are delimited and understood. Through Li's ethnographic observation, historical documentation and scenic dramatization, a fin de siècle local world—a provincial society centred around the local gentry, based on family, clan, and an urban-country habitat, with its shifting social and psycho-cultural fabric—emerges as where history takes place. In *Great Waves*, the last of the novel series, when the narrative turns to the Sichuan Railway Protection Movement, the main event that brought down the Qing Empire in Li's account, the communal as network and association is what underwrites the characterization and orchestrates the action—the development and denouement of the agitations.

The multiplicity of characters in Li's sequence confounded its readers when it was revised in the 1950s. 〔註 17〕 Sensitized in an increasingly dominant socialist realist convention that eulogies revolutionary wars and histories, they found the novel's lack of central heroic figures and a triumphant resolution unsatisfactory (Li Jieren, "Afterword", *Great Waves* 2011: 373). Early PRC criticism also dwelled on the lack of true heroic and realist types in Li's characterization as what contributed to the novel's failure to be a passable historical-materialist account of China's Bourgeois Revolution. 〔註 18〕 For Li however the need for multiple protagonists is a necessary part in crafting a capacious historical fiction. It is a formal choice to achieve a polyphonic historical voice that Ng suggests coming from the conceptual challenge of Tolstoy's idiosyncratic historical narrative of *War and Peace*, 〔註 19〕 but Li himself ascribes to examples in numerous "big (*da bu tou*)" European and Chinese novels, from *War and Peace* to the four Chinese classics (Li Jieren, "Afterword", *Great Waves* 2011: 373). More significantly, this multiplicity in characters and plots allows for the scaling from individual story to mass experience.

〔註 17〕 This essay concentrates on the 1930s versions. The revisions in the 1950s merit sustained studies of their own.

〔註 18〕 See Li Shiwen. *Life and Works of Li Jieren*, 1986: 209-234.

〔註 19〕 Kenny Kwok-kwan Ng, T*he Lost Geopoetic Horizon of Li Jieren: The Crisis of Writing Chengdu in Revolutionary China*, 2015:476.

The manifold protagonists collectively represent the communal, not as realist social types that readers of 1950s China have learned to expect, nor as the Lukácsian individuals determined and differentiated by a progressive history, but in the sense their roles and actions are dictated by the communal network of the provincial society. They acquire meaning through the latter's prism, affected by its aspirations and tensions. Unlike what Lukács sees in Scott and Tolstoy's historical fiction, Li's lead characters cannot be distinguished between world historical individuals and mediocre heroes, even though his narrative recounts the Sichuan Railway Protection Movement and related incidents as world historical events. In Li's novel sequence, the protagonists of developing events as well as local life and feelings include both known historical figures and fictional characters. As historical beings however they differ only in degrees. This is because like Lukács, Li emphasizes the spatio-temporal character of people and circumstances in his historical narrative, but unlike Lukács' understanding of Scott's local place as the primitive a priori of an all-encompassing historical progress, his vision is ethnohistorical. The geopolitical and anthropo-culturally bound place is a historical, rather than pre-historical, community. For Li's characters, their historicity is not a matter of "derivation of the individuality of characters from the historical peculiarity of their age" (Lukács, 23) but rather one of conditioned choice, bound and preceded by changes and prehistories of their geographically defined life world.

The trilogy is linked structurally as unfolding episodes in a climatic development of life and events in a fin de siècle provincial society. The characters are willing or unwilling participants in its social pandemonium, emotional turmoil and political agitation. They appear and disappear according to their role in the communal story. The two volumes (three in the 1957 revision, with a fourth unfinished) of *Great Waves* centre on the world of minor official- gentry Huang Lansheng and his family from June to December 1911, depicting in parallel narratives dramatic political events and daily existence of the city gentry and their plebeian associates. The story follows the timeline of the political movement from the establishment of the Sichuan Railway Protection Society to the declaration of the Independent Sichuan Military Government, including the September 7th massacre and subsequent riots and military uprisings. Its development is structured spatial sequentially in vignettes of human feelings and actions during that volatile half year. The two levels of narrative: details of life in and around the Huang household as well as the "social mentality" of the fin-de-siècle city glimpsed through them, and account of known historical events, are linked through this spatial construction. Under an expansive and panoramic perspective they become unfolding scenes of an on-going historical process. This way of narrating and structuring the story stages the revolution as a process of ever-evolving change. It is abrupt, unpredictable, earth-shattering and at the same time gradual and prosaic. The movement of history—the stirrings, passions and eruptions of a provincial city at the border of the vast empire gasping for its last breath—is told in shifting scenes of life and feelings of the myriad characters. The causes and effects of history seem in this way irreversible but unpredictable—with the changing scenes the momentum increases and feelings intensify, but the direction of things to come remains uncertain. The sequential narrative that accounts for the moment which ended the empire in the province juxtaposes then reconciles the two strands.

As the cumulating episode, the multi-volumed sequence of the *Waves* covers a relatively short time but broad expanse in space. It recounts the unfolding of life and events in scenes that move from private mansions to governmental compounds and the city streets of Chengdu, to surrounding country towns and villages. The full-length novel is here narrated in full-width, with its geographically shifting scenes coalescing into a panorama of a life-changing revolution spreading from the empire' end. The individual characters play their own parts in this fin de siècle drama, which nonetheless acquire meaning in the communal story: their lives and feelings become historical when seen as part of the changing fate of their life-world. The historicity of the characters, however, are not defined or differentiated by the degree to which they embody what Lukács, through Hegel, saw as the historical spirit—the inevitability of progress. Instead, in Li's ethnohistorical vision in which the local is central in world change, the array of protagonists are all world-historical individuals in the sense that they are willing or unwilling participants in events and daily transformations that have historical consequences.

The leaders of the Railway Protection movement, Pu Dianjun (1875-1935) and Deng Xiaoke (1869-1950), who are both documented historical figures, are no more visionaries like Tolstoy's Kutuzov as Lukács sees him, than Huang Lansheng, one of the novel's central but middling fictional characters. They are all average heroes in the sense their vision and action are relative to their place and time, defined by their roles and places in the community. In Li's narrative, though Pu and Deng are key figures in the political events whereas Huang is at best an opportunist revolutionary at its height, the difference in their action, perception and feelings are a matter of degrees rather than kinds. Pu and Deng are leaders of the movement because they are leaders of the provincial society. It is the on-going social transformations and political institutional changes initiated by the Qing court that made them new leaders of the community. In this fin-de siècle drama, Huang, though a minor official and unlike Pu and Deng never a figure of political prominence, became collective heroes together with other members of the provincial gentry.

Like most of his friends and family, Huang was born and raised in Chengdu. Though self-identified as of guest-origin (*ke ji*), which is common among the population of Sichuan at the time because of several large-scale Qing migrations, Huang's family has ruled as officials, owned lands as landlords and invested in businesses in the city for generations. They have become corner stones of the provincial gentry society both in social and economic standing. Huang's place in the world epitomizes the fate of the gentry class in late Imperial China. Their social and economic prowess become increasingly independent from the centre of authority of the imperial political system (Elman, 169-88). In Li's account, Chengdu gentry is not only the initiators of the movement and connivers of its escalation, their unprecedented prowess is a direct consequence of the New Policy reforms. [註20] Like other major provincial capitals of the Qing Empire, Chengdu built new-style schools, promoted commerce, trained the New Army, and sent out

---

[註20] For the impact of the New Policy Reforms in Chengdu see Kristin E. Stapleton, *Civilizing Chengdu: Chinese Urban Reform, 1895-1937*, 2000; Di Wang, *Street Culture in Chengdu: Public Space, Urban Commoners, and Local Politics, 1870-1930*, 2003.

students overseas. It is ironic that these reforms as part of the empire's last ditch self-strengthening movement actually abetted and hastened its final collapse. The most consequential in this political institutional reform is the establishment of the provincial parliament, which provided the city gentry a formal platform for contesting and dividing political power with the Qing government, and wielding greater influence in society. It is by no means surprising then that the provincial parliamentary gentries become leaders of the Railway Protection Movement. The parliamentary consultation system introduced from above through the New Policies in late Qing is short-lived, but it did give a chance for Sichuan gentry to enter official politics through society. The Sichuan Railway Protection Movement exemplifies its possibilities.

In the novel, as well as the development of the main event, Huang's central role is social rather than political. His daily ritual and social relations showcase the crucial part Late Imperial gentry plays in the Railway Protection Movement and 1911 Revolution. Huang's home is often the gathering place for local dignitaries, from influential literati to important officials. In this way Huang not only witnesses and is occasionally part of the provincial capital's political developments, the dinner parties and tea gatherings at his house are often where events are discussed and analysed. People of different social background, economic status, and political position come and go for social occasions, political briefing, business transaction or simply good food—the Huang Mansion is renowned for its epicurean provisions. Through Huang Li seamlessly links fictional characters with known historical personages, situating competing figures of authority from the provincial capital to its surrounding country and towns at the right mis-en-scène. City gentry from Huang Lansheng to his wife Mrs Huang and distant nephew Chu Yong, as well as their friends and relatives, are in this way all key figures, as participants or witnesses of the political and military events, or heroes, heroines and side characters in their own familial drama.

Joining the revolution, or becoming political in the agitating provincial society, is often a social event. For Wu Fengwu, a figure of uncertain character hovering at the edges of the city's gentry society, it is a matter of seizing a life-time opportunity.

What you say now is exactly like what I was thinking when I first heard about the goings-on of the Society-for-Railway-Protection upon my return to the provincial capital. I really took exception to the ideas and methods of Mr Luo and his friends. What do we have to do with railways? It is the Court and the Emperor's business, not something for us to stick our necks out for. I also worried about what might become of the stalemate, if the Court wouldn't budge, and insisted on carrying out what was said in the edict. Their behaviour bordered on treason. I also knew first- hand the temper of General Zhao when he was at the Sichuan border regions, thinking since he was so used to be the Son of Heaven in the wilderness how could he stand the antics of a few sour pedants? ... However after I got in touch with your dear relation Mr Liao, and went around with him to the Railway Company, heard a few lectures, watched the passionate and spirited agitations of Luo and friends on the side, I gradually changed my mind. ...Thirdly, this time when I come back I find Sichuan folks no longer what they were when I left Chengdu. Before, this was a paradise for officials. They could do what they wanted, who dared to poke their heads out and whimper. ...But nowadays things are really different. Gentry folks are having the upper hand. As soon as the provincial parliament opened up, officials cowered, not half as jaunty as they were. ...

(Li Jieren, Great Waves 2011: 132-34)

This is Wu's account of how he turned an opportune revolutionary to his surprised patron and friend Huang Langsheng. Wu, like Huang, is a middling hero in that his perceptions and actions are defined by the here and now and confined by his communal ties and standing. He came to know the movement by accident on one hand, but very much as a part of his daily communal social and economic life on the other. Wu is lower on the communal social ladder. In fact he and Huang is bond by a client and patron relationship. As a drifting urbanite, Wu is part of Huang's social and economic network, often engaged and paid by the latter for business or to act on his family's behalf. Wu is also a free-lance soldier and general man for hire. By the time the story begins, Wu just returned from a three-year failed career as a minor officer in General Zhao, the soon-to-be Sichuan Governor's Sichuan-Tibet border army. At his wit's end, he went shame-facedly to the Huang Mansion to borrow money and discuss his future with his patron. He had to escape the wrath of the general because of disciplinary issues involving one of his soldiers, cutting short an otherwise up-worldly mobile career path. But the meeting at the Huang Mansion proves a turning point. Through Huang's patronage and his familial-social network, Wu found a new path for his livelihood in the changing provincial world—becoming a man for hire for the burgeoning revolutionary cause. Wu was swayed by the passions and new-style public political agitation of the provincial gentry leaders, whose persuasion is buttressed by and in turn underwriting their increasing social-political prowess. He was also networked into the escalating Railway Protection Movement through his patron's family relations, acting at the same time for their interests and benefits in a dramatically shifting world. Wu and Huang are joined in this in a traditional client-patron relationship, but also in unforeseen new ways as they each struggle and negotiate their path in an unpredictable personal and communal life experience.

For Wu, seeing the provincial gentry gaining the upper hand is crucial in his decision for a new path. The prospect beckons a social-economically and psycho-culturally re-shuffled life world whose political institutional future Wu, like most of his fellow communal members, could not foretell. But like them, he is equally convinced that at this point even General Zhao's notoriously savage temper could not forestall the passion and prowess of the gentry-led provincial society. For Chu Yong (nom de plume Zicai), Huang's nephew, on the other hand, being socialized into the provincial revolution is almost inescapable. As a well-heeled country youth enrolled in a new-style high school for mostly gentry off-springs from around the province, Chu is taught by teachers who are traditional literati that found new outlet and expression in the newly established educational institution for their interrupted learning and political-official ambition since the abolition of the

Civil Service Examination in 1905. 〔註 21〕 Amongst them is Hao Yousan, an ardent reformer we know already from *Before the Tempest*. Hao not only teaches more reform than biology, he also occasionally acts as a direct liaison between the rebellious students and the Railway Protection Society. Most importantly, he is a family friend of the Huangs at whose place Chu stays. Thus Chu, surrounded by fellow students who are becoming new elites through new schooling, including physical education on the newly established sportsground, which proves excellent preparation for the well-muscled bravery of the Student Army in the later armed rebellion, and dependent on the emotional and familial support of relations who made a business decision to join the agitations that seem to sway the provincial society in one direction, is inexorably swept into the unfolding events. To do otherwise requires a hard-headed and hard-hearted decision against his family, clan and essential living environs that is beyond him as a middling sort. Chu is practically arm-twisted into being an ambassador and agitator for the Society because of his family clan relations (his maternal grandfather is a county-branch head of the local Paoge brotherhood, of whose loyalty and support the Protection Movement is trying hard to engage) and forcibly swayed by his school friends to return to his country home to carry it out, even though he prefers to linger at the Huang Mansion to continue his affair with his aunt-in-law.

The provisional assembly of the Sichuan Railway Protection Society convened on July 1 of the *Xin Hai* year of the lunar calendar, or the third year in the Xuan Tong reign of Qing, or the first year of the Republic of China, at two o'clock in the afternoon. … Chu Zicai did not expect the Railway Company compound to be so crowded today. …Starting from Shuwa North Street, carried forward in the middle of a band of strong and pushy young men …he shoved his way

---

〔註 21〕 The Chinese Civil Service is "the administrative system of the traditional Chinese government, the members of which were selected by a competitive examination… The examination system was finally abolished in 1905 by the Qing dynasty in the midst of modernization attempts. The whole civil-service system as it had previously existed was overthrown along with the dynasty in 1911/12" (https://www.britannica.com/topic/Chinese-civil- service, accessed 25/8/2016).

to the gate, passing a crowd of at least a thousand. …Chu found the back of his long gown torn away, and the fan in his hand stuck. What is the worst is that pinned by the bodies of the thronging multitude it is unbelievably hot and the air stank. He couldn't run away even if he wanted to. …Only when he elbowed his way inside, did Chu Zicai heave a sigh of relief. He felt lighter in the body, and he could finally move his arms and legs. He is not really a representative, he did not have to go in… But he felt he need to. This maybe his sense of responsibility, but he also felt agitated, egged on by the crowd's enthusiasm… (Li Jieren, *Great Waves* 2011: 172-74)

Chu indeed was "carried forward" into the revolution and "egged on" by its throbbing passions, with other Sichuan gentry young men like him, as well as Sichuan young men unlike him—the more plebeian urbanites who are nonetheless as "pushy" to see and join the action. In Li's account of the *fin de siècle* Chengdu, not only is the new-style school as part of the gentry social network a fertile playground for the provincial revolution, residents are socialized into the Railway Protection Movement at both the new and the old communal spaces—from recently established city and provincial newspapers to age-old street rituals (Di Wang, 163- 245). Through these communal institutions the agitation is orchestrated and organized by new political technology as well as traditional means of communication. Wu and Chu had listened to many a passionate public political speech, witnessed the increasingly consummate agitating skills of the leading parliamentary gentry, before they are affected and egged on into action. When the Provincial Government and Governor prohibited the telegraphic communication of events in Chengdu to other parts of the province and empire at the height of the movement, two underground revolutionary leaders sent wooden tablets carved with messages downstream along the Jin River to alert their comrades-in-arms as their ancestors did once upon a time. In fact, from Wu and Chu's story, as well as Li's sometimes omnipresent account, military riots and armed rebellion are organized and carried out through folk organizations and underground brotherhoods, around but sometimes beyond the network of the provincial gentry. Whilst other kinds of emerging or traditional social players occasionally enter and control the scene (such as those the readers met in *Ripples*) and negotiate their interests. Fu Longsheng, the *Waves*' other middling but significant character, also joined the revolution through the persuasive prowess of the provincial gentry. He read their stirring arguments on the mushrooming popular newspapers and was convinced of their cause, then listened to the same public political speeches and was moved to tears and action. The process of Fu's enlistment is one of reaffirming his communal identification. He is invited into the eagerly inclusive and public political movement as communal social events, despite his limited communal standing as a small-time traditional umbrella maker and shop-owner. Once there, through reading, listening and being in physical and emotional proximity to the centre of agitation, he is convinced that the provincial gentry, from the parliamentary leaders to school students, are truly performing their communal duties and advocating its interests. However he is also equally ready to confront them the moment he sees them failing, taking things into his own hands—once he organized a mob and rushed into an unwilling gentry family mansion to demand and force their action (Li Jieren, *Great Waves* 2011: 217-219). If Fu's initial introduction to the revolution is through his first-time venture into new-style public urban and elite political institutions—he read the news and comments on the Railway Protection Movement by accident from popular newspapers his peddler friend was recruited to sell, and went into the meeting ground that is newly open to elites and plebeians alike out of curiosity, his actual revolutionary political activities are carried out in his familiar urban environ: on the streets and in the form of performing traditional communal duties such as neighbourhood worship rituals. These street and neighbourhood activities prove a crucial part in the development and final outcome of the events that changed the fortune of his world and beyond.

The 1911 Revolution from its main events to accumulative social underpinning in Li's novel narrative is indeed communal. As agitations that germinate from local world change and culminate in the crumpling of the empire, their development and denouement is underwritten by the Sichuan provincial community as network and association—through characterization and the orchestration of action as well as the gazetteer style narrative. The fin de siècle provincial society is a historically significant life world that not only enables the members to communicate with one another but also to organize in groups both traditional and novel. Continuing the communal sagas of the *Ripples* and *Before the Tempest*, *Great Waves*' process of narration builds up to the formation of an agitating crowd, from the city to the surrounding towns and countryside, with its final eruption back in the provincial capital. From its first formation to its expansion through and beyond the province, this crowd throbs with the same enthusiasm as Chu Yong first felt it in the Railway Company compound and carries the escalating action. Its ebbings and surgings not only menaced the institutions of the empire's political establishment. Spurred on by increasingly divergent political, social and personal interests, with violent tidal waves spilling well beyond the political aspirations of either the Constitutional Monarchist or the Republican causes in the Railway Protection Movement, they brought the system to its ruin. In this sense it is indeed an engulfing and all-consuming crowd not unlike those figured and feared by Li's contemporary Inter-War European writers. But this provincial revolutionary crowd in Li's figuration is not a historically unconscious mass opposite the knowing, thinking and feeling individual as historical being. Hao Yousan was indeed differently affected by the spectacle of the public execution from most of the cheering crowd because of his delicate disposition. But as one of a group of gentry-youths who attended the event together with many other parties—as social groups, families or individual urban residents, he experienced its shock with them similarly as exhilaration, as indications of impending life change. Neither he, nor his friends, nor the other Chengdu residents who witnessed or heard about the event remained the same since, even though their courses of action diverge. Chu Yong is almost physically nudged into action by the enthusiasm of the throbbing mass, but the crowd that egged him on is comprised as much of the "pushy" plebian young men unlike him as by perceiving, feeling, and hesitating young and old literati like him. Whereas Fu Longsheng rushed to the scene of the massacre together with thousands of other city plebeians like him out of one and the only motivation: fulfilling their duty to save their community leaders whose lives are rumored to be endangered for fulfilling their communal duties. "People surged and became feverish. They all came simply to save Mr. Pu and Mr. Luo. They did not care if they actually could or not. Nor the fact that even if they could, what good it would do them. They only had one thought in mind: Butcher Zhao caught Mr. Pu and Mr. Luo and will kill them, we have to rush to the Southern Compound for the rescue! ...One man yelled in the street, and the whole street uproared..." (Li Jieren, *Great Waves* 2011: 273). "... [P]erhaps people did not even have these calculations, they just pushed with all their might as their duty demanded, and shouted with all their might as their duty demanded; it did not occur to them to worry about the consequences" (276). In the process Fu is not always fully conscious of his actions and reactions, but proves single-minded in his motivation with the rest of the crowd. Here the individual is a definitive part of a mass experience, whether they are named or anonymous. Each is bonded with the other and the rest as willing or unwilling participants of a shared historical process.

Li's agitating crowd is organized and enacted through the community that orchestrates individuals as well as geographically demarcated social groups into a though often unpredictable but historically meaningful mass. It is the communal crowd of a life world whose actions reach beyond its immediate environs. In Li's ethnohistorical perspective, the Sichuan provincial society as a communal network is a set of social and cultural interactions and behaviors that have meanings and expectations between its members. What it enables is not simply action, but actions based on shared expectations and meanings between individuals. In *Great Waves*, the array of characters as members of the community build up their repertoires of political action through their communal association, their individual but intersecting acts lead to the final communal eruption. In this way Li's novel sequence on one of the seminal events in modern Chinese history indeed shares the Lukácsian conception of modern history as individually significant mass experience. Though Li's mass is namable—even at its most amorphous moment, deeply locally and historically rooted. It is not the ontologically mythical modern crowd that Elias Canetti simultaneously dreads and longs for, 〔註22〕 but as capable

---

〔註22〕 Elias Canetti, *Crowds and Power*, 1962.

of great spontaneous eruption. The crowd in Li's sequential novel history of Chengdu in 1911 is a development of the interpenetration of a dramatically changing communal social mentality and the historical political contingencies of the fin de siècle Qing Empire. Through his manifold plot and multiplicity of characters, cumulating in the formation, expansion and final eruption of a communal crowd, Li scales history from individual to mass experience and vise versus with a contending ethnohistorical perspective. In this ethnohistory as a spatial-scenically structured serial novel Li figures the local as the present site of history and the communal subject of historical change. His "historical real" comes not so much from his protagonists as world historical individuals or mediocre heroes but from the intertwining of political upheavals and the "stirrings in people's lives and feelings" of a particular place. This interpenetration shows itself in his gazetteer-style scenic descriptions and narratives of life and events; in his figuration of local characters who become makers and riders of historical "great waves" through processes of socialization within an inherited but changing communal network. The communal framework underwrites both Li's historical vision and his novelistic orchestration—in his account the geographically rooted and spatially narrated multifariousness of human feelings and action escalated to an ending with uncertain and multiple political prospects. As such Li's trilogy alternates the version of the 1911 Revolution as bourgeois and national that inevitably progresses to a modern Chinese nation. Its narrative heralded in a modern Chinese historical novel with formal and affective possibilities that became all the more significant because of its loss in the second half of the twentieth century.

Works Cited:

1. Canetti, Elias. *Crowds and Power*, New York: Farrar, Straus and Giroux 1962.

2. Chen, Pingyuan. *Transformations in the Narrative Mode of the Chinese Novel*, Beijing: Beijing daxue chubanshe 2010.

3. Dening, Greg. *Performances*, Melbourne: Melbourne University Press 1996.

4. Dillon, Michael. *China: A Cultural and Historical Dictionary*, London: Routledge 2003.

5. Ding, Fan. *A History of the Chinese Local-Colour Fiction*, Beijing: Beijing daxue chubanshe 2007. Duara, Prasenjit. "Local Worlds: The Poetics and Politics of the Native Place in Modern China," *South Atlantic Quarterly* Vol. 99, No. 1 2000: 12-45.

6. Elman, Benjamin A. 'Late Traditional Chinese Civilization in Motion, 1400-1900,' Ofer Gal and Yi Zheng eds. *Motion and Knowledge in the Changing Early Modern World*, Heidelberg: Springer Dordrecht 2014: 169-188.

7. Esherick, Joseph W. *The Origins of the Boxer Uprising*, University of California Press 1988.

8. Guo, Moruo, 'Waiting for the Chinese Zola,' *Chinese Literature and Art*, Vol. 1, No. 2, June 15 1937,

9. *Selected works of Li Jieren*, Vol. 1, Chengdu: Sichuan renmin chubanshe 1980: 5-17.

10. Heathcote, Owen. *Balzac and Violence: Representing History, Space, Sexuality and Death in La Comédie humaine*, Bern: Peter Lang 2009.

11. Jonsson, Stefan. *Crowds and Democracy: the Idea and Image of the Masses from Revolution to Fascism*, New York: Columbia University Press 2013.

12. Li, Jieren. 'Postscript: *Great Waves* Vol. 2', *The Complete Works of Li Jieren*, Vol. 4b, Chengdu: Sichuan wenyi chubanshe 2011: 767-770.

13. Li, Jieren. 'Preface to *Ripples in a Dead Pond*', *The Complete Works of Li Jieren*, Vol. 9, Chengdu: Sichuan wenyi chubanshe 2011: 241-243.

14. Li, Jieren, 'My Writing Experience,' *The Complete Works of Li Jieren*, Vol. 9, Chengdu: Sichuan wenyi chubanshe 2011: 244-251.

15. Li, Jieren. 'Postscript: *Great Waves* Vol. 3', *The Complete Works of Li Jieren*, Vol. 4c, Chengdu: Sichuan wenyi chubanshe 2011:1165-1167.

16. Li, Jieren. *Ripples in a Dead Pond*, *The Complete Works of Li Jieren*, Vol. 1, Chengdu: Sichuan wenyi chubanshe 2011.

17. Li, Jieren. *Before the Tempest*, *The Complete Works of Li Jieren*, Vol. 2, Chengdu: Sichuan wenyi chubanshe 2011.

18. Li, Jieren. *Great Waves*, *The Complete Works of Li Jieren*, Vol. 3a and 3b, Chengdu: Sichuan wenyi chubanshe 2011.

19. Li, Jieren. 'French Novels and Novelists after Naturalism', *The Complete Works of Li Jieren*, Vol. 9, Chengdu: Sichuan wenyi chubanshe 2011: 143-181.

20. Li, Shiwen. *Life and Works of Li Jieren*, Chengdu: Sichuan kexueyuan chubanshe 1986.

21. Lu, Xun. 'Preface to Tian Jun's *Village in August*', *the Complete Works of Lu Xun*, Vol. 6, Beijing: People' Literature Press 1991.

22. Lukács, Georg. *The Historical Novel*, Hannah and Stanley Mitchell trans. London: Merlin Press 1962

23. Mitter, Rana. "1911: The Unanchored Chinese Revolution," *The China Quarterly*, Vol. 208, December 2011.

24. Ng, Kenny Kwok-kwan, *The Lost Geopoetic Horizon of Li Jieren: The Crisis of Writing Chengdu in Revolutionary China*, Leiden: Brill 2015.

25. Owen, Stephen. Remembrances: *The Experience of the Past in Classical Chinese Literature*, Cambridge: Harvard University Press 1986.

26. Prusek, Jaroslav. *The Lyrical and the Epic: Studies of Modern Chinese Literature*, ed. Leo Ou-fan Lee. Bloomington: Indiana University Press 1980.

27. Rowe, William T. *China's Last Empire: The Great Qing*, Cambridge: the Belknap Press 2009.

28. Shi, Bing. *Telegraph and Political Changes in Late Qing and Early Republican China*, Shanghai Jiaotong University: PhD Dissertation, 2010.

29. Skinner, G. William ed. *The City in Late Imperial China, Studies in Chinese society*. Stanford: Stanford University Press 1977.

30. Stapleton, Kristin E. *Civilizing Chengdu: Chinese Urban Reform, 1895-1937*, Cambridge: Harvard University Asia Center 2000;

31. Wang, Dewei. "The Fall and Temptation of the South: On Su Tong's Fiction", *Foodstuff for Angels*, Taibei: Maitian Publishing Limited 2002:11-36.

32. Wang, Di. *Street Culture in Chengdu: Public Space, Urban Commoners, and Local Politics, 1870- 1930*, Stanford: Stanford University Press 2003.

33. Yang, Lianfen. *The Moving Moments: Late Qing and May Fourth Literature*, Taiwan: Xiuwei Communications 2006.

34. Yang, Tianshi. *End of the Empire*, Changsha: Yuelu shushe 2013.

省城，他鄉，革命

　　李劼人（1891～1962）的系列小說《死水微瀾》（1935），《暴風雨前》（1936）和《大波》（1937）被同時代的作家郭沫若稱爲小說近代史，「小說的近代《華陽國志》」。「作品的規模之宏大已經相當的足以驚人，而各個時代的主流及其遞嬗，地方上的風土氣韻，各個階層的人物之生活樣式，心理狀態，言語口吻，無論男的女的老的少的，都虧他研究得那樣透闢，描寫得那樣自然。……把過去了的時代，活鮮鮮地形象化了出來」。〔註1〕李氏三部曲的規模的確宏大，既有歷時的涵括時代主流變遷的史詩，又有空間呈現的「地方上的」日常生活，末世社會的男女眾生，以及他們的心理狀態，言語行爲。李劼人自己也在《死水微瀾》的《前記》中解釋說他的小說系列寫的是中國近代史：「從一九二五年起，一面教書，一面仍舊寫些短篇小說時，便起了一個念頭，打算把幾十年來所生活過，所切感過，所體驗過，在我看來意義非常重大，當得歷史轉捩點的這一段社會現象，用幾部有連續性的長篇小說，一段落一段落地把它反映出來。我想，直接從辛亥革命入手太倉促了些。這個革命並不是突然而來的，它有歷史淵源，歷史上積累了很多因素，積之既久才結這個大瓜。要寫，就必須追源溯流，從最早的時候寫起。寫鴉片戰爭，我不熟習，熟習的是庚子年以後的事。聽見過八國聯軍的事情，也看見過當時成都所受的影響。第二年成都鬧紅燈教，殺紅燈教的首領之一廖觀音，打教堂，這些事我最清楚，我就從這時候寫起，從庚子年寫到辛亥革命，寫所聞，寫所見，寫身所經歷，三段一系列。這就是大家所講的三部曲。第

〔註1〕郭沫若，《中國佐拉之待望》，《中國文藝》1937年第一卷第二期。見《李劼人選集》第一卷，第5頁。

一部叫《死水微瀾》，第二部叫《暴風雨前》，第三部叫《大波》，從書名可以看出當時革命進程的。」〔註 2〕這樣的歷史敘事追源溯流，著重展現革命作為歷史事件的進程，並且鉅細皆備，尤其重要的是作者要寫的是他所熟習，經歷過或耳熟能詳的事件，情勢。「有連續性」的系列小說是這種敘事的最好形式。對李劼人而言，這樣的歷史過程和社會情勢必須經由「地方上的風土氣韻」及「各個階層的人物之生活樣式，心理狀態，言語口吻」透視。這不僅因為他強調小說作者的歷史見證人身份，更重要的是在他的小說史中，地方是歷史的唯一現場。

地方於中國現代小說並不陌生。以故鄉為焦點的鄉土小說是五四新文化運動現代意識的載體，也是文化人現代焦慮的體現。在此，鄉土是「被固態化了的農業文明縮影」，成為思想家文人各類主義思潮及價值判斷的必爭之地。〔註 3〕沈從文（1902～1988）一九三四年創作的田園詩風的《邊城》是這種原鄉追憶的最好體現。小說中美麗小城和周圍鄉村中田園牧歌的消逝隱喻了現代社會人的根本流失，也顯示了沈從文的現代小說嘗試。其中不難看出他對現代主義原始田園傾向的借鑒。茅盾（1896～1981）一九三三年的《子夜》雖以在中國現代文學中不多的長篇城市小說著名，其中對現代中國社會之命運的思索也是通過城鄉兩個對立的範疇展示的。四面楚歌的農業文明的原鄉雖然只是工業，現代，充滿活力的上海的常常缺席的反照，卻是小說敘事的起點。茅盾也寫過同時代的小鎮鄉村變化的中短篇小說。《春蠶》（1932）《林家鋪子》（1932）的原鄉是歷史變化的場地，卻仍然是固態化了的農業文明的縮影被外來的動態的勢力威脅破壞。在這裡和在大多數的現代鄉土小說或地域文學裏一樣，既定空間——地方上——的變化，被展示為時間上的不同。城鄉的距離成了新舊時代的對比。兩者的差異變為歷時的線性軌道上向新文明過渡的不同點。可以說，現代中國文學的地域敘事是一種隱喻，一種集體文化焦慮。

李劼人的地方是歷史的，是世界變化的直接場域。其歷時性表現在空間範疇的世事變遷中。除風土人情和現世眾生百相，還有歷史沿革，地理座標。作為三部曲發生地的晚清帝國邊境省府的成都和周圍鄉村城鎮以及它們的關係，在李的描述中可以歸類為施堅雅的晚期中華帝國城市中心大區域的模

〔註 2〕李劼人，「《死水微瀾》前記」，《李劼人全集》第九卷，第 241 頁。
〔註 3〕丁帆，《中國鄉土小說史》，第 6 頁。

式。在一個區域中不同等級的城市，城市與鄉村，與鄉市間的集鎮的關係既是階梯結構的，上下有別，又因同屬一個分工不同的政治經濟體系而結爲休戚相關的有序的一體。而省城是這個政治經濟體的中心。〔註4〕李的三部曲的世界是由天回鎮，一個城鄉間的集鎮開始的：

> 由四川省會成都，出北門到成都附屬的新都縣，一般人都説有四十里，其實只有三十多里。路是彎彎曲曲畫在極平坦的田疇當中，雖然是一條不到五尺寬的泥路，僅在路的右方鋪了兩行石板；雖然大雨之後，泥濘有幾寸深，不穿新草鞋幾乎寸步難行。……然而到底算川北大道。它一直向北伸去，直達四川邊縣廣元，再走過去是陝西省的寧羌州，漢中府，以前走北京首都的驛道，就是這條路線。並且由廣元分道向西，是川甘大鎮碧口，再過去是甘肅省的階州文縣。凡西北各上進出貨物，這條路是必由之道。
>
> 以前官員士子來往北京四川的，多半走這條路。……
>
> 路是如此重要，所以每日每刻，無論晴雨，你都可以看見有成群的駝畜，載著各種貨物，參雜在四人官轎，三人丁拐轎，二人對班轎，以及載運行李的扛擔挑子之間，一連串的來，一連串的去。在這人流當中，間或一匹瘦馬，在項下搖著一串很響的鈴鐺，載著一個背包袱挎雨傘的急裝少年，飛馳而過，你就知道這便是驛站上送文書的了。不過近年因爲有了電報。文書馬已逐漸的少了。……
>
> 這鎮市是成都北門外有名的天回鎮。志書上，説它得名的由來，遠在中唐。……

（李劼人，《死水微瀾》，2011：13～14）

在李的筆下一九零零年的天回鎮並非死氣沉沉的內地鄉村的縮影。和它所屬的省會成都一樣，集鎮雖然地處龐大的清帝國的一隅，卻也是帝國遽變的一部分。它是僻鄉，也是數代中華王朝四通八達交通樞紐的重要一環，尤其是從晚清至關緊要的邊防重鎮四川省會成都至帝國各地及中心的必經之地。故事開始的時候小鎮的地位有了改變——「有了電報。文書馬已逐漸的少了。」但是變化的微瀾以及引發的滔天巨浪，對部分小鎮人——故事的主角們——生死攸關，卻並非『外來』對『本地』，『新』對『舊』的簡單侵襲和蠶食。

〔註4〕G. William Skinner, ed. *The City in Late Imperial China, Studies in Chinese Society,* 253～289.

外來的物事在小鎮柴米油鹽的生活中漸漸變得習以爲常。鄉場上洋貨土貨和產自帝國其他地方的貨物羅列在一起的，供小鎮及周圍鄉村的人們選擇。「小市上主要貨品，是家織土布。這全是一般農家婦女在做了粗活之後，藉以填補空虛光陰，自己紡出紗來，自己織成。⋯⋯但近來已有外國來的竹布，洋布。那眞好，又寬又細又勻淨，⋯⋯只是價錢貴得多，買的人少，還賣不贏家織土布。⋯⋯小市鎮上，也有專與婦女有關的東西。如較粗的土葛巾，時興的細洋葛巾；成都桂林軒的香肥皂，⋯⋯也有極惹人愛的洋線，洋針，兩者之中，洋針頂通行，雖然比土針貴，但是針鼻扁而有槽，好穿線，⋯⋯也有蘇貨，廣貨，料子花，假珍珠。⋯⋯」（李劼人，《死水微瀾》，2011：49～50）。在李劼人的陳訴中，洋土的較量是由當地人的喜好定勝負的。其優劣貴賤與強勢的生產方式和經濟行爲有關，也取決於地方日集月累的生活方式，一時一地隨著內外世界共時變遷而變的經濟社會力量。洋貨在內地的大量出現是晚清世界大變動最直接的物化體現之一，它們變成省城鄉鎮日常生活的一部分顯示了近代中華帝國歷史轉折的「世界背景」。〔註 5〕這種世界背景也可以從形容詞「洋」在十九世紀中頁以來的歷史語言熱中體會到。〔註 6〕洋的原義爲海洋的，海洋性的。是一具有空間特指性的詞，意指所有洋那邊的，漂洋過海的，海（洋）外的物和事。與後來更流行的形容境外人事物或風格的「外」不同，洋不僅顯示區分，內外有別，還保留了其源自遠方闊大世界的空間指謂，提醒人們中華之地與海外世界變爲一體的過程。

李劼人的天回鎮並未因洋針洋布成爲全球性的大同世界。但是外面世界變爲小鄉鎮物質生活的一部分展示了被喻爲死水的社會也漣漪陣陣。洋貨在省城城鄉的流行不僅是世道變化的物化標誌，也折射出人們心靈和社會情勢的悸動。作爲欲望的對象與社會身份的象徵，它們在帝國末期地方士紳的心理情感波動和對帝制以及他們生活的整個世界的態度的變化中起了相當的作用。三部曲的主角之一官紳郝達三在庚子事變（1900）的關鍵時刻游移於對帝制的忠誠和已成爲省城望族家庭日用必需品的舶來貨的留戀。郝和他的朋友們習慣性地傾向於支持義和拳民，因爲他們聽說當政的慈禧太后支持拳

〔註 5〕 Antonia Finnane, "Yangzhou's 'Modernity': Fashion and Consumption in the Early Nineteenth Century', *positions: east asia cultures critique,* 392.

〔註 6〕 W. Feng, "Yi, Yang, Xi, Wai and Other Terms: the Transition from 'Barbarian' to 'Foreigner' in Nineteenth Century China", *New Terms for New Ideas: Western Knowledge and Lexical Change in Late Imperial China,* 95～124.

民。同時他們也爲日益上升的基督教民在本地的勢力而擔憂，尤其是後者和教堂對田地和財富的爭奪。但在爲拳民們的行徑喝彩後，郝達三突然意識到：「若把北京使館打破後，不曉得洋人還來不來？不來，那才糟哩！我們使的這些洋貨，卻向哪裏去買？」（李劼人，《死水微瀾》，2011：168）他的擔憂並非沒有緣由。對相當部分有資財或收入豐厚的成都士紳和市民來說，沒有舶來品的日常生活已經難以想像：

> 郝公館裏這些西洋東西，實在不少。至於客廳裏五色磨花的玻璃窗片，紫檀螺鈿座子的大穿衣鏡，這都是老太爺手上置備的了。近來最得用而又爲全家離不得的，就是一般人尚少用的牙刷，牙膏，洋葛巾，洋胰子，花露水等日常小東西。洋人看起來那樣又粗又笨的，何以造的這些家常用品，都好，只要你一經了手，就離它不開？

> （李劼人，《死水微瀾》，2011：162）

當然省城和周圍鄉鎮的一般居民們還無法像郝大公館一樣天天用上進口的牙膏牙刷，不過中上層市民都愛逛的新開張的成都商業場裏洋貨充足且廣受歡迎。郝達三和他的世交好友們在這死水微瀾的時候也並未因爲偏愛洋貨而擁護清庭爲自新自強而推行的新政，他們不通也看不上康梁的新學。但在他們的生活中，舶來品從奇技淫巧變成了日常必需。物質世界的多樣化也使他們和帝國末世的其他臣民一樣心動情移。到《暴風雨前》開始的時候，郝達三不光成了通過新政建立的省諮議局議員，他還送兒子女兒去成都彼時遍地開花的新式學堂學習。他的女兒們成了省城最早的女學生之一。塞滿洋貨的郝公館甚至還半睜眼半閉眼地爲一激進革命黨人提供了庇護。至《大波》，郝達三及兒子郝又三都成了風起雲湧的四川保路運動的積極參與者，大清帝國直接的掘墓人。

　　從天回鎮的《死水微瀾》到成都省的《暴風雨前》至《大波》，李劼人的近代小說史寫的是省城革命。大清帝國辛亥年間從最後的掙扎到瞬間煙消雲散其起始和過程都是地方性事件。其中公認的關鍵事件之一，就是歷時半年的四川保路運動。在這個意義上，被後世稱爲辛亥革命的一九一一年的帝制的消亡是一系列或突發或日集月累的，與晚清政府的新政息息相關的地方性事件的結果。地方是帝國消亡和中國由此開始革命不斷的現場。以方志寫近代史是李要堅持表現的歷史眞實的必須。也許這也是郭沫若爲什麼既把李的三部曲定義爲「小說近代史」又稱作「小說的近代《華陽國志》」的原因。李劼人的歷史眞實涵括翻天覆地的大事件和日常生活的漸變，即社會生活，結構和社會心理的變化。「你寫政治上的變革，你能不寫生活上，思想上的變革麼？你寫生活上，思想上的脈動，你又能不寫當時政治，經濟的脈動麼？必須盡力寫出時代的全貌，別人也才能由你的筆，瞭解到當時歷史的真實。」〔註7〕地方是這種歷史觀的立足點。李劼人方志式的歷史敘事不僅在空間內呈現時間，將歷史敘述於鄉土上；在人物行為和事件發展的結構上或縱向探根溯源，或橫向品類呈現，縱橫交錯間讓歷史的歷時性展現於空間的共時性上。讓大事件的史落實到日常空間的全景裏，使歷史的巨變庸常史詩兼備。而且更重要的是這種方志式的敘事顯示出地方是歷史發生的唯一場所，無論是改天換地的遽變還是日常生活的日新月異。地方志因此成為大歷史的最好載體。只有通過方志式的空間化的庸常史詩兼備的全景呈現，才能洞悉和再現近代中國革命史的歷史真實。彰顯宏大歷史生發衍變的地域場景和空間限定也凸現了歷史因緣及結局的偶然性。這也許是李劼人在歷史的轉折關頭幾次撰寫成都地方志的原因。李不僅在他的系列小說中陳鋪描述了大量成都及四川的地理座標，歷史沿革，風土人情。他的三部曲可以因此被看作帝國末世邊隅省城的變化史。他還在一九四九年寫下了《二千餘年成都大城史的衍變》，一九五三年《成都歷史沿革》，一九五八年《成都的一條街》等，在另一個新世界開始的時候以方志追索歷史的變遷。

　　作為歷史現場的地方在李劼人的方志式小說近代史裏既有原鄉也有他鄉。這不僅表現在省城作為遽變和漸變同時發生的歷史現場早已有從政治到情感和物質生活的世界背景，還在於這場史變的主角們既是土著又和他鄉有著千絲萬縷的聯繫。遊學境外彼時已成了地方士紳入仕甚還維生的重要途徑。他鄉在這裡不是外部世界對本土的威罔，而是本土變遷的背景和在場。李的歷史視野中的四川保路運動及其引發的辛亥革命是士紳革命。作為晚清政府新政的一部分，成都也和帝國許多其他的城市一樣，建學校，興實業，練新軍，派遣留學生。極具諷刺意味的是這些自救改革舉措，加上諮議局等士紳由社會議政涉政空間的建立，促使了帝國和千年帝制的大江東去。四川士紳送子弟留學的熱情極高。一九〇六年四川留學生占全國留日學生總數的十分之一，居全國之首。〔註8〕『出洋』是科舉廢除後士紳子弟求出身的有限的門道之一。對『洋』

〔註7〕李劼人，「大波第二部書後，」《李劼人選集》第二卷，第 953 頁。

〔註8〕張金蓮，《走出夔門──論清末四川留日學生〉，內江師範學院學報，No. 7 Vol. 24, 2009。

的嚮往也是士紳階層對帝國末日和世道變遷自十九世紀中期以來論辯思索的結果。其中『東洋』除了是通向今世富強文明象徵的『西洋』的捷徑，也是率先西洋化擠入世界強權的榜樣。留日成為當時官派或自費出洋的首選因此並不奇怪。「從 1901 年到 1911 年，每年留日學生的人數都高於留學其他各國人數的總和。」二十世紀初的日本不僅聚集了成份最複雜的中國留學生，「也匯聚了這些知識分子中最複雜的理想形式——政治的，思想的與文學的，保皇的與革命的，保守的與激進的，青年學子式的與流亡刺客式的。」〔註 9〕回歸的留日學生在地方的政治、經濟、教育、軍事等許多領域都發揮了重要作用，川籍的回歸學人也是如此。保路運動的領袖人物蒲殿俊（1875～1935）和鄧孝可（1869～1950）在事件發生前都剛從日本遊學歸來。

在李劼人筆下，蒲殿俊、鄧孝可作為有史可查的保路運動的領袖人物是文獻式處理的，也就是說他們的言行是作為歷史事件發展的一部分敘述的，而他們並未成為小說的主要人物。但留學或遊宦日本是李的省城地方敘事的很重要的組成部分。它是人物心理行為的注釋，也是晚清社會地方情勢變動的標誌之一。在三部曲中，幾乎所有的官紳商家庭都有出東洋和出過東洋或想出東洋的子弟。東洋在《暴風雨前》是以「我們老大帝國」的救藥由一即將留日的青年介紹給主角之一的郝達三的：「日本與我們同文同種，而在明治維新前，其腐敗也同，其閉關自守也同，……一旦效法泰西，努力維新，而居然達其目的。又是我們的東鄰，我們只要學它，……它怎樣做，我們也怎樣做……我們既有成法可取，當然用不著那麼久的時間，多則五年，少則三年，豈不也就富強了？」〔註 10〕這位微末鄉紳出身的正在努力成為新少年的少年口中的東洋當然不過是對當時時新文明話語的重述。其中強國富民的訴求加上了國夢家夢的急功近利。「維新」與「稱霸東亞」是在此初次出場的日本形象的關鍵詞。雖然郝在當時對新政新學及新派少年都似懂非懂，也隨即悟出了中國欲求富強，只有學日本的道理。更重要的是，在曾經遊宦日本幾個月的好友葛寰中幫助下，很快認識到了出洋與在這個新世界上安身立命的關係。雖然他的兒子郝又三因母親不捨等原因未能成行，這位向郝家第一次介紹了東洋的新少年蘇星煌多年留學回來後成了郝家的女婿。蘇在日本留學的期間關心時政，和保路運動的領袖們一樣成了立憲派。歸國後官做到了帝

〔註 9〕李怡，《日本體驗與中國現代文學的發生》，13～14。
〔註 10〕李劼人，《暴風雨前》，第 6 頁。

國的中心北京。而且他在北京的家也是新式的：他的太太，郝家在成都上過新學的大女兒，常常在男女同處的社交場合大發政見。

其實李劼人小說系列中更重要更有意思的留日人物是尤鐵民。尤和蘇一樣是四川士紳背景的新派少年。但旅日後加入了同盟會，成了激進的革命人物。回川後東躲西藏冒險搞革命活動。在被搜捕期間隱居郝家與郝大小姐搞自由戀愛，爾後不辭而別。有意思的是這個書中至始至終的激進人物，在保路運動以及引發的全民大暴動中卻無絲毫作為。除了早期暗中準備搞爆炸起事，失敗後就緲無下落。但作為小說系列的主要人物之一，他的作用卻非常重要。他的激進和留日經歷在李的敘事計劃中是用以表現地方情勢，社會關係，人物行為的漸變的，是地方變化與其異質和世界背景關係的呈現，而不是對歷史事件的直接表述。在李劼人的小說省城革命史裏，尤和其他的激進革命黨人在事件進程中的作用有限，他們的經歷，行為，情感卻是世紀末地方社會情勢，思想傾向，人物行為方式變化的具體呈現點。他們的東洋留學背景更是彰顯了這種變化的歷史特殊性。尤鐵民的激進活動在保路運動以及其引發的歷史大變動中的直接作用可有可無，但他在郝家以及省城的士紳子女圈中留下的情感和思想行為的漣漪卻不僅僅是微瀾。郝家父子甚還女兒們都成了維新或革命的身體力行者。在《大波》中才出現的留日歸國學生周宏道是全面維新的。他真心實意地想在省城推行實施法政。但他對省城社會最大的貢獻是給公館生活帶來了更新更洋化的日常起居和吃喝玩樂的方式，並使一位官紳家的老小姐有了性和婚姻的歸宿。李劼人在這裡並非反諷士紳的革命不徹底性。日常起居和兩性關係在小說中與歷史大事件相輔相成。周宏道和其他留學生的留（東）洋和回歸其歷史作用並不局限於他們在革命事件中的具體表現和用處。作為個體和頗為可觀的群體，他們是地方變化的世界背景的心理，行為，文化主體的體現。他們的重要性在於他們是省城社會生活，生存方式，情感的漸變過程中異質性（來自異鄉的，新奇的）變為同質性（本地生活情感方式）的一部分。

李劼人的方志式省城革命史可以被看作格里格·鄧寧所定義的地方社會的族群史。其要點不僅在於所謂的國族大歷史都是有時間地點的，受不同所在地的社會文化所制約，更關鍵的是要通過抓住這樣的歷史中最重要也是其內涵最含混不清的時刻來審視它們彼時和現在的意義。〔註11〕李劼人筆下的

〔註11〕Greg Dening, *Performances*, 44～45.

四川保路運動和辛亥革命毫無疑義是中國近代史上這樣的關鍵時刻，其歷史意義需要不斷重新審視。在這樣族群史中，革命，暴動，改朝換代的大歷史同時具有民俗人類學的意義。革命不僅是政治形式，國族制度的遽變，而且是地方世界生存方式，生命形態的變異。他鄉在地方遽變中所起的複雜作用，包括留日學生在清末社會變化中所扮演的角色，都讓讀者不得不重新思考這些歷史事件和對它們的表述的意義。既以物化的形式出現又是新的正在形成的地方心理情感文化主體的一部分的他鄉在李的三部曲中是省城革命史和二十世紀初中國社會，政治，經濟，文化大變動的背景，參照，是在場的引發變動的勢力之一。

參考文獻

1. Dening, Greg. *Performances,* Melbourne: Melbourne University Press, 1996.

2. 丁帆。《中國鄉土小說史》，北京大學出版社，2007。

3. Finnane, Antonia. "Yangzhou's 'Modernity', Fashion and Consumption in the Early Nineteenth Century" *positions: east asia cultures critique,* 11, 2003: 395～425.

4. Feng, W. "Yi, Yang, Xi, Wai and Other Terms: the Transition from 'Barbarian' to 'Foreigner' in Nineteenth Century China" *New Terms for New Ideas: Western Knowledge and Lexical Change in Late Imperial China,* ed. M. Lackner, I. Amelung and J. Kurtz, Leiden: Brill, 2001: 95～124.

5. 郭沫若。《中國佐拉之待望》，《中國文藝》1937 年第一卷第二期，1937 年 6 月 15 日。

6. 李劼人。「《死水微瀾》前記」，《李劼人全集》第九卷，成都：四川文藝出版社，2011：241～243。

7. 李劼人。「大波第二部書後，」《李劼人選集》第二卷，成都：四川人民出版社，1980：951～955。

8. 李劼人。《死水微瀾》，《李劼人全集》第 1 卷，成都：四川文藝出版社，2011。

9. 李劼人。《暴風雨前》，《李劼人全集》第 2 卷，成都：四川文藝出版社，2011。

10. 李劼人。《大波》，《李劼人全集》第 3，4 卷，成都：四川文藝出版社，2011。

11. 李怡。《日本體驗與中國現代文學的發生》，臺灣：秀威信息公司，2008。

12. 茅盾。《子夜》，北京：人民文學出版社，2008。

13. 沈從文。《邊城》，北京：中國青年出版社，2014。

14. Skinner, G. William Ed. *The City in Late Imperial China, Studies in Chinese society.* Stanford: Stanford University Press, 1977.

15. 張金蓮。《走出夔門——論清末四川留日學生》，《內江師範學院學報》，No. 7 Vol. 24，2009。

庸常與史詩：李劼人的「小說近代史」

一、歷史敘述與小說形式

　　在中國文學史上，歷史與小說的關係源遠流長。小說作為一種敘事性的文類被認為是私人制史，野史筆記中發展出來的，即作為正統史書的補遺和參照。歷史小說則被認為是史傳中的歷史描寫，尤其是其中帶有想像性描述的篇章〔註1〕。雖然宋元時「小說」一詞與「講史」有別，指與歷史題材無關的較短篇的故事敘述，而講史話本才是現代概念中以歷史為題材的小說〔註2〕。講史話本奠定了元、明之後傳統歷史小說的敘事模式，以兩種方式——口頭說書和文字刊印書籍一流傳下來〔註3〕。作為現代歷史小說前身之一的明清歷史小說則是在此基礎上發展起來的，以斷代史為藍本，根據其內容分為兩種類型：一種是以重大的歷史事件為中心，按照正史的歷史進程展開敘事的歷史演義小說，重點敘述歷史事件，人物描述和刻畫居於次要地位，如《三國志通俗演義》，貼近由史書本紀衍化而成的講史話本。另一種是以一

〔註1〕張中良：《20世紀三四十年代中國小說敘事》，臺灣：秀威信息科技股份公司，2004年，第96頁。

〔註2〕楊聯芬認為作為現代文體的「歷史小說」一詞首次出現於1902年《新民叢報》為雜誌《新小說》所做的廣告文中。此廣告將歷史小說作為雜誌內容之一列出，並將其定義為「專以歷史上事沐為材料，而服演義體敘述之。」楊聯芬。《流動的瞬間：晚清與五四文學關係論》，臺灣：秀威信息科技股份公司，2006年，第159～160頁。

〔註3〕魯德才：《古代白話小說形態發展史論》，天津：南開大學出版社，2002年，第19頁。

個或一群英雄人物爲中心的英雄傳奇小說，如《水滸傳》，強調重要人物對歷史的影響，原型是由紀傳體史傳和列傳衍化的講史話本〔註4〕。

顧明東由此在他的《中國小說理論》中得出結論說中國小說發展史是一部小說從歷史中脫胎而出的獨立史〔註5〕。David Rolston 也指出傳統小說評注早就注意到歷史的影響對小說的發展是一種負擔〔註6〕。顧氏近一步提出中國小說成熟的標誌一方面是其內容由講述眞實歷史人物和事件轉到虛擬敍述無史可考的故事，另一方面是作爲敍述文體在角度，觀念及審美經驗上的全方位改變〔註7〕。這種中國小說史論當然難以涵蓋歷史小說發展的全部，卻彰顯了作爲文體小說與歷史敍述的緊密關係。

從文類發展史看來，作爲敍述文體，歷史小說不可避免地同時具有史詩性和庸常性：雖然狹義的史詩——敍述英雄傳說或重大歷史事件的長篇敍事體詩——被認爲是非典型的中國傳統文體〔註8〕，但歷史小說，無論是講史話本還是英雄傳奇的史詩性似乎毋庸置疑：作爲中國歷史小說的原型，《三國演義》和《水滸傳》都背景龐大、人物眾多，涉及大量的虛構空間，時間跨度大，再現某特定歷史時期的生活面貌且規模宏恢，並吸收了神話、傳說、故事等，描繪帝（王）國興衰，天地輪迴，講述英雄傳奇，可謂典型的史詩式敍述文本。但也涉及飲食男女，市井生活，其傳奇性也包括非（反）英雄的，尤其是後者，情節多圍繞眾好漢打家劫舍，雞鳴狗盜的生涯。如果史詩性指詩意規範的敍事，修辭情感莊嚴高尚，吟頌英雄業績，常爲氏（國）族集體過去的讚歌，爲後世定義可傳世的事件，人物，意義，庸常則指小說（話本，故事）的細節性，日常性，描述性，作爲文體必需的從內容到形式上的非詩意成分，甚至可以說最基本的成分。黑格爾認爲這種文體的庸常性是時代的。在他看來，「敍事文」時代的開始，包括小說的興起，是庸常的現代世界的開始，其本質是反詩意，反藝術的〔註9〕。巴赫金卻認爲敍事散文的興起並非一

〔註4〕同上。

〔註5〕Gu, Mingdong. *Chinese Theories of Fiction: A Non-Western Narrative System*, Albany: SUNY, 2006:6.

〔註6〕Rolston, David L. *Traditional Chinese Fiction and Fiction Commentary: Reading and Writing between the Lines*, Stanford University Press, 1997: 131～165.

〔註7〕Gu, Mingdong. *Chinese Theories of Fiction : A Non-Western Narrative System*, Albany: SUNY, 2006 : 7.

〔註8〕朱光潛：《朱光潛全集》第8卷，合肥：安徽文藝出版社，1993年。

〔註9〕G. W. F. Hegel, *Aesthetics ： Lectures on Fine Art*, trans. T. M. Knox, Oxford: Clarendon Press, 2 Vols, 1:10.

袪魅或流失的過程，而是社會眾聲對話式聚集的正面形成過程。散文形式是
文學語言成熟的標誌，其散文性，就是庸常性，是喧囂的生命和文化衍化成
歷史的標誌。而小說是蘊含「庸常思維」，「庸常視野」，「庸常智慧」的最好
文學形式〔註10〕。

　　中國現代歷史小說的源頭可追溯到晚清，聞立飛認爲「小說界革命」
在追求新文學觀念與創作方法的同時也促使歷史小說開始向現代擅變。在
這一過程中，曾樸（1871～1935）是第一個從事全景式歷史小說創作的作
家〔註11〕。曾樸的《孽海花》全景式歷史敘述主要表現在它開放兼容的視
野：「小說的場景從蘇州、上海和北京一直轉到柏林和聖彼得堡；培根和盧
梭與中國大詩人李白和蘇東坡、隋場帝與路易十六被相提並論，中國革命
者與俄國虛無黨人被相提並論；改良主義的公羊哲學與聖西門的社會革命
哲學形成對照；才子佳人的浪漫史與俄國虛無主義的情人們的愛國和無私
的激情形成對。在《孽海花》的宏闊視野中，可以發現作者著力以寫實的
現代風格描繪處在激蕩變化中晚清全景歷史的全新意圖」〔註12〕。聞還指
出曾樸對全景式歷史小說的探索是以傳統觀念來接納並改造外來的歷史小
說形式，它的現代性在於傳統觀念與外來形式（以司各特爲代表的十九世
紀歐洲歷史小說）的折衝鯢齫中，如全景式歷史圖象的主題與所謂「珠花
式」結構（「連綴多數短篇成長篇」）之間的衝突。另外，小說的進化史觀
與其預言性敘事框架之間有著內在的矛盾。《孽海花》把對晚清社會頹敗局
面的描繪與革命黨的興起聯繫起來，二者之間的因果關係表達了曾樸的進
化史觀，即晚清社會革命的必然性。但這種線性發展的現代進化史觀，在
小說裏卻被曾樸納人更爲廣闊的預言性敘事框架中，「不僅金、傅愛情故事
一開始就被預言了結局，奴樂島最終沉人孽海的故事也預言了晚清社會的
結局，這樣，傳統敘事陰陽相剋、興衰交替的循環觀念籠罩了整部小說，
並與進化的歷史觀念形成抵梧之勢」〔註13〕。

〔註10〕M. M. Bakhtin, *The Dialogic Imagination: Four Essays*, University of Texas Press, 2010: 404.
〔註11〕聞立飛：《現代中國歷史小說的發生》http：//www.literature.org.cn/Article.aspx？id=60985, 27/2/2014.
〔註12〕同上。
〔註13〕同上。

二、李劼人的長篇「小說近代史」

　　李劼人（1891～1962）的連續性近代史長篇小說《死水微瀾》（1935）、《暴風雨前》（1936），《大波》（1937；1957 重寫，未完）開拓了中國現代長篇小說的新格局，它們在二十年代五四後小說創作轉向以「自我」「抒情」及「書信體」「日記體」爲主的背景下，重新奠定了長篇歷史小說作爲現代文學形式和文體的地位。以短篇小說和散文見長的魯迅曾感歎：「即以前清末年而論，大事件不可謂不多了：鴉片戰爭，中法戰爭，中日戰爭，戊戌政變，義和拳變，八國聯軍，以至民元革命。然而我們沒有一部像樣的歷史著作，更不必說文學作品了」〔註 14〕。在魯迅看來，歷史，尤其是中國現代史，應該是重要的現代文學題材。而大事件須有相對應的（文學）敘述文體。李的三部曲因其「宏闊的場景」和「超長的表現時代的長篇敘事」被稱爲現代中國「大河小說」〔註 15〕。李氏敘事開闊的流動性和他對某時某地大變動期間宏大主題及細碎瑣事的歷史興趣確實令人聯想起阿爾貝・蒂博代（Albert Thibaudet 1874～1936）的「循環小說」〔註 16〕。但他的三部曲無論從寫作動機，文體和審美效應來看都遠非對這樣或那樣類型小說的模擬。李也不曾提及有創作中式「大河小說」的野心，他與法國文學的關係遠遠超於對個別文類的興趣。在三部曲的寫作修改過程中，李所感興趣並借鑒的是古今中外的「大部頭」小說：「一九五八年五月起，我又病了一場。……藉此機會，便把以前曾經看過的若干部中外古今大部頭小說，搬出來溫習。從這中間，得到很大啓發。懂得細節應該如何處理，方不嫌其累贅，討厭；插敘應該如何擺法，有時順理成章地小小插一段，接著便回顧到正文，…」〔註 17〕。顯然，李需要考慮的是「大」作爲篇幅和長度所需的相應的敘述策略和技巧，在對歷史的重構和敘述中庸常的細節怎樣和大事件互爲「插曲」和「正文」。李在《死水微瀾》的《前記》中寫到：「從一九二五年起，一面教書，一面仍舊寫些短篇小說時，

〔註 14〕魯迅：《田軍〈八月的鄉村〉序》，《魯迅全集》第 6 卷，北京：人民文學出版社，1981 年，第 286～389 頁。

〔註 15〕司馬長風：《新中國文學史》，香港：昭明出版有限公司，1976 年，第 455～457 頁。

〔註 16〕A. Thibaudet, "Une vole e" (1 er novembre 1935), *Réflexions sur Ia littérature*, 2007 : 1574.

〔註 17〕李劼人：《〈大波〉第二部書後》，《李劼人全集》第四卷，成都：四川文藝出版社，2011 年，769 頁。

便起了一個念頭，打算把幾十年來所生活過，所切感過，所體驗過，在我看來意義非常重大，當得起歷史轉披點的這一段社會現象，用幾部有連續性的長篇小說，一段落一段落地把它反映出來」〔註 18〕。這一創作意圖來源於李對「歷史」、「革命」和「長篇小說」不斷衍變發展的理解。「我想，直接從辛亥革命人手太槍促了些。這個革命並不是突然而來的，它有歷史淵源，歷史上積累了很多因素，積之既久才結這個大瓜。要寫，就必須追源溯流，從最早的時候寫起。寫鴉片戰爭，我不熟悉，熟悉的是庚子年以後的事：聽見過八國聯軍的事情，也看見過當時成都所受的影響。第二年成都鬧紅燈教，殺紅燈教的首領之一廖觀音，打教堂，這些事我最清楚，我就從這時候寫起，從庚子年寫到辛亥革命，寫所聞，寫所見，寫身所經歷，三段一系列。這就是大家所講的三部曲。第一部叫《死水微瀾》，第二部叫《暴風雨前》，第三部叫《大波》，從書名可以看出當時革命進程的」〔註 19〕。李的歷史是大事件：革命及其進程，但同時又是所有他作爲個人及歷史見證人所經歷體驗並有所感的各種社會現象。在李看來，理解革命需追源溯流。而追溯事件的源頭是一個反思選擇的過程。斷定事件的起始發展和記敘作者熟悉或所聞所見的社會生活及情感都是李對「小說近代史」寫什麼和怎麼寫的思索嘗試。可以說李對「大部頭」小說的興趣來自於他對描述變化過程的形式結構的探索。他認爲與鉅細皆具的革命進程相對應的是系列及段落性的歷史小說。多卷體和長篇幅使空間時間的容量極大，且可停可續，適宜於既壯闊又瑣細的歷史敘事。李劼人寫作修改《大波》三部曲的過程可以說是一個探索描述前所未有的歷史變革的現代小說形式和結構範式的過程，旨在描繪敘述清帝國無可挽回的衰亡崩潰及其引發的一系列中國二十世紀的革命和不斷的社會文化變動。其形式結構既有對「大河小說」的借鑒也有對章回小說的利用。李直接提到的適宜《大波》題材內容的敘述形式的可參照小說有狄更斯的《大衛科波菲爾》，左拉的《勞動》，托爾斯泰的《戰爭與和平》和「中國的占典長篇」《三國》、《水滸》、《紅樓夢》、《金瓶梅》，並認爲其中尤以《戰爭與和平》和《三國》的篇幅鋪展和人物塑造最有借鑒價值〔註 20〕。

〔註 18〕李劼人：《〈死水微瀾〉前記》，《李劼人全集》第九卷，第 241 頁。
〔註 19〕李劼人：《談創作經驗》，《李劼人全集》第九卷，第 246～247 頁。
〔註 20〕李劼人：《〈大波〉第三部書後》，《李劼人聖集》第四卷，第 1166～1167 頁。

在三部曲中，李劼人的歷史視野涵括翻天覆地的大事件和日常生活的漸變：李把兩者都叫做歷史的眞實，即社會生活，結構和社會心理的變化。「你寫政治上的變革，你能不寫生活上，思想上的變革麼？你寫生活上，思想上的脈動，你又能不寫當時政治，經濟的脈動麼？必須盡力寫出時代的全貌，別人也才能由你的筆，瞭解到當時歷史的眞實」〔註21〕。表達這種歷史視野的小說形式必然既有其史詩性又有其庸常性。全景式長篇敘事無疑最適宜描述從飲食男女，社會眾生的心理情感悖動到翻天覆地的政治革命的「時代的全貌」。因爲全景式敘事具有史詩性的開放的（空間性的）敘述流動，又有細節的具體展現。全景小說常被定義爲具有全方位視角的在地理及社會場景方面都鉅細包容的小說，展現大面積的無限制視野下的場景或一系列事件。在李的小說中這種全景展現表現爲一種對能容納史詩性庸常性兼具的中國現代歷史，尤其是革命過程的小說敘述結構的嘗試。

《大波》，三部曲的最後一部，是這種歷史敘述的最好例證。如果說《死水微瀾》戲劇性地展現了省城外小鄉鎮社會眾生在翻天覆地前隨著帝國衰亡的悸動，暴風雨前》揭開了省城作爲前所未有的變動的歷史現場的情感文化，個人欲望及社會心理的漸變，《大波》則講述描繪了後來被視爲辛亥革命先聲的四川保路運動的全過程。其中帝國一隅的王朝末世的頹敗的政治生活，漲落的社會和個人情緒，生活方式和行爲的漸變，群體的躁動（暴動）都是構成革命作爲歷史事件連綿不絕的（情節）組成部分。

三、《大波》的兩個敘述層面

像《暴風雨前》一樣，《大波》（原初本兩卷，改寫本三卷）繼續以省城成都風搖雨墜的大清帝國末期的士紳爲主角，以客籍官紳黃瀾生一家從一九一一年六月到十二月半年的生活經歷爲中心，全景展現了遽變在帝國的一隅的發生發展過程。雖然敘述依照四川保路運動從起始到四川獨立軍政府成立的時序，其多卷長篇的篇幅是以空間（場景）結構的。小說敘述的兩個層面——黃家生活細節及其透視的社會情勢和歷史事件的直接描述一是通過這種空間結構連接起來的，成爲全篇連綿不斷的場景。這種敘述結構和方法使革命清楚地呈現爲一個前所未有的變化過程：既突兀，驚天動地，又鉅細間雜，

〔註21〕 李劼人：《〈大波〉第二部書後》，《李劼人選集》第二卷，第953頁。

反覆無常。歷史的脈動——邊隅古城在帝國末日的江河日下和無常的在即遽變時的亢奮一在場景的演變中逐步展現出來。歷史事件的因緣因此顯得既偶然又難以逆轉。

在初版《大波》中，敘述的這兩個層面在結構上相對獨立，頗有花開兩朵，各表一枝的痕跡。這在早期的評論中，被看成是李的自然主義藝術觀在作崇，即他過於拘泥於細節的真實〔註22〕。李劼人對自然主義是感興趣的〔註23〕，左拉的《勞動》是《大波》寫作的坻本之一。但與曾樸不同，他對中國現代歷史小說敘述方式的嘗試不在於對外來形式或藝術觀的好奇和引用。小說中兩種敘述層面在形式上的分離也非傳統觀念與外來形式的衝突，而直接體現了作者對「小說近代史」的文體探索，從中可以看出作者對「新小說」敘事形式探索的承繼和拓展。由空間展開的生活場景和據時發展的歷史事件兩個層面來敘述末日帝國的邅變可以看出社會世情小說與歷史演義的結合。全方位地表現寫作者作為歷史當事人或見證者的所經歷，所見，所聞，所感是李寫歷史小說的初衷。庸常的，無一不包的社會和個人生活細節，影響大眾的激進活動，日漸衰敗的帝國政務，暴發的全民運動，都是作者要描述的歷史真實。虛擬的黃家生活和有史可查的保路運動系列事件在這個意義上是互補的不可或缺的兩部分。李對傳統小說敘事方法的借鑒——花開兩朵，各表一枝——保持了三部曲持衡的空間結構，又凸顯了兩個敘述層面的有機互補性。通過一個場景一個場景的分開但連續不斷地講述，歷史真實不分鉅細地或時巨時細地被空間性地呈現出來。黃家，郝家，以及相關的幾個下層市民家庭的飲食男女，生老病死和一發不可收拾，愈演愈烈的四川保路運動是一株花的兩朵。大清帝國的衰亡崩潰及其引發的持續不斷的政治革命和社會變動不僅是一系列的大事件也是日常生活，個人情感的量變質變。《大波》原初版和重寫版對這兩個層面的處理不同之處源自李劼人對歷史小說作為文類和敘述形式的不斷探索和變化的觀念。初版的寫法與「新小說」的關係明顯，也能看出作者改寫傳統演義體的企圖。黃家及其相關人物的生活部分為社會言情，其中對個人欲望和社會心理的描寫可看出十九世紀法國小說的影響。歷

〔註22〕李士文：《李劼人的生平和創作》，成都：四川科學院出版社，1986年，第209～234頁。

〔註23〕李劼人：《法蘭西自然主義以後的小說及其作家》，《李劼人全集》，成都：四川文藝出版社，2011年，第143～181頁。

史事件的描述部分可被形容爲文獻體—作者常常全篇或部分引用歷史文獻，以呈現方式記敘史實的企圖明顯。重寫版則體現了李劼人衍變的歷史小說觀和對其現代形式，尤其是對「小說近代史」的歷史性和小說性的表現方式的不斷探索的結果。從李列出的古今中外可供借鑒的「大部頭」小說也可看出他對重寫作爲現代歷史小說的《大波》的設想：社會小說與歷史演義並重。他對它們作爲敘事坯本的興趣也主要在於它們的敘述結構：細節怎樣與大事件互補，怎樣互爲正文與插曲。簡言之，重寫版《大波》以全景式結構與視角融社會小說和歷史演義爲一體，在以空間場面連接的全景敘述格局中兩個層面的故事發展不再自成一體，而是作爲互補的場景戲劇性地呈現革命的庸常和史詩性。在李式現代歷史長篇小說——「小說近代史」中，士紳男女微妙的心理變化，省城眾生生活方式的衍變與全民暴動一樣重要。

　　和《暴風雨前》一樣，隱居省城的士紳是《大波》的主角。從這個角度來看，小說敘述的兩個層面在初版中也難以被視爲游離的兩部分，而是通過核心人物的生活和視野連接在一起。生活細節和社會情勢通過他們的日常活動，歷史事件—難以收拾的政局和愈演愈烈的全民運動——通過他們的視角（或所聞或轉述），以各表一枝的方式講述出來。以黃瀾生作全書的主角因此是必然的選擇。雖然在帝國末世的邊隅省城黃官微位低，且是捐的，而且自認是客籍。但黃不僅生長於成都，幾代爲官爲宦爲糧戶（且投資金融）經營下來，在經濟和社會地位上早已是省城士紳的中堅。黃瀾生的境況可以說是晚期中華帝國時期士紳命運變化的縮影，即越來越多的士紳的經濟地位和社會勢力與帝國政治權力制度脫節〔註24〕。如果說小說中黃是政治生活的觀察者，在社會生活中他卻是主角。這在李劼人的「歷史眞實」中是非常重要的。因此黃既可爲敘述遷變及其因緣過程的核心當事人，又可爲旁觀者。他的眼耳口鼻和心理情緒均爲敘述結構的整合點：初版從黃瀾生在一九一一年五月某初夏夜對世事無常的感歎開始，引出變動在即的成都日常生活的蘊籍平靜，再介紹了正在醞釀的四川保路運動及其因緣，尤其是末日帝國的新政在邊隅省城的影響。由於歷史事件的敘述由黃的微妙心理活動和個人感歎引入，雖然黃不是事件的主角，但黃家及親朋好友的衣食住行，愛恨情仇都變

〔註24〕Benjamin A. Elman, "Late Traditional Chinese Civilization in Motion, 1400～1900", Ofer Gal and Yi Zheng eds. *Motion and Knowledge in the Changing Early Modern World*, Heidelberg; Springer Dordrecht 2014:169～188.

得與進行式的鐵路事變息息相關。作為省城士紳階層的重要成員的黃家人等不僅或多或少地參與了保路運動，他們的日常作息，情緒欲望都與運動的漲落關係密切。歷史真實在初版中主要通過相關眾生的微妙心理活動，個人與社會情勢的相互滲透，和大事件的發生發展在同一時段內分枝展現：其中人的欲望變化，社會情緒的漲落與歷史事件的進展同樣重要並相輔相成。可以說在初版的描述中兩者是並行的，由人物聯繫起來。

四、庸常的史詩：辛亥──省城的士紳革命

因此，以黃瀾生為中心的，包括黃太太，楚用等在內的省城士紳男女，無論是歷史事件的當事人，目擊者，或是家庭情景喜（鬧）劇的主配角，作為小說人物都十分重要。這些士紳人物的重要性不僅在於他們是敘述結構，視角和情節發展的核心，更重要的是他們是李劼人「歷史的真實」的一部分。李的三部曲，尤其是後兩部的主角是士紳，由他們身上展演開來的帝國末日的歷史遞變與士紳階層與帝國政治中心關係的分離密切相關。《大波》由黃瀾生在歌舞升平的省城夜遊以及無謂的對世事無常的感歎開始，很快引入即將暴發的保路運動並溯其源到清末的新政。在李的筆下，成都（周近）的士紳不僅是保路運動的始作俑者和事端急速擴展的蘊釀者，而且他們前所未有的影響力（這是風潮能以起始的重要原因）是新政施行的直接結果。諮議局的建立給了他們與官府分庭抗禮的正式建制和規儸其他地方社會力量的平臺。議紳成為四川保路運動的領頭人因此毫不奇怪。另外，至清末，大量士紳通過仕途外的不同路徑聚集了可觀的財力物力。他們的經濟地位和社會影響雖游離於政治中心外，卻足以威儸地方，左右情勢。新政由上至下引入的議政制，其實施雖然短暫，卻給了地方士紳由社會介入政局的機會。四川保路運動的興起發展就是典型的例證。《大波》初始時的成都省城就是這樣一個末世的，官紳互相抗衡卻也互相依賴，社會其他勢力也在不安悸動的社會。黃瀾生雖然是省城政治生活的旁觀者，卻是社會生活的中心。他財力可觀，他家的宅院常常是顯紳，有時也是顯官聚集的場所。他不僅可以在官場見證政局，他家的飯局茶座常常是事件發生發展的討論分析處，不同身份，見解，立場的人來來往往：通過他不僅可以不露痕跡地連接虛構人物和史載歷史人物，還可以連接省城及周圍鄉鎮社會的各種勢力。以黃瀾生和他的家庭社會關係

來表現士紳階層在保路運動甚或辛亥革命中的核心作用是李劼人歷史真實的必然選擇。

《大波》展現的保路運動以及由它引發的大變動是末世歷史事件，社會情勢影響和推動了政治形勢發展：雖然清廷自十九世紀中葉以降就開始了眾多「自救」改革，包括猶猶豫豫的憲政實驗，卻無法挽回帝國的江河日下。新政等一系列改革措施甚至加速了社會力量（包括經濟力量）與政治中心的分離。「新」的實驗雖不一定成功，卻打破了幾千年來被視為正統的制度和社會基礎的傳統。權力越來越分散的社會成了左右變化過程的主要因素。在這種背景下的變革常常由庸常開始。成都的市民雖然反感卻變得離不開路燈和警察對他們生活的干預。新式學堂的運動會和廣場上的操練成了學生同志會形成的生理和心理溫床。議紳們越練越利的口才，對新詞匯加上舊格局愈來愈熟練的掌控，和對怎樣適時變得聲淚俱下的把握，更是在各類會場鼓動激發群情的直接要素。社會情勢由個人日常生活，行為習慣，心理情感構成，同時又影響改變個人情緒和行為選擇。它的波動引發和制約群體行動，聚集社會力量，左右政治局勢，同時又難以預料和逆轉，常常引起整個社會的大波動。這樣的變動因此又是史詩性的。初版對這種社會情勢引發的大變局的敘述處理是用社會世情小說來注釋歷史演義：透視常常顯得突兀的事件，給呈現正史的文獻加上心理甚至生理的人間情勢注腳。革命和暴動的起因後果雖未因此變得一目了然，但起碼有了聲，有了色，有因緣可尋，也變得更複雜，更難以理清，更有了「歷史的真實」。省城各階層士紳男女的飲食男女，情感糾結因此十分重要。黃的社交圈中的官僚葛寰中的多變的嘴臉和交際手腕，家道殷實的歸國留日學生周宏道對罐頭鰻魚新做法的精到，都是變化的政局和社會情勢的日常體現，也折射出士紳們身處其中的心理波折和自覺不自覺的生活方式的改變。在三部曲中，李花了大量筆墨來描寫省城及周圍鎮鄉的服飾變遷。《大波》更是不厭其煩地描述了亂世冗奮的時尚。黃瀾生堅持從頭到腳的舊派（傳統裝束）卻也欣賞周宏道的新派（日式西服）。革命的過程也是服飾變化的過程。從參加廣場會議以至暴動穿長衫的不便，到從軍要穿短打還是長衣，甚至軍政府宣佈獨立後男性的頭髮該剪不剪，剪多長，都是《大波》記敘的事件發展的組成部分。這種對亂世亂穿衣的興趣或困惑主要是男性的，士紳的，雖然「反正」後的服飾大解放滿街遍巷，遍及社會各階層，巡防軍甚至穿著戲裝遊街走巷。而新近嘗到逛街樂趣的黃太太不僅和她同階層的太太小姐們一樣是這種極亢奮的時尚的實踐者，而且是評論人。黃太太對新近時興，在省城成都由新派日本女人開先的旗袍全無興趣，她笑罵的對象是亂穿漢服的年輕士紳男性。黃太太的時尚不在服飾新派。作為生活優渥的官紳太太她的裝束時髦卻不亂規矩。她與其他出現在男女混雜的社交場所的上層女性大都不是所謂的新女性。在亂世的省城新女性的代表是由更邊緣的，外來的，被明確指認為日本女人的女性擔任的。她的新表現在穿著開始流行的旗袍公開講演女性在早期兒童教育中的重要作用。黃太太的歷史真實在於她的言論，行為以及由其表現的思想情感的驚世駭俗。而且這種驚世駭俗不僅在她的家庭內部親朋好友間變得見怪不怪，而且漸漸被省城的士紳社會所接受。黃瀾生作為他的丈夫只是對她的言論時感尷尬，卻也不無驕傲，甚至公開讚賞。對她的行為，尤其是與表侄的畸戀，也只是不願公開特別是由下人談起而已。由女性不合規矩的情和欲來表現社會，尤其是亂世的情勢在中國近代社會小說傳統中由來有之。甚至可以說是中國小說現代性的重要標誌之一：從馮夢龍的三言到《紅樓夢》，《金瓶梅》，多情或縱慾的女性不僅警世驚世，是時代情感心理變遷的先驅，也是小說敘事的核心。黃太太的身上也有包法利夫人的影子，但她的身心悸動不是時代轉換期新舊道德的齟齬。她的情感爆發和她男女平權的言論一樣都是斬釘截鐵的，一發不可收拾的，卻也被她遊刃有餘地納入日常生活中。這種不管不顧和不守規矩在李的筆下不是社會轉型期人物性別角色和社會身份的轉變。黃太太和三部曲中類似女性人物的驚世駭俗有其地域性〔註25〕，更有其歷史性：對舊規矩的淡漠甚還懷疑否定和對新規矩好奇熱情是末世生活的一部分。更重要的是，不論新派還是舊派，在事件的進程和前所未有的社會變化中都意識到規矩本身不再不可置疑，而有了重新界定的可能。比她們的男性親友更遠於政治中心，卻也是帝國社會精英一部分的士紳女性成為此類社會情感欲望革命的先驅似乎順理成章。不過黃太太和香荃等的革命是她們社會性別角色內的革命—士紳女性由此有了和變化的物質生活同軌的新的感情社會生活的可能。她們的世界並未隨著帝國的結束天翻地覆，而是隨著帝國末期開始的漸變擴展為能展演她們社會性別角色的更寬泛的舞臺。

〔註25〕 李怡：《現代四川文學的巴蜀文化闡釋》，長沙：湖南教育出版社，1995 年，第 79～97 頁。

　　重寫版的變動體現的並非像早期李評所斷定的李劼人改變了的史觀〔註26〕，而是他對歷史小說及其敘述形式不同的理解和把握。在新舊版中李對歷史真實——社會生活和事件發展的瑣碎尋常細節和史詩式不可抑止的演進——的堅持毫無改變。二十世紀五十年代漸成主流的歷史唯物主義進化史觀對他的影響也僅在於他對士紳家庭生活的主傭關係的描寫中加了些許模棱兩可的階級意識。重寫版對《大波》最大的改變在敘述手法。以黃瀾生及其他幾個士紳家庭生活和保路運動發生發展過程的兩個敘述層面依然存在，但不再爲兩條分開的線索。由於這兩個層面的主角都是寓居或來往於成都的從官僚到擁護立憲或傾心革命的士紳男女，他們理所當然地成爲全景描述社會生活和歷史事件的集中點和結構中樞。他們的日常生活和「非常」活動——以不同程度介入保路運動——都成爲全景式描述的空間場景組合，由全知式視角正面講述。因此重寫版敘述的幅度增大，空間結構畫面廣闊，涉及省城及周圍城鄉政治社會生活的各方面，甚至一縣一鄉地講述武裝暴動的過程。這種全景式敘述手法體現了李劼人不斷衍變的對長篇歷史小說的看法，從類型上融社會言情於歷史演義中，使小說的敘述更趨於史詩般的壯闊的展現，並且把黃瀾生之類的人物更多地變爲敘述結構的一環，眼看耳聞口述或評論直接參與的或道聽途說的運動進程和官府應對。但在這樣更全景式的敘述中李並未減少對非事件的社會日常生活甚或個人心理的描述，雖然刪除了部分被攻迂爲自然主義的人物和事件的「欲」或「生理性」的描寫。黃太太的心理悸動少了欲便難以對應廣場會堂眾生人擠人生理的亢奮，割指流血和滂渤眼淚引起的衝動，革命和變化便少了史詩性與庸常性的持衡的張力和互補。但重寫的《大波》——以士紳爲主角的四川保路運動及其引發的大清帝國的崩潰的地方志式的史詩——和初版一樣鉅細皆容，既言情又正面演義事件。無論是初版還是二十年後的改寫，李劼人堅持的歷史真實都是兩個層面的。歷史波瀾壯闊的發展也是省城眾生在新舊間的日常生活和超常的爆發。李的「小說近代史」是史詩，但貫穿其中的是一種審視歷史和敘述真實的「庸常的智慧」。

〔註26〕李士文：《李劼人的生平和創作》，成都：四川科學院出版社，1986年，第237～243頁。

從《里門拾記》到《果園城記》：
師陀小說原鄉志系列

　　二十世紀三十年代是中國現代小說的黃金歲月似乎已成定論（Yiyan Wang 2016：199～200）。這與中華民國的第二個十年以及第一次世界大戰後中國的經濟繁榮，城市建設和文化的現代性進展密切相關（張中良 2013：17）。它的多元和異彩紛呈也與諸多文藝思潮並存、紛爭的現象〔註1〕緊密相聯，不同文學派別之間的對峙與互滲加速並加深了各種文類文體的實驗出新。其中最引人注目的是中長篇小說和系列小說的重新崛起和數量的激增。這不僅顯示了由晚清新小說起始的新文學經由近三十年的發展已經開始形成自身的傳統和逐漸成熟的作家群，長篇和系列小說重新成為主要的小說形式也是對二十年代小說文類以「抒情」和「書信體」短篇為主的反動。其發展更是三十年代的作家及文化人在二十世紀中國及世界歷史大事件：辛亥革命（1911），第二次世界大戰（1937～1945）等及其引發的大動盪的短暫間歇醞釀期，在承襲反思新文學二十年發展的基礎上，對歷史，尤其是當代史及其敘述形式的關注和思考的結果。他們對長篇和系列敘述的可能性的追求來源於他們把握，再現，重塑現代史的願望（魯迅 1991：287）。小說作為一種敘事文體與歷史的關係成為許多作家創作的動因：茅盾的《蝕》、《農村三部曲》，巴金的《激流三部曲》，李劼人的「大波」系列，蕭紅，師陀的中短篇系列等。三四十年

〔註1〕張太原的《〈獨立評論〉與20世紀30年代的政治思潮》以個案的方式展現了這一時期中國思想界的這種矛盾、衝突的複雜局面。見張太原，《〈獨立評論〉與20世紀30年代的政治思潮》，2006。

代中國現代小說的發展方向似乎重新肯定了中國小說生發的原初動力：以一種邊緣化的文體敘述言說歷史（Owen 1986：141～43），也重續了新小說對史的依託和野心（陳平原 2010：195～221）。

這種試圖通過小說把握，重塑中國現代史的企求同時也與三十年代小說發展的另一引人注目的趨向──地域書寫──密切相關〔註2〕。地域於中國現代小說並不陌生，以故鄉為焦點的鄉土小說是五四新文化運動現代意識的載體，也是文化人現代焦慮的體現（丁帆 2007：6）。由鄉土小說發展而來的三十年代的地域敘事，雖也繼續著眼於區域文化，詠敘作者或真實或想像的原鄉，寄寓他們對故土的依戀甚或啟蒙者式的恨其不爭，如沈從文的湘西山水，艾蕪的南疆風情，吳組緗的皖南鄉村和李劼人的四川民風。但這裡的區域描述更明確自覺地表現了作家的歷史時空觀，或者說體現了現代中國小說對歷史敘事的空間性自覺回歸。作者或真或假的鄉愁是其對歷史的感悟和把握的空間展現和切入點。這裡回歸的原鄉不再是或需被懷念或需被改造的過去的象徵，而是現時歷史的在場。王德威在評論幾十年後蘇童的南方小說時把這樣的敘事叫做「虛構的民族志學」〔註3〕。王氏的結論是以建立在以鄉土及地域表述中「想像的鄉愁」為始來「綜論沈從文以降，鄉土文學逐漸顯露的美學自覺」。在王的闡釋中，想像的鄉愁「除了是真情流露外，也代表了文學傳統的溯源尋根，更暗示了文學寫作『望鄉』姿態的搬演……」，所展現的是一種文學的浪漫想像魅力（王德威 2002：18）。通過建述沈從文已降鄉土文學的自覺，王要證明的是個人，個性化的抒情傳統在中國現代文學中的重要性。這種美學的有情是一種對無情的大歷史的文學拯救。地域文學的重要性體現在它以空間──「抒情視景」──拯救時間。「蘇童的故事是可卑可怖的，但他以有情的眼光，娓娓敘述各個人物的生死悲歡，並將其融入香椿樹街四季輪轉的神秘循環中。在小說最動人的時刻，蘇童終能將不堪一顧的生命抽樣，幻化成陰森幽麗的傳奇。。所謂化腐朽為神奇，蘇童這樣的抒情集錦風格，堪稱重對沈從文（《湘行散記》），蕭紅（《呼蘭河傳》），師陀（《果園城記》）這一脈小說傳統，賦予一世紀末的詮釋」（王德威 2002：18）。王在此不僅把

〔註2〕吳國坤把這種趨向叫做原鄉在三十年代的回歸。見：Kenny Kwok-kwan Ng, *The Lost Geopoetic Horizon of Li Jieren: The Crisis of Writing Chengdu in Revolutionary China*, Leiden: Brill 2015：48～51.

〔註3〕王德威，〈南方的墮落與誘惑──小說蘇童論〉，《天使的糧食》，臺北：麥田出版有限公司，2002：18。

蘇童置於現代中國文學史上可圈可點的作家之列，而且作爲一個舉足輕重的
逐漸自覺的二十世紀中國文學傳統的繼承者，從而追塑了這個傳統。王的解
構性閱讀是爲了彰顯現代文學的抒情傳統，以及這個傳統相對於（無情的）
歷史動盪的傳承性和美學（有情的）拯救性。「抒情視景」呈現出歷史／時間
的無情和地域／空間有情的可能性。如果我們不把這種文學相對於歷史的有
情性局限於對中國文學抒情傳統的重新認可，或個體對歷史的反動──美學
拯救，以及背後所隱涵的歷史與個人的二元對立關係，也許我們可以把這種
有情性看作一種現代中國文學對現代中國史及其世界背景的述說企求和把
握。三四十年代系列或長篇小說地域敘事的方興未艾顯示出的正是文學通過
對空間性虛構敘事文體的探尋來對現代史的把握。李劼人（1891～1962）系
列小說《死水微瀾》（1935），《暴風雨前》（1936）和《大波》（1937）的出版
和接受是很好的例證。李的系列長篇一經發表就被同時代的作家郭沫若稱爲
小說近代史，「小說的近代《華陽國志》」〔註4〕。郭看到的正是李的實驗性現
代歷史小說的空間性敘述對近代中國史的企求，即李的地域小說式歷史敘事
重新肯定了中國小說和歷史敘事的本原性糾纏，以及方志對於史的「視景」
式可能性。郭指出在李的系列「視景」敘述中，歷史過程和社會情勢經由「地
方上的風土氣韻」及「各個階層的人物之生活樣式，心理狀態，言語口吻」
透視（《李劼人選集》第一卷：5）。李的現代地域歷史小說重新確立了長篇歷
史小說作爲現代中國文學文體的重要性，同時顯示了方志這一傳統的空間性
歷史敘述爲現代小說對歷史的把握提供的可能性。這不僅因爲像方志的編撰
者一樣，李通過融志傳的視野及敘述模式於小說的描述與結構中強調了小說
作者的歷史見證和記敘人身份，更重要的是在他的小說史中，地方是歷史的
唯一現場。這裡原鄉作爲歷史現場不僅是美學的自覺和抒情的立場，作爲一
個地域指稱它是國族與個人二元對立之外的不可或缺的歷史空間，更重要的
是它強調了地方作爲一個特指但同時不斷衍變的群體的生存環境的歷史存
在。李劼人的「大波」系列所例證的三四十年代中國小說對歷史地域的長篇
或系列性敘述的追求，不是通過地方拯救歷史，空間解構時間，而是在對現
代史的思考中重現地方是歷史現場。由視景托起的，不僅僅是文學的抒情對
歷史動盪想像性拯救的可能性，正史書寫外的「虛構的民族志學」才是這類

────────────

〔註4〕郭沫若，《中國佐拉之待望》，《中國文藝》1937年第一卷第二期。見《李劼人
選集》第一卷，四川人民出版社1980年版，第5頁。

敘述文體興起的主旨。更確切地說，這樣以地域爲核心的小說史敘事建述的不是「國族」「個人」架構內的本.安德森式的想像社群的民族志，而是文學的原鄉志。原鄉這裡是作者或眞實或自覺以文學想像的方式認同的有特定地域指向的故土，相對於想像的國族，它具有地域和群體意義上的歷史先在性，指認的是由地域指稱的享有共同歷史的某個生命群落作爲政治，經濟，文化共同體的生存環境。在三四十年代的自覺的小說地域敘事中，地方既是有機原生的又是歷史的，對它的虛構——文學想像——是對它的過往歷史（包括文學史）的追贖重塑又是對它當代史的介入。原鄉小說志以故鄉社群個人和群體的生命體驗來描述它作爲歷史現場的世界變遷。

　　師陀（1910～1988）是這樣的小說原鄉志傳統的起始者之一〔註5〕。他的系列小說集《里門拾記》（1937）和《果園城記》（1946）「有情」地描述了故鄉——一個既是虛擬又是實指的空間——中原鄉村和小城的現代變遷。用師陀自己的話說，這樣的分篇結集描述是「浮世繪」式的：《里門拾記》的創作衝動始於一九三五年。這年師陀回故鄉杞縣化寨住了半年，近距離地觀察到街坊鄉鄰們的現世生存，「因此發下了願心，打點把所見所聞，仇敵與朋友，老爺與無賴，總之，各行各流的鄉鄰們聚集攏來，然後選出氣味相投，生活樣式相近，假如有面目不大齊全者，便用取甲之長，補乙之短的辦法，配合起來，畫幾幅素描，亦即所謂『浮世繪』的吧。日後積少成多，機會來了，編印成書，雖不怎麼偉大驚人，倒也好算作一幅《百寶圖》」〔註6〕。這種以人生場景再現原鄉生態歷史變遷的文學述求也是同時代李劼人，蕭紅等人的系列地域小說的共同企望。師陀的創作論顯示了這種傾向的歷史美學自覺。師陀用「浮世繪」來譬喻自己的創作意圖，不僅因爲它是一種通過描繪特定地域的特定生存群體生活形態的視覺藝術形式——十七世紀江戶世風民情的寫照，它的選題所表現出的現世關懷，它對地方眾生日常生活場景——遷變的歷史中稍縱及逝的空間片斷——的捕捉定格，以及其場景式系列結構，都可以看作是記錄表現鄉鄰「生活樣式」以及由此構成的故鄉生態總體衍化的最好形式。師陀對系列性地域敘事的追求也可以從《里門拾記》的寫作過程看出。他是年秋返回北京後開始寫作，自第三篇《過客》開始每篇都加上了「里門拾記」的總標題，到一九三六年六月完成十篇，加上此前所寫的兩篇

〔註 5〕王德威，2002：18。
〔註 6〕師陀，《〈里門拾記〉序》，《師陀全集》第 1 卷，第 96 頁。

共計十二篇，一九三七年一月出版爲系列小說集，其積少成多，分篇結集爲鄉里撰志的意圖貫穿始終。《里門拾記》的意義並不在於它開啓了一種集錦式抒情風格的鄉愁小說傳統。鄉里在這裡不僅像李劼人的省城一樣是歷史的現時場景，而且是片斷式描述的人物故事地方風情背後系列敘述的主角。作品自覺的分篇結集式寫作雖也能看出晚清新小說長短篇系列敘事結構形式實驗的影響，卻並非對所謂集錦式敘述的直接承繼。師陀對系列性地方小說志的嘗試，和李劼人，蕭紅等人的地域方志式歷史系列敘事一樣，旨在通過故鄉世界的拓變，其中各色人物的生死掙扎及喜怒哀樂，演示作爲歷史大動盪一部分的原鄉「生活樣式」的變遷。他們對視景式，風俗畫式敘事的追求，體現了作者試圖通過小說篇幅結構的實驗來把握歷史──故鄉世界生態變化──的願望。這種相對於歷史的有情不是個人對無情歷史的美學拯救，而是一種把故鄉及故鄉人重置於歷史視景的努力。這樣的文學述求所涉及的不僅是文學傳統的溯源尋根或重新創造，也彰現了小說作爲一種敘述形式對歷史敘述本身的追索，甚或是本源性挑戰的回歸。也許這也是《里門拾記》和稍後的《果園城記》都有明顯的史傳筆法的原因。百寶圖式的人物風貌系列代表了中國文學對歷史最原初的介入和改寫。

　　雖然不少評論者都意識到「浮世繪」式寫作是師陀系列小說的關鍵，但他們大多把它解釋爲一種現實主義的表現手法。唯有解志熙注意到了這樣的形式探索與作者對現代中國「生活樣式」的關注的聯繫。解提出師陀有意把《里門拾記》寫成一部反田園詩的小說化的村落志，因揭示鄉里村落社會種種生活樣式的病態和整個鄉土中國社會生態的惡化，與當時廢名、沈從文等的田園詩式鄉土敘事大異其趣〔註7〕。不過這種對照是建立在解對沈從文等人的田園詩式鄉土敘事的約定俗成的誤讀上的。與師陀，沈從文同時活躍於三十年代文壇的李健吾（1906～1982）是第一個作這種對比的。他從有師屬關係的兩人作品中看出的是相似的抒情風格和對立的鄉土中國性：「沈從文和蘆焚〔註8〕先生都從事於織繪。他們明瞭文章的效果，他們用心追求表現的美好……」但「沈從文先生做得那樣輕輕鬆鬆……他賣了老大的力氣，修下了一條綠蔭扶疏的大道，走路的人不會想起下面原本是坎坷的崎嶇。我有

〔註7〕解志熙，《現代中國「生活樣式」的浮世繪──師陀小說敘論》，《清華大學學報：哲學社會科學版》2007年第3期：5～19頁。
〔註8〕作者按：師陀筆名。

時奇怪沈從文先生在做什麼……沈從文先生的底子是一個詩人」。而師陀的《里門拾記》則用不無詩意的抒情筆墨讓人感到那個鄉里村落世界的「一切只是一種不諧和的拼湊：自然的美好，人事的醜陋」，以至於「讀完了之後，一個像我這樣的城市人，覺得彷彿上了當，跌進一個大泥坑，沒有法子舉步……這像一場噩夢。但是這不是夢，老天爺！這是活脫脫的現實，那樣眞實」〔註9〕。李氏的對照一面是對所謂直面現實的寫作態度的讚賞，一面是對沈從文的歷史詩情的誤斷〔註10〕。師陀和沈從文的抒情鄉土志對歷史的有情實屬異徑同歸。沈的「出世」的田園詩與師陀「入世」的「浮世繪」一樣都是對歷史——現世的變化衍生——的文學審視。

　　《里門拾記》是師陀小說風物志的第一部。作爲其人物風俗視景的村落世界確實不似沈從文虛構追溯的湘西桃花源，而展現了一種「不諧和的拼湊。」但這裡的不諧和並非簡單的「自然的美好，人事的醜陋。」師陀的現世不是現實主義視野中的社會現實，而是一個更爲廣闊的包括他摯愛的「大野」（《里門拾記——序》，《師陀全集》第一卷：95）上下土地山川的生存世界。《毒咒》，合集的第一篇，也是師陀回鄉後決定爲靜心而寫作的第一篇小說，確有志傳的成份：「以一雙族祖夫婦作標本，又參考幾位絕嗣（si）的鄉鄰的事蹟，」但它「又似乎是一篇廢稿的改裝」（同上，96），最初定名爲《墟》。師陀寫原鄉志的初衷的象徵主義趨向十分明顯。不論是最初的《墟》和後來的《毒咒》都是他對原鄉世界現代衍變情感判斷的形象暗示，他的神秘的充滿誇張的生和死的村落似乎是艾略特「客觀對應物」理論的印證：「頹坍了的圍牆，由浮著綠沫的池邊鉤轉來，崎嶇的沿著泥路，畫出一條疆界。殘碎磚瓦突出的地上，木屑發黑，散出腐爛氣息。一到春天，小草便從冬季中蘇醒。隨後夏來了，莒麻，莠草和蒿歡聲號喧，還有艾，森林般生長著了……太陽像燃燒著的箭豬，顫抖著將煙火的光撲過來……晚霞靜悄悄的停在天空。霞的光最先落在這裡，照著瓦礫的碎片反光，將這廢墟煊耀得如同瑰麗的廣原一般。浮綠沫的池塘驟然臃腫了，反射出凝結了脂肪似的光彩」（《毒咒》，《師陀全集》第一卷：98）。這裡作者表現情緒的唯一途徑是借助聯想尋找客觀對應物。不

〔註9〕劉西渭（李健吾）：《讀〈里門拾記〉》，《文學雜誌》第1卷第2期，1937年6月1日出版，第2頁。引自郭榮榮，《師陀小說研究述評》，http：//qk.laicar.com/Home/Content/2334020

〔註10〕見本文1～2頁。

光有聞一多《死水》似的浮著綠沫泛著脂光的池塘，頹坍的牆那邊，發著腐爛氣息的土地上一到春夏艾草會像森林般地瘋長。最讓人吃驚的是「太陽像燃燒著的箭豬，顫抖著將煙火的光撲過來」。不同尋常的聯想不僅讓讀者看到萬物生死運作的突兀強暴，也具有波德萊爾式「感應」和「通感」的效應：人與自然、精神與物質、形式與內容之間都存在著感應的關係。且在象徵的世界裏，各種感官的作用彼此互通，無論哪一種感官受到刺激都會產生兩種和兩種以上的感覺經驗，用一種感覺對另一種感覺進行描寫，如色彩對聲音，氣味對色彩等是對這種經驗的最好描述。讀者看著太陽形狀詭異的烈焰，彷彿也聞到燒焦的箭豬毛的惡臭，預感到大野村落生命故事的不祥。艾略特《荒原》的全文翻譯完成出版於 1937 年〔註11〕，與《里門拾記》幾乎同時。此前也有不少的評論介紹〔註12〕。正致力於探索自己寫作風格的師陀對其意象手法內涵的熟悉並不奇怪。師陀自己的敘述實驗的詩意性是論者公認的。這種詩意不僅是秋原的青蒼高朗、點綴著白雲的天空，和正午陽光照耀下的溫暖的原野對荒誕人事的偶而點綴，也是一種陌生化聯想式暗喻性敘述意願的自覺。這裡作者竭力塑造的，用以捕捉感覺經驗的可以在不同感官和不同物種間互通的意象，是這種詩意的載體，而非抒情的田園畫。

師陀對現代主義手法的實驗性運用，與他對史傳筆法的興趣一樣，旨在為故鄉的土地鄉鄰作傳，探索原鄉生命世界的現代生存。不論是定名為《墟》或是《毒咒》，師陀鄉土志的開篇是講鄉鄰絕嗣的。把大野上生命無謂循環的瘋狂與村中人類歷史性承傳的絕望相對照，想表現的是一種歷史的宿命。「這塊地上有毒：斷子絕孫，滅門絕戶。有毒！」（《毒咒》，《師陀全集》第一卷：98）。這是故事的主角之一畢四奶奶對自己和村人生息的土地的判斷和詛咒。畢四奶奶更像張愛玲或幾十年後蘇童筆下的人物，誇張的中國文明發展的歷史犧牲品演化成的迫害狂：中國女性的歷史宿命。畢四奶奶的丈夫畢四爺和他的祖輩一樣，是這片土地上的望族，錢，權，勢皆備。無論是在原鄉的土地上還是在現代的官衙中他和他的兄弟們都如魚得水。但他卻無嗣。他想通過娶妾生產男性繼承人的企圖不斷被因為絕望而逐漸瘋狂的畢四奶奶以及他

〔註11〕 趙蘿蕤譯，上海新詩社出版，1937。
〔註12〕 最早的是葉公超：1932 年，葉公超在《施望尼評論四十週年》一文中第一次提到艾略特，《愛略特的詩》，《清華學報》第 9 卷第 2 期，1934 年 4 月。http：//202.112.126.101/jpkc/zgxddwxs/content/ktjy/pe2zjy/0205.htm#_ftn15

們的四個女兒們超乎尋常的激烈反對挫敗。他最終娶到的甚至也懷了孕的「小」也被他越來越狂暴的妻女虐打身亡。與張愛玲和蘇童的類似故事中的男性人物不同的是，畢四爺似乎是一個令人同情的角色。起碼在敘述者「我」的眼中。作為既是成人回憶者又是童年事件經歷觀察者的「我」對畢四爺的同情不是社會性的也不是性別的，雖然有一些後者的成份。童年的「我」明顯地是村中孩子群中的一員（他們總是在村裏或原野上觀望著偶而也參與著原鄉世界的生命故事和愛恨情仇），是正在成長的男性少年，對村裏的「小」們懷著弱者的同情和模糊的欲的嚮往。他對畢四爺的感情是複雜的。既有對他作為權勢者（包括男權權勢）的判斷，也有對他無嗣的同情。這種同情是對原鄉生命延續的焦慮，不是男性性別間跨社會階層的對家族承傳的焦慮，而是一種生命物種間的通感，一種對生命被毒害，被詛咒的命命相通的恐懼。有意思的是這種恐懼最後還是被寓意成了女性的歷史宿命：她們是生命承傳的欲的始作俑者，犧牲者和破壞者。歷史對原鄉的詛咒也就自然而然地由牟四奶奶口中發出。而生死恣意的大野是現代原鄉人生命承傳無望的共盟。那裡生命的狂烈瘋長更像是土地被毒殺的另一例證。物種的互通添加了敘述者和讀者對原鄉歷史毒咒的恐怖絕望。不少論者都注意到了師陀小說中的戲劇性和散文化同在。《里門拾記》裏這種陌生化聯想式的詩意同時存在於故事人物的鬧劇和大野的田園散文中，又讓他們之間充滿了張力。《毒咒》彌漫著擾攘不寧和神秘、紛亂而瘋狂的戲劇氛圍，突發性的事件和緊張的故事情節突兀地出現在暗喻性敘述中，詩意和情節分享小說的中心。

　　師陀為故鄉大野和大野上的人事撰寫的志傳，雖然以陌生的意象和鬧劇般情節的發展肆虐式地向讀者展示那裡生命過程及結局的殘酷無常，「但也掩不了它字裏面的和善。」這種和善首先再現於他對大野的描寫。除了《毒咒》裏狂躁的萬物外，他的浮世繪中也有靜謐的風物丹青：「河水在蔥綠的岸間懶洋洋流去。魚時常躍出平靜的水面，拋一閃銀光，渦一個圓渾，但水仍旖旋前進，彎過為樹林遮隱，沉溺於古代迷夢的村莊經過如煙的柳蔭，分開浩茫的田野，發出閃閃的一派白光。啄木鳥在林中不倦的敲擊。河上升起溫膩的蒸汽。氣朗雲淡，野曠天晴，風微且醉人」（〈村中喜劇〉《師陀全集》第一卷：139）這裡的動是恆古的，現世和過去一樣都融入它旖旋的過程。生命如常且不倦地變化著。這也許是作者疏離的敘述中暫時的情感回歸。但更是一種作者對自己繼續是故里一員的宣示。和善的視景式視野重新強調了師陀的系列小說是文學的原鄉志，大野，大野上的人事，它們的志傳的撰寫人，都是原鄉世界變化的生命形式的一部分。物種間的通感讓志傳作者能完全感受並領會到大野和大野上的人事的存在衍變。他像外來者樣審視描繪他們的生存世界和生命方式，但又像他們中的一員一樣懂得他們的狂暴和靜息，他們的經驗也是他可能的經驗。對他們歷史性的審視也是對自己以及共有歷史的審視。在生生不息同時又暴虐寥落的大野上，人們目的不明卻也饒有興味地演繹著日常生命。《秋原》上爭戰剛結束，「壕溝還不曾填平」，但「原野確是豐饒」，「血泊上已蓬蓬地生起五穀」。男性鄉民們對陌生闖入者的猜忌，加上雄性欲望的膨脹，使他們捉住偶然在豆叢中歇腳的漢子，將他弔在墳園，盡興賞玩，感到無趣後，一哄而散，只留下夕陽中的異鄉漢子默默地注視著自己的腳尖（《師陀全集》第一卷：114～119）。《倦談集》中的人們已習慣每天兩到五個地槍決犯人，人們對此麻木的同時並開始報以欣賞性的眼光。有古董收藏癖的「老者」和生活百無聊賴的兩個學徒爲破碎的腦袋訂立著名目，觀看著泥坑中的頭顱「捉迷藏」的「遊戲」。牧師華盛頓更是早已習慣並愛上了這裡「中國式」的生存方式（《師陀全集》第一卷：161～173）。《倦談集》，《秋原》，《霧的晨》，《村中喜劇》等篇目的故事背後展現的似乎是大野上人們麻木、殘酷的看客心理。但這樣的看客心理似乎也不同於魯迅《藥》裏傳統村民對現代革命者犧牲的觀望不解。《過客》裏的人們莫名奇妙地向著人群湧去的方向一路跑去，在河裏發現了屍體時隨意猜測，滿足著自我，也欣賞著別人。當他們發現撈上來的屍體不是他們所希望的女屍時，雖有些失望，但仍然觀看著並議論著，種種有趣故事雖未落實卻因講得頭頭是道而留在聽者（和讀者）的記憶裏。那睜著烏藍色眼睛的屍體也在看大家。自始至終看客心理存在於在場的每一個人，但導致被看者不幸的眞正原因卻被忘卻了，看的行爲轉化成了人們日常生活中的調劑。作者對大野人事生存方式的審視在此不是悲憫的。悲憫是一種高高在上的局外人的情感。這裡審視者也是觀望人群的一員，審視也是觀望。作者讀者都無一例外。《里門拾記》作爲師陀文學原鄉志的第一部審視並反思的也是文學歷史審視作爲一種審美行爲的本身，也可以說是對中國現代文學望鄉傳統的諷喻。

　　師陀高度自覺的原鄉志裏的原鄉確實不是「鄉土文學」中那或需哀惋或需改造的現代歷史的過去。過去和現在在這裡存在於同一生命世界的變化過

程中。這裡的原鄉既是歷史的——有年月有日期有戰亂的二十世紀現世生活
——又是比現世長久的原初的生命恣意。誰說更久遠的生存世界不會與現代
歷史的演變同存且共時變化著，就像河水總會「在蔥綠的岸間」村旁或湍急
或懶洋洋地流淌。游移於諷喻的浮世繪人生和「和善」的丹青風景也許是希
望現世也能靜靜地旖旎前行，但更是作者對原鄉是歷史現場的強調。故里和
它周圍的世界是亂世——躲不開的，歷史的。《受難者》裏伊的苦難從頭至尾
和現時的戰爭和官府的徵兵直接相關，就連她因爲丈夫的嗜賭敗家除了忍受
無法改變愛子和自己的悲劇命運也是常見的中國女性的歷史宿命。但《里門
拾記》和後來的《果園城記》一樣是文學的原鄉志，作者對故里生命形式及
其歷史衍變的審視是有情的。除意象語言敘述的陌生化，故事的鬧劇化和人
事物間通感的營造，這種有情也呈現在作者不時筆觸的和善裏，尤其是在他
對故鄉各色人等的娓娓述說中。他懂得他們，不論篇幅的長短都讓他們的心
理情感與他們的現世存在一起再現於他們的形象故事裏。在他的筆下，酒徒、
女巫、寡婦等都有著頑強的生命力，哪怕屬於他們的故事是他們現世生活樣
式和生命本身的毀滅。他還塑造了一個迥異於眾人的抓。「這裡有一個例外，
即《巨人》裏的抓。是至今還活著的人，且不曾在他的『生傳』中雜入他人
的事蹟」（《里門拾記序》，《師陀全集》第一卷，2008：97）。巨人抓的「生傳」，
就像他生存的世界，作者的鄉里一樣，是現世的，現在進行時的。儘管作者
說他不喜歡他的家鄉但懷念著那廣大的原野，而抓是在那廣大原野上出生長
大的，他的生命故事仍然是在這個「雞，貓，狗爭吵的世界」（130）發生發
展的。與他人不一樣的是他挑戰式地活在那裡，獨自住在荒宅裏，但「他愛
著狗和貓」（130）。抓確實是不甚可愛的原鄉世界的邊緣人。如果說他有著大
野的魂靈，它的痕跡也是散佈在他在家鄉的現世生活中的。抓的邊緣性不是
原生的，而是一種自覺。原鄉的習俗給與他的是心靈的傷害：與他青梅竹馬
的戀人因爲習俗嫁給了他的兄長。抓傷心卻無抱怨，只是默默離開了家鄉和
大野。離鄉其實是本篇的主題之一，是抓挑戰式原鄉生存的前提。敘述者年
少時曾以爲抓的不一樣是緣於他是外鄉人。「最初他一口『下邊』口音把我帶
進了幻想的世界……，總以爲他是漂洋過海的異鄉客人，一定見過不少世
面，……」（128）這裡原鄉外鄉的對應是理解師陀「鄉土」描寫歷史觀的關
鍵。少年敘述者的幻想世界和抓眞正去過生活過的「下邊」與本土的區別在
作者的描繪中（本鄉少年的幻想和抓的親身體驗中）不是時間性的。離開本

土到異鄉可以見世面，漂洋過海開闊的是生命體驗的不同的空間可能性（見世面的內涵）而不是時間或歷史的後置。在抓的生存過程和師陀的志傳裏，原鄉不是外面世界的過去，「下邊」也不是它的可能或不可能的現在和將來。它們互為背景，同時存在於共有的歷史中。抓本是「本鄉兒男」（128），在經歷了本土不經意的殘忍後，見了世面：有了異鄉的背景和口音，方可以重新找到一種在原鄉的生活樣式。抓的邊緣性是一種選擇後的忠誠。我們不知道他在「下邊」經歷感悟，卻知道他的回歸不是為了對故土進行啟蒙性的現代改造，也不是哀歎它田園本色的無奈逝去。他只是面對原鄉雞狗貓吵的現世不一樣地生活著。他的生活樣式的不一樣也不是對原鄉以過去文明或現代文明進行道德判斷——他既賭錢也喝酒，只是勞作著且不加區分地愛著那裏所有的（小）生命。抓是另一種原鄉人。他的「生傳」告訴讀者在故鄉不同的生存方式的可能性是與現世大世界緊密相連的。原野的生和愛只有在和它世界互為背景的條件下方能不一樣地歷史地存在於鄉土上，而這個鄉土是變化的現世的核心構成。

《里門拾記》起始的師陀「系列小說」敘述形式不僅標誌著作者寫作的真正起步：他終於找到屬於自己的題材、思路和相應的敘述形式、結構方法，也標誌著由「新小說」實驗開始的中國現代系列小說作為一種現代小說敘述結構形式成熟的開始。在完成《里門拾記》一個月後——一九三六年七月底，師陀從北京赴上海的途中，繞道到河南偃城縣城住了半月。那裏的所見所感讓他有了續寫原鄉系列的衝動，但這一次他並沒有立即動筆，而是經過了整整兩年的醞釀。從一九三八年九月開始到一九四六年初，蟄居上海的師陀用了差不多八年時間創作了又一部十八篇的系列小說《果園城記》，分篇陸續在《萬象》等刊物發表，一九四六年五月全書由上海出版公司出版。全書一經刊出，《文藝復興》雜誌的編者便贊其「優美深刻，得未曾有；純靜、凝練、透明，反覆閃光的水晶」（劉增傑，1984：23）。顯然，《果園城記》是《里門拾記》思路與寫作方式發展的結果。師陀在日據的上海凝心八年繼續的是他的系列文學原鄉志。這一次的描寫對象的不是他真實的故里，而是一個他偶而客居，更是在鄉土文學中常見的小城。師陀的不同是把這個他想像的有象徵寓意也有歷史地域特指的小城明確地指認為他的小說志傳的主角：

> 這小書的主人公是一個我想像中的小城……我有意把這小城寫
> 成中國一切小城的代表，它在我心中有生命、有性格、有思想、有

> 見解、有情感、有壽命，像一個活的人。我從它的壽命中切取我頂
> 熟悉的一段：從前清末年到民國二十五年，凡我能瞭解的合乎它的
> 材料，我全放進去。這些材料不見得同是小城的出產：它們有鄉下
> 來的，也有都市來的，要之在乎它們是否跟一個小城的性格適合。
> 我自知太不量力，但我說過，我只寫我瞭解的一部分。現在我還沒
> 有將能寫的寫完，我但願能寫完，即使終我一生。

選擇小城作為續寫現代文學原鄉志的主角不僅因為它是特指的有歷史，社
會，文化地理意義的地域，而且因為它是形形色色城鄉皆有的「生活樣式」
的凝聚點。更重要的是這裡師陀「有意」要寫的是它的生傳，與巨人抓的一
樣，「有生命、有性格、有思想、有見解、有情感、有壽命」。而這樣的生傳
的重點──作者所熟悉的與之有共同生命體驗的──是它的現代史：從前清
末年到民國二十五年。並且像李劼人一樣，師陀強調歷史為生存經驗的一部
分，因此「我只寫我瞭解的」。這樣自覺為之、全力以赴創作的《果園城記》
系列的原鄉志不是對風俗加風格的地方特色的追求，而是對作為生活樣式以
至於社會生態總體的現代中國原鄉世界衍變的寫照。

　　因此《果園城記》和《里門拾記》一樣，可以說是體現了師陀文化人類
學式的原鄉關照，又繼續了他用浮世繪式「志傳」手法於現代系列小說敘述
的實驗。師陀對現代原鄉世界變遷這種社群史式的關照，可能與當時的中國
人文及社會科學思潮，尤其是起始於二十年代在三十年代方興未艾的中西文
化論戰有關（解志熙 2007）。如他所傾心描繪的原鄉社會「生活樣式」的演化，
其中對鄉土中國社會的思考很難說與梁漱溟的「生活的根本在意欲而文化不
過是生活之樣法」〔註 13〕及其發表於一九三六年的《鄉村建設理論》無觀念
上的策應。但師陀的文學原鄉志並非是建立在現代與傳統，先進與落後相對
應觀念上的對所謂鄉土中國的封閉自足、傳承有序而又循環往復、日漸惡化
的社會生態困局的揭示。他的原鄉世界是現世的，與他鄉，「下邊」及其他的
外部世界相連：《里門拾記》裏充滿了他鄉客，「本鄉男兒」也毫不猶豫地離
鄉還鄉，而《果園城記》裏的果園城的重要地標是書中人物頻繁來往的火車
站。這個世界傳承艱難──人們或許絕嗣或許愁嫁或許為愛獨身或許因為戰
爭白髮哭葬黑髮。師陀描繪的的確是原鄉世界生活樣式和生命形態的現代困
局。但他對這個世界現代變遷的關照不是以三十年代中國社會性質論戰的概

────────────────

〔註13〕梁漱溟，《東西文化及其哲學》，1987 年，第 54 頁。

念爲參照的，與稍後費孝通對「鄉土中國」的社會人類學研究以及梁漱溟在《鄉村建設理論》中以鄉村爲中國傳統文化最後的殘留地建立的鄉村分析建設理論也並不相似。他雖在《果園城記》的開篇中說他的果園城是「是一個假想的西亞細亞式的名字」（《果園城記》，《師陀全集》第二卷：454），他爲它寫的志傳卻並無對這些論戰中常見的生產力、生產關係、階級關係的考慮。他描述的現代原鄉生活樣式包括了它們的久遠，又呈現了這種久遠的現世艱難。它們變化遲緩卻難以循環往復。這種生存困局在《里門拾記》裏被描繪爲艾略特式的現代荒原，但師陀有情的文學歷史關懷所營造的並非完全的絕望。他對描寫對象諷喻後的和善，一種同一歷史進程內物種間的感同身受，讓他在荒原上通過抓及其他類似人物的不一樣的生傳讓讀者也看到了原鄉另類生活樣式的可能性。抓和他既新又舊的邊緣性的生存方式與張愛玲傾城後廢墟上的蹦蹦戲女人一樣表現的是文學對歷史的現代性批判，也是作者對自己和同一生存群體及地域的生命和生活樣式繼續生存可能性的審美想像。

　　《果園城記》的原鄉想像循此而進。不過師陀這裡對原鄉作爲特定的歷史空間的詩意審視有了明顯的風格上的轉變。《果園城記》的敘述追求確實可以被形容爲蘇童式化腐朽爲神奇的地域歷史文學書寫的前身。師陀在此娓娓敘述的各個小城人物的生死悲歡仍然是和善的諷喻，沒有蘇童故事中那種刻意的歷史與人事交匯的可卑可怖。但敘述風格的轉換──從《里門拾記》的陌生化現代主義象徵性語言及敘事實驗到《城記》語言敘事優美熟習化與人物故事陰森神秘化的對照──的確顯示了作者現代原鄉志之二的化現世人物志爲傳奇的傾向。這裡所謂的化腐朽爲神奇是一種不同的歷史詩意追求。《城記》是作者三十年代末戰爭初期構思，戰時八年穴居於墳墓般的日據上海逐篇寫成的：「接著是所謂『七.七事變』，北方先打起來了……而我自己也叢此流洛洋場。如夢如魘，如釜底遊魂，一住八載……我不知這些日子是怎麼混過去活過來的。民國二十七年九月間，我在一間像棺材的小屋裏寫下本書第一篇《果園城》……第二年──民國二十八年更不得了下去：我搬進另一間更小，更像棺材，我稱之爲『餓夫墓』，也就是現在的『舍下』的小屋。就在這『墓』裏，我重又拾起《果園城記》，六月間寫成《葛天民》……」（《果園城記.序》，《師陀全集》第二卷：452）。這裡原鄉人物的生傳顯得凄美陰森，與他鄉──作者客居地──的現世生存狀況息息相關。如果師陀在《果園城記》裏續寫的仍然是原鄉生存的現代困局，這種困局是他在他鄉──與原鄉空間相隔但時間相同更重要的是同屬於一個歷史進程的「洋場」——共享的。原鄉傳奇不僅是作者現世生存感受的投射，也是作者有情歷史詩意的載體。《城記》系列作為原鄉傳奇的歷史性在於它所描繪的生存困境不僅與他鄉同時而且是後者預兆性的前身。師陀對果園城生傳傳奇性的構造首先在於他在塑造一種城裏生活樣式沉滯感的同時強調它們的現世性，在一特指時間內的不同人物的浮世繪使小城傳奇成為顯示正在進行的中國現代史的橫斷面。正是這種傳奇性使淒美的果城故事有了歷史示範性。表現小城現代生活的沉滯——變化艱難——讓讀者看到原鄉不僅不在巨變的歷史外，而且是巨變困局的先兆象徵。小城人物現世生存的隔世穴居感與作者（讀者）他鄉現世的穴居互相呼應。

　　果園城的傳奇有隨著年輪往復的美麗的自然：「假使你恰恰在秋天來到這座城裏，你很遠很遠就聞到那種香氣，葡萄酒的香氣。累累的果實映了肥厚的綠油油的葉子，耀眼的像無數小小的粉臉，向陽的一部分看起來比搽了胭脂還要嬌豔。」「果園正像雲和湖一樣展開，裝飾了這座古老的小城。」（《果園城》，《師陀全集》第二卷：458，459）。果園城甚至還有自己的神話傳說，它的千年高塔就是從一個過路神仙的袍袖中遺落下來的（457）。它也有久遠的歷史：帝制時代果園城也曾人才輩出，進士第或布政第的胡馬左劉四大家族主導了城鄉庶民的生活，甚至連「門房」也是「世襲罔替」（《城主》，《師陀全集》第二卷：473）。然而除了作為背景引入現世的故事外，作者對果園城的過去並無書寫的興趣。他要寫的是「從前清末年到民國二十五年」間果園城的「生活樣式」和承載這些生活樣式的人事自然的衍變。自然的現代傳奇依然是一樣的優美，雖然作者的描繪用了他鄉的物事作比，抒情的筆觸更似油畫而不是丹青。與之對照的果園城裏各色人物的傳奇卻有墓誌銘般的陰淒。這些傳奇的主角大多為現代人物，嫁不出去的老小姐素姑除外。但素姑的故事除了給不太可靠的敘述者馬叔敖提供在景色美麗的果園城尋找舊夢感歎時光流逝的契機外，與張愛玲的同類故事相比，並不能印照中國女性的歷史宿命。用了素姑繡品的其他年輕女性畢竟都嫁出去了。素姑的愁嫁和傷春很難說有現代和傳統糾結的意味。葛天民是新式農校培養出的現代式實驗農場的場長，自殺的油三妹是新式女教師，甚至城主朱魁爺也是在小城現代社會結構中如魚得水的地頭蛇。而這些果園城現代傳奇的大部分是由又是作品人物又是敘述者的馬叔敖用第一人稱以散文式的形式記述的。

　　如果說《里門拾記》有戲劇化的傾向，突發性的事件和突兀的情節發展與象徵性的情景描寫共同佔據小說的中心，《果園城記》則可以被形容爲一種散文化情節淡化的小說實驗。作者拾取的是普通的日常人生場景和平凡瑣碎的生活細節，以生活的常態取代了《拾記》對變態的依賴。這也許是作者墳墓式的他鄉現世生存使他對原鄉的審視有了變化，使他對人生的常態有了劫時的留戀嚮往？但《城記》裏原鄉的生命常態與作者的他鄉存在一樣是陰淒無望的。原鄉有著與他鄉一樣的日常生存困局。劫時的師陀似乎更無須爲作新詞強作愁。他在此的化腐朽（小城的穴居式的人生常態）爲神奇（淒美的系列文學故事）再次展示了原鄉的現代歷史宿命和一種自覺的對中國現代史的美學審視──一種和善的對原鄉加上作爲它現世生存背景的整個現代生命世界的無望的焦慮，以及對原鄉敘事本身的進一步探視。

　　這種探視在很大程度上是通過對敘述者馬叔敖的設立和審視進行的。與《里門拾記》中的或以「我」出現或作爲不在場的觀察敘述者不同，馬叔敖並不是果園城的「鄉里男兒」，雖然他曾在此度過童年。在《果園城記》的大部分故事里師陀通過他以第一人稱敘事，讓原鄉的人事透過「我」重回果園城後的所見、所聞、所憶、所感和所思表述出來，一方面有散文般的自由、隨意和從容，一方面讓常態的生老病死和從革命者到地頭蛇的悲歡情仇都顯得如夢如魘。「我」在果園城的志傳裏像「織梭」，勾連小城的過去和現在的生活片斷，由零散到集中地顯現出生活在小城裏的人物的面影或側影，以散文化的敘述，由「我」的感情情緒的「經線」，把人物的背景、遭際、經歷、變故和命運的「緯線」編織起來，以「我」的感情情緒的潛在的起伏變化所左右。在首篇《果園城》裏，「我」──馬叔敖──帶著童年的留戀之情來到了這個「我」「熟悉」、「熟知」的小城。這個小城就像親昵的老友，等著他，讓他來去自由。然而，當他眞的接近果園城的人和事時，甚至在故舊孟林太太用出人意料的很大的聲音對他說話和作爲「老女」的憔悴的二十九歲的素姑出現前，「一陣哀傷的空虛已經在等待我了」（《果園城》，《師陀全集》第二卷：461）。果園城人相遇時的招呼和道別聲也使他悵然，覺得自己是一個蕩子，本該「沒有人知道的來了一次，又在沒有人知道中走掉，身上帶者果園城的泥土」（460）。「我懊悔沒有這樣辦……悄悄離開……」（461）「我」的躊躇，還沒開始就有了的哀傷，使他一個又一個的訪友尋舊，一次又一次的失望乃至絕望，顯得動機不清，目的不明。「我」對小城和人的情感判斷甚至觀

察視角都變的不太可靠。馬叔敖在他出現的故事系列中確實是一個靠不住的
敘述者。最關鍵的是與《里門拾記》的敘述者不同，他與果園城及其人事間
沒有物種間生命的通感。他舊地重遊是衝動於親切美好的少時回憶。重溫美
好不遂是他對小城現世失望的首要原因。他與他所觀照的小城人物間無深層
的溝通。他們的生老病死，悲歡離合是他情緒起落，情感波動的載體。他拒
絕把他們置於他與他們共享的歷史。油三妹的自殺確實讓他為女性的現代命
運不平。但在《期待》中他面對革命者犧牲後父母的掛念不知念念不忘的是
自己不能言語的愧疚。講述著葛天明因職業政治而夭折的新式實驗農場生涯
他心懷難平，但他同時想著的卻是：

> 在牆外面，當我們講著話的時候有一個小販吆喝。還有什麼是
> 比這種喊聲更親切更值得回憶的呢，當我們長久的離開某處地方，
> 我們忽然聽見仍舊沒有改變，以前我們就在這樣靜寂的小巷裏聽慣
> 了的聲調。我們從此感到要改變一個小城市有多麼困難，假使我們
> 看見的不僅僅是表面，我們若不看見出生和死亡，我們會相信，十
> 年，二十年，以至五十年，它似乎永遠停留在一點上沒有變動。
>
> ……
>
> 我們繼讀〔續〕坐在葡萄棚下面。四圍是靜寂的，空中保持著
> 一種和諧，一種鄉村所有的平靜氣息。這城裏的生活是仍舊按著它
> 的古老規律，從容的一天一天進行著，人們還一點都不感到緊張。
> 太陽已經轉到西面去了，我們可以想像到太陽每天在這時候都這樣
> 的轉到西面去了。（《葛天民》，《師陀全集》第二卷：470）

馬叔敖看到的是變化，感歎物是人非，美好難繼；可熟習親切的市聲又讓他
突然以啓蒙者慣用的腔調抱怨改變小城的不易。作者讓讀者注意到是在不太
可靠的敘述者的抒情感謂中小城被說成是被時間遺忘了——那裡日落日出，
生活「從容的一天一天進行著。」而且敘述者一面和頑強的市聲一樣親切不
減的老友分享著原鄉的從容，一面例行職責般地責怪原鄉人生活的不緊張。
他的原鄉視野和情感確實顯得模凌兩可。但作者也讓不可靠的馬叔敖說出「在
這個彷彿被時間忘卻了的小城中也有變動」（《狩獵》，《師陀全集》第二卷：
544）。系列中大部分的故事講述的都是這樣的變化。只是這裡的講述沒有戲
劇性，像短篇史詩，或凄美的墓誌銘，結局已定：中心是悲劇的結尾，美好
和掙扎只存在於倒敘裏，再加上敘述者常常彷彿是循例老調重彈般的散文式

抒情。有些故事確實限於例行的墮落與無奈的沒落，彷彿與時間無關：傳統
世家的墮落遵循的是例行的模式──門第顯赫的胡馬左劉四大家族在紈絝子
弟的揮霍和兄弟鬩牆的內耗中紛紛敗落，但「布政第」胡家的千金小姐淪落
風塵卻和傳統政治社會結構的現代轉變直接相關，傳統業者每況愈下的沒落
也是難免的收場──由於現代物事的衝擊，一向安分守己的小城平民漸漸難
以維持傳統的生計，手藝高超的錫匠淪為乞丐，技驚四座的說書藝人貧病而
死。馬叔敖由此哀怨地感歎：「凡是在回憶中我們以為好的，全是容易過去的，
一逝不再來的」（《說書人》，《師陀全集》第二卷：536）。馬念念不忘的「以
為好的」其實還是久遠的從容的原鄉生存。這是他舊地重遊的動機。但作為
一個已經確立的現代文學傳統所界定的文類敘述者，他似乎對另一種原鄉書
寫的運作也相當稔熟。他的原鄉抒情不斷游移於兩者之間。而在故事中，傳
統的生活方式和生命態度在果園城難以為繼，它們的改變進程艱難同時也難
以逆轉。問題並不在于果園城人對這種轉變是否自覺。順著習慣成自然的傳
統慣性生存固然常以悲劇告終，有意做現代人過現代式生活的果城人同樣命
運多舛。不甘平庸的現代文學青年賀文龍文學夢難成只好繼續做中學教師；
受過新式農業教育的農事改革家葛天民屢經挫折之後變成了一個不問世事的
隱士。但他們的現代生存企圖卻並不是被所謂習慣勢力扼殺的，它們不能善
終是因為現世生存本身的不易。賀文龍是因鬥不過庸常放棄的，而葛天民完
全無意也不會職場政治。他們也並不曾就此回到某種傳統中生活。賀繼續著
他的教師生涯，教的也是現代的科目；葛雖像自足的隱士，卻也繼續著他的
新式農業實驗。重要的是他們繼續從容地在原鄉生存著，像不息的市聲一樣
親切地等著善待著焦躁無根，多愁善感又愧疚的來訪者。其他果城人的現代
生活更具悲劇性：在外感染了新式思想的「傲骨」回到家鄉的改革舉措──
植的樹造的林，被他雇來種樹的窮苦鄉下人在夜裏連根拔掉當柴燒了；兩個
革命者徐立剛和小張被迫逃離果園城，徐的父母在他犧牲後都不知其下落。
最悲哀的是女性的命運彷彿命定，無論她們是現代的還是傳統的：率性可愛
的女教師油三妹因為欲望萌動行為舉止大膽而被迫自殺了；美麗的大劉姐只
因為被一個莽撞小子強吻了一下而被迫遠嫁為他人妾。果城生活樣式變化的
艱難的和難以逆轉（其他和馬一樣回鄉尋舊的人──包括大劉姐──都失望
而去）使敘述者馬叔敖無法達到他重遊的目的：果園城的變和不變都讓他難
尋舊夢。他浪漫地在小城漫遊享受著人事故舊的親切卻義正詞嚴地感歎抱怨

著小城的不變，尤其是小城人在他看來習慣成自然的生活態度。作爲敘述者的他的情感判斷以及觀察視野游移變換，顯得十分不可靠。這種不可靠一方面顯示了原鄉現代生命存在和生活樣式的複雜性，一方面是對原鄉書寫傳統本身，尤其是其慣用的觀察視野和情感結構的反思。師陀對馬叔敖式敘述者的設立，以及他的不可靠的散文式抒情作爲果園城人事浮世繪的結構性串聯的運用，是一種作者對文學原鄉志書寫的自覺以及其現存傳統的諷喻。《果園城記》代表的文學原鄉志既無創造「烏托邦」世界的審美衝動，也無啓蒙者式的批判意識。有的是對兩者的諷喻和對無邊無際的廢墟般的故鄉場景和生命在無望的現世歷史中存在的展示。它滲透著作者對原鄉個體及群體生命的現代歷史存在可能性的關注。

馬叔敖作爲敘述者的不可靠性反而加強了《果園城記》系列的情感，視野和作者歷史美學判斷的複雜性。這種複雜性貫穿了整部作品，浸潤著作品的敘述節奏，影響著作品的意義生成。《城記》的大部分篇章是由馬叔敖對果園城既富於感情也暗含著評判的觀感串聯成整體的。馬的抒情和敘述同步的漫遊同時還具有結構的功能和導讀的作用——讀者正是透過他的善感的心與眼，逐步進入「果園城」世界，一點一滴地積累著印象、深化著認識，最終形成一個複雜的「果園城」整體印象。但馬作爲作品的人物之一，他的有局限性的觀照，敘事，抒情同時又是讀者觀照審視的對象。讀者一方面接收著他呈現的果園城的生態人事，一方面又隨著他的講述感歎感受到他的視野和情感判斷的游移不可靠性，進而重審他的敘述和抒情。這種敘述和抒情的複雜性是師陀續寫的文學原鄉志系列敘述的關鍵。而小城作爲「這本書中的眞正主人公」是由這種自覺的系列小說的敘事體式完成的。系列小說有意識地把多個短篇結構成一個富有內在聯繫的系統整體，其內部的每個敘述單元雖然採取短篇的形式，但從整體來看系列並不是短篇的簡單集合，而是一個互文共在的有機整體。這使它具有不亞於甚至大於長篇小說的容量，但在結構和敘述上更爲自由靈活，具有不拘一格、寓合於分、互文互補的特長和整體大於部分之合的優勢。如果說魯迅的「魯鎮系列」、沈從文的「湘西系列」都是後來批評家、研究者的歸納概括而非作家當初的自覺創作，師陀的原鄉系列，無論是《里門拾記》還是《果園城記》都是有意爲之的。師陀對現代中國小說原鄉敘事傳統的探索貫穿著他對這個既久遠又是歷史的空間世界種種生存方式的獨到觀察與審視。在他的構造的抒情視景中，形形色色的原鄉人物不是國民性的載體、階級性的典型或人性美的化身，而是其現世衍化的「生活樣式」的代表。各式各樣的「生活樣式」在共同的空間背景上構成了一個既有區分又相互依存且可以相互轉化的小社會結構，一種具有共同文化習俗、行爲習慣以至於情感意識的人類小群體。而師陀對這一切的觀照顯示出一種分析性的綜合意識——他有意識地刻畫出了一幅幅人物素描（志傳）並有機地將其結構爲一整套「生活樣式」的浮世繪。讀者透過他的觀照所看到的是一幅長卷的現代中國原鄉世界的生態畫卷。而且這個畫卷是以整個現代世界爲背景和參照的。原鄉生態的轉變是現代歷史的中心場景。這樣一種從「生活樣式」著眼來對現代原鄉「社會生態」進行整體觀照的敘事路徑，的確迥異於既有的鄉土敘事範式，使人們得以在既有的而且幾成定式的敘事範式——文化批判、階級分析以及田園牧歌抒情——之外，能夠既審視又同情地理解中國原鄉的種種生活樣式及其社會生態；體會到那一切也是淵源有自的人類活動、自成一體且生生不息的人類社會，同時關注它現代生存的可能性，和作者一起通過文學的形式（敘事抒情）及其意義空間（生命經驗開掘、形象世界呈現）理解，闡釋並想像原鄉和原鄉人（將）怎樣在變化無常的現代歷史中衍生。

參考書目

1. 陳平原，《中國小說敘事模式的轉變》，北京：北京大學出版社，2010。丁帆，《中國鄉土小說史》，北京：北京大學出版社，2007。

2. 郭沫若，《中國佐拉之待望》，《中國文藝》1937 年第一卷第二期。引自《李劼人選集》第一卷，四川人民出版社 1980 年版，第 5 頁。

3. 梁漱溟，《東西文化及其哲學》，北京：商務印書館，1987。

4. 劉增傑，《師陀生平年表》，劉增傑編：《師陀研究資料》，北京：北京出版社，1984。

5. 劉西渭（李健吾），《讀〈里門拾記〉》，《文學雜誌》第 1 卷第 2 期，1937 年 6 月 1 日出版，第 2 頁。引自郭榮榮，《師陀小說研究述評》http://qk.laicar.com／Home／Content／2334020。

6. 魯迅，《田軍〈八月的鄉村〉序》，《魯迅全集》第 6 卷，北京：人民文學出版社，1991。

7. Ng, Kenny Kwok-kwan. *The Lost Geopoetic Horizon of Li Jieren: The Crisis of Writing Chengdu in Revolutionary China*, Leiden: Brill 2015.

8. Owen, Stephen. *Remembrances: The Experience of the Past in Classical Chinese Literature*, Cambridge: Harvard University Press, 1986.

9. 師陀，《師陀全集》第一卷上，開封：河南大學出版社，2004。師陀，《師陀全集》第一卷下，開封：河南大學出版社，2004。

10. 王德威，〈南方的墮落與誘惑──小說蘇童論〉，《天使的糧食》，臺北：麥田出版有限公司，2002：11～36。

11. Wang, Yiyan. "Fiction in Modern China: Modernity through Storytelling", Yingjin Zhang ed. *A Companion to Modern Chinese Literature,* Chichester: Wiley Blackwell, 2016：195～213.

12. 解志熙，《現代中國「生活樣式」的浮世繪──師陀小說敘論》，《清華大學學報：哲學社會科學版》2007 年第 3 期：5～19。

13. 張太原，《〈獨立評論〉與 20 世紀 30 年代的政治思潮》，北京：社會科學文獻出版社，2006。

14. 張中良，《中國現代小說的敘事風貌》，臺北：秀威，2013。

二、危機的詩意——
現代中國文學的歷史審美建構

Poetics of crisis and Historical Redirection
Guo Moruo's Modern Nirvana

Yi Zheng

中文摘要：

　　本文探討歷史危機作爲概念和意象對郭沫若詩歌中壯美詩學的形成的重要性。通過系統分析郭氏早期詩歌創作《鳳凰涅槃》和時代精神的關係，尤其是對「暴風驟雨」式文化的引進嚮往，作者提出，郭沫若對歷史危機的詩性誇張，一方面開創了現代中國壯美詩學的先河，另一方面也使現代詩歌的歷史美學野心——讓新詩帶來新世界——變得更加困難。

The literary revolution of early twentieth-century China, the height of which usually marked by the New Culture Movement of the May Fourth, 〔註1〕 is noted in modern Chinese literary history 〔註2〕 for its antipathy to tradition and passion for rebellion. Consequently, the project of modern Chinese literature is envisioned to wrest whatever is literary and cultural from its age-old cocoon, and poetry is seen as the last to be disentangled from its traditional bondage. But "notwithstanding this dedication to modernity, tradition persisted ..." 〔註3〕 This, however, is attributed less to the lack of individual talent on the part of the poets and more to

---

〔註1〕 Chow Tse-tsung, *The May Fourth Movement: Intellectual Revolution and Modern China,* 1960.
〔註2〕 Wang Yao, *Zhongguo xiandaiwenxue shilunji (Essay Collection on the History of Modern Chinese Literature),*1998.
〔註3〕 Julia Lin, 31.

the tradition from which they tried to wrestle themselves free. The early modern Chinese poets are weighed down by "the great legacy of the traditional poets", 〔註 4〕 especially its thousand-years of refinement. Understood in this way, tradition looms doubly ominous for the aspiring modern poets both as an overwhelming heritage and as a lack. For "one must bear in mind that the new poetry was not built directly upon the old, as were modern Chinese fiction and drama, both of which had a long and remarkable vernacular tradition in their favor". 〔註 5〕 The new poetic rebellion had to be groundbreaking not only in rejecting *wenyan* as its poetic medium, together with all the conventional verse forms and prosodic rules. It also had to master *baihua*, the vernacular, before it could `elevate' it to the status of the only acceptable medium for the new verse, and create its own new prosody. The modern Chinese poetic revolution thus cannot be understood as a poetic revolt against the antiquated and worn, nor a regenerative cycle between the new and the old. This is probably why influence studies in poetic form and prosody, no matter how eruditely and intricately accomplished, can at best explicate the particular aesthetic choices of the poets and their implications, cultural and formal, with a perhaps. 〔註 6〕 What is often missing in the otherwise excellent prosodic and formalist studies, in the careful tracing of influences and inventions in the revolutionary experiments, is their historicity. For the May Fourth New Culturalists and modern poets of early twentieth-century China, the question of what is modern Chinese poetry is emphatically and passionately formal as well as cultural, but above all timely.

I. The Sublime as the Cultural and Poetic Spirit of the Times

The modern Chinese poets' preoccupation with the timely spirit and their fascination with the Romantic sublime as its aesthetic figuration 〔註 7〕 can partly be

---

〔註 4〕 Julia Lin, 31.
〔註 5〕 Julia Lin, 31.
〔註 6〕 Marian Galik, 177-90.
〔註 7〕 See Yi Zheng, *From Burke and Wordsworth to the Modern Sublime in Chinese Literature*, 2010.

explained by Richard Bourke's understanding of Romantic aestheticism in late eighteenth century England—that is, it is a modern aesthetic attempt to inaugurate "an era which disowns the historical inheritance that defines it". 〔註8〕 As an inaugural aesthetics it aims at a historical disjunction but is nonetheless burdened with the same history's precedents. Similarly afflicted with the anxieties of a traumatic modernity, modern Chinese poets and other advocates of new culture also imagined their cultural aspirations and practices as aesthetic reaction against the onslaught of history, and in this sense aesthetic regeneration as historical re-direction. Their ambition is thus concerned as much with the invention of genres and erection of aesthetic doctrines as it is with the possibility "for an entirely new social function for the writer...and consequently for a different society". 〔註9〕 This historical redress has at its centre a deliberate hyperbolization of literary and aesthetic agency, which is predicated on a sense of national crisis. In his preface to the opening issue of *Chuangzao jikan* (The Creation Quarterly), published in July 1921, Guo Moruo (1892-1978), one of the vanguards of modern Chinese poetry, declares that "The Creator – I will call upon the might of the "erupting volcano" and the "*Sturm und Drang* of the Universe" to "create a bright world". 〔註10〕 Guo's exaltation of "*Sturm und Drang*" as the most properly modern aesthetic ideal, poetic subject, style and sentiment is no mere idiosyncrasy. In the history of modern Chinese literature, it has always been exalted or derided as the spirit of the times.

With Guo, the Romantic poets of the Creation Society, "with their exaggerated, heroic, crude, and fearless momentum, pushed open a new frontier for Chinese literature." 〔註11〕 This new frontier is the much-needed poetic spirit for modern Chinese poetry, which has by then established its chosen language and medium – the celebrated switch to vernacular and abolition of regulated forms – but needs new subject matter and most importantly new moods, sentiments and ways of expression to match the tempo and scope of the raging cultural revolution.

〔註 8〕 Richard Bourke, 199.

〔註 9〕 Lacoue-Labarthe and Nancy, 5.

〔註 10〕 Guo, "Xu" ["Preface"] 1-2.

〔註 11〕 Shen, Congwen. "Lun zhongguo xiandai xiaoshuo chuangzuo (On the Creation of Modern Chinese Fiction)". *wenxue yuekan* (The Literary Monthly) 2.4 (1931): 4, qtd. in Long, 9.

Guo and the Creation Society poets championed the content, sensibility and expressions of Romanticism as something that can bring new ideals and possibilities to New Chinese Poetry. In line with the demand of the times, their exaggerated passions and crude heroism, especially as embodiment of a youthful hope after destruction, have not only reshaped Chinese poetic composition but also the structure and modes of feelings of an entire generation. In this sense it is seen aesthetically and historically as part of the volcanic eruption of the sweeping cultural revolution. *Sturm and Drang* had since become the slogan of the day among the cultured youth. And as Ou-fan Lee demonstrates in his study *The Romantic Generation of Modern Chinese Writers* (1976), it had shaped the psycho-cultural tempo of modern Chinese literary movements as well as individual authorial choices.

What the desire for a cultural *Sturm and Drang* ushered in aesthetically is the Romantic sublime. To inaugurate an era which disowns the historical inheritance that defines it is a sublime task. To re-create a Chinese sublime becomes the demand of the times. When the pioneer of modern Chinese aestheticism Wang Guowei (1877-1927) expounded on the relation between the aesthetic and emotional depth earlier in the century, he was proposing "a cure for an emotionally depressed and morally degenerate society". 〔註 12〕 The innermost psyche and emotional depth Wang was concerned with were the psychic and affective ills caused by the trauma of a violent modernity. Thus his exposition of the sublime in Kantian and Schopenhauerian terms is an historical aestheticism: "When an object hostile to our will confronts us and violently tears up our will and dissolves it, so that our cognitive faculty assumes independence and we penetrate deep into the thing itself, we call this object 'sublime' and the feeling that of sublimity'". 〔註 13〕 In Wang's reconstruction of the sublime, the violence of terror and destruction are requisite and overwhelming. It "tears up our will." The subsequent ascendance of cognitive faculty and its "penetration" to the essence of things, which is the requisite closure for the sublime aesthetics, is at most a post facto understanding.

〔註 12〕 Ban Wang, 24.
〔註 13〕 Wang Guowei, 1635.

Wang was so caught up with the sublime's function to tear us away from the anxieties and tensions of a traumatic modern Chinese life that the ultimate moment in his feeling of sublimity is the moment of death. This is why Wang Ban describes Wang Guowei's venture into a historical-aesthetic redemption as "sublimation unto death". 〔註14〕 From Wang Guowei to the May Fourth Romanticists, the pursuit of the sublime had undergone considerable change; it was pursued with a different "spirit" of the times. As champions of a raging cultural revolution that was set to redeem a failing social and political modernization, the New Culturalists struggled with a sublime discourse less hesitant, more ferociously heroic and destructive, marked with unbound defiance and unabashed yearnings for greatness. However, as I elaborate later, it nonetheless carried on the preoccupation with death initiated by the earlier melancholic Wang Guowei.

In terms of poetics, the search for a modern sublime in early twentieth century China is defined as matters of both structure and sentiment, congregating on the grandness of scope and loftiness of feelings, which in turn constitutes the greatness of the poet. In a letter to Guo Moruo in 1920 while editing and publishing his earliest poems, the aesthete and critic Zong Baihua wrote: "Your poems tend to be conceptually lofty and forceful; it shows that you should be good at writing big poems, the sublime kind… There are very few people who are capable of doing this in China. It will prove your greatness". 〔註15〕 A new Chinese poetry of "the sublime kind" which constitutes the new "great" poet should be conceptually "lofty "and "forceful," structurally "big," and often heroic or at least defiant in subject matter. Zong's call for poetic composition and sentiments of a different kind seems to echo the Romantic construction of the expressive a priori of artistic manifestations. It also echoes such construction's aspiration towards the sublime as well as with its insistence on the correspondence between the poetic quality and the greatness of the poetic mind. And the demand here is not only presented as an aesthetic one, it is seen, definitely and more emphatically, as a demand of the times, as something necessitated by the spirit of the age.

〔註14〕 Ban Wang, 17-54.
〔註15〕 Tian, Zong and Guo, 27.

For the May Fourth Culturalists as well as later critics and historians, how to understand and define the timely spirit is synonymous with understanding the quintessence of the cultural revolution and its historical implication. In its contentious definition and re-definition, the timely spirit becomes a necessary preamble in the discourse of modern Chinese literature. Beyond the New Culturalists' Romantic entanglement, the preoccupation with the spirit of the age attests to the prevalent sense of the present as a moment of crisis. As James K. Chandler shows in his study of Romantic historicism, the term spirit of the age is "one of the most self-consciously novel and distinctive coinages of that (Romantic) period". 〔註 16〕 Its novelty coined "precisely to identify its own novelty and is in the fact that it established the legitimacy of the preoccupation with contemporaneity". 〔註 17〕 As Chandler shows, what is established by the numerous Romantic writings on the "spirit of our times" is precisely the importance and difference of "our age."

The evocation and transposition of the spirit of the age by modern Chinese writers and critics as a "dominant idea" certainly derives from their sense of their very own historical situation. It puts into focus their feeling of national as well as personal crisis. In fact, the preoccupation with crisis defines their contemporaneity as distinction, whereby "modernity" acquires an unequivocal sense of urgency, as something tantamount to ultimate difference. The New Culturalists' exultant obsession with the spirit of the times also testifies to their uneasy relation with tradition as something they know defines them but from which they desire nothing less than complete disentanglement, at least rhetorically. The discourse on the timely spirit, highlighting the notion of contemporaneity, seems to offer them that sense of distinction, and the inevitability of change, which is as much future-oriented as crisis-driven. The contention on its definition is thus emblematic of the struggle in the construction of modern Chinese cultural history.

Wen Yiduo (1899-1946), Guo's famous contemporary poet and poetry critic, has summarized the spirit of his age in five cardinal points: the spirit of movement,

---

〔註 16〕 Chandler, 105-14.
〔註 17〕 Chandler, 106.

the spirit of rebellion, the spirit of science, the spirit of *datong* (universal equity), and the frustration of youth. 〔註 18〕 Wen's construction privileges the spirit of movement and rebellion as much as the frustration of youth. This last point, however, is erased decades later when He Qifang (1912-1977) tries to re-historicize the spirit in his comment on the timeliness of *Goddess*, the earliest poetry collection of Guo Morou:

The timely spirit of the *Goddess* lies mainly in this: it has expressed, emphatically, the hopes and aspirations of the Chinese people, in particular of the young Chinese intellectuals, for the regeneration of their homeland; it has expressed their revolutionary spirit and their optimism. It writes about their discontents and curses towards the old China, but more significantly it portrays the dreams, prophecies and acclamations for a future new China... All these can be said to be the manifestations of the spirit of May Fourth and its optimism. (He 442-43)

He's reconstruction emphatically subsumes the frustrations and struggles of the May Fourth New Culturalists into a grand evolutionary narrative of a Chinese revolutionary nation building, in which the sense of crisis dissipates in inevitable progress. His contemporary Zhou Yang (1908-19$9), however, though as optimistic and future-oriented, nonetheless describes the May Fourth spirit and its literary manifestation as bordering on an almost irascible ferocity. 〔註 19〕

The spirit of the May Fourth, often identifiable as the Romantic sublime in the figuration of the New Chinese poets, and which has come to stand for the beginning of a modern Chinese cultural tradition is thus best described as a spirit of destruction as well as creation. Though in the retrospective representations of it literary historians tend to downplay the shared sense of anxiety, of desperation, of pain and anger which sometimes turn into vigorous protest, sometimes melancholia, that attends the historical trauma, and the sense of crisis which prevails in the writings and moods of the young intellectuals. Yan Huangdong's more recent delineation of the progress of the modern Chinese poet, however, echoes closely what is found in the self-image and imagination of the New Culturalist poets

〔註 18〕 Wen, 3.
〔註 19〕 Zhou, *Jiefang ribao* Supplement 16, 1941.

themselves. Like in the progress narratives, the poet in this is the first seer that awakens to the new world. But what is the new world he sees?

> An ugly, cold world without light, without warmth, without freedom and without happiness! He sees around him Hell and prison houses, oppression and deception, crimes and suffering. Thus he suffers and weeps. Then his suffering turns to hatred, his weeping anger, and when they became uncontainable, he bursts forth into a most fierce protest, and begins a violently passionate struggle that culminates into an ultimate "No." He not only wants to break away from the old world, but also wants to tear it apart, crumble it and crush it to pieces! His anger burns like fire, his protest turns into a storm, and he strikes at the whole old world, old system, like a thunder. (Yan 275)

Although Yan's portrayal of the poet's progress as the coming-to-be of the modern Chinese subject champions what has become known as positive Romanticism in its revolutionary fervor, it nonetheless foregrounds the feelings of pain and anger. It highlights anxious desperation and savage ferocity spurred on by historical crisis as the underwriting affect of modern Chinese aesthetics and grounding passion for the spirit of the age. Modern Chinese aesthetics, as seen pioneered and embodied by the May Fourth spirit, can thus be summarized as that which "typically celebrate the energetic, the obscure, the disruptive, the unlimited, the powerful, and the terrible as a new set of positive aesthetic terms". 〔註20〕 Or they can be understood in the way Guo Moruo describes his two volcanic years of poetic eruption immediately after May Fourth: "Whitman's poetic spirit which seeks to do away with everything old and restrictive is especially suitable for the *Sturm and Dung* of May Fourth, I am completely shaken by his majestic and unconstrained tone. Under his influence, and spurred on by Baihua (Zong), I composed `Yelling at the Edge of the Earth,' 'Earth, My Mother,' 'Ode to the Bandit,' 'Good Morning,' 'Nirvana of the Phoenix,' 'Heavenly Dog,' 'Lamp of the Heart,' 'Coal in the Furnace,' 'Lesson of the Cannon,' and so on, poems of masculine savagery." 〔註21〕

〔註20〕 Furniss on eighteenth and nineteenth century English Sublime, 20.
〔註21〕 Guo, *Guo Moruo on Creation*, 204.

This perception of a violently disruptive but unlimited sublime as the only possible cultural reaction against the crisis of modernity explains why the search for the sublime, or the great, the lofty, the powerful, and the excessive, is perceived to embody the spirit of the times. Such an understanding of the aesthetic reprieve also demonstrates that the modern Chinese sublime, at its earlier poetic inception, which coincided with the roaring furor of the New Culture Movement, is invoked and refigured predominantly with the sense of the defiant, the savage and the terrible. The modern aesthetic turn for those in quest of a sublime poetics in early twentieth century China is definitely an affective construction that is predicated on feelings and passions, its end the building up of the social function of the writer and a new society through its aesthetic and moral affect. However, with the figure of crisis and feeling of terror at its center, the formulation and refiguration of the sublime in modern Chinese poetry are too often too "aggressively destabilizing" to resolve the "flashed up" fears and disruptions to achieve its historically envisioned ends. The "sublime humanity" that Schiller fancies, 〔註 22〕 as well as the historical ends and modern poetic beginnings Chinese new poets aspire to, are often momentarily patched up as forced poetic closures.

II. Nushen (The Goddess) and the Nirvana of Modern Chinese Poetics

Yan Huandong's depiction of the making of modern Chinese poet as ferocious and savage can easily be a close reading of Guo Moruo's figuration of *Qu Yuan* in his historical verse drama. 〔註 23〕 However, it is Guo's first poetry collection Nushen (*the Goddess*, 1921) that is credited to have fulfilled the ambition of poetic epoch-making aspired to by early twentieth century Chinese poets. Whatever its reception, the collection is regarded unequivocally as the first though experimental but "realized" poetry collection of the New Literature Movement, and as the culmination of the longings and aspirations of a whole generation of heroic quest.

〔註 22〕 Schiller, 38.
〔註 23〕 Guo, *Study of Qu Yuan*, 1957.

〔註 24〕The appearance of *Nusen* is as much an advent as a fulfillment, and in this sense an historical event, marking the arrival of a Chinese poetic "modernity."

What is so different about Guo's *Nushen* that it is hailed as an historical monument, and what is so "modern" about it that discussions of the spirit of the times are literally predicated on it? As Guo's first poetry collection, it consists of his poems composed during the period from 1919-1921: one poetic prologue, fifty-three "free style" verses that vary in subject and formal structure, and three verse dramas. One of the most noticeable features of the volume is that almost all its consequential works are composed at the height of the May Fourth, the "hurricane" (Guo) period of the New Culture Movement. The coincidence of Guo's poetic outbursts with the raging waves of the times made him the poet of the age, and his poems embodiment of the "modernity" that he passionately championed. Although Guo is credited as the first *baihua* poet who truly achieved the poetic freedom that the movement set out to attain—his composition marks the emergence of a Chinese "free verse" and verse drama—he is not lauded mainly for his stylistic and generic innovations. Above all things, he is remembered as the vanguard *par excellence* of modern Chinese literature and his poems the metonymy for "new poetry." Even in 1923, only two years after the collection's publication by Shanghai Taidong Book House, it was already eulogized by fellow poet and critic Wen Yiduo as the very embodiment of the spirit of the age: "If we talk about the New Poetry, only Mr. Guo Moruo's compositions can be called by such a name. This is not only because formally and stylistically his poems are the most remote from the old poetry, what is most important is that the spirit of his poetic work is the spirit of the times—the very spirit of the twentieth century. Someone said that literacy works are products of the times, and *The Goddess* is unabashedly its prodigal son". 〔註 25〕Wen's comment has since become the standard in Guo criticisrn. 〔註 26〕

Nushen, or more exactly its spirit and timely birth, is indeed the prodigal son of its age. Its rearing process encompasses the "hurricane" and raging waves of

---

〔註 24〕Bian Zhilin, 152-57.
〔註 25〕Wen, "His Spirit is the Spirit of the Times," 432.
〔註 26〕See Yan 272-73.

early modern Chines history, and it is born out of the modern trauma as its redress. Guo has repeatedly described the deluges and torrents of this particular period of Chinese history as his poetic inspiration, an "influence" that is felt and remembered in almost both terms: "During the months between the end of 1919 and the beginning of 1920. I was almost immersed in poetry every day. And every onslaught of poetic influence put me in a state of high fever. I was shivering between heat and cold so hard that I could hardly hold my pen. When I said 'poems are written. not made up,' it was based on my feelings then". 〔註27〕 *Nushen* in this sense is both an offspring of and a hymn to May Fourth, and as such, understanding of its formal revolution and poetic subject-object has become metonymic in understanding the "spirit" of Chinese modernity. It becomes synonymous with the aspirations for the "new" in form, subject and feelings of the New Poetry movement. As many have argued, *Nushen* had succeeded for the first time in crafting what has come to be called a Chinese free verse, a verse form that is neither loosened lines of an otherwise classical structure　nor imitations of its Western counterpart. The poems are often read as examples of the hope and longing of the age, of its passions and vitality, and for their unsurpassed audacity to break away from the familiar, the conventional, and the old. With images from the self-incinerating phoenix to the dog that barks at the sun, from the blazing coal to the sun-creating goddess, which has earned Guo the title of the "tidal wave" poet, the experiments in the collection also mark a revolution of "sentiment" in Chinese poetic history. Aside from its manifested concerns about what to write and how to write it, the publication of *Nushen* symbolizes a revolution in what should or can be appropriate poetic "sensibilities," ushering in a poetics of ferocity. However, amid the exclamatory superlatives that laud Guo's "creative" poetic revolution of the modern form and content, and easy identification between his "revolutionary" poetic affect and the "spirit" of the age, little heed is paid to the sense of historical and personal crisis which Guo emphasizes in pathological terms as the driving force for his composition and affective impetus of the collection's poetics. The collection is noted for its "positive" Romanticism because of its overflowing

---

〔註27〕 Guo, Wode *zuoshi jingguo*, 144.

optimism and tone of uncontrollable vehemence; its "explosive," roaring expressions and vast galloping imagination; for its extreme hyperbole and fantastic language. These, as I argued elsewhere, 〔註 28〕 are part of Guo's original transformation of the sublime as an aesthetic ideal in itself. Close analysis suggests that *Nushen*'s sublime poetics is a reformulation of the excessive propensities of an aesthetics centered on pain and desperation, on the disruptive and limit of death. The lasting poetic images and sequences from the collection, for instance, are the self-destruction of the phoenixes before their regeneration; the striving of *Nushen* (the Goddess) to create a new world upon the ruins of the old; Poet Qu Yuan's passionate but desperate search for liberty; Nie Rong's and Nie Zheng's self-sacrifice (the heroism in the collection is almost always suicidal). The affect of the "explosive" passions rendered through Guo's bombarding verses is thus more defiant than "positive". And I argue hence Guo's sublime poetics is an exclamation, a compositional and affective struggle for the great. But in its strife to break away from the confines of tradition and search for freedom of form and poetic subject, his compositions remain under the shadow of national crisis and personal desperation, figured more than convincingly in the celebration of melancholia and death. The verses in the collection no longer maintain the symmetry, harmony, refinement, and poised delicacy of both form and sensibility assumed for classical Chinese poetry. Instead, they hyperbolize a stylistic and affective ferocity, ruggedness, simplicity, and sheer power. What the collection has achieved, as many Guo critics have pointed out, is a sense of poetic audacity and vigor lacking in Chinese poetic history. But what is most striking in these exalted and exalting verses are traces of turbulence, of tremendous, sweeping movement that carries home rather than away, darkness of images and feelings. The sublime transfigured in Guo's new verses is a sublimity of destruction and savage abandon. The crisis of Chinese history writ large as the necessary backdrop for the composition of modern poetry, its new imagery and new feelings remains large in the composition. It overshadows the poetic resolutions devised for new aesthetic and historical direction.

〔註 28〕 Zheng, 83-103.

"*Fenghuang niepan* (Nirvana of the Phoenix)" is most thematically emblematic of the collection. It typifies the "spirit" of *Nushen* and hence the very "spirit" of May Fourth. The verse is celebrated for its passions of idealism, uninhibited imagination, fantastic imagery, audacious exaggeration, grand scope, vehement tones and turbulent rhythms. And these are qualities that come to be regarded as the staples of a "Chinese" "positive" Romanticism, and which certainly seem to have established the theme of regeneration in the poem. 〔註 29〕 What is often unnoticed, however, is the poem's structural and thematic attempt at epic making, Guo's search for new cultural icons and his effort to re-create a "modern" Chinese legend in due process. In his notes before the "Prelude," Guo tells his readers that the image of the "Phoenix" in the poem comes from the "Realm of the Beyond" (*Tian fang guo*), which is an archaic name for Arabia and often evoking associations of fantasy and legend. But the name itself is equivalent to the Chinese *fenghuang* (*feng*: male, *huang*: female), which are believed to have originated from Mount Danshe. So the poetic-epic hero here is conceived as a legendary bird from the "beyond" but translatable to what is also originary and "Chinese," and who, after five hundred years of life burns itself with sandalwood and reincarnates from the ashes. Guo's poetic epic begins as an elegy to the birds' impending death. The "Prelude" is a choral narrative of the preparations of the *feng* and *huang*'s self-destruction: "In the night sky, of the approaching Chuxi (Chinese New Year's Eve), /A pair of *fenghuang* is hovering to and fro. /They fly away singing melancholy and low, / And with branches of sandalwood. /They flutter back atop Mount Danshe" (Guo, *xuanji* [Selected Works] 3 22: 1-5).

The dirge of the narrator sets the tone for the ritual. The setting, for all its evocations of the New Year's eve, is bleak and desolate: "On the right of the mountain there are withered *wutong* (Chinese parasols), /On the left of the mountain a sweet spring drains, /In front of the mountain stands the boundless sea, /Behind the mountain lies the vast prairie, /And on the mountain is the wintry sky where a piercing wind blows" (Guo, 22: 6-10). Mount Danshe re-created in these lines is no longer full of jade and gold as it once was, though the images Guo sets

---

〔註 29〕 See Chen Li 8-24.

up included all the commonplaces of the sublime. On the vast wintry ruins of mountain, sea, prairie, sky, trees and spring, the backdrop of the *fenghuang*'s self-destruction is a world in proximity with death. It is a world near dusk, and like its old and tired protagonists, moribund. The "Prelude," which sets the tone for the ballad-epic, with its reoccurring refrain of the darkening night and "The *feng* has flown tired, /The *huang* has flown tired, /Their death is nigh" (13-15), successfully builds up the atmosphere of the impending end, but without any hint of beyond. The *feng* and *huang* continue their last sublime though nonetheless woeful song, while a flock of their more profane fellow beings watch vacuously: "Ah Ah! /The mournful *fenghuang*! /The *feng* dances, bending low but defiant! /The *huang* sings, sublime! /The *feng* dances once more, /And so sings the *huang*, /A flock of worldly birds, / Come to watch the funeral song" (Guo, 24: 29-36).

In keeping with the tone set up in the "Prelude," "The Song of the *Feng*" and "The Song of the Huang," which make up the main body of the poem, accumulate in intensity and passion. As the swan song of the legendary birds, they build up the theme of exaltation in defiance. In face of impending terror, the *feng* and *huang* revel in the sublimity of destruction. The sense of terror divulged in the two "Songs," however, does not come so much from the birds' approaching death, which, after all, is self-chosen, a choice with hope for the beyond, but rather from their narrative. In preparing their own cremation, the birds soar towards the sky and circle towards earth, hover between the past and present, and roam the vast space of the poet's imagination, which is also the expansive ruin of Chinese civilization. They sing separately and in unison, their songs penetrate four corners of the earth, bewailing and cursing the world of their being. The "Songs," which are the birds' death throbs of anger and sorrow, are actually the poet's lamentation for five hundred years of (pre) modern Chinese history and the conditions of human existence. In the present "universe" in the "songs," the old world is described as the ``butcher house," "prison," "graveyard," and "Hell": "You, the vast universe, as cruel as cast-iron! /You, the vast universe, as dark as black pigment! /You, the vast universe, as odorous as blood!" (24: 39-41). The *feng* begins his mourning song as a denunciation of the world from which he and the *huang*, as symbols of the glory of Chinese civilization, are impelled to depart. But the *feng*'s indictment is not constrained to the wrongs of his immediate existence. Like it is in Qu Yuan's "*Lisao*" ("Sorrows at the Departure"), the protestations and requisitions of the *feng* are directed against the whole universe, it is a reiteration of Qu's "Tian wen" ("Query to Heaven"). What the *feng* questions and laments, are the conditions of our very human existence, and what he professes is a fundamental skepticism of the ways of being in the world, of China's adherence to the ultimate unchangeability of things which is believed to be the historical cause of its lethargy: "Oh, the cosmos, /Why do you exist? /And whence do you come? /Where do you sit yourself? /Are you a limited hollow ball, /Or a boundless entity?... /What other things exist beyond your perimeter?" (Guo, 24: 42-51)

Guo's query to heaven, however, is not intended to be a reflection on the nature of things and being or any a *priori* cosmic principle. The universal questions are posed only to lead to the rightful rage that heaven knows naught and thus cannot provide answers to human suffering and the ways of the world, especially the onslaught of the direction of modern history: "Raising my head I ask the sky, /But the sky, haughty and high, knows naught. /Bending low I ask the earth, /The earth is dead, without breath. /Stretching my neck I ask the sea, /The sea is sobbing, choked by its own tears" (Guo, 25:58-63). "The Song of the *Feng*" is dominated by rage, a rage given vent to in bitter protest and shrill curse. Guo, through the wailings of the dying *feng*, certainly does not begrudge "high colors" of description and "vicious imagery" in an otherwise rather plain, almost colloquial ballad form. With little hint of the hope or joy of transcendence, the *feng*'s fury is vindictive: "Ah, the universe, and the world, /I will persevere to put you under my cursing-spell: /You thick-blood soiled butchery /You sorrow infected prison! /You shrieking/ghost-filled grave! /And you Hell with dancing devils! /Why have you come to live on earth?" (Guo, *xuanji* [Selected Works] 3 26: 68-73). If the *feng*'s despair is at the pain and terror of the world and the universe in general, "The Song of the *Huang*" is a lamentation of the five-hundred years of Chinese history in particular. She bewails its tears and humiliations, and its present place in the vast ocean like a lonely sinking boat.

Five-hundred years of tears pour like waterfalls.

Five-hundred years of tears drip like a burning can

The tears that are inexhaustible,

The filth that is unwashable,

The passions that are inextinguishable,

And the shame that is inerasable.

…

Ah, Ah!

The last stretch of our dim and floating life,

Is like the lonely sinking boat amid the vast sea.

…

The sail is broken, The mast cracked, The oars scattered,

The girder rotting away. (Guo, 27: 86-104)

The huang's summation of recent Chinese history is not unlike its popular contemporary assessment. But besides accreting and enumerating the pain and sorrow of the last five-hundred years, which is a `historical' period deliberately set up and aside to accentuate its abrupt and successive traumatic modern turn and the thousands of years `before,' it intensifies the despair and hopelessness, the feelings of endless suspense. The generally lamented national and historical crisis is here intensified into utter desperation, the course of China moribund without redemption (a sinking boat with broken sail), aesthetically in the stanza and historically by implication. The poetics of the sublime, as Guo figures and uses it, is a precarious play of the dark obscurity of the terrible. It is a historical-aesthetic play different from the cathartic sublimation elaborated earlier by Wang Guowei. Although both these refigurations (Wang's and Guo's) are part of "the aesthetic search for meaning in cultural crisis". 〔註30〕 The imagery and sentiment of the song, following and dramatizing the setting up of the "Prelude," tell a story of boundless terror and humiliated impotence which are so real, that they threaten to exceed the boundaries which posit them as mere prerequisites for the sublime moment beyond: "Ah, Ah! /… /On the left the sea is flowing boundless and nigh,

---

〔註30〕 Ban Wang,17.

/On the right the sea is flowing boundless and nigh, /In front there is no lighthouse, /Behind the coast is nowhere to behold" (Guo, 27:14-17). Death, in such an emphatic configuration and with such lifelike omnipresence, can no longer be read as a ruse or necessary ploy for subsequent transcendence: "Folly! Folly! Folly! /What are left are sorrow, frustration, solitude, and decay, /Those spirited corpses that surround us, /Those spirited corpses that are woven through us. /…Gone! Gone! Gone! /Everything is gone. /All is gone. /So will be us, / And so will be you" (Guo, 27: 39-52).

After such breathless and hyperbolic variations on death, decay, and despair, the chorus of the *feng* and *huang* finally does strike a note of defiance and heroism, at least they know they are at the limit and have no hesitation in devising a dignified end. The end they envision has no hint of the beyond, but a slight hope of redemption. They hope to bring with them in a final act of (self) destruction all that is unseemly and depraved from the familiar world of their origin and existence: "Ah, Ah! /The flame is up. /The fragrance arises. /Time has come! /Death is knocking on the door! /All that is in us! /All that is outside us! /All things and everything! /Please! Please!" (Guo, 29: 139-47). The legendary birds valiantly embrace their end, if not with joy, at least with nonchalance and glee: the inferno they unleash with their self-sacrifice can at least bring about the destruction of all that is dilapidated, despondent, and hideous. However, the audience of their ritual vitiates the reader's expectation of the sublime: as onlookers of the *fenghuang*'s gesture beyond, the group of "prey of the mundane"—from the homely pigeon to the thuggish eagle—do not responds with the anticipated terror, awe or the sense of narrow escape, which are requisite for the aesthetic completion of a sublime process. They simply fail to comprehend the sublime spectacle: after witnessing the legendary birds' death chant and self-incineration they hasten to celebrate and compete for their replacement in the feathered realm. For the unenlightened birds of the world, the *fernghuang*'s "staged" death is a foolhardy act or a capitulation to fate. Since they cannot comprehend the stagedness of the staged death and consequently its meaning, they can only gloat over the *fenghuang*'s misfortune. "Ha ha, *fenghuang*! *fenghuang*! /You have been our feathered sovereign in vain!

/So you are really dead? You are really dead? /From now on I will be the chieftain!" (30: 148-151) sings one "vulgar" bird after another.

The failure of the "prey of the mundane" to participate metaphorically in the sublime spectacle may be the result of the very difficulties in the all too earnestly transfigured ruse. In the poet's attempt to bring the terrors of the modern world home, the fervently enumerated and authenticated wounds of history have become so real that it is difficult for the spectators to acquire that necessary distance—the possibility of differentiation between themselves and the actors which makes good effectively the spectacular show. After their emphatically repetitive construction as the main feature of Guo's ballad-epic and seemingly artless bombarding statement, the immediacy of the historical terrors and the intensity of the poet's/protagonist's pain in the end overwhelm the stagedness. Because it is this stagedness that grounds the very implication of will, choice, agency and hope of overcoming in the *fenghuang*'s death, failure in its perception makes the act falling short as a gesture beyond. Or this simply illustrates the very problem of transfiguring the sublime as an historical aesthetics. As redress to the modern trauma, Guo seems to have translated and refigured the very paradox of the Romantic sublime. Just as it is exemplified in the Burkean definition of the sublime ruse and Kantian structure of the a priori, this aesthetic construction simultaneously aspires to its verifiability by everyone (the universal) and which, by its very strenuousness, excludes the weaker subject. Guo's configuration is further compounded by his share of the Romanticists' ambition to refigure the modern epic culture-hero. In his quest for a devastating heroism as the only force of redemption, he has to resort to the divine bird, which, despite the transfigured cross-cultural origins soars far beyond the realm, hence comprehension, of the earthly multitude. In his choice of utter defiance, and at the moment of consuming rage and uncontrollable passion for total destruction/revolution, Guo, like many of his fellow radical modern Chinese cultural critics and poets, has failed to establish the sympathetic correspondence between hero and audience. A failure which not only resulted in the worldly birds' inability to participate in the *fenghuang*'s sublime play but also in the fate of modern "vernacular" Chinese poetry—a genre that has never quite resolved the paradox of its striving for stylistic and affective avant-garde and its desire for democratization, which is the very premise of its coming-into-being. The disjunction between the *fenghuang*'s act and the home birds' response has vitiated the project of transfiguring the modern sublime as aesthetic healing of the cultural wounds of history. It attests to the conceptual and structural difficulties inherent in the strenuous affective demand of the formulations of the modern sublime and its transport. It also foregrounds the contrary impulses of the radical May Fourth intellectuals to both enlist and differentiate themselves, as defiant epic culture heroes, from the multitude. And this has proved the irresolvable dilemma of both the original and Guo's transfigured sublime cultural avant-guardianism.

"The Song of Nirvana." when it does come, after the conclusive celebration by the Lowly prey of the happy demise of their more heroic fellow creatures, comes more as an appendix, an epilogue rather than the poem's end. After a cock pronounced the dawn, the spring tide rises and the light that died the previous night awakens again. In chorus, the *feng* and *huang* sing forever with mounting joy, of their reincarnation, of the dewy new life of everything and being; of freshness, cleanliness and fragrance. But above all things, they sing in and about harmony, of the oneness in being and in eternity: "We are reincarnated. /We are again alive. /One in everything, alive. /Everything in one, alive, /... /We are fresh, we are clean, /We are magnificent, we are fragrant. /... /We are sincere; we are full of love. /We are blissful, we are harmonious. /One in everything, in harmony. /Everything in one, in harmony. /Harmony is you, harmony is me. /Harmony is him, harmony is fire" (Guo, 32-33:181-210). The beyond in Guo's imagination sounds strangely familiar. After all, "Nirvana" has always promised transcendence in death, as long as one practices differentiating (from the multitude) self-discipline. In Guo's idealization, the *feng* and *huang* have also aspired to bring with them regeneration of the world at large. But in the pantheistic heaven where the born-again birds sing like angels, and where the influence of Goethe is unfailingly pointed out by a host of critics, the scene of universal bliss doggedly reminds one of the Confucian utopia of *Datong shije*—the world of universal equality, where harmony is at the center of things and being. Thus the "beyond" actualized and affixed as the end of the *fenghuang*'s' (the poet's) sublime gesture not only seems nebulous, a hyperbolic space without "content" (as opposed to the earlier songs, there is literally no imagery in the last chorus), hence highly improbable. It also threatens to resurrect with it an origin, an all-too- puissant cultural source the poet and his fellow modern Chinese literary practitioners vowed to do away with. Guo's phoenix, transported like this, resembles neither the Hegelian Western nor Asiatic bird. 〔註 31〕Its poetically affixed reincarnation complicates rather than helps the historical vision of the May Fourth New Culturalists originated from acutely felt national and personal crisis. It also reminds us that historical visions are not always confined in cultural manifestos. Instead, they are often redefined in poetic practices that diversify their course.

Guo's project of a sublime poetics thus indeed unleashes the original aspirations and burdens of the Romantic sublime, in that it fully displays the possibilities and limitations of the modern "aesthetic reprieve" of history. This reprieve is made possible but at the same time compromised by the capacious aesthetics of the sublime. Guo's attempt to resolve aesthetically the cultural and historical dilemma of Chinese modernity by supplementing and transfiguring "pathos" of crisis and "`the spirit of the times," beautiful tears and sublime terror, tradition and modernity is partially successful. At the end of the nirvana there is indeed a new poetic spirit and beginnings of a modern Chinese poetics. But the historical crisis of modernity that is both the cultural driving force and aesthetic underpinning of the poetic revolution remains a dominant and threatening poetic figure, affectively irresolvable in Guo's composition, and becoming more than the necessary backdrop and prelude to modern Chinese poetry.

Works Cited:

1. Bian, Zhilin. "The Development of China's `New Poetry' and the Influence from the West." *Chinese Literature: Essays, Articles, Reviews* 4.1 (1982): 152-57.

2. Bourke, Richard. *Romantic Discourse and Political Modernity: Wordsworth, the Intellectual and Cultural Critique*, Prentice-Hall, 1993

〔註 31〕Shu-mei Shih, 52.

3. Burke, Edmund. *A Philosophical Enquiry into the Origin of Our Ideas of the Sublime and Beautiful*. Ed. James T. Boulton. Oxford: Basil Blackwell, 1987.

4. Chen, Li. "Shengming shengdian de chengzuikuanghuan" ("Intoxication in the Carnival of Life"). *Guo Maruo zuopin duoyuanhua jiedu* (Pluralist Interpretations of Guo Moruo's Major Works). Ed. Chen Li and Xiaocun Chen. Chengdu: Sichuan daxue xhubanshe, 2006. 8-24.

5. Chow, Tse-tsung. *The May Fourth Movement: Intellectual Revolution and Modern China*. Cambridge: Harvard UP, 1960.

6. Chandler, James K. *England in 1819*. Chicago: U. of Chicago P, 1998.

7. Furniss, Tom. *Edmund Burke's Aesthetic Ideology: Language, Gender and Political Economy in Revolution*. Cambridge: Cambridge UP, 1993.

8. Galik, Marian. *The Genesis of Modern Chinese Literary Criticism, 1917-1930*.

9. London: Curzon, 1980.

10. Guo, Moruo. "Xu" ("Preface"). *Chuangzao jican* (The Creation Quarterly) 1.1 (1921):1-3.

11. Guo, Moruo. *Guo Moruo lun chuangzuo* (Guo Moruo on Creation). Shanghai: Shanghai wenxue chubanshe, 1983.

12. Guo, Moruo. "*Qu Yuan yanjiu* (On Qu Yuan)." *Moruo wenji* (Collected Works of Guo Moruo). Vol.11. Beijing: renmin wenxue chubanshe, 1959. 331-430.

13. Guo, Moruo. "Wode zhoshi jingguo (My Poetic Career)." *Moruo wenji* (Collected Works of Guo Moruo). Vol. 11. Beijing: renmin wenxue chubanshe, 1958. 137-48.

14. Guo, Moruo. "Fenghuang Niepan (Nirvana of the Phoenix)", *Guo Moruo xuanji*: Shige (Selected Works of Guo Moruo: Poetry). Chengdu: Sichuan renmin chubanshe, 1982. 22-34.

15. He, Qifang. "Shige xinshang" ("Poetry and Its Appreciation"). *He Qifang wenji* (The Collected Works of He Qifang). Beijing: renmin wenxue chubanshe, 1983. 442-63.

16. Kant, Immanuel. *Observations on the Feeling of the Beautiful and Sublime*. Trans. John Goldthwait. Berkeley: U of California P, 1965.

17. Lacoue-Labarthe, Philippe, and Jean-Luc Nancy. *The Literary Absolute: the Theory of Literature in German Romanticism*. Traps. Philip Barnard and Cheryl Lester. Albany: State U of New York P, 1988.

18. Lee, Ou-fan. *The Romantic Generation of Modern Chinese Writers*. Cambridge: Harvard UP, 1973.

19. Lip, Julia C. *Modern Chinese Poetry: An Introduction*. Seattle: U of Washington P, I 973.

20. Long, Quanming. *Zhongguo xinshi liubianlun* (On the Trends and Changes of the Chinese New Poetry). Beijing: renmin wenxue chubanshe, 1999.

21. Schiller, Friedrich. *On the Aesthetic Education of Man, in a Series of Letters.* Trans. Reginald Spell. New York: Frederick Ungar, 1965.

22. Shih, Shu-mei. *The Lure of the Modern Writing Modernism in Semicolonial China 1917-1937.* Berkeley: U of California P, 2001.

23. Tian, Han, Baihua Zong, and Muoro Guo, eds. *Sanye Ji* (The Shamrock Collection). Shanghai: Shanghai shuju, 1982.

24. Wang, Ban. *The Sublime Figure of History: Aesthetics and Politics in Twentieth-Century China.* Stanford: Stanford UP, 1997.

25. Wang, Guowei. *Wang guantang xiansheng juanji* (Complete Works of Guantang Wang). Tas-bei: Wenhua chuban gongsi, 1968.

26. Wang, Yao. *Zhongguo xiandaiwenxue shilunji* (History of Modern Chinese Literature). Beijing: Beijing daxue chubanshe, 1998.

27. Wen, Yiduo. *"Nusen zhi shidai jingshen"* ("The Timely Spirit of the Goddess"). Chuangzao zhoubao (The Creation Weekly) 3 June 1923: 3-7.

28. Wen, Yiduo. "Tade jingshen shishidaijingshen" ("His Spirit is the Spirit of the Times"). *On Guo Moruo.* Ed. Fang Xiangdong. Beijing: dacong wenyi chubanshe, 2001.430-36.

29. Yan, Huang-dong. *Fenghuang, nushenjiqita: lun Guo Moruo* (Phoenix, Goddess and Others: On Guo Moruo). Beijing: renmin wenxue chubanshe, 1990.

30. Zheng, Yi. From Burke and Wordsworth to the Modern Sublime in Chinese Literature, West Lafayette: Purdue University Press, 2010.

31. Zhou, Yang. "Guo Moruo he fade nushen" ("Guo Moruo and His Goddess"), *Jiefang Ribao* (The Liberation Daily) 16 November 1941, *Guo Moruo yanjiu zhiliao (Reference Materials for Guo Moruo Studies)*, Ed. Xunzao Wang, Zhengyan Lu and Sao Hua, Beijing: Zhongguo shehui kexueyuan chubanshe, (1987): 208-215.

32. Zong, Baihua. "Qingshi wenti" ("The Question of Love Poetry"). *Xinshi bao* (The New Current Post): *Xuedeng* (Learning Light) 8.22 (1920).

Ailing Zhang and her Drifting Heroines: an Aesthetics of Existence

Yi Zheng

Born in the foreign concessions of Shanghai, Ailing Zhang (1920-1990) was educated in colonial Hong Kong, and inspired by "the meeting place of the East and the West, of tradition and modernity, the new and the old; of good and evil, light and darkness, civilization and barbarity". 〔註1〕 Ailing Zhang is a writer of the Chinese semi-colonial metropolis. In her fantastically brilliant but brief creative career—during and immediately after the Second World War—she has chronicled nothing less than the crumbling of "old" Chinese civilization, its monstrous modern emergence, and "the small men and women" in between. Alone and in exile, she died at the age of seventy-five in Los Angeles. Because of her appearance in Shanghai during the Japanese Occupation and her rebuttal of the tragic and heroic as seen befitting her times, she and her stories are more often regarded as the passing of a beautiful comet than anything that merits mention in Chinese literary history. Recently however, both her writings and writings about her are making a comeback. For instance, the publication of *Eileen Chang Reader* is underway by the University of California Press. 〔註2〕 In the following essay, I reflect on the

---

〔註1〕 Ke Ling, "An Embroidered Portrait of the Ten-Mile Playground (*Wei Shili Yangcang Xouxang*)," *China Daily*, Taiwan, January 9 1994. Quoted from Shao, Yingjian, *Romance Literature and Whispered Life* (*Chanqi Wenxe yu Liuyan Rensheng*), Beijing: Life/Books/New Knowledge the Three Unity Press, 1998.

〔註2〕 It is worth noting, though, that C. T. Hsia had recognized her talents and recommended her as one of the best Modern Chinese writers in his *A History of*

long due possibility of cross-cultural appreciation and understanding of her essays and fiction which arise from and are about the fissure between the ruins of civilizations.

I. Introduction: Ailing Zhang and the Revelation between the Ruins

In a time of low atmospheric pressure, a place of alienated soil, there is no fantasy, and no longing for the blossoming of wondrous flowers.

But the more important stories of life often crop up like accidents. They catch you unaware.

Fu Lei, "On the Fiction of Ailing Zhang," 2

This is how Fu Lei alludes to the mid 1940s, the milieu in which Ailing Zhang and her stories "crop up like accidents." The emergence of Zhang and her writing, like a wondrous flower, appears to many literary historians as a miracle rather than a natural growth. The splendor of the miraculous flowering, however, for them, also foreshadows its own more usual withering. Thus Fu, one of the most celebrated modern Chinese literary and art critics, warns Zhang and the reading public of the rarity of good endings for miraculous splendors in China. The dazzling charm of Zhang's *Shanghai and Hong Kong Stories*, for Fu, is in the fragile brilliance over-laden with the original sin of an alienated soil at a time of low atmospheric pressure, hence merits wary cultivation. The danger of its over-blossoming imperils the very chastity of the artistic muse, and Fu warns the reader that "to protect her is to protect yourself" (Fu, 419). Fu's judicious admiration of and, yet, profound unease with Zhang's uncanny effulgence has set the tone for the charting of Zhang's place in the memory of a literary posterity as the passage of a beautiful, but treacherous comet. 〔註3〕

Modern Chinese Fiction published decades ago. As this volume of *Annals of Scholarship* is going to press, Linda Norton informs us that the *Chang Reader,* edited by Karen Kingsbury will be ready for publication by Spring 2003.

〔註 3〕 Fu Lei. well-known modern Chinese translator, art and literary critic. Unless otherwise noted, all translations in the text are mine.

The unease with Zhang's exorbitant and vagarious appearance on the literary scene actually attests to the anxiety of the modern Chinese intellectuals about the beginning, the end, and the direction of their cultural modernity. Hence, her charm is also her undoing. When Fu lauds her as the delightful stylist that catches the literary scene unaware, he both offers her as a corrective to his fellow literary practitioners who are unduly preoccupied with the battle of "isms" and as a warning against the treachery of extravagant stylization which seems to inhere in an effeminate, decadent "Chinese" cultural tradition. Thus as a true guardian of the tradition set up by the "New Culture" movement since the May Fourth revolution in 1919, both Fu's fascination of and chagrin with Zhang's literary flowering predictably fall on the charm and "caprice" of her stylization, and on her limited "variations upon a theme" — "the defunct aristocracy or petty bourgeoisie entangled in the nightmares between man and woman" (Fu, 413).

Zhang's variations upon the modern Chinese theme seem to lack the tragic and heroic dimension, which according to Fu and his fellow cultural critics are the necessary constitutive properties of a redemptive modern Chinese literature. Thus it is not surprising to find that for all her dazzling brilliance, Zhang has literally no place in the modern Chinese literary history. 〔註 4〕Her literary exuberance/ extravagance seems to embarrass, if not to imperil, a laboriously instituted and vigilantly professed collective modern Chinese cultural memory, not only because of her unfamiliar stories, but also because of the troublesome ambivalence of her very literary emergence in the semi-colonial Shanghai under "Foreign (Japanese)" occupation. Even her most venerating feminist critics have hallowed her presence within the modern Chinese literary scene as a "desolate and reckless smile." 〔註 5〕

〔註 4〕 In the more official modern Chinese literary history, she is simply written off as a flower of evil, for the fact that she flourished as a stylist during the last two years of Japanese occupation.

〔註 5〕 In the "diasporic" Chinese literary circles, Zhang is more or less lauded as the exquisite stylist who is loved not only for her charming, feminine stories but also for her own sensational life story, except the serious critical attention paid to her by C. T. Hsia. The more recent critical studies on her works have been mostly written by mainland and overseas Chinese feminists. For example, see Men Yue and Dai Jing-hua, *Fuchu Lishi Dibiao (Emerging Out of the Historical Surface: Studies in Modern Chinese Literature by Women,*), "Na Changliang de Waner Yixiao (Ailing Chang: That Lonely and Reckless Smile)", 321-339.

To relegate Zhang's presence as a smile or an unwitting but beautiful passing is to underscore her difference, and for the "New" cultural critics, her impenetrable unfamiliarity. Zhang's choice of the limited variations upon one theme is by no means unwitting. "Literary folks generally prefer to concentrate on the heroic aspect of life and disregard the everyday and mundane," Zhang declares in "My Own Writings (*Ziji de Wenzhang*)." And "to stress the heroic is to aspire to the height of the superman ...", whereas "I dislike the sublime. I could do with the tragic, but prefer the desolate." 〔註6〕 Zhang's choice of the mundane disavows the monumentality of history, which the new Chinese cultural critics have transposed from the West. It is a radical re-vision, in Rey Chow's words, of a different modernity. 〔註7〕

> I have no wish to write history, and no right to direct or comment on the proper attitudes of historians. But I always hoped in private that they would pay more attention to the irrelevant details of life. Reality is not something one can systematize. It is more like the turning on of seven or eight loudspeakers at once, each sings by itself but somehow all mixed together. Only in the thick of such sound and fury, there sometimes comes to pass an instant of heart-rending illumination...

> (Zhang, "End of the Ember (Jin Yu Lu)," *Collected Works* 53)

But Zhang's radical re-vision is not simply a modernity of details that fragments the wholeness of history. She searches for the moment of illumination through the rupture of the ruins of human civilization; a wisdom for life against the odds of history, or, as Michel Foucault formulates it, an aesthetics of existence woven through an extravagance of textual details in the wandering narratives of her drifting heroines. If Foucault's formulation is a projection of a certain ideal but attainable practice of life, Zhang's schema is to procure through re-configurations of textual practice an art of historical and cultural existence for her displaced women. This is what most of her critics fail to understand in their veneration of her

---

〔註6〕 Zhang, *Zhang Ailing Wenji* (Collected Works of Eileen Chang), vol. IV, 173.

〔註7〕 Rey Chow, "Modernity and Narration in Detail," Woman arid Chinese Modernity: the Politics of Reading between West and East, Minnesota University of Minnesota Press, 1991, 84-120.

ingenious integration of a fiercely "Western" "modernist" sensibility and a formal, older, ephemerally "Chinese" "lyricism", in their appraisal of her excess of details and the intensity of her evocative verbal images. As Yvonne Zhang points out in her discussion of the "rage" over Zhang by contemporary Taiwanese "feminine" writers, that in their appropriation of "Zhang's peculiar sense of history" as cultural nostalgia, they have missed the poignancy, the "disconcerting truth" of "Zhang's caustic criticism of life in both the feudalist and Communist societies." In other words, Zhang's details and images and the history woven out of them are anything but "lyrical reminiscences." However, even as she takes serious notes of Zhang's "peculiar sense of history," Yvonne Chang also defines that sense as at best an acute self-consciousness of her own powerlessness, capsulated in the term "*wunai*," and filtered all too ephemerally through such aesthetic strategies as "poised evasiveness, passivity with heightened consciousness, and self-indulgence in subjective sentiments." 〔註 8〕

The texture of Zhang's aesthetics of existence, manifested in the structured, highly stylized over flow of details, does come from her "peculiar sense of history." However, its peculiarity and derivative aesthetic schema is not a choice of "*wunai*" (choice without choice) but a deliberate, brazen aside from the monumental variations on the modern Chinese theme. It is interlaced with her perspicacity into the traumatic complexities of modern Chinese life. Zhang's sense of history has been compared to that of the modernists, in the sense that her vision, like theirs, is relentlessly cast upon a post-war, post-civilization wasteland, and in the sense that "Modernism" is known for its attraction to the marginal, the exile, and the "other," for its "narrative of unsettlement, homelessness, solitude and impoverished independence." 〔註 9〕 It may not seem far amiss, then, to characterize Zhang as a modernist on the margins, since she seems to share modernism's obsession with

---

〔註 8〕 Sung-sheng Yvonne Chang, "Yuan Qiongqiong and the Rage for Zhang among Taiwan's Feminine Writers," *Gender Politics in Modern China*, ed. Tani E. Barlow, Durham: Duke University Press, 1993, 215-237.

〔註 9〕 See Chana Kronfeld's excellent work on marginality and modernism, *On the Margins of Modernism; Decentering Literary Dynamics*, Berkeley: University of California Press, 1997.

deviant atypical examples, with "the marginal as exemplary, in its choice of stylistic and intertextual models, in its   selection of paragons, and its thematics" (Chana Kronfeld 71). But the analogy stops here, and this is not only because Zhang's discordant minor tones are composed in major keys, as Kronfeld so eloquently describes marginal modernisms. Zhang may have shared the modernist sensibilities, but both her historical vision and aesthetic schema differ from the known properties of modernism significantly. In the course of her writing career, Zhang did not disclose self-conscious inclinations toward participation in any "international" modernism movement. And just as her vision of the modern world as wasteland is by no means apocalyptic, her aesthetics of existence is neither an aesthetics of marginality nor minimalist in its stylistic choices. In fact, one of the major critical complaints about Zhang's writing is her propensity for extravagant stylization, which is seen as a result of her all too-clear memory of a "traditionalist" "Chinese" cultural heritage that is at odds with the modern. 〔註 10〕 Her aesthetics derive directly from her peculiar vision of history and her cross-cultural heritage. It is excessive, "capricious," and defies categorization.

Zhang's aesthetics of existence, which favors the excessive, mundane minutiae of everyday life and what might be called moments of historical illumination, is woven into the ideal of the Clown Woman. A figure taken from the "lowly," vivacious Northern country "Bengbeng Opera", 〔註 11〕 it seems to resemble the modernist configuration of the marginal as exemplary. The figure is introduced in Zhang's "Forward to the Second Edition of *Romances* (Chuanqi Zaibanxu)." Despite her acclaimed "exquisite lyricism," Zhang is also notorious for her fascination with the "vulgar" art forms. Her "taste" is said to be that of the contrast between scarlet and garish green. In "Forward," she re-frames and re-centers her story collection   *Romances* (Chuanqi) with the "outdated Bengbeng opera" staged in Shanghai—with her own romance with the mini-drama of the

---

〔註 10〕 Fu, 417-18.
〔註 11〕 An old-fashioned popular country opera called "Bengbeng Xi (Bouncing Drama)", originated from north China. The genre is generally considered rustic and unrefined. It is not usually frequented by the literati.

Clown Woman: "I've always wanted to see it (Bengbeng Opera), at least once, but I can never find anyone to go with; I can't possibly confess and persuade anyone that I am actually interested in such vulgar pursuits. Only until recently I've discovered a Mrs. X whose family refused to stoop so low as to accompany her to see Zhu Baoxiao in the Shanghai heat, so we went together" (Wenji, *Collected Works*, Vol. IV, 135). The country opera is introduced with no apparent reference to the story collection but a clear awareness of the genre's humble origin and stubborn oddity of existence in the hyper-cosmopolitan colonial metropolis. It is introduced as a deliberate confession of a quest for the "low" community of irreverent women. In the narrative, Zhang re-presents the Bengbeng opera in primordial brutality, as the sound and fury of the wasteland that is overshadowed by its "trivial" prelude, which revolves around the irreverent and irrelevant singing of the Clown Woman. In fact, the meaning of the drama resides completely in the aside of the Clown Woman. In Zhang's structure of the mini-drama, the prelude—a farce starring the Clown Woman on the theme of husband murdering—is actually the centerpiece. In excessive detail and with the fierce preposterous witticism of the Clown Woman, it simply takes over. As the Taiwanese critic Zhang Jian points out in his appraisal of Zhang's stylistic cunning: "After all this, whether the husband is murdered, or the presence of the official-judge in the sedan chair, all seem rather pointless. What is left is the crude and Herculean woman! Only she emerges as the real master of the new barbarian world." [註12] Zhang's Clown Woman, however, is not Herculean. Her predominance comes not from mastery but from a tenacious irreverence to the rules of the game (she refuses on all account to answer the judge's question but irrelevantly insists on singing). She does not emerge as the master of the new world—after all, hers is only the sideshow, and she remains the clown, never the heroine—but a farcically insignificant wandering woman in-between. In an unusual move, Zhang has spelled out her role between the fissures of the new and old

---

〔註12〕 Zhang Jian, "Zhang Ailing de Zixuxing Xiaoxiaoshuo," Zhang Ailing Xinlun, ("On the ministories of Eileen Chang-Forward to the Second Edition of Romances, "New Commentary on Eileen Chang),Taipei: The Book Spring Publishers, 1996, 195.

barbarian world which serve as both the backdrop and center-stage of her *Romances*: "On the wasteland of the future, under the broken tiles and remaining walls, only the woman like the Clown Woman in the Bengbeng Opera can survive unscathed, anytime, anywhere, she makes it home" (*Collected Works*, 137). As the central metaphor of Zhang's romances of the drifting Chinese women between the modern ruins, the figuration of the ideal Clown Woman departs significantly from the modernist idealization of the marginal as exemplary. It does not poeticize the "marginality" of the wretched woman, but highlights her side-song. The meaning of her alterity, which is also the meaning of the mini-drama, results not so much from her in-betweeness as in her irreverent and irrelevant singing and insistence on disregarding the rules of the game. Zhang does not practice a poetics of marginally in her figuration of the Clown Woman, but an aesthetics of existence that hinges on her side song. This aesthetics is derived not only from the figure's historical alterity, but also her determined irreverence, from her peculiar wisdom developed between the fissure of the historical ruins. And this is how Zhang's central metaphor, as the revelation between the ruins, and as what makes sense and frames the narratives of her drifting women, should be understood.

II. Historical Alterity and the Freakish Wisdom of the Fallen Cities

Zhang is the writer of "fallen" cities. The fall of Shanghai actually occasioned her transient literary efflorescence. As Meng Ye and Dai Jinghua eloquently put it, the existential possibilities of the "fallen" cities is for Zhang a revelation of the "broken tiles and remaining walls" that re-emerge as the aftermath of historical catastrophe, not only about women, but also about a moribund Chinese civilization lingering on its death bed. 〔註 13〕But if Zhang's variations on the modern Chinese theme are centered on that revelation, they are never apocalyptic. Her ruins are the "broken tiles and remaining walls" which emerge as death and bespeak no regeneration. As the outcast daughter of an

〔註 13〕 Dai and Meng, 321.

opium-addicted, degenerate and doomed aristocracy, Zhang's nostalgia can best be described as a revelry in figuring the death of that aristocracy. She fancies the semi-colonial, fallen, and occupied "old" but lingering China as ruins upon which her desperate yet recklessly defiant heroines roam in quest for a living. Her backward gaze turns into a ruthless scrutiny, which is devoid of tenderness. It is always tinged with a desperate hatred, a hatred for the killing effect of that very past as well as its irreversible passing. Her fictional world, though often likened to an ephemeral and beautifully faded antique painting, 〔註 14〕involves, nonetheless, a relentless (self) critique, a bitter protest, and a probing reflection on an imposed and imposing Chinese modernity.

> People live in their times. But times sink like shadows, and one feels deserted, like an outcast. To prove one's existence, to grasp that last bit of the tangible and the essential, one has to resort to the memories of the old, resort to any memory of the times when one has lived. This, at least, is much more distinct and endearing than gazing into the future. Then, only then, she attains an extraordinary perception, an estranged familiarity with the surrounding world, sensing, suspecting that this is after all an absurd world of antiquity dark and brilliant at the same time. It is this embarrassment, this disharmony between reality and memory, that spawns the first slight but solemn tumult, that begins the fervent and earnest but nameless struggle. (Wenji, *Collected Works*, IV, 174)

Such speculations about time, memory, and the human struggle against history explain Zhang's variations upon the modern Chinese theme. Yet she is not writing an elegy. Zhang accepts the collapse of an "old" "Chinese" civilization in its traumatic encounter with the modern world as a matter of course. Her concern revolves around the possibility of a new beginning and survival of her female subject upon such ruins. Zhang's narrative use of "one" easily and categorically skips into that of "she." Her backward gaze illustrates her desperate but strategic recourse; she is fully aware that the renderings of history have placed her at odds

---

〔註 14〕 Chinese (sur)realist painting is characterized by fine brushwork and an almost exaggerated attention to details.

with both the present and the future. She turns the memory upon the ruins into a new beginning and survival of her female subject upon such ruins. Julia Kristeva argues that the alterity and estrangement of women flows from their relationship with language and from the desire for their privileged position within the symbolic, the "alterity within." 〔註 15〕Zhang's interest in her displaced, estranged and self-estranging heroines, however, is with history as catastrophic events and ruins. Like Kristeva, Zhang seeks, through a poetics of exile and (dis)location, the flash of an epiphany, that moment of striking perception, but her pursuit of the illumination does not rest with the *jouissance* of tongues or the infinity of language that woman as exile so readily and conveniently embodies. Zhang's fascination with estrangement and dislocation is part of the construction of an aesthetics of existence. Above all, she expresses a longing for that tumultuous epiphany which alone will compel the desperate but nonetheless defiant struggle for survival. It is her response to an historical displacement on the part of those who are like her: the "always already" displaced Chinese women.

Zhang's revelation between the ruins is not apocalyptic. In her world, death does not bring regeneration, and her remembrance of the past does not foster a reincarnation of what took place long ago or far away. She merely pieces together an assortment of split images, a pastiche of the disintegrating world for that moment of striking perception. It is simultaneously an epitaph and an overture. This is the quintessence of Zhang and her heroines' apparent nonchalant spatial and temporal movement: they seem to drift between the cracks left open by the collapse of an old civilization and the thrust of a semi-feudal, semi-colonial "modern" China, with that "not so healthy," but "curiously remarkable wisdom" ("Those Shanghainese," *Collected Works*, 20).

That wisdom comes only with the heroine (s) insistence on a historically placed but no less self-imposed estrangement. It is an aberrant and fantastic wisdom that is evident in the peculiar milieu of the fallen cities of Shanghai and Hong Kong—"a freakish fruit of the disharmonious intermingling of various deformities, new and

---

〔註 15〕See *Ethics, Politics and Difference in Julia Kristeva's Writing*, Ed. Kelly Oliver, New York Rutledge, 1993.

old" (*Collected Works*, 20). As the outcast daughter of the last of a dying breed, and a "modern" woman who drifts between the occupied and colonial metropolis, Zhang literally dwells on the very cutting edge of the crash and rupture between the moribund "old" Chinese civilization and its "modern" displacement from the colonizing West. Her stories are as much about the death of a civilization as they are about its aberrant "new" existence and the perilous possibilities that lie between. This is probably why they are no less farce than tragedy like in a "Peking opera," because "Chinese tragedies are usually farcical and noisy, full of lively clamor," and "in the operas even the most sad scenes are filled with brilliant, flaming colors" ("On Foreigner Watching Peking Opera," *Collected Works*, 26). Zhang's world is tragic, or rather pathetic, yet it is in a farcical way by no means an unsympathetic world. The wasteland of death is not rendered barren or minimalistically dreary. Rather it is minimalistically pinned down by an extravagance of colors, presented with a striking perception and the ripping agony of acceptance of an imposed "historical" "fate." The structure of Zhang's feelings as they emerge from the relationship between her heroines and their world is best captured in the passage describing Bai Liusu's sensation upon entering the hall in her family home, a big house in the concession of Shanghai in which her entire bankrupt gentry clan live together as refugees since the formation of the Republic:

> One can almost see in the hall along the high walls tall bookcases, darn red sandalwood with green engraved emblems. On the display table in the middle, inside a glass case, stands an enamelled Occidental grandfather clock whose mechanism has long stopped working. On its sides hang two scarlet scrolls of antithetical couplets, with gold longevity round flower background, each flower holds up one big dripping, inky character. In the dim light, every word seems floating in the air, far from the paper. Liusu feels like a character on the couplet herself, drifting, fluttering, far from the ground. ("Love in the Fallen City *(Qingcheng Zilian)*," *Wen* Ji, II, 53-54)

Liusu's "home" is a canopied, cloistered kingdom of decay, where the faded splendors of color only recall, pathetically, mockingly, the already desecrated sumptuousness of a past. With added layers of gray and dirt bestowed by modern history, the leftover colors of the past are inevitably stained and filthy, often menacing: "Beverly Nichols has a line about the haziness of the crazed: `In your heart sleeps the moonlight,' whenever I read it, I cannot help thinking about the blue moonlight on our ceiling, full of quiet murderous intent" ("Whispers (Liuyan)", *Collected Works*, 108).

Out of such colors Zhang emerges, like many of her heroines, with that "not so healthy" but "curiously remarkable wisdom," a wisdom of critical estrangement. She simultaneously embodies and defiantly struggles against the always already alien, always already exiled, and always already anomalous existence. But her re-coloring of that world is without self-pity. She has not only accepted her alterity, but deliberately, critically rewritten it: in a world where a woman can only live as daughter, wife or concubine, or mother and mother-in-law, she has refused all by becoming a stranger, a homeless wanderer. It is with such "dubious identity," such critical estrangement that Zhang scrutinizes her world and arranges the fate of her heroines in between its ruins.

A drifting narrative translates chilliness and quiet desperation into an "ephemeral" but nonetheless defiant and relentless aesthetics of dis-coloration, and dis-location. Zhang's drifting narratives, no matter how varied, are invariably variations on the theme of the "fallen" modern Chinese story. But her tales are seldom direct protests or outbursts of anger. Many have been wary of her "poise" and "evasiveness", of her indulgence in "ephemeral" details. Such lack of nakedness (Zhang loves clothes), of explosion, however, is by no means nonchalant. Zhang's stylistic "ephemerality" is only her structure of feelings—the reflective layering of a "chilling sadness" and "quiet agony" ("Poetry and Hallucination," *Collected Works,* 132), experienced and re-presented after witnessing the killing effect of the "modern" "Chinese" trauma, the pain and destruction it inflicts, and the discovery that the victims are "used to it."

III. The Historical Escapement: the Drifting Daughters between Shanghai and Hong Kong

The only resolution of Zhang's world seems to be its further disintegration, like a broken mirror, it has to be crushed to pieces. There are two kinds of species that populate its ghostly space: ephemerally beautiful and recklessly desperate women, and faceless, ageless men of eternal youth. 〔註 16〕 The men are ``infantile corpses soaked in distilled alcohol" (*Collected Works*,135)—in Zhang's structure of feelings, men as a species have no life or feeling, and therefore no presence, except as symbols and props of an endless farce. Her story is essentially one of crushing, of splitting and leaving behind, and men, as bodies and embodiments of that crushing world, are incapable of separation. They have no dreams therefore no longing, nor that sense of tumultuous uprooting which alone would compel them on a quest for a different existence.

Zhang's domain, then, is a world of women—her story are women's stories—which feminist critics have suggested are her unconscious attempts to create a fatherless world that symbolizes the crumbing of a whole civilization. Whether she does it deliberately or not, Zhang's world is an expanse of fatherless ruins. But her story of the displaced and floating Chinese women is not a re-telling of the maternal legend. In the crumbling but no less smothered kingdom, the mothers are either the "embroidered birds on the silk screen—a white bird nestling in the golden nest, vividly woven on melancholic purple satin. With the passage of time, the feathers are faded, molded, and eaten by worms; but even when it dies, it dies on the screen" ("Bitter Jasmine Tea," *Collected Works*, 54). Or they rule in place of the Fathers inside the canopied bed. However the mother on the bed does not rule like the legendary earth mother who exudes primordial love; instead, she wields her power like the absent (dead) Father, if not directly, through her sons and upon her daughters and daughters-in-law. Thus Zhang's stories of splitting, of *being* between the ruins only belong to the outcast daughters (add self-imposed, self-willed, rebellious and reckless). The strife between mothers and daughters, though, in Zhang's symbolic language structure, is not a replication of Freudian

---

〔註 16〕 Meng and Dai, 326-27.

complexes. Their battle is the struggle between the possibility of escape and its negation.

The daughters' story, however, is not simply one of escape. Unlike their counterparts in the stories of the May Fourth writers, Zhang's heroines' displacement and exile does not foretell the emergence of "modern women." Going places does not mean deliverance. In "Going Upstairs," Zhang warns her readers that the act of departing might very well be just going upstairs, "they will all come down when the dinner gong is struck" (*Collected Work*, 73). In Zhang's perception, the ruins outside the canopied bed embody a new barbarian world in which the daughter might dream of escape. Only those like the Clown woman, however, can live with their side song, irreverently and irrelevantly between its cracks, and attain that "not all together healthy, but curiously remarkable wisdom."

"The Embers of Eaglewood—the First Incense" is the first of Zhang's Hong Kong stories, the first weave in the fabrication of the romances of the Clown Woman. The story takes place immediately before the war, before the "fall" to Japan of the British colony of Hong Kong. "At the beginning of the story, Ge Wilong" is "an ordinary girl from Shanghai" (*Collected Works*, II, 1). Like many of Zhang's heroines, she is an ambitious but unlucky female descendent of the old and fallen Chinese gentry who, driven by (mis)fortune, has drifted to Hong Kong in search of new life and place. But the Hong Kong she finds is an even stranger place: looking out from the verandah of her aunt's grand mansion on top of the Hills, "the garden is like a gilded tray held abruptly out in the midst of the wilderness of the hills… Here not only the dizzy stark contrast of the colors seem fleeting and unreal—the contrasts appear everywhere; the blunt intermingling of different places and different times thrusts one into a phantasmagoric world" (*Collected Works*, II, 2). The phantasm, however, does not belong to the usual domain of traditional tales. It is the curious but unique phantom of the Colony. Wilong's aunt's house looks like the newest of the most modern "Western" cinemas but for its roof of mock-antique green "Chinese" tiles. The drawing-room, though furnished in the Western style, is not completely devoid of "Oriental" decorations: "But these Oriental colors are apparently garnished for the foreign friends. Since the English has come all the way to See China, one has to oblige. The China served here is the China dear to the heart of her Western friends: absurd, fragile and farcical" (ibid.). Wilong is fully aware that though new to the Colony, she cannot avoid becoming a reflection of its shadows: "Ge Wilong glanced at herself… she has also turned into bits of the Oriental colors. At the moment she is wearing the extraordinary uniform of the Nanying High School…in late Mandarin fashion; it is as though they wanted to dress all their girls as the late Dearer-than-the-Golden-Flower, or maybe it is only part of the Hong Song authorities' ploy to attract European and American tourists" 〔註 17〕 (ibid.).

Wilong came to Hong Kong initially with her family to avoid the "Fall" of Shanghai into the Japanese hands, and continues to stay for a better fortune away from her "fallen" but nonetheless "steadfast" parents. She dreams of escape and of starting anew in Hong Kong with her aunt. For Wilong, to appeal to her aunt's sympathy is by no means merely opportunist. The latter, an aging but active Socialite amongst the rich of the Colony, is herself a rebel of sorts: "You know who I am to your family? a self-willed sinner wallowing in degeneration; shame and disgrace to   the clan; refusing all the good families my brothers can find me only to become a concubine of Lian, humiliating my great bankrupt kindred…." (*Collected Works*, II, 9). Mrs. Lian wields vengeance upon her brothers to further her own fortune, not only in money but also in "love." She literally turns herself into the evil flower of Hong Kong. Wilong's escape appears a detour back to a new-canopied kingdom fostered under the shades of the Fragrant Colony. 〔註 18〕 After their first encounter, "She sees that her aunt is   a capable woman, who holds the giant wheel of time in one hand. In her own small world, she has saved the air of lewd luxury of the late Mandarins all to herself, like   the Dowager Empress behind the canopy" (*Collected Works*, II, 11). Wilong, however, has different aspirations. With unusual ingenuity and hardiness, she plans a life in between as a "new" "modern" "independent" woman by learning from her outwitting, decaying

---

〔註 17〕 Famous courtesan of the late Qing Dynasty, rumored to have pleased the German General during the invasion and occupation of Beijing by the troops of the Eight-Nation Alliance after the Boxer Rebellion.
〔註 18〕 In Chinese language Hong Kong means the Fragrant Harbor.

aunt, and within both the old and new barbarian world: "as to me, since I've walked into this ghostly world with open eyes. I've nobody to blame if I am possessed… But if I walk straight and stand erect, she'll have to deal with me in decency. Rumors are rumors, if only I just study hard…" (ibid.). Wilong's downfall, therefore, is not that she is complacent with her historical fate, that she has not planned and executed her own flight. It is rather that she has not grasped the odds against her historical escapement, that she has failed to comprehend the force of the "filthy, complex and inexplicable reality" (II. 17) of the new barbarian world which takes shape upon the ruins. Ni-er the servant girl has tried to initiate her into such wisdom:

> "It's not that I want to disappoint you… This is just high school, there is only one university in Hong Kong, even the college graduates can't find work. There are jobs, fifty to sixty Yen a month, like teaching in the elementary school of the Nunnery, being bullied by the foreign nuns all the time, it's really not worth it!"… "Don't be mad with me if I tell you something. For your own good, you'd better sharpen your eyes and catch someone while you are allowed out." Wilong sneered: "Among aunt's friends? They are either smooth young men like gigolos, or patriarchs with their own harem. Then there are the English soldiers, even them, anyone who is somewhere near a lieutenant will not mix up with us Yellows! And this is your Hong Kong! …" (*Collected Works*, II, 18- 19)

Wilong's folly is that she believes she can beat them at their own game. She is unwilling to repeat the life of her aunt, but the unwillingness is not enough to compel her out of the latter's kind of game. Lured by Hong Kong's glories and a new sense of freedom (to play), she becomes too fond of its trappings, and worse still, too fond of one of the male players. Wilong's final trapping is an inability to break loose from the conventions of love. In this new modern world, Wilong plays a traditional, romantic game of women's surrender, which, ironically, she sought to escape earlier. To sustain and pay for her hopeless `love' and lover/husband, Wilong gradually deteriorates into a high-class prostitute. Yet her story differs from the usual tale of betrayal of the innocent woman in the city of evil because of her acute perception and disconcerting self-awareness. More than once she tries to break free and start again: "I know I've changed. I never liked my old self, but even less the new I'll go back and begin afresh....It is easy to think that one can go back and begin a new person...a new life...but she is no longer so simple. Study hard and then look for a job is not necessarily the proper way out for a pretty but talentless girl like her.⋯Thus a new life means a new man...a new man?" (II, 41-42) Wilong has left home and tried to re-emerge in the new barbarian world upon the ruins, but she cannot achieve the status of the Clown woman, because on the new playground she places the old game. The survival of the Bengbeng Opera's heroine is dependent on her side song, which evokes the conventional wisdom, insists on its irreverence and irrelevance, and totally disregards the roles of the game. Wilong has perception but no illumination, whereas the latter alone can compel her to journey through the fissure of the ruins. Thus she voluntarily, almost ironically, embarks on her own sacrifice in the nightmarish entanglement between the ghostly man and ghostly woman. Wilong's journey concludes Zhang's first Hong Kong story and represents her first variation upon the "modern" "Chinese" theme.

"Love in the Fallen City" is the only one of Zhang's drifting narratives in which the daughter/woman achieves success in her historical dis(re)-location. However, the story is not a romance of the flight of the white bird out of the golden clouds on the embroidered screen, but rather a historical accident. The brutality of war destroys the infinitely intricate heavy screen allowing a dead woman to be "resurrected" by chance. 〔註 19〕 Not coincidentally, "Love in the Fallen City" is also one of Zhang's stories that displeases Fu most, not least because it is a romance without the serious and noble fatality of tragedy, which for him is the only proper genre for such great historical events as world wars and the destruction of civilizations. Zhang's writing, however, purports to embrace but only plays with this genre in a stylish cynicism. Rather it is the novella's plot line and narrative structure, which centers on a nightmarish entanglement between a man and woman

---

〔註 19〕 Dai and Meng, "Civilization, History, and Woman," 333.

that serves as an index for Fu's abhorrence toward the limited variations upon one theme. Furthermore, what irks Fu more is Zhang's insistence on not allowing any tragic dimension or "passion" in a love story with an almost apocalyptic background when combining world historical events with such a small man and woman, who with their "petty wisdom" cannot become tragic heroes (Fu, 411). Moreover, her insistence on not allowing them and the "history" they enact any redemption or catharsis in addition to her refusal to bring about the possibility of apocalypse—since there is not even "love" in this purported love story—appears problematic to Fu.

Many contemporary critics (if and when they paid any heed to Zhang and her writings) tend to read the story of Bai Liusu as that of a woman *in* history—a rewriting of the male legend in which a *femme fatale* topples the city. Thus, in their reading, the symbolism of the fallen city and its broken walls becomes the center of the narrative's signification. As is evident in the following prototypical quotation:

> …looking towards it, the wall is tall and imposing, without end. It looks craggy and cold, the colour of death. Her face is framed on the wall, and seems changed by contrast—red lips, moist eyes, and a flesh and blood face full of its own thoughts. Looking at her, Liuyuan said: "I don't know why this wall makes me think of the far away and the Long ago….one day, when our civilization is destroyed, when everything ended-burnt up, bombed, and collapsed, maybe this wall will remain. Liusu, if we meet then under this wall… Liusu, maybe you will be more sincere, and maybe I will be more sincere" ("Love in the Fallen City," *Collected Works*, 65)

Even Fu, who otherwise laments the "pettiness" of theme and over- sophistication of style of the novella, finds the paragraph briefly redeeming, as it unexpectedly but promisingly reveals that even Zhang is capable of glancing into the realm of the majestic. "In the novella, in the endlessly plain field there suddenly appears a vast sand storm. But like a sand storm, its tumult is instantaneous. When the feared destruction eventually comes and ends, Liuyan has only added upon his numb nerves some more fatigue. The moment of epiphany is long forgotten…" (*Fu,*

Collected Works, 411). On the other hand as Zhang's feminist critics, Meng and Dai see the symbolism as a rewriting of the myth of the earth mother, as an alternative modern apocalypse, even though they have perceptively pointed out earlier that Liusu's narrow escape is accidental rather than necessary. For them too, to focus on the most apocalyptic but very obviously uncharacteristic moment as the center of Zhang's otherwise irrelevant narrative, is to classify her rendering of history, civilization and woman as yet another, though different, male/patriarchal legend of the *femme fatale*/earth mother/whore woman, a reconstruction of the archetypal Troy-Helen mythos. Thus in their reading, Liusu's face, framed on the wall, though emphatically captured with its "flesh" and "blood" "red lips and moist eyes," is reduced to a body, whereas the dead gray craggy wall seems to have acquired some of her flesh color and a sinister, bloody life. For them it is upon such exchange of life and death that Zhang's modern apocalypse is written: on the back of the woman on the ruins man/human race is resurrected. In the reconstructed legend the cliche of the *femme fatale* is turned into an alternative earth mother, the Ark of human regeneration. Thus the story of the woman on the ruins becomes both a critique and a celebration of the human flight upon the back of the woman. It becomes, in its end, a sacred story. In their interpretation, though, Meng and Dai emphasize that Zhang's re-telling of the authoritative male myth about history/civilization/woman is not only ironic but also almost literally deconstructive. If, in the Homeric epic, Helen, as cause and trophy of the toppling of Troy, is absent from the narrative, Liusu is from beginning and end the omnipresent narrative center of Zhang's story. She is not only "present" but also the sole mover of the narrative action and consciousness.

However, even Meng and Dai's sympathetically perceived and exquisitely executed readings have missed the point of Bai Liusu's romance. To begin with, Liusu's story in the fallen city is by no means a sacred apocalypse—by the end of the narrative the woman has not rescued the human race from catastrophe. It is rather the calamities of war that have temporarily saved the woman from madness and destruction. The irony and deconstruction of the Helen/Troy mythos, on the other hand, is only the departure of Zhang's romance, not its culmination or denouement. Liusu's tale is not an anti-epic. It is an irrelevant story with an accidental ending. But for the calamities of history, Liusu would have repeated the destiny of Wilong or that of many an Ailing Zhang heroine. "The fall of Hong Kong has abetted her. But in this inexplicable world, who knows what is cause, what is effect? Who knows it is not just to complete her story that a city is toppled? Thousands die, and thousands suffer; then there are the earth-shaking changes. . . But Liusu has no sense of any particular place in that history. Smiling, she stood up and kicked the mosquito-repellent incense under the table... In the romances the femme fatales that topple the cities are always like this" (*Collected Works*, II, 84).

But Liusu is not a femme fatale (it is hard to miss the irony in Zhang's evocation of the cliche), in Zhang's romance the role is reserved for her foil, a self-acclaimed wandering Indian princess (who actually lives as a socialite and mistress to a rich English man). Instead, she is a divorcee driven out of her ex-gentry household by her bankrupt siblings, and has to win the battle with her prospective lover/husband with wit in order to find herself a place in the world. Her romance, in its sly tit-for-tat, its slight flirtation, its selfish calculation and its commonplace ending—marriage, is full of "petty' wisdom and truly mundane. Unlike Helen, she is no cause for the historical toppling of the city, nor has she any sense of place in that history, which, as eventful calamities, has gone ahead against or despite of her existence. Only in its ironic, indiscriminate destruction it has toppled the city for her and has aided unwittingly in her historical escapement. However, in her rather commonplace story, Liusu's lonely exodus seems tenacious, obstinate, if not heroic. Before the story begins, she has already escaped once. Against all odds she has divorced her depraved husband. But her flight then is only a flight "upstairs", or rather a detour back into the canopied backrooms of her mother's and her own original historical place. Liusu's second flight, her historic drift from Shanghai to Hong Kong is compelled but not without a reckless and relentless courage. The mother's house is seldom a sanctuary for the fleeing daughter, especially when her brothers share her inheritance. Liusu has to leave in order not to be absorbed back into the filthy scarlet background of the past with its faded golden drops. The (dis) relocation to Hong Kong is at least a gambling with chance, an attempt to take matters into her own hands: "Liusu's hands have never touched any chips nor the dice, but she also likes to gamble. She decides to gamble with her fate" (Collected Works, II, 60). At least she has nothing to lose.

Liusu's "slight" but "fervent and earnest struggle" is punctured by moments of illumination. But they are not instances of transcendence as grasped by critics like Fu (who tend to forget that the well-worn apocalyptic exclamation in the story is given by Fang Liuyan, the male protagonist who is only a prop in Liusu's story). What Liusu attains through her desperate drift between the fallen colonial metropolises is that "not so healthy" "but curiously remarkable wisdom." Before the flight, locked up inside her "own" home, the dilapidated but still there Bai Mansion, Liusu's feverish and bright eves see everything with a peculiarly sharpened focus:

> You are still young? But it doesn't matter here, here youth is no rare commodity. They have plenty of the young and the lively-children are born one after another, new bright eyes, new tender red lips, new wisdom. But as years go by they are worn out, the eyes darken, life darkens; with the birth of another generation, they are absorbed into the glittering scarlet background of the past splashed with golden drops, and the golden drops are the dim peeping eyes of the long dead. (*Collected Works*, II, 54)

Confined within the proximity of a present past, Liusu's vision may be tinted, but not without a peculiar wisdom. Familiarity with the "dim peeping eyes" of the ghostly past makes her skeptical of the possibilities for regeneration and revolving change. As she arrives at the Hong bong harbor aboard a Dutch passenger ship, Liusu has a sudden epiphany about the Fragrant Colony and her own traversal: "It was a fiery hot afternoon. The first things that caught her eye are the giant billboards, red, orange, pink, reflected in the green sea, patches and strips of hostile colors, rushing up, tumbling down, battling under water with unabated clamor. Liusu wondered if in this exaggerated city when one falls it will not be heavier than anywhere else. Her heart began to pound…" (*Collected Works*. II,60). Unlike Wilong, Liusu has no illusions about the Colony as her new playground or about her freedom to play. She understands with anguish and a sense of self-irony that she is playing the desperate old game on the new barbaric ruins, a nightmarish game Zhang insists as the only one available for most of her heroines—the outcast, disinherited, but relentlessly rebellious young gentry women who have the longing for but not the "skill" (Liusu's own words) to enter as players into their imposed modern game. Ironically, it is the brutal and endless barbarity of the modern ruins which Liusu apprehends upon her arrival, and which eventuates in its most drastic form on the eve of her re-ascent "upstairs," that has momentarily saved her from her "fate." For all her superior understanding, delicacy of feeling and intricate maneuvering, she has lost the battle and become Liuyan's mistress. It is the war that dramatically destroyed her new house "upstairs" and halted her in her re-absorption back into the bloody scarlet background of the long dead. But her ending does not bring regeneration. Zhang does not grant modern barbarity or the savagery of history apocalyptic redemption for the human race. Not least for her outcast, displaced and devastated heroines. What Zhang is willing to allow her headstrong and struggling heroine, between the fissure of the ruins, is a flash of illumination, a moment of tenderness and a mundane denouement—wartime marriage with uncertain endings:

> Liusu sits up and wraps herself in the quilt, listening to the mournful wind. She knows the grey brick wall near the Fresh Water Bay must still be there, towering and indifferent.... Drifting, as in a dream, she walks towards it's depth, and sees Liuyan coming rushing. She's finally met him...She suddenly climbs beside Li uyan, separated by his comforter; nestles against him. He holds out his hand and grabs hers. Instantaneously they seem to see through each other. It is only a flashing moment of complete under-standing, but the moment, the flashing instant is enough for them to live harmoniously for ten or eight years. (Wenji, *Collected Works*, II, 82)

At the moment of mass destruction, in the narrow space between death and the lowest form of existence, men and women seem finally leveled to an equal footing.

That is the only ground for Liusu's euphoria. What Zhang is willing to grant her drifting heroine at the end of an atrocious human destruction is nothing more than "ten or eight years" of mundane existence. But it is a new assignment not without dignity. And that hard-won, scanty dignity is not without Liusu's own agency. Her romance offers no catharsis of redemption, either for herself or mankind. After all, as yet another aside of the denouement of her story, the smart, shrewd, but repressed Mistress Four figures she should also divorce her good-for-nothing husband—if Liusu has done so well, how can anyone blame others for following suit? "Liusu stoops down in the shadow of the lamp and lights the mosquito-incense. Thinking about Mistress Four, a smile flickers on her face" (II, 84)

Liusu, in her euphoria of a momentarily mundane existence, is not a Bengbeng Opera heroine, though in some respect she is like the Clown Woman who insists on her irrelevant story, on singing the side song, on irreversibly and relentlessly crossing the rules of the game. Zhang, in her construction of the aesthetics of dislocation, an aesthetics between the fissure of the ruins, has relegated the role to a different kind of woman, or perhaps more accurately, to a different class of women. After all, the Bengbeng opera and its playing women belong to the margins of the "cultivated" society: they entertain the plebeian. In that setting, Liusu and her fellow "gentry" female travelers can only be its chance visitors. For all the devastating tumbling and endless dislocation between the ruins, Zhang concludes with her sympathetic relentlessness, they are incapable of complete separation from their cultivation, from that intricately enclosed moonlit high ceiling "full of quiet murderous intent," as   Liusu cries out aloud to Liuyan: "It is much better like that, seeing it for the first time. No matter how wicked, how filthy, it is people outside, things outside. But suppose you grow up inside, with it everywhere around you, how can you tell which are they, which are you?" (II, 66)

IV. The "Clown Woman" among the "Broken Tiles and Remaining Walls"

In contrast, A Xiao, like most of Zhang's drifting heroines, is adept. But unlike them, she is an outsider of the waned but still glaring scarlet background: a Shuzhou maid in the foreign concession of Shanghai. "The Osmanthus Heat: A Xiao's Autunm Lament " 〔註20〕 is one of the few stories in modern Chinese literary history *of* a servant woman. The clever, wry, impervious A Xiao is not only the focus but also the eye and conscience of Zhang's narrative, which moves with and is filtered through the structure of her feelings and perception. A Xiao's narrow, long eyes pass through, observe, register, and scrutinize the incongruous existential possibilities of the wartime semi-colonial Shanghai through and around the kitchen of her English master.

Unlike Zhang's gentry heroines, A Xiao is incapable of nostalgia. She is a fiercely self-proclaimed urbanite: "To cope with the wartime restriction of running water, every household has acquired a day water jar, and on its sauce-yellow surface there is painted a light-yellow dragon. Any woman who sees herself in the water somehow looks like an ancient, classic beauty. But A Xiao is an urban woman, she'd rather take a peep at herself in the broken pocket mirror (taken from a purse) pasted on the powder green wall beside the door" (*Collected Works,* I, 175). A Xiao's non-relation to "old" cultural memory and her peculiar urbanity as a waged nanny in the metropolis is enforced. The only link between her and the old country from which she is permanently dislocated, since her employment as a servant in the city, is her limited economic exchange with her mother, who neither acknowledges her common-law husband nor her son (it is rather significant to note that A Xiao and her husband did not go through any accepted ritual of marriage). The absence of cultural ritual is ensued by qualifications of her institutional status as a wife and a woman—both her son's and her own livelihood depend solely on her servitude: "Looking at Baisun, her heart is filled with a widow's sorrow even though she has her man, and it's better than having none, she has to depend on

---

〔註20〕 "Osmanthus Heat" is a vernacular expression used in Shanghai to refer to the humid and hot days at the beginning of autumn.

herself' (I,184). But A Xiao's lament entertains no illusion about the age-old institution of marriage: "at the same time she finds it rather tasteless to mull over it. After all her son has grown so big, why sulk? If her man cannot support her, even if they are wed in red regalia he also doesn't have to do it. Who can she blame if she is born to be busy? The money he earns can hardly sustain himself. Sometimes he has to borrow her money to join the guild" (I, 185) A Xiao's lament about and adamant clinging to her peculiar urbanity is her fervent though slight struggle amid the harsh incongruities of an imposed "modern" life where neither the old nor the new offers a woman of her kind any respite or alleviation. But it is also such relentless existential possibilities that make her wise. Surpassing all other Zhang heroines, A Xiao is an irreverent but expert interpreter of the phantasmal realities of the colonial metropolis, even in moments of despair she maintains her independence of judgment.

Armed with her curiously remarkable wisdom, A Xiao observes with shrewd perception the world of the new barbaric ruins which has brought her and her nauseatingly petty but suave English master together. In their relation of master and servant, A Xiao is certainly the one for whom understanding and judgment is reserved. For A Xiao, her master's house is very much the epitome of the fallen, incongruous realities of the semi-colonial China, and his petty quotidian life is similar to those of the other ordinary, small-time colonials. Characteristic of Zhang's "cinematic blown-up of details" (Rey Chow), A Xiao sums up her master with wry, cutting humor and irreverent, exaggerated minutiae: "the flesh on the master's face is like a piece of medium-rare steak, reddish with blood strips. What with the newly cultivated mustache, his face looks like a particularly nourishing half-hatched egg, with little spots of yellow wings visible." And his bedchamber "is filled with knickknacks, like the boudoir of an upper-class white Russian whore, who has pecked pieces of brunches and leaves of China to decorate her nest" (I, 1176-180). A Xiao's biting perception of her master is far from personal venom, nor is it merely the judgment of a merciless sharp-eyed, sharp-tongued woman. Her assessment of him also reflects her attitude towards the fallen condition of the new ruins and the context of his being there : "(quoting him) `Shanghai is really getting worse! The Chinese, even the servants have learnt how to cheat and bully the foreigners!' But if he is not in Shanghai, all foreigners in their own, real foreign places have to go fight each other, he would be long dead!" (I, 181).

A Xiao, with her wry wisdom and irreverent judgment, is the interpreter of Shanghai's semi-colonial realities. Her vision is confined, irrelevant, by no means Godlike, and her lament does not aspire to any wasteland profundity. Both A Xiao's wisdom and sadness are limited, and her frustration is most often about the daily defeat of her life between the margins of her futile ambition to maintain a basic dignity for living. As A Xiao scrutinizes, ponders and labors through the irritating and incongruous life in wartime Shanghai, she is angry, defeated but nonetheless benevolent. Her benevolence extends not only to her fellow servant women, her son, her ne'er-do-well husband, but also to her rather unsavory English master, and the whole train of his pathetic foreign and Chinese consort women. It is as though with her peculiar perception from the margins she has `seen through' the existential state of herself and her fellow creatures. Her vision is with distance but not transcendence. Amid her myriad lamentations, A Xiao has achieved a certain dexterous art of life between the fissures of the ruins. It is a dexterity of a very limited kind, as her life story, including her acute perception and fierce independence of judgment, is filtered through the typical Ailing Zhang "trivialized and privatized affective structure" (Chow,116). Like "Love in the Fallen City," A Xiao's relation with and perception of the "Fallen City" is always and only through her kitchen and her master's apartment building. World historical events—World War II, and the fall of the city, are only pervasive but secondary clamors to A Xiao's daily lamentations. Thus by its very design her story is insignificant. It is irrelevant to the ragings of *history out there*, except as something they insouciantly, ruthlessly impinge upon. Tumbled along and thrown between the "historical" ruins, A Xiao laments but reserves her judgment. Her lamentation is not nostalgic, nor has it any hint of self-pity. She laments, by way of the daily irritations of the incongruities of life in wartime Shanghai, within the confines of her English master's apartment rooms, the *fallen* conditions of "modern" Chinese life. As for herself she has made do with irreverence and remarkable wisdom. What she has achieved, in the relentless "heat" of the war-ravaged, occupied metropolis, is nothing less than living with perceptive and dignified benevolence.

It will not be far amiss, then, to assume that it is through the ingenuity of A Xiao's art of life, that Ailing Zhang has woven her aesthetics of existence for her drifting heroines between the fissures of the ruins. After all, she has declared rather unequivocally, that "the woman who prevails in the new barbarian world is not the wild rose that everybody imagines, with big black fiery eyes, tougher than man and always wipe in hand, ready to strike, ...On the wasteland of the future, under the broken tiles and remaining walls, only the woman like the Clown Woman in the Bengbeng Opera can survive unscathed, anytime, anywhere, she makes it home" (*Collected Works*, 137). A Xiao, with her critical but non-transcendent vision and her cunning for life, is closest to Zhang's ideal of the Clown Woman. And her vision closest to Zhang's own. As previously noted, Zhang's place in relation to her heroines and their miniature drama is not that of the stage director but that of the voice-over. 〔註21〕 It is a voice-over simultaneously offstage and enmeshed with the voices of her center stage characters': a critical scrutiny as well as a sympathetic echo of their slight but tumultuous struggle, of their "curiously remarkable wisdom." It is a voice-over woven in and out of the side song of the Clown Woman, in the figuration of an historical aesthetics that depend upon her irreverent but insistent singing. The insistence on voice, on singing tenaciously aside, is the quintessence of Zhang's aesthetic schema and historical vision. It makes her ideal of the Clown Woman and the narrative of her drifting heroines as an aside from the stereotypical figuration, both by contemporary critics and classical modernists, of "marginal prototypes," which is always ready to be re-absorbed by an invisible center. 〔註 22〕 Zhang's voice, over but with the voices of her (non)heroines', persistently irreverent and emphatically "trivialized," is nonetheless critical and visionary in the midst of the sound and fury of the variations upon the "modern" Chinese theme. What she offers, brazenly and obstinately, is a critique, and a vision, of the historical condition of Chinese modernity and its manifold life and death

---

〔註21〕 Yu Qin, "Zhang Ailing zhuanlue, ("Biographic Sketches of Eileen Chang," *Wenji*, (*Collected Works*,) IV, 430.
〔註22〕 Kronfeld, 225-26.

minutiae for some of her female and other non-heroic fellow beings; a critical vision made all the more poignant for its desolate defiance and non-transcendence, for its contemporary as well as posterior receptive misconception. After all, even though she is declared the next seeker (of the truth of Chinese modernity) after Lu Xun (Yu Qing, *Works*, IV, 430) her search is not for the direction of History but an aesthetics of existence between the historical ruins. Zhang's aspiration, like that which she charts for her desolate but ambitious heroines with their inexorable longings to make it, is that of the Clown Woman, who never tries to master history but defies its catastrophes.

Chinese Modernisms

S. H. Donald, Yi Zheng

Political and Cultural Modernity

The following short account of Chinese modernisms is neither complete nor without contention, but we do hope that three useful starting points will emerge. First, the modern is and has always been a political project, or a series of projects that emerge as part of a seismic shift in the way in which a social world experiences itself and the encroachments of the wider world, but also a direct result of action and decisions made by a new generation of intellectuals and artists. In China, the role of the intellectual has been closely related to political innovation and that relationship cannot be laid aside in literary history. Second, despite the political impetus to much of what we describe below, and much else besides, one must also recognize as independently valuable the aesthetic adventures on which so many writers, artists, and film-makers embarked over the1920s-1940s. Whether or not one subscribes to the tendencies and groups as coherent movements, or as literary adventurers and enthusiastic experimenters, the best of the work of the period has had powerful effects on contemporary art and literary practice and provides startling aesthetic links across the phases of twentieth-century history and back into the imperial past. Third, the role of film in the shaping of a modern sensibility in China is a subject that we do not address here to the degree that the medium deserves, although it has been discussed in more detail elsewhere. 〔註 1〕 We would therefore ask the reader to account for film in the Chinese modern, when pursuing the subject beyond this introduction. Finally, we acknowledge that the Chinese modern has had a separate rendition across the years between the Socialist Liberation in 1949 and1980. This revolutionary modernity and its accompanying aesthetics are, however, so discrete from the Chinese modern of the early twentieth century that it would take a longer work to justice to this complexity. Again we can only exhort the reader to bear in mind not only the current Reform era, but also the works of revolutionary consciousness (including, for example, the poster art of the 1950s-1970s) when investigating the formations of modernity in Chinese art and literature of the past century.

It is impossible to separate key periods of Chinese sociopolitical change from the modernist interventions of Chinese artists, writers and scholars. From the early rnodernity of the late Qing dynasty (1644-1911) to the Reform era of today (1976-), highly charged debates on China's place in the modern world have been coterminous with cultural practice and political activism. And, while the contemporary avant-garde is not always as radical as one might expect, nonetheless, the habit of discussing politics through art continues. As a rule of thumb, there is a continuity across Chinese modernist experiments in literature and aesthetic theory that reiterates and critiques China's perceived mistakes on the political scale, however contradictory. On this trajectory, China's mistakes include succumbing to colonial interference from the West, resisting the benefits of modernization through the key decades of 1950-80, and then falling headlong into the consumer modern in the Reform era. 〔註 2〕

〔註 1〕 S. H. Donald and P Voci, 'China: Cinema, Politics and Scholarship; in J. Donald and M. Renov (eds), *The Sage Handbook of Film Studies* (London: Sage, 2008): 54-73.

〔註 2〕 See Shu-mei Shih, *The Lure of the Modern: Writing Modernism in Semicolonial China*, 1917-1937, (Berkeley: University of California Press, 2001), and Xudong Zhang, *Chinese Modernism in the Era of Reforms* (Durham, NC: Duke University Press, 1997).

Despite the seeds of modern thinking evident in the poetry of the nineteenth century, the painting of the Ming (1368-1644), and their materialization in the political thoughts of Kang Youwei and Liang Qichao in the 1890s, 〔註3〕 extant histories generally cite the New Culture movement (1917) as the beginning of cultural modernity in China. The New Culture movement was an intellectual cultural revolution culminating in the May Fourth (1919) student protest against the Treaty of Versailles and the continuing influence of Japan in China's trade and current affairs. 〔註4〕 Here we would concur with those such as David D. W. Wang who consider the modern to date from the Qing period, 〔註5〕 while noting that the literary scholar and historian Wang Hui traces modernity's economic and cultural emergence in China to a much earlier period—to to late Ming and the last Chinese imperium. 〔註6〕 Wen-hsin Yeh, on the other hand, emphasizes that the spread of modernity in China rested on material and cultural change in the everyday sphere, which arose from gradual industrialization and new forms of urban organization. There was no single revolutionary moment prior to 1949 when the world turned upside down. 〔註7〕

Nevertheless, most historians and interpreters of Chinese modernity agree that certain events since late Qing (roughly the mid-nineteenth century) have imposed a

〔註3〕 See Kang Youwei, Ta T'ung Shu: *The One-World Philosophy of K'ang Yu-wei*, trans. Laurence G. Thompson (London: Allen & Unwin, 1958); Teng Ssu-yu and John K. Fairbank, *China's Response to the West: A Documentary Survey, 1839-1923* (Cambridge, Mass.: Harvard University Press, 1979); Liang Qichao, *History of Chinese political thoughts during the early tsin period*, trans. L.T. Chen (New York; ams Press,1969) , Liang Qichao, 'Selections from Diary of travels through the new world', trans, Janet Ngt, Earl Tai and Jesse Dudley, Renditions, 53-4 (Spring-Autumn 2000), 199-213.

〔註4〕 Wang Yao, *Zhongguo xinwenxueshi chugao* (A Draft History of New Chinese Literature); Hong Kong: Bowen shuju,1972), Lin Yushen et al. (eds), May Fourth: A Multi-Angled Reflection (Hong Kong: United Publishers, 1989).

〔註5〕 Wang David Der-wei, *Fin-de-Siècle Splendor: Repressed Modernities of Late Qing Fiction, 1848-1911* (Stanford, Calif.: Stanford University Press,1997); see also Jon Kowallis, The Subtle Revolution: Poets of the `Old School' During Late Qing and Early Republic China (Berkeley: Institute of East Asian Studies, 2006).

〔註6〕 Wang Hui, "Dao Lun (Introduction)", in *Zhongguo xiangdai sixiang de xingqi* (`The Rise of Mode Chinese Thought), 4. Vols (Beijing: Sanlian Shudian, 2004), 1-102.

〔註7〕 Wen-hsin Yeh, "Introduction"; in Yeh (ed.), *Becoming Chinese: Passages to Modernity and Beyond* (Berkeley : University of California Press, 2000), 1-30.

direction upon how the modern is experienced and understood. The Opium Wars, also known as the Anglo-Chinese Wars, lasted from 1839 to 1842 and 1856 to 1860 respectively. China's defeat in both wars forced the Qing court into signing the Treaty of Nanking and the Treaty of Tianjin, also known in China as the Unequal Treaties. These agreements included provision for the opening of additional ports to foreign trade, for fixed tariffs, and the secession of Hong Kong to Britain. The British also gained extraterritorial rights. Several countries followed Britain and sought similar agreements with China. Many Chinese found this situation humiliating, and such sentiments are considered to have contributed to the Taiping Rebellion (1850-64), the Boxer Rebellion (1899-1901), and, eventually, the downfall of the Qing dynasty in 1911. 〔註 8〕 Thus, it is understandable that, while modernity and attendant modernisms were well under way in the nineteenth century, their provenance and context made it preferable to nominate a later inception, which could allow for radicalism without any imperial content. However, there was strong modern opposition to national humiliation far earlier than 1919.

The first collective political and intellectual response to the challenge of Western military and technological superiority was the Self-Strengthening movement (1860s-1870s). This arose when a number of Chinese officials and intellectuals became convinced that China needed to adopt the technologies and military practices of the West if it were to remain a sovereign state. From the 1860s to the 1890s, the Qing court instituted reforms designed to achieve these goals. Furthermore, the defeat in the First Sino-Japanese War (1894-5) convinced radical thinkers that sociopolitical changes were needed if the technological and military advancements were to succeed. Their response was the Wuxu Reform, or the Hundred Days' Reform, a 104-day national cultural, political, and educational reform movement in 1898, led by Kang Youwei and Liang Qichao. The reformists advocated the imitation of measures taken in Japan and Russia regarding how best to manage political and social systems under imperial power. Their efforts ended in failure with a coup d'état, the Coup of 1898, by powerful conservative opponents.

〔註 8〕 J. Mason Gentzler, *Changing China: Readings in the History of China from the Opium War to the Present* (New York: Praeger, 1977).

Despite the immediate disappointment, this failed reform did lead to far-reaching institutional and cultural changes. The most influential was the abolition of the Imperial Civil Service examination (1905), which until that point had determined the membership of the ruling class and the structure of the bureaucracy, and was the bedrock of the imperial system of officialdom. As a replacement to the examination system, the Qing government started building what they understood to be modern colleges. There were 60,000 of these by the time of the Republican Revolution in 1911. Meanwhile, the constitutionalism campaign started out with an elaborate outline of constitutionalism but ended with an already powerful prince (from the Qing imperial line) being chosen as prime minister, and seven out of the thirteen members of the cabinet being drawn from the imperial family. Radical constitutionalists changed their political methods after this failure, supporting revolution instead of constitutionalism in their effort to save the nation. Despite their limited success, these reform measures, plus the formation of new, Western-style, modern armies and rampant anti-Manchu (non-indigenous ruling class of the Qing) sentiment, were important precedents to the Xinhai Republican Revolution, which began with the Wuchang Uprising on October 1911 and ended with the abdication of Emperor Puyi on 12 February 1912. The Xinhai Revolution effectively ended the Qing dynasty and millennia of powerful imperial rule. It is generally considered to have ushered in a new era and marked the beginning of Chinese political, economic, and cultural modernity.

Concurrent with these political and social upheavals, radical advocacy for cultural reform augmented the sense of crisis. There were those who questioned traditional Confucian values and facilitated the introduction of Western ideas through translation, both sentiments in turn supported by the rise of journalism and changing social expectations towards literature. The latter in particular resulted in the late Qing-early Republican boom in fiction as political tool and social critique. Of most lasting consequence to modern Chinese cultural history in both literary and visual domains, and including revolutionary modernism and post-revolutionary postmodernism, was the beginning (1895-1911) of what later became the Vernacular (baihua) movement of the 1910s and 1920s. In October 1919, the

National Federation of Education Associations called for the government to sanction educational use of the vernacular language, instead of classical Chinese. In the first half of 1920, the Ministry of Education ordered that the written vernacular replace classical language in all grades of primary school. There are no exact equivalents to the magnitude of this shift, but Europeans might compare the move from Latin to the local vernacular as a primary form of written communication, and Arab speakers could reference the gap between modern spoken Arabic and the language used in classical Arabic scripture and literary texts. In all these cases, contemporary users of the older language must undertake instruction and long years of effort to access their written heritage. Likewise, older systems excluded all but the most privileged readers.

May Fourth and Modernist Beginnings

The years immediately following the1911 Revolution are remembered as a series of failed promises. The resulting de facto warlord governments (1916-27) proved no more promoters of modernization than guarantors of national interests. Recently, however, scholars have argued that there were elements of democratization evident in the leadership of some local power brokers, and indeed point out that 'warlordism' is a term that suits the historical perspective and self-legitimization of the Chinese Communist Party. Frank Dikotter has suggested, indeed, that the history of warlordism is 'counterfactual' and that a genuine comparison with the Qing era and the post-1949 period would suggest that 'dispersed government' was far from perfect, but not as much a failure as generally opined. ﹝註 9﹞ Furthermore, Louise Edwards has suggested that the gendered politics of the period were superior in some ways and some places to the generalized assumptions of chaos and corruption sustained through historical summaries written after 1949. ﹝註 10﹞

﹝註 9﹞ Frank Dikotter, *The Age of Openness: China Before Mao* (Hong Kong: Hong Kong University Press, 2008), 7-14.
﹝註 10﹞ Louise Edwards, *Gender, Politics and democracy: women's suffrage in China* (Stanford: Stanford University Press, 2008)

With these caveats in mind, and recognizing that the history of the May Fourth movement is a legitimizing foundation of the Chinese Communist Party and is therefore politically sacrosanct, some of the historical given are still warranted. The main issue that young intellectuals held against the federal system was continuing weakness in the face of foreign powers, and poor integration of regional and national interests. It was against this background of disenchantment that the intellectual revolution, the New Culture movement (1917), began. It was led by intellectuals who had decided that political reform should be preceded by a far-reaching cultural enlightenment. Thus, they held up for critical scrutiny nearly all aspects of Chinese culture and tradition. Inspired by alien concepts of individual liberty and equality, and the ideals of democracy and science, they sought a far more serious reform of China's institutions than that which had resulted from the self-Strengthening movement and the early promise of the Republican revolution. They directed their efforts particularly to China's educated youth.

Young Chinese fury at the concessions to Japan embedded in the Treaty of Versailles, and especially at the continuation of colonial rule in Shandong Province, culminated in what was later called the May Fourth Incident. The anti-imperialist student protest which began on 4 May 1919 became a major cultural and political movement. It was no less than an attempt at a combined intellectual and sociopolitical movement to achieve national independence, the emancipation of the individual, and a just society. These huge aims were to be achieved through the modernization of China. The movement's leaders operated under the assumption that intellectual changes would lead to modernization through an embrace of intellectual, artistic, and industrial development. 〔註11〕 In reality, although the movement's iconoclastic attack on the socially fragmented, hierarchical structure of Chinese society may have contributed to the eradication of cognitive and social barriers to the consolidation of a nation state and to domestically driven industrialization, it was at heart a cultural revolution. Most significantly, although variously characterized as a Renaissance, the Chinese Enlightenment, or a

---

〔註11〕 Chow Tse-tung, *The May Fourth Movement: Intellectual Revolution in Modern China* (Cambridge, Mass.: Harvard University Press, 1960), 338-55.

Romantic Era, 〔註 12〕 the movement led to the embrace of Marxism both in the cultural sphere and as a political ideology. May Fourth is now considered the foundational cultural legacy of the second revolutionary war and victory, which established the People's Republic of China in 1949.

Cultural iconoclasm was a key mobilizing force within the events and activities of the movement. Passionate critiques of Confucianism, traditional customs and habits, oppression of women, superstition (*mixin*), and the ethical system of ritual (*li*) dominated the cultural debates and were the major themes of literary creation. They were aided by 'translingual practices' that translated, appropriated, and transformed Western ideas, systems of thought, and cultural forms. 〔註 13〕 While major universities, notably Peking, served as the location for the intellectual ferment, journals such as New Youth (1915-26), edited by Hu Shi and Chen Duxiu, functioned as the foundational forums for the New Culture movement, promoting science, democracy, and vernacular literature.

Modernist experimentation in literature and aesthetic thought was central to the May Forth movement. 〔註 14〕 European and Japanese modernist writers had been translated and introduced to China from the beginning of the twentieth century. Modern Chinese literature is indeed self-defined as a component part of world literature. And while key figures of both the New Culture movement and

---

〔註 12〕 Vera Schwarcz, *The Chinese Enlightenment: Intellectuals and the Legacy of the May Fourth Movement of 1919* (Berkeley: University of California Press, 1986).

〔註 13〕 Lydia H. Liu, *Translingual Practice: Literature, National Culture, and Translated Modernity—China, 1900-1937* (Stanford, Cali#: Stanford University Press, 1995).

〔註 14〕 Kirk Denton, *Modern Chinese Literary Thought: Writings on Literature 1893-1945* (Stanford, Cali: Stanford University Press, 1996). As Denton shows, there have been different waves of modernist movements in art, architecture, cinema, literature, and aesthetic theory in China since the beginning of the twentieth century. This present chapter focuses on the early twentieth-century Chinese modernist aesthetic and literary practices with brief discussions of their fin-de-siècle revival as a post-socialist avant-garde movement. For comprehensive accounts of Taiwanese modernist literature in relation to the cultural history of Taiwan, see David Der-wei Wang and Carlos Rojas (eds), *Writing Taiwan: A New Literary History* (Durham, NC: Duke University Press, 2007); Sung sheng Yvonne Chang, *Modernism and the Nativist Resistance: Contemporary Chinese Fiction from Taiwan* (Durham, NC: Duke University Press, 1993).

New Chinese literature such as Lu Xun and Guo Moruo are claimed as defining figures in the more dominant modes of social realism and Romanticism in received histories, they should be simultaneously credited as modernist in their aesthetic vision and formal practices. 〔註 15〕

Modernist invention was significant in the years after the May Fourth movement. In 1920 Tian Han and Shen Yanbing, through the journals *New Youth* and *Transformation*, introduced neo-Romanticism as the newest development in modern Western literature. 〔註 16〕 They observed that, since the end of the nineteenth century, while capitalist material civilization had become highly developed, its social limitations were also apparent. The First World War was, in their opinion, the culmination of the social decay of capitalism. It led to a need for spiritual consolation rather than material wealth. This was for them the social-historical raison d'etre of neo-Romanticism. Their position is especially interesting from the perspective of contemporary Chinese art practice, where the Reform era now evidences some dissatisfaction with wealth-based value systems and a generation of young people disillusioned with a post-ideological existence.

Neo-Romanticism was a reaction to nineteenth-century Naturalism, and emphasized the symbolic representation of the subjective and mythical realms of life. It was subsequently referred to as aestheticism, literature of decadence, and Symbolism, and its essence was epitomized for Chinese neo-Romantics by the works of Charles Baudelaire, Paul Verlaine, Arthur Rimbaud, and Stephane Mallarme. Futurism, Expressionism, Dadaism, Imagism, Surrealism, all followed the defeat of Naturalism. 〔註 17〕 Shen Yanbing (Mao Dun) in particular emphasized that the set path for the New Chinese Literature was neo-Romantic. He argued that if modern Chinese literature were to join the literatures of the

---

〔註 15〕 Marston Anderson, *The Limits of Realism* (Berkeley: University of California Press, 1990); Leo Oufan Lee, *The Romantic Generation of Modern Chinese Writers* (Cambridge, Mass.: Harvard University Press, 1973).

〔註 16〕 Tian Han, `Xinlangman zhuyi jiqita' (`Neo-Romanticism and Other Things'), *Youth of China,* 1/12 (June 1920), 24-52; Shen Yanbing, `A Suggestion for the New Literature Specialists', Transformation, 3/1 (sept.1920), quoted in Ma Liangchun and Zhang Darning et al., *Zhongguo xiandai wenxue sichao* ('The History of Modern Chinese Literary Development); Beijing: Shiyue wemuie chubanshe, 1995), 908.

〔註 17〕 Ma and Zhang ed al., *Zhongguo xiandai wenxue sichao*, 906-7.

world, then it must engage in a period of emulation of Western literary experiment. 〔註18〕

The early practices of modernism on the Chinese literary scene may be characterized as attempts at coherence with the literary development of the outside world, reflecting the sense of belatedness and urgency that plagues late-developing modernities. This has been pointed out by a number of critics and is sometimes perceived as a lack of critical originality. Some even conclude that this demonstrates that the Chinese modernist impulse is defined and limited by its semi-colonial condition. 〔註 19〕 However, their eagerness to be modern and culturally relevant in the international sphere did not necessarily indicate a lack of critical judgment on the part of Chinese intellectuals. The choices made by the innovators demonstrated not only an appreciation of newness but also an unmistakably critical approach to foreign cultures and sources. Modernism operated as a cultural inoculation against the overweening imperial power derived from European modernization, and thus especially as a riposte to the imperialism and sub-imperialism of China's own governance in the long period of humiliation leading up to the First World War and its immediate aftermath.

Dissonance and Continuity

Our contention is, then, that early twentieth-century Chinese modernists made evaluative and critical distinctions among different modernist movements. Chinese neo-romanticism in 1920 involved a critical rethinking of capitalist modernity and its literary implications. Futurism, for instance, was introduced even though Chinese interpreters decided it was somewhat ridiculous and glossed it as such. As early as 1914, Zhang Xichen had already translated and presented Futurism in the context of transnational movements from Italy to Japan. In an article he translated from an unknown Japanese author, 'World-Wide Futurism', the subtitles captured the defining qualities and national presumptions of these aesthetic experiments:

〔註18〕 Ibid
〔註19〕 *See e.g. Shih, The lure of the modern.*

'What Is Futurism?', 'Destruction of Old Civilization', 'Eulogizing Modern Mechanical Civilization', 'Eulogizing War Literature', 'English, American, and French Futurisms', 'Russian Futurism', 'Futurist Menu', and 'Japanese Futurism'. 〔註20〕 In 1921 Song Chunfang translated Futurist plays and characterized them as mad and farcical. 〔註21〕 Guo Moruo disavowed Futurism as a cultural expression, commenting that it was 'a freak birth out of extreme materialism... It believes all that is now is worth representing. All human desire and ambition worth affirming, even the money-grabbing instincts. Therefore capitalism, even war, becomes something praise-worthy'. 〔註22〕

Guo's critique may be more reductionist than aesthetically discerning, but it does show that, even in their eagerness to catch up with the modernized world, the early twentieth-century Chinese modernists marked their differences and made their choices. Ambivalence to capitalist modernity as well as to its cultural expression runs throughout their judgments. Mao Dun, while he appreciated the aesthetic impulses of Futurism, most especially its fascination with power, speed, noise, and chaos, similarly critiqued its blind worship of these qualities, which he felt demonstrated the Futurists' wrongful capitalist consciousness. 〔註23〕

Symbolism, meanwhile, became one of the most influential aesthetic and poetic movements in the history of modern Chinese literary culture. It similarly began as a translated, transplanted modernist practice modeled on European prototypes, but it gradually emerged as a major creative component in the formation and transformation of modern Chinese poetry. From 1919 onwards,

---

〔註20〕 Zhang Xichen, `Worldwide Futurism', *Dongfang zaozi* (Oriental Journal), 11/2 (1 Aug. 1914); quoted in Ma and Zhang et al., *Zhongguo xiandai wenxue sichao*, 911.
〔註21〕 *Dongfang zaozi* (Oriental Journal), 18/13 (10 July 1921); Xiju `Drama', 1/5 (30 Sept. 1921); both quoted in Ma and Zhang et al., *Zhongguo xiandai wenxue sichao*, 911.
〔註22〕 Guo Moruo, `Weilaipai de shiyue jiqi piping (The Poetic Covenant of Futurism and its Critique)', *Chuangzao zhoukan* (`Creation Weekly'), 17 (Sept. 1923) quoted in Guo, *Moruo wenji* (Collected Works of Guo Moruo), (Beijing: Renmin wenxue chubanshe, 1959), 38-41.
〔註23〕 Fang Bi, *Xifang wenxue jieshao* (`Introduction to Western Literature') (Shanghai: Shijie shuju, 1930): 244-5. Ma and Zhang et al., *Zhongguo xiandai wenxue sicao*, 370-81.

Symbolist poetry and drama were systematically translated and introduced. Translators of Symbolist poetry noted its emphasis on suggestion and ambiguity, and its reliance on the use of evocative subjects and images rather than explicit analogy or direct description. They also, however, pointed to Symbolism's interest in the concept of the inner life, the macabre, the mysterious, and the morbid, all of which were central to the fascinations of the European *fin de siècle*. The Chinese advocates of Symbolism unsurprisingly lauded the images of the profane, the decadent, and the sensual, introduced by poems such as those collected in Baudelaire's *Les Fleurs du mal* (1857). 〔註 24〕 What is of most interest, perhaps, is that, although many commentators and translators highlighted the timely quality of the movement as anti-Romantic and anti-realist, they also pointed out that the typical Symbolist practices of suggestion, ambiguity, and evocation were reminiscent of classical Chinese poetry. The latter was, of course, the target of the modern poetic revolution. Nonetheless, in the manner of the `almost symbolic' mannerisms of Ming dynasty scholar painting, it now appeared that Chinese poetic practice had been modernist centuries before the event. Thus, the continuity between the late imperial Chinese modern and translated post-imperial modernism was especially evident in the Symbolist movement.

Symbolism is a rare instance in modern China where a non-mainstream literary trend has become relatively established and influential. It was introduced in the first decade of the New Culture and New Literature movement, and continued to be a noted literary practice until the late 1940s, just before the establishment of the People's Republic of China. In the later years of the Second World War and the post- war years, when nationalism and then a radicalized left cultural turn held sway, it had begun to sound a more dissonant note. Nonetheless, its imprint on modern Chinese poetry is irrevocable.

Li jinfa, whose poetic career is mostly limited to the few years when he was studying in Paris, is usually regarded as the first Chinese Symbolist poet. His poetry collections *Wei Yu (`Drizzle')* and *Sike yu xiongnian (`The Gourmand and*

〔註 24〕 Ma and Zhang et al., *Zhongguo xiandai wenxue sicao*, 370-81.

the Year of Ill Fortune') were completed between 1920 to 1923, and published in 1925 and 1927. When he came back to China, 〔註25〕 Li had aimed to seize the best of both the Chinese and European poetic traditions and to create new poetic possibilities in their harmonious correspondence. This, shown most often in a mixture of classical and modern diction, underpins his claim that poetry is not the clarion call of the times but a product of sensations and emotions. His insistence that the poet should capture images, record inspirations, and re-create them according to his associations free from external objects and consciousness, strikes a discordant note in the rhetoric of the modern Chinese literary revolution, and poses a particular problem for post-1949 literary historians. Even standard histories cannot discount him as a simple admirer of decadent Western traditions, for he was also critical, and powerfully so. He wrote in 'Life's Ennui' that the Europe he was witnessing was a morass, where massacres of history

> shrieks of hunger,
>
> forever harass me outside my door,
>
> my heart and soul cower. 〔註26〕

Li, however, was most devoted to recording the poet's sensations, expressing his unnamable moods, capturing human dreams and psychosexual details. He used symbols to describe melancholia, to suggest the soul's struggle through verse notorious for its mystery, emptiness, and obscurity. The first poem in *Drizzle*, 'woman Forsaken', is an internal monologue of a forsaken woman. The poet expresses her sorrowful bitterness as a social outcast. For Li, the image of the forsaken woman is not a sign of proto-feminist outrage, but a misticr symbol of human fate, wherein life is no more than a woman forsaken, hovering between life and death at the graveyard. Choosing the trope of a woman forsaken by men as the epitome of tragic inevitability, the poet rewrites modern life as unjust and lonely, and retains its masculinist centre.

〔註25〕 Li Jinfa, *Wei Yu* (`Drizzle') (Beijing: Beixin shuju, 1925) and *Sike yu yiongnian* ('The Gourmand and the Year of Ill Fortune') (Beijing: Shangwu yinshuguan, 1927).

〔註26〕 In Ma and Zhang et al., *Zhongguo xiandai wenxue sicao*, 467; trans. modified.

Poetic Modernism

There are recurrent themes and frequently used metaphors in Li's poems: the graveyard, death, grey dreams, the lonely traveller, evening bells, moss, the mad soul, melancholia, the Devil, hell, and a fallen flower petal. All would appear anathema to the progressive modernization themes of the New Culture movement. While opening up new poetic horizons both in terms of imagery and sensibility for the modern Chinese poetic experimentation, these figures and metaphors also earned Li the title of 'the poet of anomaly', which is perhaps code for historians having no idea how to place him effectively in the legitimate historical teleologies established after 1949. 〔註27〕

Dai Wangshu is acknowledged not only as a mature Symbolist but also as a major modern Chinese poet. 〔註28〕 His influence crosses over different schools and extends over several decades. Dai studied French literature in Shanghai Zhen Dan University in the 1920s. He was an avid reader of Verlaine and Baudelaire in the original. He went to France in 1932 to study and travel, and returned to China in 1935. Dai started writing and publishing poetry in 1922. His acknowledged Symbolist years are the two decades after 1925. He published altogether ninety poems in four collections, *Wode jiyi* ('My Memory'), *Wangshu cao* ('Wangshu Grass'), *Wangshu shige* ('Poems of Wangshu'), and *Zainan de suiyue* ('The Disastrous Years'). 〔註29〕 Dai was also a major translator of modern French, English, and Spanish poetry into Chinese. Almost all his translations have supplementary explanations detailing technical considerations as well as characterizing the translated poets and their practices. As a supplement to his translation of Baudelaire's *Les Fleurs du mal*, Dai comments, 'as to those who censure Baudelaire's work and claim it to be poisonous, who worry that he will mislead new Chinese poetry, the proven history of literature will give them a

〔註27〕 Li Jinfa, 'Woman Forsaken'; in Michelle Yeh (ed.), *Anthology of Modern Chinese Poetry* (New Haven: Yale University Press, 1992), 18.

〔註28〕 Ma and Zhang et al., *Zhongguo xiandai wenxue sicao*, 477.

〔註29〕 Dai Wangshu, *Wode jiyi* ('My Memory'; Shanghai: Shuimo shudian,1929); *Wangshu cao* ('Wangshu Grass'; Shanghai: Xiandai shuju, 1933); *Wangshu shige* ('Poems of Wangshu'; Shanghai: Xiacm-iai shuju, 1937; *Zainan de suiyue* ('The Disastrous Years'; Shanghai: Xingqun chubanshe, 1948).

better answer. A more profound understanding of Baudelaire himself will also lead to a different opinion. This will be true if one does not imitate him superficially.' 〔註 30〕

Dai's poetic vision and theory centred on the idea of poetic moods. The poet's mood defines the poem's content and its form. The change of moods determines changes within a poem, its colour, and its rhythm. A poem is thus 'an expression of the harmony of moods in words'. 〔註 31〕 Mood swings literally constitute the rhythm and rhyme, the musicality, of the verse. Also, in Dais schema, poetry is not the sensory enjoyment of sound, vision, taste or touch alone. Rather, it provides the summation of all sensual or super-sensory pleasures. Dai emphasizes the movement and structure of moods as both poetic form and content. Just as moods always change, so are they always in flux, and thus should all external poetic form move and sway. The same flower, grass, tree, leaf, ray of light, and bird in nature may produce different moods and poetic expressions if seen and experienced in different frames of mind and heart. This is the basis of Dai's symbolic correspondence, and again we recognize here the echoes of visual art practice in the landscape (*shanshui*) traditions, and in Buddhist-inspired renditions of tree, water, and stone in particular.

Dai's best-known poem, 'Alley in the Rain', can be described as a demonstration of the poet's pursuit of a modern musicality in the new vernacular lyrical form (as opposed to the classical Chinese metric system). It displays his poetic ideal of fluidity of form and suggestive thematic ambiguity. As a poem that emphatically embodies the poet's moods into suggestive but ambiguous symbols, it reveals subtle fusions of the late Tang (827-860) mode of poetic lamentation of life's inevitable melancholia and Verlaine's scheme of the necessary mixing of ambiguity and accuracy in poetic imagery:

> With an oil-paper umbrella, alone I
> Wander in a long

〔註 30〕 Dai, `Houji' (`Supplement'), in Les Fleurs du mad (Shanghai: Huaizheng wenhua chubanshe, 1947).

〔註 31〕 Dai, `Wangshu lunshi' (`Wangshu on Poetry'), Xiandai (Les Contemporaines), 2/1 (Nov.1932), 92-4.

> Lonely alley in the rain
> Hoping to meet
> A melancholy girl
> > Like a lilac…
> She drifts by like a lilac
> > In a dream;
> > The girl drifts by me.
> She walks farther and farther
> Until she reaches the broken fence
> At the end of the alley in the rain. 〔註32〕

The poem has seven stanzas. It describes a lonely youth, presumed to be the poet, who wanders in an alley waiting for the passing of a girl who is like a lilac. Except for the sound of the raindrops on the umbrella, the alley is quiet and melancholic, as is the lilac-like girl in the youth's eyes. The poet-youth's moods take first priority in the poem. They are suggested in the image of the girl in transience, whose lilac-like melancholia is identified and coveted by the poet. The girl herself is drifting outside, indifferent to the poet's feelings and resisting the schema of the poem. The poet's moods are projected onto the drifting of the lilac-like girl, the lonely alley, and the dripping rain. They are ambiguous and unclear, the melancholy and the poet's loneliness are conveyed but unnamable. The images, as symbols of these transient moods and feelings, are also drifting and dripping; they appear only in passing.

Dai's moods and form are now considered the orthodox manifestation of Chinese Symbolism. This is something of a breakthrough, as for years they were judged by official literary historians in Mainland China to be too reminiscent of the old, the Western and the unhealthy to be representative of the progressive Chinese modern. Dai's poetic vision and practice are also considered by his contemporaries, as well as later Chinese modernists, as the forerunner and cornerstone of a Chinese modernist poetry movement (xiandaipai) that became prominent in the 1930s.

〔註32〕 Dai, 'Yu Xiang' ('Alley in the Rain'), in Yeh (ed.), *Anthology of Modern Chinese Poetry*, 31-2.

Poets and critics who identified with this movement described themselves as being no longer content to introduce particular strands of European modernisms, unlike the earlier neo- Romanticists or Symbolists. Rather, they intended to create a `pure' and `purely modern' poetry which would capture `modern life' and `modern moods' for `modern people' with `modern vocabulary' and in `modern form'. 〔註33〕 The modern life to which they referred was that experienced in the fast-paced, noisy, greedy, and brutally competitive trappings of modernization in the early decades of the twentieth century. This was a modernity shared with their European and Japanese counterparts (industrial harbours, noisy factories, department stores, jazz clubs, and the First World War are the manifestations of modernity most frequently referenced in their poetic manifesto and practice).They pursued various poetic forms but concentrated on a free-verse form different from both the prosaic tendencies in the earlier vernacular poetic experimentations of the New Culture movement and the strict lines regulated by the classic metric system. They explicitly rejected the functionalist conception of poetry as a tool or weapon for social reform and politics, a stricture which was beginning to take hold in the 1930s in China, and would reach fruition at the Yan'an Talks in 1942, and implementation in the years post-1949. 〔註34〕 But for now, for both the theorists and poets, modernist poetry, as the most desirable form of modern poetry, should pursue nothing else but pure modern poetic form and moods.

Besides Dai Wangshu, the most notable poets of this self-conscious poetic modernism were Bian Zhilin, Fei Ming, and Xu Chi. The first three were also the acknowledged precursors of the Taiwanese modernist movement in the 1960s. As presaged in Yan'an, this promising beginning of the maturation of modern Chinese poetry was soon ended by the Second World War and by subsequent nationalist and, crucially, socialist political and aesthetic demands. 〔註35〕

〔註33〕 Shi Zhecun, 'You guanyu benkan de shi' ('Again about the Poetry in Our Journal'), *Xiandai* (Les contemporaines), 4/1 (Nov.1933), 6.

〔註34〕 Ellen R. Judd, `Prelude to the Yan'an Talks: Problems in Transforming a Literary Intelligentsia', *Modern China*, 11/3 (1985),377-408.

〔註35〕 Ma and Zhang et al., *Zhongguo xiandai wenxue sicao*, 978-9.

Fiction and Psychoanalysis

The other notable and relatively established modernist literary practice both in its time and through subsequent Chinese cultural history is experimentation in psychoanalytical fiction. In 1920 Jun Chang introduced Freud and the libidinal in his redefinition of poetic creation as the satisfaction of sexual drive. 〔註 36〕 But it was Zhang Dongxun who systematically introduced psychoanalysis, through the work of Freud and Jung. 〔註 37〕 Throughout the 1920s, there were numerous translations and discussions of psychoanalysis and its literary cultural applications, both from European sources and through Japanese interpretation. Zhu Guangqian's studies *The Psychology of Literary Art* (1936) and *Abnormal Psychology* (1933) not only went further in systematically introducing and analysing the Freudian psychoanalytical enterprise, but also proposed that `those who study literature and art have to understand the concept of sublimation and the function of sexual drives in the human unconscious...It is therefore imperative to study abnormal psychology. 〔註 38〕 The translation and study of psychoanalytic literature was carried out through the 1940s and re-emerged at the end of the 1970s to mid-1980s in the Reform era post-Mao.

New theories and interpretations of traditional as well as modern Chinese literature and culture have resulted from the introduction of Freudian psychology. Guo Moruo was the first to use Freudian psychoanalysis to explicate the classic Yuan dynasty (1271-1368) play *Xi Xiangji* ('Romance of the Western Chamber') (by Wang Shifu). Guo seemed to agree with the Freudian explanation that all literature originates from libidinal drives, and proposed to reread classic Chinese romances as youthful and rebellious expressions of sexual repression against patriarchy. 〔註 39〕 Zhou Zuoren, on the other hand, used the theory of the

---

〔註 36〕 Jun Chang, `Xingyu de kexue' (`The Science of Sexual Desire'), *Dongfangzazh* ('Oriental Journal'), 17/15 (10 Aug.1920); quoted in Ma and Zhang et al., *Zhongguo xiandai wenxue sicao*, 931.

〔註 37〕 Zhang Dongxun, `Lun jingshen fenxi' (`On Psychoanalysis'), Mintuo, 2/5 (5 Feb. 1921); cited in Ma and Zhang et al., *Zhongguo xiandai wenxue sicao*, 931.

〔註 38〕 Zhu Guangqian, `Qian yian' (`Preface'), in *Biantai xinlixue* (`Abnormal Psychology', Shanghai: Shangwu shuju, 1933), 1.

〔註 39〕 Guo Moruo, `Xixiangji yishu shang de pipang yu qi zuozhe xingge' (`An Aesthetic Critique of the Romance of the Western Chamber and the Personality of the Author, 1921); in *Guo Moruo quanji* (`Complete Works of Guo Moruo'; Beijing: Renmin wenxue chubanshe, 1985), xv. 322-3.

unconscious to defend his contemporary Yu Dafu. He argued that Yu's controversial novella *Chenlun* (`Sinking; 1921), 〔註40〕 which records in detail the protagonist's conflicts between the flesh and the soul, is a genuine work of art, a bold psycho-emotional revelation of the self and the collective, and not at all immoral (as many alleged). For him it is an excellent example of the artistic sublimation of unconscious sexual repression and personal depression shared by young people at the time. It is consequently the most representative work dealing with the frustrations of modern Chinese youth. 〔註41〕 Guo Moruo described his own novella *Canchun* (`The Remains of Spring') 〔註42〕 as a delineation of the characters' psychological movement rather than a plot narration. He suggests that the story is best read in terms of psychoanalysis or as an explication of dreams. 〔註43〕

Many fiction writers quickly understood the creative potential of the psychoanalytic turn in characterization and in the depiction of emotive, internal life. They realized that the realms of human psyche, the conscious and unconscious, as well as instincts and desires, were invaluable resources for fictional representations of life as yet unexplored in Chinese literature. Lu Yin's *Li Shi riji* (`Li Shi's Diary; 1923) is a poetic exploration of the friendship between two young women. Its homoerotic overtones, although explicit, are nonetheless conveyed in symbols and dreams. One day Li Shi finds herself falling deeper and deeper in love with Wan Qing and drifts into a dream:

> I dreamt there was a little stream. By its side stood a graceful cottage; in front there were two gigantic willows, their branches gently touching the thatched roof; under the willows there was a small boat. The sun was setting then, and white clouds blocked the sky, Wan Qing

---

〔註40〕 Yu Dafu, `Chenlun'(`Sinking'), in *Yu Dafu xiaoshuo quanji* ('The Complete Short Stories of Yu Dafu'; Hangzhou: Zhejiang wenyi chubanshe, 1991), 23-34.

〔註41〕 Zhou Zuoren, `Chenlun' (`On Sinking'), *Chengbao fukan* (`Morning Post Supplement'), 26 Mar.1922; repr. In Chen Zishan and Wang Zili (eds), *Yu Dafu yanjiu ziliao* (`Research Materials on Yu Dafu, 1986), 1-5.

〔註42〕 Guo Moruo, 'Canchun' (`The Remains of Spring'), in Guo Moruo quanji, ix. 20-35.

〔註43〕 Guo Moruo, 'Piping yu meng' (`Criticism and Dreams'), *Chuangzao jikan* (`Creation (quarterly'), in Xunzhao et al. (eds), *Guo Moruo yanjiu ziliao* (`Research Materials on Guo Moruo', Beijing: Zhongguo shehui kexue chubanshe, 1986), i. 169.

and I were in the boat, rocking to and fro, we drifted further into the reeds. Suddenly it rained, we were protected by the reeds so could not see the drops, but we heard the unceasing sound of their falling......Now recalling the dream, isn't it what we always wanted?
〔註44〕

Clouds and rains are standard metaphors in classical Chinese for sexual intercourse. A thatched cottage, weeping willows, and a boat on the stream provide the typical setting for traditional love stories. These explicit references within the dream make the psychosexual evocation of the narrative very clear. Shi Zhecun, who was the editor of the journal *Xiandai* (Les Contemporaines), around which the previously discussed modernist poets gathered, not only writes about sexual libidinal drives and their effect on the human psyche, but also probes their distortion. His short story `Meiyu zixi' (`Monsoon Eve, 1933) was understood as a demonstration of the unconscious, in particular of repressed sexual settings. 〔註45〕 It tells the story of a city-man on the way back from his work in the rain, and his encounter with an unknown young woman and consequent psycho-emotional activity. The whole story is a non-sequential process of free association of the protagonist's instincts, impressions, and fantasies; his conscious musings and unconscious desires. The pre-monsoon drizzle, the pedal-cab ride, the peep of a shop girl, and the pointed, phallic umbrella which the man holds in his hand, all contribute to a revelation of the psychosexual unconscious of the protagonist and of the city streets as an active player in modern human psycho-emotional consciousness. *Cun Yang* ('Spring Sunshine, 1936) is even more direct in its depiction of the effect of sexual repression on an old spinster whose unexpected riches had ruined her chances of marriage. 〔註46〕 The narrative centres on her sudden sexual awakening one fine spring morning and the disturbing consequences thereof. The Freudian reference is here thematic rather than structurally employed. As an avowed modernist, Shi

〔註44〕 Lu Yin, `Li Shi riji' (`Li Shi's Diary'), in Ren Haideng (ed.), *Li Shi riji* (Beijing: Beijing yanshan chubanshe, 1998), 37.
〔註45〕 Shi Zhecun, `Meiyu zixi' (`Monsoon Eve'; Beijing: Xinzhongguo shuju, 1933).
〔註46〕 Shi Zhecun, `Spring Sunshine', in *One Rainy Evening*, trans. Rosemary Roberts (Beijing: Panda Books, 1994), 99-111.

wrote numerous short stories and novellas about sexual repression, displacement, sublimation, and distortion, which also necessarily meant that he was consistently experimental in his narration. He relied on suggestive symbols, free association, and stream of consciousness, avoiding sequential accounts of temporal and spatial cause and effect. These works, and those of Li Jianwu among others, placed the individual psyche at the disposal of the first Cultural Revolution. Although dormant for most of the second half of the twentieth century, their gift has been recuperated in contemporary film, arts, and literature. The scope of this chapter does not permit us to investigate the cultural individualism of the twenty-first century, but we would suggest that the impact of the Freudian psyche is still underestimated in scholarship on Chinese culture.

New Sensationalism

The New Sensationalist school grew from the precedents offered by both psychoanalytic knowledge and Symbolism. Its first practitioner, Liu Na'ou, introduced the term and its assertions from Japan in his translation of modern Japanese literature. 〔註 47〕 Liu and his fellow New Sensationalists were interested in the sensations of the moment and the use of symbols to capture the existential quality of human experience. They emphasized the subjective and the psycho-emotional in representing the external and experiential. While this made them seem part of the psychoanalytical experiment, or Symbolist in their technical pursuit, it is their exclusive focus on the modern Chinese urban that has earned them lasting attention.

Mu Shiying, the movement's key figure, was a minor writer but one who evinced a cinematic sense of space and time. His work was noted for its depiction of new urban youth and the cityscape of Shanghai, using Sensationalist techniques to highlight the fast-moving impressions of sound, light, colour, and shape. The fragmented piece 'Shanghai de Hubuwu' ('The Shanghai Foxtrot', 1932) was, he

---

〔註 47〕 Liu Na'ou (trans.) *Sheqing wenhua* (`Culture of Eros', Shanghai: Shuimo shudian, 1928).

averred, only a technical experiment in preparation for a longer novel, and so we read it in that light. 〔註 48〕

The story has no plot, no visible structure, and breaks away from conventional narrative modes. It demonstrates the fast flow of metropolitan time, the fluidity of human consciousness, and recalls the Dada cinema of Leger and Andrews, and the photography of Man Ray. 〔註 49〕 In the story, foxtrot and waltz provide the rhythm of the piece, randomly listing contrastive urban images and objects: neon lights, dancing girls, Nestle chocolates, jazz, and high-heels clipping along the tree-lined avenues in the French Concession. Indeed, one might also cite the lessons in montage which Eisenstein's cinema had taught the world, and the shimmering associative narrative of European-Hollywood's tale of urban attractions in Seventh Heaven (Borzage, US, 1927).

Shu-mei Shih describes Liu Na'ou's narrative technique in his rendition of a nightclub scene as 'synaesthetic listing', as the narrative angle behaves as a film camera, moving from an establishing shot of the scene into medium close-ups of the types and characters that give the location human texture:

> Everything in this Tango palace is in melodious motion—male and female bodies, multi-coloured lights, shining wine goblets, red, green liquid, and slender fingers, garnet lips, burning eyes…The air is heavy with a mixture of alcohol, sweat, and oil, encouraging all to indulge in the high level of excitement. There is a middle-aged man laughing heartily with his teeth showing, a young lady speaking endearingly while her arms make charming, affected gestures… 〔註 50〕

The writings of the New Sensationalists were thus, from the perspective of literary historians perhaps, indebted to the international and local cinematic cultures in which they developed and from which they learnt how to embody the speed and disorientation of the modern city in their prose. And, as befits the

---

〔註 48〕 See `The Shanghai Foxtrot (A Fragment)', trans. Mu Shiying, comm. Sean MacDonald, *Modernism/Modernity*, 11 (2004), 797-807.

〔註 49〕 See Malculm `Purvey, `The Avant-Garde and the "New Spirit": *The Case of Ballet Mechanique*, October, 102 (Autumn 2002), 35-58.

〔註 50〕 Liu Na'ou, *Dushi fengjingxian* (`Scene', Shanghai: Shuimo shudan,1930), 3-6; quoted in Shi, *The Lure of the Modern*, 288.

output of China's cinematic city, New Sensationalism is widely studied as representative of Chinese modernism and of the avant-garde of modern Chinese city literature. 〔註 51〕 The writers' pursuit of modern urban themes and modernist narrative techniques and their high- pitched manifesto of `decadent, urban sensation', or perhaps `art for art's sake' as long as it is truly meaningless, have marked them out as an important alternative cultural movement in the two decades before Liberation in 1949.

Modernist Confrontation

Even a brief and incomplete account of Chinese modernism indicates that the relationship between sending and receiving cultures 'involves a far more complicated process than the simple transmission of a literary model from one culture to another; [and] that reception of influence is frequently predicated on intrinsic conditions and needs, that an influence cannot take place unless there is pre-existing predisposition'. 〔註 52〕 In his study *Milestones in Sino-Western Literary Confrontation*, Marian Galik defines `influence' as `confrontations', as a process to be understood `in the broadest possible connections and parallels, in all their essential motions and contexts'. 〔註 53〕 Galik further elaborates by way of the Soviet comparativist A. S. Bushmin that 'literary continuity' (snyatie/Aufheben) in the encounter of two or more literatures is 'the highest contact-taking, which, as 'a creatively mastered tradition, is in its essence in a dissolved, or philosophically speaking, in a "cancelled" state'. 〔註 54〕 This understanding of influence, for Galik, is to shift the emphasis to the 'receiving end':

〔註 51〕 Sima Changfeng, *Zhongguo xinwenxue shi* (`History of New Chinese Literature'), ii (Hong Kong: Shaoming shudian, 1978) ,35, 85, 86; Lee Ou-fan, *Shanghai Modern: The Flowering of a New Urban Culture in China, 1930-1945* (Cambridge, Mass: Harvard University Press, 1999), 154-90; Shi, *The Lure of the Modern*, 231-370.

〔註 52〕 Michelle Yeh, `The Anxiety of Difference--a Rejoinder; *jintian* (`Today'), 1 (1991), 94.

〔註 53〕 Marian Galik, *Milestones in Sino-Western Literary Confrontation (1898-1979)*, (Wiesbaden: O. Harrassowitz, 1986), 1.

〔註 54〕 Ibid. 2.

If we divide the word Aufheben in its Hegelian connotation into its three meaningful components: to cancel, to preserve, and to lift up, then it becomes clear that the process (which may be understood as influence) may imply a new phenomenon which becomes relevantly modified in the prism of the receiving literary and social context, primarily in connection with the creative abilities of the receiving subject and the needs of the receiving literary structure. 〔註 55〕

To be influenced in this sense is to make a historically implicated choice which presupposes transformation as a component of creativity. The idea of `predisposition' foregrounds the needs and agencies of the new writers, adapters, translators, and transformers. They are not merely on the receiving end of the work of others, but became transformative and deliberative new voices referencing culturally distinct patterns of expression while finding their own timbre and reason. The case of the earl- twentieth-century Chinese modernist experimentation becomes most meaningful when understood in the prism of its historical and social context, that is, vis-a-vis its relations with China's protracted modernization process. Early twentieth-century Chinese modernist movements often strike discordant notes in the major tunes of their particular times. They have never been institutionalized as the highest achievement of modern literary development and, unlike their European counterparts, remain marginal in Chinese cultural history.

Reform and its Avant-garde Literary Reflection

The economic Reform in Mainland China in the late 1970s was a political movement to change the historical direction of socialist modernization. It aimed to adopt reform measures that would rebuild a Chinese modernity then considered by both the state and the populace to have gone severely astray during many years of political strife and ideological cleansing. This political-economic revolution also sparked a literary reformation. Modernist forms and practices were once again

---

〔註 55〕 Ibid. 4.

appropriated as aesthetic and cultural interventions against the mainstream of reform and post-reform culture. Where mainstream reform literature functions predominantly as the thematic and affective testing ground for the new vision of developmental modernization, it is still as social-realist in form as it has been for the past thirty years. Modernist experiments, under such circumstances, intervene directly in both politics and the politics of culture. Wang Meng's trail-blazing exploration of the stream of consciousness is an outstanding case in point. His novellas *Chun zhi sheng* ('The Sound of Spring, 1980) and *Hu Die* ('Butterfly', 1980) are written as free associations of the psycho-emotional activities of reformed and reinstated party officials and ordinary people in the aftermath of the Cultural Revolution, and reveal great ideological scepticism and post-ideological ennui. 〔註 56〕 The free-flowing associative internal monologues of his characters evince doubt and disillusionment in the wake of political extremism, rather than shared hope for the new era. Wang's own sense of disillusionment, aided by the psycho-emotional depth achieved by his use of the stream of consciousness, hints that the failure of thirty years of socialist modernization may not be merely tactical, but fundamentally historical. Wang's modernist formal experimentation, however, is pioneering in itself, as his free-flowing narrative structure showcased for the first time the possibility of multiple narrative forms in the literary history of the People's Republic of China. Wang's modernist exploration has finally allowed historical narrative its personal psychological manifestation.

The much-studied *Menglongshi* (Misty Poetry) movement is paradoxically hailed as the beginning of the literature of this new era. While 'the New Era' is an affirmative naming of the mainstream culture of the time, *Menglongshi* actually began as an underground poetic movement of political protest. Its targets were the institutions of the state and the cultures that they encouraged. Despite being the most forceful avant-garde of the literature of the New Era, its experimental form and deep scepticism quickly returned it to the margins in the reform and

---

〔註 56〕 Wang Meng, 'Chun zhi sheng ('The Sound of Spring') and 'Hu die' ('Butterfly'), in *Wang Meng xiaoshuo baogaowenxue xuan* ('Selected Novellas, Stories and Reportage by Wang Meng', Beijing: Beijing chuhanshe, 1981), 200-49

post-reform Chinese literary and artistic scene. 〔註 57〕 Bei Dao, Mangke, Duoduo, Gu Cheng, Su Ting, the leading poets of this movement, all consider themselves, and are considered by others, as cultural rebels. Not only does their poetry demonstrate their devotion to the creative and literary in restrictive circumstances, but the act of writing is itself the way by which they directly ponder, engage with, and counter social reality Although the individual poets differ widely in their aesthetic visions and stylistic choices, the *Menglongshi* movement is in the avant-garde of contemporary Chinese literature owing to its collective breakaway from conventions of the socialist era, which might be briefly characterized as direct expression of positive emotions for politically sanctioned themes in simple metric systems and folksy language. Their reliance on metaphors and suggestion is as much political necessity as aesthetic deliberation. Thanks to the *Menglongshi* poets, Chinese poetry need no longer be a political tool. It is this aesthetics of political resistance that has laid the foundation for a different kind of modern Chinese literature. While the modernist formal experiments of these poets, from the use of complicated and elusive imagery to free-associative internal monologues, to the re-creation of free verse and epics, may not have gone very far beyond the limits of their predecessor modernist poets from the 1920s and 1930s, their achievement is nonetheless substantial. Their predecessors wrestled with the confines of tradition that were so tenacious in the past, while they have confronted the political and aesthetic restrictions of the present.

The most recent notable modernist literary movement in contemporary China is the avant-garde fiction experiment beginning in the 1980s. Writers such as Mo Yan, Yu Hua, Su Tong, and Ge Fei self-consciously experimented with narrative techniques and formal language, and pushed the limits of novelistic practice. Their works claim heritage from Latin American magical realism but also from a reconstructed classical Chinese narrative reliance on details. Novels, novellas, and short stories, sometimes dubbed meta-or anti-fiction, are wilfully deconstructive, either of the extant grand narratives in theme or of the mainstream storytelling

---

〔註 57〕 Chen Xiaoming, *Anxiety of Expression: Historical Disillusionment and Contemporary Literary Reform*, (Beijing: Central Translation Press, 2002), 29-30.

conventions in style. Thus, they are sometimes considered postmodern pioneers. 〔註58〕The end of these experimental fiction writings, which came sooner than expected, was brought about not by complicity with the reform and post-reform cultural politics as is sometimes charged, but by the very successes of the reform of cultural institutions in post-socialist China. 〔註59〕That is, what began as aesthetic interventions in the cultural politics of an extremist socialist modernization became formulaic cultural productions in a thriving market. Now, the formal experiments of these avant-garde writers no longer pose challenges to the norms or conventions of oppressive political and cultural institutions. These late twentieth-century modernist practitioners, like their early-century predecessors, have become another dissonant echo of the modern in the great hall of China's modernization.

〔註58〕Chen, *Anxiety of Expression*, 90-111.
〔註59〕Zhang, *Chinese Modernism in the Era of Reforms*, 150-200.

讀李怡主編的《詞語的歷史與思想的嬗變》

　　李怡主編《詞語的歷史與思想的嬗變》由巴蜀書社出版，這是一部集中國學界多位中國現代文學專家研究之大成的論著，該書的出版無疑意義重大。其主旨是「追問中國現代文學的批評概念」，著作的內容範疇及涵括的議題都是當下中國現代文學批評和文學史研究急需梳理探討的概念、史實和問題。它以文學批評概念關鍵詞在現代中國的流變爲線索，通過詞語的歷史來追索思想的嬗變。有史，有文學，有理論梳理和辨析，也有作者編者個人對中國現代文學文化及思想的理解和評價，是不可多得的史、論、索引工具及教學輔助材料。

　　《詞語的歷史與思想的嬗變》最重要的貢獻是對現代中國文學文化研究關鍵詞彙的歷史演變的梳理和重估。「追問」不僅是全書的組織方式，也是作者由當代進入歷史概念及歷史——文學史、思想史和文化史的切入點。但這種追問不僅是對具體詞語的來源，其變化發展的史實及背景的追索審視，同時也是對它們作爲中國文學研究當代批評關鍵概念的質疑反思。對史的重溫、梳理在此同時也體現爲對當代思想文化及學科建設的一種思辨。

　　在這個意義上，由重估中國現代文學的現代性作爲開篇也就順理成章了。正如作者所指出的那樣，「現代」是指稱中國現代文學、文學研究及文學史的最基本名詞，也是業內長期慣用、但對其起源、歷史、外延、內涵尚無認眞勘探的一個概念。作者由二十世紀末展開的「現代性重估」大論辯開始，探尋這一辯論對中國現代文學學科發展及約定俗成的中國現代文學觀的影響。由此開始的討論當然涉及中國現代文學研究界乃至整個中國現代學術思想界對於「現代」作為一個歷史思想概念的認識的複雜過程，包括「五四」以後中國文學與文化對「現代性」的自覺追求。與書中其他篇章不同，作者並未就此展開對中國現代文學或文化史及其現代性形成演變過程的梳理和討論。在這裡，論者重梳現代文學史，是由對在重估現代性思潮中中國大陸學界走紅的幾家理論的評論和辯駁開始的。作者討論了詹姆遜的「寓言說」、「兩種現代性」、「後殖民」理論與中國現代文學的他者性以及由此而來的局限性等問題，由此揭示了由理論導讀和套讀文學文本所形成的誤區。不過，需要我們進一步探討的問題可能也在這裡：指出用新興理論對文學文本的套讀過於「簡明」，認定這些當代理論與中國現代文學的歷史文本間存在「深刻的隔膜」，這固然正確，但如若僅僅如此，中國現代文學難道就成了集生存體驗之成的純「感性」文本嗎？ 現代文學有百年之長的、與現代思想史文化史緊密相連的歷史，也有經由數代作者、學者、思想者論辯思索形成的文論，它們的位置又在何處呢？ 所謂的現代中國文學傳統究竟還有哪些內容，它在「強勢」的西方當代理論面前難道就剩下零零落落由個別作家個人體驗文本所組成的肉身？ 沒有系統性，沒有理論？ 或者站在今天來看，它在經過包括國家機器在內的權力或學術文化機構長期不斷編選，成為經典和既定的教育內容後也非強勢？所有這些問題疊加起來都相當複雜，需要我們繼續在「現代性」的糾纏中展開。

　　作者提出，要深入總結和考察中國現代文學自身的現代性，就必須由對其時間性的追索轉向對其空間性的探討，這一點在我看來非常之重要。較之時間， 尤其是現代和當代中國所接受了的線性進步時間的單一性和同一性，空間彰顯特定時空範圍內各構成部分的豐富性及其相互之間的張力，確實是探討具體文學話語和系統，包括作家作品特殊意義的更具「寬度」和「厚度」的觀念。但需要記住的是不同的空間之間，尤其在世界範圍內的現代歷史的形成過程中，有著千絲萬縷的聯繫。其形成變化常常是相輔相成的。因此「他者」「自身」甚或「民族性」之類的概念都不是簡明的，有其特定的來龍去脈和歷史內涵，也有其空間性。它們的應用也應受其時空規定的歷史定義和所指的約束。

　　所以，回到中國現代文學的歷史，通過其關鍵話語在半個世紀內的演變所顯示的立論，來探詢辨析其作為一個特殊的但和其他傳統相關的文學文化傳統，是很有意義的。這也是《詞語的歷史與思想的嬗變》的精彩所在。作為對整個中國現代文學史論的梳理，它所選擇的詞匯和概念範疇是依據現代中國文學的常用經典詞匯和概念組織限定的，強調了現代中國文學作為一個複雜的不斷演變的文學傳統的歷史主體性和自覺性。第一章是對中國現代文學作為一個已形成的傳統的總體特徵的探討，第二章是對文體概念的辨析追述，第三章是對現代中國文學演進的思想概念的逐條清理評論，第四章是對二十世紀文學思潮、創作方式與批評術語的史實考察和分析，第五章是對與革命和左翼文學有關的詞語的專門整理和評析，它們都體現了《詞語的歷史與思想的嬗變》的組織理念——正視並闡釋中國現代文學的豐富性、複雜性和歷史性。如第二章對話劇在中國的定名以及對散文作為一種現代中國文體的史實的挖掘，確實為中國現代文學文體的命名形成——其不可否定的原創性——正了名。第三章通過對一系列思想概念的梳理總結了中國新文學批評傳統的形成及經由的複雜道路。此章極有洞見地在對「民族」和「世界」兩個關鍵概念在現代中國的形成運用的討論中加入了對被很多中國文學史和批評史忽略的思想和思想史的「地域性」的清理，指出後者在前兩者作為現代歷史文化觀念的形成中的至關緊要的意義，而這種地理空間體驗的追求是中國現代文學和文化的核心構成之一。

在對這種構架及其意義的分析中，作者特別總結了比較文學的發展在改革開放後的中國現代文學研究中所起的重要作用，也指出了影響研究的局限性。當然，如果能脫開彼時「走向世界」的急切而此時又視世界為他者的焦躁，比較文學的視野和方法對現代中國文學研究的深入還是有許多可用之處，如對不同傳統及其產生、發展（斷裂）空間的關係的比較研究，探討它們作為不同的文化傳統在共時的歷史壓力下的不同或類似的反應。比較文學的存在，也能夠提醒我們慎用 「西方」「東方」之類含混的歷史地理思想，並以此作為比較的雙方等等。這樣我們也就不再會用「影響說」來作繭自縛了。

第五章把「革命辭語」作為專門史加以清理分析，這與全書以現代中國文學及相關文化論辯中常用並形成了規範意義的詞匯為理析對象一樣，具有開拓性的意義。因為，只有重新正面梳理、反思現代中國文學發展的真實歷程及其重要背景和已形成並傳承下來的觀念語彙，才能正確認識理解文學的歷史性和文學形式，文學史存在與發展的意義。「革命」作為貫穿現代中國整整一個世紀的重要詞匯應該是現代中國文學和文學史研究的重要課題。對其指稱的歷史事件及激進熱情的後果的質疑不應成爲放棄相關的史論梳理，以及拒絕對相關作品展開研究的藉口。論者在書中對「革命」及相關詞匯之於近現代中國的使用和演變的追述，爲這一方面的研究打下了基礎。革命和革命文學也可以從審美角度進行研究。其中不僅有激情，也有歷史觀、認識論和文學形式的問題。審美審視及價值判斷和文化、文化史研究不應該脱節。審美並非僅僅屬於所謂「純文學」的範疇。這也是《詞語的歷史與思想的嬗變》一書給我們的啓示。

總之，作爲一名在海外從事中國文學研究與教學的學者，我覺得《詞語的歷史與思想的嬗變》除了作爲思想、文論、觀念史給讀者（尤其是業內的同人） 啓迪外，也是一部有用的中國現代文學教學參考書。